Evelyn Martinengo-Cesaresco

Essays in the Study of Folk-songs

Evelyn Martinengo-Cesaresco

Essays in the Study of Folk-songs

ISBN/EAN: 9783744768344

Printed in Europe, USA, Canada, Australia, Japan

Cover: Foto ©Andreas Hilbeck / pixelio.de

More available books at **www.hansebooks.com**

ESSAYS IN THE STUDY OF FOLK-SONGS.

Will no one tell me what she sings?
Perhaps the plaintive numbers flow
For old, unhappy, far-off things,
And battles long ago :
Or is it some more humble lay,
Familiar matter of to-day?
Some natural sorrow, loss, or pain,
That has been, and may be again !

W. WORDSWORTH.

ESSAYS IN THE
STUDY OF FOLK-SONGS.

BY THE

COUNTESS EVELYN MARTINENGO-CESARESCO.

LONDON:
GEORGE REDWAY,
YORK STREET, COVENT GARDEN.
MDCCCLXXXVI.

CONTENTS

515

INTRODUCTION.

Wo man singt da lass dich ruhig nieder,
Böse Menschen haben keine Lieder.

INTRODUCTION.

IT is on record that Wilhelm Mannhardt, the eminent writer on mythology and folk-lore, was once taken for a gnome by a peasant he had been questioning. His personal appearance may have helped the illusion; he was small and irregularly made, and was then only just emerging from a sickly childhood spent beside the Baltic in dreaming over the creations of popular fancy. Then, too, he wore a little red cap, which was doubtless fraught with supernatural suggestions. But above all, the story proves that Mannhardt had solved the difficulty of dealing with primitive folk; that instead of being looked upon as a profane and prying layman, he was regarded as one who was more than initiated into the mysteries—as one who was a mystery himself. And for this reason I recall it here. It exactly indicates the way to set about seeking after old lore. We ought to shake off as much as possible of our conventional civilization which frightens un-educated peasants, and makes them think, at best, that we wish to turn them into ridicule. If we must not hope to pass for spirits of earth or air, we can aim at inspiring such a measure of confidence as will per-suade the natural man to tell us what he still knows of those vanishing beings, and to lend us the key to his general treasure-box before all that is inside be reduced to dust.

This, which applies directly to the collector at first hand, has also its application for the student who would profit by the materials when collected. He should approach popular songs and traditions from some other stand-point than that of mere criticism ; and divesting himself of preconcerted ideas, he should try to live the life and think the thoughts of people whose only literature is that which they carry in their heads, and in whom Imagination takes the place of acquired knowledge.

I.

Research into popular traditions has now reached a stage at which the English Folk-Lore Society have found it desirable to attempt a classification of its different branches, and in future, students will perhaps devote their labours to one or another of these branches rather than to the subject as a whole. Certain of the sections thus mapped out have plainly more special attractions for a particular class of workers : beliefs and superstitions chiefly concern those who study comparative mythology; customs are of peculiar importance to the sociologist, and so on. But tales and songs, while offering points of interest to scientific specialists, appeal also to a much wider class, namely, to all who care at all for literature. For the Folk-tale is the father of all fiction, and the Folk-song is the mother of all poetry.

Mankind may be divided into the half which listens and the half which reads. For the first category in

its former completeness, we must go now to the East;
in Europe only the poor, and of them a rapidly de-
creasing proportion, have the memory to recite, the
patience to hear, the faith to receive. It was not
always or primarily an affair of classes : down even to
a comparatively late day, the pure story-teller was a
popular member of society in provincial France and
Italy, and perhaps society was as well employed in
listening to wonder-tales as it is at present. But there
is no going back. The epitaph for the old order of
things was written by the great philosopher who
threw the last shovel of earth on its grave :

> O l'heureux temps que celui de ces fables
> Des bons démons, des esprits familiers,
> Des farfadets, aux mortels secourables !
> On écoutait tous ces faits admirables
> Dans son château, près d'un large foyer :
> Le père et l'oncle, et la mère et la fille,
> Et les voisins, et toute la famille,
> Ouvraient l'oreille à Monsieur l'aumônier,
> Qui leur fesait des contes de sorcier.
> On a banni les démons et les fées ;
> Sous la raison les grâces etouffées,
> Livrent nous cœurs à l'insipidité ;
> Le raisonner tristement s'accrédite ;
> On court, hélas ! après la verité,
> Ah ! croyez-moi, l'erreur a son mérite.[1]

Folk-songs differ from folk-tales by the fact of their
making a more emphatic claim to credibility. Prose
is allowed to be more fanciful, more frivolous than
poetry. It deals with the brighter side ; the hero and
heroine in the folk-tale marry and live happily ever
after ; in the popular ballad they are but rarely united

---

[1] Voltaire.

save in death. To the blithe supernaturalism of elves and fairies, the folk-poet prefers the solemn supernaturalism of ghost-lore.

The folk-song probably preceded the folk-tale. If we are to judge either by early record or by the analogy of backward peoples, it seems proved that in infant communities anything that was thought worth remembering was sung. It must have been soon ascertained that words rhythmically arranged take, as a rule, firmer root than prose. "As I do not know how to read," says a modern Greek folk-singer, "I have made this story into a song so as not to forget it."

Popular poetry is the reflection of moments of strong collective or individual emotion. The springs of legend and poetry issue from the deepest wells of national life; the very heart of a people is laid bare in its sagas and songs. There have been times when a profound feeling of race or patriotism has sufficed to turn a whole nation into poets: this happened at the expulsion of the Moors from Spain, the struggle for the Stuarts in Scotland, for independence in Greece. It seems likely that all popular epics were born of some such concordant thrill of emotion. The saying of "a very wise man" reported by Andrew Fletcher of Saltoun, to the effect that if one were permitted to make all the ballads, he need not care who made the laws, must be taken with this reservation: the ballad-maker only wields his power for as long as he is the true interpreter of the popular will. Laws may be imposed on the unwilling, but not songs.

The Brothers Grimm said that they had not found a single lie in folk-poetry. "The special value," wrote Goethe, "of what we call national songs and ballads, is that their inspiration comes fresh from nature : they are never got up, they flow from a sure spring." He added, what must continually strike anyone who is brought in contact with a primitive peasantry, "The unsophisticated man is more the master of direct, effective expression in few words than he who has received a regular literary education."

Bards chaunted the praises of head-men and heroes, and it may be guessed that almost as soon and as universally as tribes and races fell out, it grew to be the custom for each fighting chief to have one or more bards in his personal service. Robert Wace describes how William the Conqueror was followed by Taillefer, who

> Mounted on steed that was swift of foot,
> Went forth before the armed train
> Singing of Roland and Charlemain,
> Of Olivere, and the brave vassals
> Who died at the Pass of Roncesvals.

The northern skalds accompanied the armies to the wars and were present at all the battles. "Ye shall be here that ye may see with your own eyes what is achieved this day," said King Olaf to his skalds on the eve of the Battle of Stiklastad (1030), "and have no occasion, when ye shall afterwards celebrate these actions in song, to depend on the reports of others." In the same fight, a skald named Jhormod died an honourable death, shot with an arrow while in the act of singing. The early Keltic poets were forbidden to bear arms : a reminiscence of their sacerdotal status, but they, too, looked on while others fought, and encouraged the combatants with their songs. All these bards served a higher purpose than

the commemoration of individual leaders: they became the historians of their epoch. The profession
was one of recognised eminence, and numbered kings
among its adepts. Then it declined with the rise of
written chronicles, till the last bard disappeared and
only the ballad-singer remained.

II.

This personage, though shorn of bardic dignity, yet
contrived to hold his own with considerable success.
In Provence and Germany, itinerant minstrels who
sang for pay brought up the rank and file of the
troubadours and minnesingers; in England and Italy
and Northern France they formed a class apart,
which, as times went, was neither ill-esteemed nor ill-
paid. When the minstrel found no better audience he
mounted a barrel in the nearest tavern, or

> At country wakes sung ballads from a cart.

But his favourite sphere was the baronial hall; and
to understand how welcome he was there made, it is
only needful to picture country life in days when
books were few and newspapers did not exist. He
sang before noble knights and gracious dames, who,
to us—could we be suddenly brought into their
presence—would seem rough in their manner, their
speech, their modes of life; but who were far from
being dead or insensible to intellectual pleasure when
they could get it. He sang the choicest songs that
had come down to him from an earlier age; songs of
the Round Table and of the great Charles; and then,
as he sat at meat, perhaps below the salt, but with his
plate well heaped up with the best that there was, he
heard strange Eastern tales from the newly-arrived pil-

grim at his right hand, and many a wild story of noble love or hate from the white-haired retainer at his left.

I have always thought that the old ballad-singer's world—the world in which he moved, and again the ideal world of his songs—is nowhere to be so vividly realised as in the Hofkirche at Innsbruck, among that colossal company who watch the tomb of Kaiser Max; huge men and women in richly wrought bronze array, ugly indeed, most of them, but with two of their number seeming to embody every beautiful quality that was possessed or dreamt of through well nigh a millennium: the pensive, graceful form of Theodoric, king of the Ostrogoths, and the erect figure whose very attitude suggests all manly worth, all gentle valour, under which is read the quaint device, "Arthur *von England*."

If not rewarded with sufficient promptitude and liberality, the ballad-singer was not slow to call attention to the fact. Colin Muset, a jongleur who practised his trade in Lorraine and Champagne in the thirteenth century, has left a charming photograph of contemporary manners in a song which sets forth his wants and deserts.

> Lord Count, I have the viol played [1]
> Before yourself, within your hall,
> And you my service never paid
> Nor gave me any wage at all;
>   'T was villany :

---

[1] Sire cuens, j'ai vielé
  Devant vous, en vostre osté;
 Si ne m'avez, riéns doné,
 Ne mes gages aquité
     C'est vilanie ;

By faith I to Saint Mary owe,
Upon such terms I serve you not,
My alms-bag sinks exceeding low,
My trunk ill-furnished is, I wot.

Lord Count, now let me understand,
What 'tis you mean to do for me,
If with free heart and open hand
Some ample guerdon you decree
     Through courtesy ;
For much I wish, you need not doubt,
In my own household to return,
And if full purse I am without,
Small greeting from my wife I earn.

"Sir Engelé," I hear her say,
"In what poor country have you been,
That through the city all the day
You nothing have contrived to glean !
See how your wallet folds and bends,
Well stuffed with wind and nought beside ;

Foi que doi Sainte Marie !
Ainc ne vos sievrai je mie,
M'aumosniere est mal garnie
Et ma malle mal farsie.

Sire cuens, quar comandez
De moi vostre volonté.
Sire, s'il vous vient à gré
Un beau don car me donez
     Par cortoisie.
Talent ai, n'en dotez mie,
De r'aler à ma mesnie.
Quant vois borse desgarnie,
Ma feme ne me rit mie.

Ains me dit : Sire Engelé
En quel terre avez esté,
Qui n'avez rien conquesté
     Aval la ville ?
Vez com vostre male plie,
Ele est bien de vent farsie.

Accursed is he who e'er intends
As your companion to abide."

When reached the house wherein I dwell,
And that my wife can clearly spy
My bag behind me bulge and swell,
And I myself clad handsomely
   In a grey gown,
Know that she quickly throws away
Her distaff, nor of work doth reck,
She greets me laughing, kind and gay,
And twines both arms around my neck.

My wife soon seizes on my bag,
And empties it without delay ;
My boy begins to groom my nag,
And hastes to give him drink and hay ;
My maid meanwhile runs off to kill
Two capons, dressing them with skill
   In garlic sauce ;

 Honi soit qui a envie
 D'estre en vostre compaignie.

 Quant je vieng à mon hosté
 Et ma feme a regardé
 Derier moi le sac enflé,
 Et ge qui sui bien paré
   De robe grise,
 Sachiez qu'ele a tot jus mise
 La quenoille, sans faintise.
 Elle me rit par franchise,
 Les deux bras au col me lie.

 Ma feme va destrousser
 Ma male, sanz demorer.
 Mon garçon va abruver
 Mon cheval et conreer.
 Ma pucele va tuer
 Deux chapons por deporter
   A la sause aillie ;

My daughter in her hand doth bear,
Kind girl, a comb to smooth my hair.
Then in my house I am a king,
Great joyance and no sorrowing,
Happier than you can say or sing.

Ballad-singing suffered by the invention of printing, but it was in England that the professional minstrel met with the cruellest blow of all—the statute passed in the reign of Queen Elizabeth which forbade his recitations, and classed him with "rogues, vagabonds, and sturdy beggars."

" Beggars they are with one consent,
And rogues by Act of Parliament."

On the other hand, it was also in England that the romantic ballad had its revival, and was introduced to an entirely new phase of existence. The publication of the *Percy Reliques* (1765) started the modern period in which popular ballads were not only to be accepted as literature, but were to exercise the strongest influence on lettered poets from Goethe and Scott, down to Dante Rossetti.

Not that popular poetry had ever been without its intelligent admirers, here and there, among men of culture : Montaigne had said of it, "La poësie populere et purement naturelle a des naïvetez et graces par où elle se compare à la principale beauté de la poësie parfaicte selon l'art : comme il se voit es villanelles

Ma fille m'apporte un pigne.
En sa main par cortoisie
Lors sui de mon ostel sire,
A mult grant joie, sans ire,
Plus que nus ne porroit dire.

de Gascouigne et aus chançons qu'on nous raporte
des nations qui n'ont conoissance d'acune science, ny
mesme d'escripture." There were even ardent collectors, like Samuel Pepys, who is said to have
acquired copies of two thousand ballads.[1] Still, till
after the appearance of Bishop Percy's book (as his
own many faults of omission and commission attest),
the literary class at large did not take folk-songs quite
seriously. The *Percy Reliques* was followed by
Herder's *Volkslieder* (1782), Scott's *Minstrelsy of the
Scottish Border* (1802), Fauriel's *Chansons Populaires
de la Grèce* (1824), to mention only three of its more
immediate successors. The "return to Nature" in
poetry became an irresistible movement; the world,
tired of the classical forms of the eighteenth century,
listened as gladly to the fresh voice of the popular
muse, as in his father's dreary palace Giacomo
Leopardi listened to the voice of the peasant girl over
the way, who sang as she plied the shuttle:

> Sonavan le quiete
> Stanze, e le vie dintorno.
> Al tuo perpetuo canto,
> Allor che all opre femminili intenta
> Sedevi, assai contenta
> Di quel vago avvenir che in mente avevi.
> Era il Maggio odoroso : e tu solevi
> Così menare il giorno.
>
> • • • • •
>
> Lingua mortal non dice
> Quel ch' io sentiva in seno.

---

[1] Not to speak of Charlemagne, who ordered a collection to
be made of German songs.

The hunt for ballads led the way to the search for every sort of popular song, and with what zeal that search has since been prosecuted, the splendid results in the hands of the public now testify.

III.

A brief glance must be taken at what may be called domestic folk-poetry. In a remote past, rural people found delight or consolation in singing the events of their obscure lives, or in deputing other persons of their own station, but especially skilled in the art, to sing them for them. Thus there were marriage-songs and funeral-songs, labour-songs and songs for the culminating points of the pastoral or agricultural year. It is beyond my present purpose to speak of the vintage festivals, and of the literary consequences of the cult of Dionysus. I will, instead, pause for a moment to consider the ancient harvest-songs. Among the Greeks, particularly in Phrygia and in Sicily, all harvest-songs bore the generic name of Lytierses, and how they got it, gives an instructive instance of myth-facture. Lytierses was the son of King Midas, and a king himself, but also a mighty reaper, whose habit it was to indulge in trials of strength with his companions, and with strangers who were passing by. He tied the vanquished up in sheaves and beat them. One day he defied an unknown stranger, who proved too strong for him, and by whom he was slain. So died Lytierses, the reaper, and the first " Lytierses," or harvest-song, was composed to console his father, King Midas, for his loss.

Now, if we regard Lytierses as the typical agriculturist, and his antagonist as the growth or vegetation genius, the fable seems to read thus: Between man and Nature there is a continual struggle; man is often victorious, but, if too presumptuous, a time comes when he must yield. In harvest customs continued to this day, a struggle with or for the last sheaf forms a common feature. The reapers of Western France tie the sheaf, adorned with flowers, to a post driven strongly into the ground, then they fetch the farmer and his wife and all the farm folk to help in dragging it loose, and when the fastenings break, it is borne off in triumph. So popular is this *Fête de la Gerbe*, that, during the Chouan war, the leaders had to allow their peasant soldiers to return to their villages to attend it, or they would have deserted in a body. It may not be irrelevant to add that in Brittany the great wrestling matches take place at the *fête* of the " new threshing floor," when all the neighbours are invited to unite in preparing it for the corn. In North Germany, where the peasants still believe that the last sheaf contains the growth-genius, they set it in honour on the festive board, and serve it double portions of cake and ale.[1] Thus appeased, it becomes a friend to the cultivator. The harvest "man " or " tree " which used to be made by English reapers at the end of the harvest, and presented to master and mistress, obviously belonged to the same family.

We have one or two of the ancient Lytierses in what is most likely very nearly their original and

---

[1] A fuller description of German harvest customs, with remarks on their presumed meaning, will be found in the Rev. J. Van den Gheyn's " Essais de Mythologie et de Philologie comparée," 1885.

popular form. One, composed of distiches telling the story of Midas' son, is preserved in a tragedy by Sosibius, the Syracusian poet. The following, more general in subject, I take from the tenth Idyl of Theocritus :—

Come now hearken awhile to the songs of the god Lytierses.

Demeter, granter of fruits, many sheaves vouchsafe to the corn-field,
Aye to be skilfully tilled, and reaped, and the harvest abundant.

Fasten the heaps, ye binders of sheaves, lest any one passing,
Call out, "worthless clowns, you earn no part of your wages."

Let every sheaf that the sickle has cut be turned to the north wind
Or to the west exposed, for so will the corn grow fatter.

Ye who of wheat are threshers, beware how ye slumber at mid-day,
Then is the chaff from the stalk of the wheat, most easily parted.

Reapers, to labour begin, as soon as the lark upriseth,
And when he sleeps, leave off, yet rest when the sun overpowers.

Blest, O youths, is the life of a frog, for he never is anxious
Who is to pour him his drink, for he always has plenty.

Better at once, O miserly steward, to boil our lentils ;
Mind you don't cut your fingers in trying to chop them to atoms.

These are the songs for the toilers to sing in the heat of the harvest.

Most modern harvest songs manage, like that of Theocritus, to convey some hint of thirst or hunger. "Be merry, O comrades!" sing the girl reapers of Castcignano dei Greci, a Greek settlement in Terra d'Otranto, "Be merry, and go not on your way so downcast; I saw things you cannot see; I saw the housewife kneading dough, or preparing macaroni; and she does it for us to eat, so that we may work like lions at the harvest, and rejoice the heart of the husbandman." This may be a statement of fact or a suggestion of what ought to be a fact. Other songs, sung exclusively at the harvest, bear no outward sign of connection with it; and the reason of their use on that occasion is hopelessly lost.

IV.

I pass on to the old curiosity shop of popular traditions—the nursery. Children, with their innate conservatism, have stored a vast assemblage of odds and ends which fascinate by their very incompleteness. Religion, mythology, history, physical science, or what stood for it; the East, the North—those great banks of ideas—have been impartially drawn on by the infant folk-lorists at their nurses' knees. Children in the four quarters of the globe, repeat the same magic formulæ; words which to every grown person seem devoid of sense, have a universality denied to any articles of faith. What, for example, is the meaning of the play with the snail? Why is he so persistently asked to put his horns out? Pages might be filled with the variants of the well-known invocation which has currency from Rome to Pekin.

English:

I.

Snail, snail, put out your horn,
Or I'll kill your father and mother the morn.

2.

Snail, snail, come out of your hole,
Or else I'll beat you as black as a coal.

3.

Snail, snail, put out your horn,
Tell me what's the day t'morn :
To-day's the morn to shear the corn,
Blaw bil buck thorn.

4.

Snail, snail, shoot out your horn,
Father and mother are dead ;
Brother and sister are in the back-yard
Begging for barley bread.

Scotch :

Snail, snail, shoot out your horn,
And tell us it will be a bonnie day, the morn.

German :

1.

Schneckhûs, Peckhüs,
Stäk du dîn ver Horner rût,
Süst schmût ick dî in 'n Graven,
Da freten dî de Raven.

2.

Tækeltuet,
Kruep uet dyn hues,
Dyn hues dat brennt,
Dyn Kinder de flennt :
Dyn Fru de ligt in Wäken : ·
Kann 'k dy nich mael spräken ?
Tækeltuet, u. s. w.

3.

Snaek, snaek, komm herduet,
Sunst tobräk ik dy dyn Hues.

4.

Slingemues,
Kruep uet dyn Hues,
Stick all dyn veer Höern uet,
Wullt du 's neck uetstäken,
Wik ik dyn Hues tobräken.
Slingemues, u. s. w.

5.

Kuckuch, kuckuck Gerderut,
Stäk dîne vêr Horns herut.

French :

Colimaçon borgne !
. Montre-moi tes cornes ;
Je te dirai où ta mère est morte,
Elle est morte à Paris, à Rouen,
Où l'on sonne les cloches.
Bi, bim, bom,
Bi, bim, bom,
Bi, bim, bom.

Tuscan :

Chiocciola, chiocciola, vien da me,
Ti darò i' pan d' i' re ;
E dell'ova affrittellate
Corni secchî e brucherate.

Roumanian :

Culbecu, culbecu,
Scóte corne boeresci
Si te du la Dunare
Si bé apa tulbure.

Russian :

Ulitka, ulitka,
Vypusti roga,
Ya tebé dam piroga.[1]

---

[1] Mr W. R. S. Ralston has kindly communicated to me this Russian version, which he translates : "Snail, snail, put forth thy horns, I will give to thee cakes."

Chinese :

> Snail, snail, come here to be fed,
> Put out your horns and lift up your head ;
> Father and mother will give you to eat,
> Good boiled mutton shall be your meat.

Several lines in the second German version are evidently borrowed from the Ladybird or Maychafer rhyme which has been pronounced a relic of Freya worship. Here the question arises, is not the snail song also derived from some ancient myth? Count Gubernatis, in his valuable work on *Zoological Mythology* (vol. ii. p. 75), dismisses the matter with the remark that " the snail of superstition is demoniacal." This, however, is no proof that he always bore so suspicious a character, since all the accessories to past beliefs got into bad odour on the establishment of Christianity, unless saved by dedication to the Virgin or other saints. I ventured to suggest, in the *Archivio per lo studio delle tradizioni popolari* (the Italian Folklore Journal), that the snail who is so constantly urged to come forth from his dark house, might in some way prefigure the dawn. Horns have been from all antiquity associated with rays of light. But to write of " Nature Myths in Nursery Rhymes " is to enter on such dangerous ground that I will pursue the argument no further.

V.

Children of older years have preserved the very important class of songs distinguished as singing-games. Everyone knows the famous *ronde* of the Pont d'Avignon :

> Sur le Pont d'Avignon,
> Tout le monde y danse, danse,
> Sur le Pont d'Avignon
> Tout le monde y danse en rond.
>
> Les beaux messieurs font comme ça,
> Sur le Pont d'Avignon,
> Tout le monde y danse, danse,
> Sur le Pont d'Avignon,
> Tout le monde y danse en rond.

After the "messieurs" who bow, come the "demoiselles" who curtsey; the workwomen who sew, the carpenters who saw wood, the washerwomen who wash linen, and a host of other folks intent on their different callings. The song is an apt demonstration of what Paul de Saint-Victor called "cet instinct inné de l'imitation qui fait similer à l'enfant les actions viriles"[1]—in which instinct lies the germ of the theatre. The origin of all spectacles was a performance intended to amuse the performers, and it cannot be doubted that the singing-game throws much light on the beginnings of scenic representations.

Rondes frequently deal with love and marriage, and these, from internal evidence, cannot have been composed by or for the young people who now play them. There are in fact some which would be better forgotten by everybody, but the majority are innocent little dramas, of which it may truly be said, *Honi soit qui mal y pense.* It should be noticed that a distinctly satirical vein runs through many of these games, as

[1] "Les deux Masques," tome i. p. 1.

in the "Gentleman from Spain,"—played in one form
or another all over Europe and the United States,—
in which the suitor would first give any money to get
his bride, and then any money to get rid of her. Or
the Swedish *Lek* (the name given in Sweden to the
singing-game), in which the companions of a young
girl put her sentiments to the test of telling her that
father, mother, sisters, brothers, are dead—all of which
she hears with perfect equanimity—but when they
add that her betrothed is also dead, she falls back
fainting. Then all her kindred are resuscitated without the effect of reviving her, but when she hears that
her lover is alive and well, she springs up and gives
chase to her tormentors.

To my mind there is no more remarkable specimen
of the singing game than *Jenny Jones*—through which
prosaic title we can discern the tender *Jeanne ma joie*
that formed the base of it. The Scotch still say
Jenny Jo, ".Jo" being with them a term of endearment
(*e.g.*, "John Anderson, my Jo!"). The following
variant of the game I took down from word of mouth
at Bocking in Essex :—

"We've come to see Jenny Jones, Jenny Jones, (*repeat*).
How is she now?

Jenny is washing, washing, washing,
Jenny is washing, you can't see her now.

We've come to see Jenny Jones.
How is she now?

Jenny is folding, folding, folding,
You can't see her now.

We've come to see Jenny Jones.
How is she now?

Jenny is starching, starching, starching,
Jenny is starching, you can't see her now.

We've come to see Jenny Jones.
How is she now?

Jenny is ironing, ironing, ironing,
Jenny is ironing, you can't see her now.

We've come to see Jenny Jones.
How is she now?

Jenny is ill, ill, ill,
Jenny is ill, so you can't see her now.

We've come to see Jenny Jones.
How is she now?

(*Mournfully.*)
Jenny is dead, dead, dead,
Jenny is dead, you can't see her now.

May we come to the funeral?
Yes.

May we come in red?
Red is for soldiers; you can't come in red.

May we come in blue?
Blue is for sailors; you can't come in blue.

May we come in white?
White is for weddings; you can't come in white.

May we come in black?
Black is for funerals, so you can come in that.

Jenny is then carried and buried (*i.e.*, laid on the grass) by two of the girls, while the rest follow as mourners, uttering a low, prolonged wail.

Perhaps the earliest acted tragedy—a tragedy acted before Æschylus lived — was something like this. Anyhow, it may remind us of how early a taste for the tragic is developed, if not in the life of mankind at all events in the life of man. "What is the reason," asks St Augustine, "that men wish to be moved by the sight of tragic and painful things, which, nevertheless, they do not wish to undergo themselves? For the spectators (at a play) desire to feel grieved, and this grief is their joy : whence comes it unless from some strange spiritual malady?"[1]

Dr Pitrè describes this Sicilian game : A child lies down, pretending to be dead. His companions stand round and sing a dirge in the most dolorous tones. Now and then, one of them runs up to him and lifts an arm or a leg, afterwards letting it fall, to make sure that he is quite dead. Satisfied on this point, they prepare to bury him, but before doing so, they nearly stifle him with parting kisses. Tired, at last, of his painful position, the would-be dead boy jumps up and gets on the back of the most aggressive of his playmates, who is bound to carry him off the scene.

To play at funerals was probably a very ancient amusement. No doubt some such game as the above is alluded to in the text, " . . . children sitting in the markets and calling unto their fellows and saying, We have piped unto you and ye have not danced, we have mourned unto you and ye have not lamented."

VI.

Mysteries and Miracle Plays must not be forgotten, though in their origin they were not a plant of strictly popular growth. Some writers consider that they were instituted by ecclesiastics as rivals to the lay or pagan plays which were still in great favour in the

[1] "Confessions," book iii. chap. 11.

first Christian centuries. Others think with Dr Hermann Ulrici,[1] that they grew naturally out of the increasingly pictorial celebration of the early Greek liturgy, — painted scenes developing into *tableaux vivants*, and these into acted and spoken interludes. It is certain that they were started by the clergy, who at first were the sole actors, assuming characters of both sexes. As time wore on, something more lively was desired, and clowns and buffoons were accordingly introduced. They appeared in the Innsbruck Play of the fourteenth century ; and again in 1427, in the performances given at Metz, while the serious parts were acted by ecclesiastics, the lighter, or comic parts, were represented by laymen. These performances were held in a theatre constructed for the purpose, but mysteries were often played in the churches themselves, nor is the practice wholly abandoned. A Nativity play is performed in the churches of Upper Gascony on Christmas Eve, of which the subjoined account will, perhaps, be read with interest :—

In the middle of the Midnight Mass, just when the priest has finished reading the gospel, Joseph and Mary enter the nave, the former clad in the garb of a village carpenter with his tools slung across his shoulder, the latter dressed in a robe of spotless white. The people divide so as to let them pass up the church, and they look about for a night's lodging. In one part of the church the stable of Bethlehem is represented behind a framework of greenery ; here they take up their position, and presently a cradle is placed beside them which contains the image of a babe. The voice of an angel from on high now proclaims the birth of the Infant Saviour, and calls on the shepherds to draw near to the sound of glad music. The way in which this bit of theatrical "business" is managed, is by a

[1] " Shakespeare's Dramatic Art," 1876.

C

child in a surplice, with wings fastened to his shoulders, being drawn up to the ceiling seated on a chair, which is supported by ropes on a pulley. The shepherds, real shepherds in white, homespun capes, with long crooks decked with ribbons, are placed on a raised dais, which stands for the mountain. They wake up when they hear the angel's song, and one of them exclaims :

> Diou dou cèou, quino vèro vouts !
> Un anjou mous parlo, pastous ;
> Biste quieten noste troupet !
> Mes que dit l'anjou, si vous plait ?

> (Heavens ! with how sweet a voice
> The angel calls us to rejoice ;
> Quick leave your flocks : but tell me, pray,
> What doth the heavenly angel say ?)

The angel replies in French :

> Rise, shepherd, nor delay,
> 'Tis God who summons thee,
> Hasten with zeal away
> Thy Saviour's self to see.
> The Lord of Hosts hath shown
> That since this glorious birth,
> War shall be no more known,
> But peace shall reign on earth.

The shepherds, however, are not very willing to be disturbed : "Let me sleep ! Let me sleep !" says one of them, and another goes so far as to threaten to drive away the angel if he does not let them alone. "Come and render homage to the new-born babe," sings the angel, "and cease to complain of your happy lot." They answer :

> A happy lot
> We never yet possest,
> A happy lot
> For us poor shepherd folk existeth not ;
> Then wherefore utter the strange jest
> That by an infant's birth we shall be blest
> With happy lot ?

The shepherds begin to bestir themselves. One says that he feels overcome with fear at the sound of so much noise and commotion. The angel responds, " Come without fear ; do not hesitate, but redouble your speed. It is in this village, in a poor place, near yonder wood, that you may see the Infant Lord." Another of the shepherds, who seems to have only just woke up, inquires :

> What do you say ?
> This to believe what soul is able ;
>   What do you say ?
> Where do these shepherds speed away ?
> To see their God within a stable :
> This surely seems an idle fable ;
>   What do you say ?

" To understand how it is, go and behold with your own eyes," replies the angel ; to which the shepherd answers, " Good morrow, angel ; pardon me if I have spoken lightly ; I will go and see what is going on." Another, still not quite easy in his mind, observes that he cannot make out what the angel says, because he speaks in such a strange tongue. The angel immediately replies in excellent Gascon patois :

> Come, shepherds, come
> From your mountain home,
> Come, see the Saviour in a stable born,
>   This happy morn.
> Come, shepherds, come,
> Let none remain behind,
> Come see the wretched sinners' friend,
>   The Saviour of mankind.

When they hear the good news, sung to a quaint and inspiriting air in their own language, the shepherds hesitate no longer, but set off for Bethlehem in a body. One of them, it is true, ex- presses some doubts as to what will become of the flocks in their absence ; but a veteran shepherd strikes his crook upon the ground and sternly reproves him for being anxious about the sheep when a heavenly messenger has declared that " God has made Himself the Shepherd of mankind." They leave the dais, and march out of the church, the whole of which is now considered as being the stable. After a while the shepherds knock for admittance, and their voices are heard in the calm crisp midnight air chaunting these words to sweet and solemn strains :

> Master of this blest abode,
> O guardian of the Infant God,
> Open your honoured gate, that we
> May at His worship bend the knee.

Joseph fears that the strangers may perchance be enemies, but reassured by an angel, he opens the door, only naïvely regretting that the lowly chamber "should be so badly lighted." They prostrate themselves before the cradle, and the choir bursts forth with :

> Gloria Deo in excelsis,
> O Domine te laudamus,
> O Deus Pater rex caelestis,
> In terra pax hominibus.

The shepherdesses then render their homage, and deposit on the altar steps a banner covered with flowers and greenery, from which hang strings of small birds, apples, nuts, chestnuts, and other fruits. It is their Christmas offering to the curé ; the shepherds have already placed a whole sheep before the altar, in a like spirit.

The next scene takes us into Herod's palace, where the magi arrive, and are directed to proceed to Bethlehem. During their adoration of the Infant Saviour, Mass is finished, and the Sacrament is administered ; after which the play is brought to a close with the flight into Egypt and the massacre of the Innocents.

This primitive drama gives a better idea of the early mysteries than do the performances at Ober Ammergau, which have been gradually pruned and improved under the eye of a critical public. But it is unusually free from the absurdities and levities which abound in most miracle plays; such as the wrangle between Noah and his wife in the old Chester Mysteries, in which the latter declares " by St John " that the Flood is a false alarm, and that no power on earth shall make her go into the Ark. Noah ends with putting her on board by main force, and is rewarded by a box on the ear.

The best surviving sample of a non-scriptural rustic play is probably *Saint Guillaume of Poitou*, a Breton versified drama in seven acts. The history of the Troubadour Count whose wicked manhood leads to a preternaturally pious old age, corresponds to every requirement of the peasant play-goer. Time and space are set airily at defiance ; saints and devils are not only called, but come at the shortest notice ; the plot is exciting enough to satisfy the strongest craving for sensation, and the dialogue is vigorous, and, in parts, picturesque. One can well believe that the fiery if narrow patriotism of a Breton audience would be stirred by the scene where the reformed Count William, who has withstood all other blandishments, is almost lured out of his holy seclusion by the Evil One coming to him in the shape of a fellow-townsman who represents his city as hard pressed by overwhelming foes, and in its extremest need, imploring his aid ; that the religious fervour of Breton peasants would be moved by the recital of the vision in which a very wicked man appears at the bar of judgment : his sins out-number the hairs of his head, you would call him an irredeemable wretch ; yet it does so happen that once upon a time he gave two pilgrims a bed of straw in a pig-stye, and now St Francis throws this straw into the balance, and it bends down the scale !

So in the Song of the Sun, in Sæmund's *Edda*, a fierce freebooter, who has despoiled mankind, and who always ate alone, opens his door one evening to a tired wayfarer, and gives him meat and drink. The guest meditates evil; then in his sleep he murders his host, but he is doomed to take on him all the sins of the man he has slain, while the one-time evil-doer's soul is borne by angels into a life of purity, where it shall live for ever with God. This motive is repeatedly introduced into folk-lore, and was made effective use of by Victor Hugo in *Sultan Mourad*, the infamous tyrant who goes to Heaven on the strength of having felt momentary compassion for a pig.

In plays of the *Saint Guillaume* class, the plain language in which the vices and oppression of the nobles is denounced shows signs of the slow surging up of the democratic spirit whose traces through the middle ages are nowhere to be more fruitfully sought than in popular literature—though they lie less in the rustic drama than in the great mediæval satires, such as *Reynard the Fox* and *Marcolfo*, the latter of which is still known to the Italian people under the form of *Bertoldo*, in which it was recast in the sixteenth century, by G. B. Croce, the rhyming blacksmith of Bologna.

VII.

Epopees, *chansons de geste*, romantic ballads, occasional or ceremonial songs, nursery rhymes, singing-games, rustic dramas; to these must be added the great order of purely personal and lyrical songs, of which the unique and exclusive subject is love.

Popular love songs have one quality in common : a sincerity which is not perhaps reached in the entire range of lettered amorous poetry. Love is to these singers a thing so serious that however high they fly, they do not outsoar what is to them the atmosphere of truth. " La passion parle là toute pure," as Molière said of the old song :

> Si le roi m'avoit donné
> Paris, sa grande ville,
> Et qu'il me fallût quitter
> L'amour de ma mie :
> Je dirois au roi Henri
> Reprenez votre Paris
> J'aime mieux ma mie, oh gay !
> J'aime mieux ma mie.

An immense, almost incredible, number of popular songs have been set down during the last twenty years by collectors who, like Tigri in Tuscany, and Pitrè in Sicily, have done honour to their birthlands, and an enduring service to literature. It has been seen that Italy, Portugal, and Spain have songs which, though differing in shape, are yet materially alike. Where was the original fount of this lyrical river ? Some would look for it in Arabia, and cite the evident poetic fertility of those countries where Arab influence once prevailed. Others regard the existing passion-verse as a descendant of the mediæval poetry associated with Provence. Others, again, while admitting that there may have been modifications of form, find it hard to believe that there was ever a time, since the type was first established, when the southern peasant was dumb, or when he did not sing in substance very much as he does now.

Whatever theory be ultimately accepted, it is certain that the popular love-poetry of southern nations, such as it has been received direct from peasant lips, is not the least precious gift we owe to the untaught, uncultured poet, who after having been for long ages ignored or despised, is now raised to his rightful place near the throne of his illustrious brother, the perfect lettered poet. Pan sits unrebuked by the side of Apollo.

These introductory remarks are meant to do no more than to show the principal landmarks of folk-poetry. The subject is a wide one, as they best know who have given it the most careful attention. In the following essays, I have dealt with a few of its less familiar aspects. I would, in conclusion, express my gratitude to the indefatigable excavators of popular lore whose large labours have made my small work possible, and to all who have helped, whether by furnishing unedited specimens or by procuring copies of rare books. My cordial thanks are also due to the editors and publishers of the *Cornhill Magazine*, *Fraser's Magazine*, the *National Review*, the *British Quarterly Review*, the *Revue Internationale*, the *Antiquary*, and the *Record* and *Journal* of the Folk-lore Society, for leave to reprint such part of this book as had appeared in those publications.

Salò, Lago di Garda,
January 15 1886.

THE INSPIRATION OF DEATH IN
FOLK-POETRY.

THE Roumanians call death "the betrothed of the
world : " that which awaits. The Neapolitans give it
the name of *la vedova :* that which survives. It would
be easy to go on multiplying the stock of contrasting
epithets. Inevitable yet a surprise, of daily incidence
yet a mystery, unvarying yet most various, a common
fact yet incapable of becoming common-place, death
may be looked at from innumerable points of view ;
but, look at it how we will, it moves and excites our
spiritual consciousness as nothing else can do. The
first poet of human things was perhaps one who stood
in the presence of death. In the twilight that went
before civilization the loves of men were prosaic, and
intellectual unrest was remote, but there was already
Rachel weeping for her children and would not be
comforted because they are not. Death, high priest
of the ideal, led man in his infancy through a crisis of
awe passing into transcendent exaltation, kindred
with the state which De Quincey describes when
recalling the feelings wrought in his childish brain by
the loss of his sister. It set the child-man asking
why ? first sign of a dawning intelligence ; it told him
in familiar language that we lie on the borders of the
unknown ; it opened before him the infinite spaces of
hope and fear ; it shattered to pieces the dull round

of the food-seeking present, and built up out of the ruins the perception of a past and a future. It was the symbol of a human oneness with the coming and going of day and night, summer and winter, the rising and receding tide. It caused even the rudest of men to speak lower, to tread more softly, revealing to him unawares the angel Reverence. And above all, it wounded the heart of man. M. Renan says with great truth, " Le grand agent de la marche du monde, c'est la douleur." What poetry owes to the bread of sorrow has never been better told than by the Greek folk-singer, who condenses it into one brief sentence : " Songs are the words spoken by those who suffer."

The influence of death on the popular imagination is shown in those ballads of the supernatural of which folk-poetry offers so great an abundance as to make choice difficult. One of the most powerful as well as the most widely diffused of the people's ghost stories is that which treats of the persecuted child whose mother comes out of her grave to succour him. There are two or three variants of this among the Czech songs. A child aged eighteen months loses his mother. As soon as he is old enough to understand about such things, he asks his father what he has done with her ? " Thy mother sleeps a heavy sleep, no one will wake her ; she lies in the graveyard hard by the gate." When the child hears that, he runs to the graveyard. He loosens the earth with a big pin and pushes it aside with his little finger. Then he cries mournfully, " Ah ! mother, little mother, say one little word to me ! " " My child, I cannot," the mother replies, " my head is weighed down with clay ; on my heart is a stone which burns like fire ;

go home little one, there you have another mother."
"Ah!" rejoins he, "she is not good like you were.
When she gives me bread she turns it thrice ; when
you gave it me you spread it with butter. When she
combs my hair she makes my head bleed ; when you
combed my hair, mother, you fondled it. When she
bathes my feet she bruises them against the side of
the basin ; when you bathed them you kissed them.
When she washes my shirt she loads me with curses ;
you used to sing whilst you washed." The mother
answers : "Go back to the house, my child, to-morrow
I will come for you." The child goes back to the
house and lies down in his bed. "Ah! father, my
little father, make ready my winding-sheet, my soul
now belongs to. God, my body to the grave, to the
grave near my mother—how glad her heart will be!"
One day he was ill, the second he died, the third day
they buried him. The effect is heightened by the
interval placed between the mother's death and the
child's awakening to his own forlorn condition.
When the mother died he was too young to think or
to grieve. He did not know that she was gone until
he missed her. Only by degrees, after years of harsh
treatment, borne with the patience of a child or a
dumb animal, he began to feel intuitively rather than
to remember that it had not been always so—that he
had once been loved. Then, going straight to the
point with the terrible accusative power that lies in
children, he said to the father, "What have you done
with my mother?" He had been able to live and to
suffer until he was old enough to think ; when he
thought, he died. Here we have an instance, one of
the many that exist, of a motive which, having re-

curred again and again in folk-poetry, gets handled
at last by a master-poet, who gives it enduring shape
and immortality.   Victor Hugo may or may not have
known the popular legend.   It is most likely that he
did not know it.   Yet, stripped of the marvellous, and
modified in certain secondary points of construction,
the story is the story of "Petit Paul," little Paul, the
child of modern France, who takes company with
Dante's Anselmuccio and Shakespeare's Arthur, and
who with them will live in the pity of all time.   The
Ruthenes affirm that it was Christ who bade the child
seek his mother's grave.   The Provençal folk-poet
begins his tale: "You shall hear the complaint of .
three very little children."   The mother of these
children was dead, the father had married again.   The
new wife brought a hard time for the children, and
the day came when they were like to starve.   The
littlest begged for a bit of bread, and he got a kick
which threw him to the ground.   Then the biggest of
the brothers said, "Get up and let us go to our mother
in the graveyard ; she will give us bread."   They set
out at once ; on their way they met Jesus Christ.

> Et ount anetz, mes angis,
> Mes angis tant petits ?

"Where are you going, my angels, my so very small
angels?"   "We go to the graveyard to find our
mother."   Jesus Christ tells the mother to come forth
and give her children food.   "How would you have
me come forth, when there is no strength left in me ?"
He answers that her strength shall come back to her
for seven years.   Now, as the end of the seven years
drew near, she was always sobbing and sighing, and
the children asked why it was.   "I weep, my children,

because I have to go away from you." "Weep no
more, mother, we will all go together ; one shall carry
the hyssop, another will take the taper, the last will
hold the book. We will go home singing." The
Provençal poet does not tell us what happened when
the resuscitated wife came back to her former abode ;
we have to go to Scandinavia for an account of that.
Dyring the Dane went to an island and wed a fair
maiden. For seven years they dwelt together and
were blessed with children ; but while the youngest
born was still a helpless babe, Death stalked through
the land and carried off the young wife in his clutches.
Dyring went to another island and married a girl who
was bad and spiteful. He brought her home to his
house, and when she reached the door the six little
children were there crying. She thrust them aside
with her foot, she gave them no ale and no bread ; she
said, "You shall suffer thirst and hunger." She took
from them their blue cushions, and said, "You shall
sleep on straw." She took from them their wax
candles, and said, "You shall stay in the dark." In
the evening, very late, the children cried, and their
mother heard them under the ground. She listened
as she lay in her shroud, and thought to herself, "I
must go to my little children." She begged our
Lord so hard to let her go, that her prayer was
granted. "Only you must be back when the cock
crows." She lifted her weary limbs, the grave gaped,
she passed through the village, the dogs howled as
she passed, throwing up their noses in the air. When
she got to the house, she saw her eldest daughter on
the threshold. "Why are you standing there, my
dear daughter ? Where are your brothers and
sisters ? " The daughter knew her not. She said

her mother was fair and blithe, her face was white and pink. "How can I be fair and blithe? I am dead, my face is pale. How can I be white and pink, when I have been all this time in my winding-sheet?" Answering thus, the mother hastened to her little children's chamber. She found them with tears running down their cheeks. She brushed the clothes of one, she tidied the hair of the second, she lifted the third from the floor, she comforted the fourth, the fifth she set on her knee as though she were fain to suckle it. To the eldest girl she said, "Go and tell Dyring to come here." And when he came she cried in wrath, "I left you ale and bread, and my little ones hunger ; I left you blue cushions, and my little ones lie on straw ; I left you waxen candles, and my little ones are in the dark. Woe betide you, if there be cause I should return again ! Behold the red cock crows, the dead fly underground. Behold the black cock crows, heaven's doors are thrown wide. Behold the white cock crows, I must begone." So saying she went, and was seen no more. Ever after that night each time Dyring and his wife heard the dogs bark they gave the children ale and bread ; each time they heard the dogs bay they were seized with dread of the dead woman ; each time they heard the dogs howl they trembled lest she should come back. Two universal beliefs are introduced into this variant : the disappearance of the dead at cock crow, and the connection of the howling of dogs with death or the dead. The last is a superstition which still obtains a wide acceptance even among educated people. I was speaking of it lately to an English officer, who stated that he had twice heard the death howl, once while on duty in Ireland, and once, if I remember right, in India. It was, he said, totally unlike any other noise produced by a dog. I observed that all noises sound singular when the nerves are strained by painful expectancy; but he answered that in his own case his feelings were not involved, as the death which occurred, in one instance at least, was that of a perfect stranger.

The interpretation of dreams as a direct intercourse with the spiritual world is not usual in folk-lore; the people hardly see the need of placing the veil of sleep between mortal eyes and ghostly appearances. In a Bulgarian song, however, a sleeping girl speaks with her dead mother. Militza goes down into the little garden where the white and red roses are in bloom. She is weary, and she is soon asleep. A small fine rain begins to fall, the wind rustles in the leaves; Militza sighs, and having sighed, she awakes. Then she upbraids the rain and the wind: "Whistle no more, O wind; thou, O rain, descend no more; for in my dreams I found my mother. Rain, may thy fount be dried; mayst thou be for ever silent, O wind: ye have taken me from the counsel my mother gave me." The few lines thus baldly summarized make up, as it seems to me, a little masterpiece of delicate conception and light workmanship: one which would surprise us from the lips of a letterless poet, were there not proof that no touch is so light and so sure as that of the artificer untaught in our own sense—the man or the woman who produces the intricate filigree, the highly wrought silver, the wood carving, the embroidery, the lace, the knitted wool rivalling the spider's web, the shawl with whose weft and woof a human life is interwoven.

I have only once come upon the case of a father who returns to take care of his offspring. Mr Chu, a worthy Chinese gentleman, revisited this earth as a disembodied spirit to guard and teach his little boy Wei. When Wei reached the age of twenty-two, and took his doctor's degree, his father, Mr Chu, finally vanished. As a general rule, the Chinese consider the sight of his former surroundings to be the worst penalty that can befall a soul. Mr Herbert Giles, in his fascinating work on the Liao-Chai of P'u Sing-Ling, gives a full account of the terrible See-one's-home terrace as represented in the fifth court of Purgatory in the Taoist Temples. Good souls, or even those who have done partly good and partly evil, will never stand thereon. The souls of the wicked only see their homes as if they were near them : they see their last wishes disregarded, everything upside down, their substance squandered, the husband prepares to take a new wife, strangers possess the old estate, in their misery the dead man's family curse him, his children become corrupt, lands are gone, the house is burnt, the wife sees her husband tortured, the husband sees his wife stricken down with mortal disease ; friends forget : "some perhaps for the sake of bygone times may stroke the coffin and let fall a tear, departing with a cold smile." In the West, this gloomy creed is perhaps hinted at in the French proverb, "Les morts sont bien mort." But Western thought at its best, at its highest, imagines differently. It imagines that the most gracious privilege of immortal spirits is that of beholding those beloved of them in mortal life—

> I am still near,
> Watching the smiles I prized on earth,
> Your converse mild, your blameless mirth.

Happy and serene optimism !

The ghosts of folk-lore return not only to succour the innocent, they come back also to convict the guilty. The avenging ghost shows himself in all kinds of strange and uncanny ways rather than in his habit as he lived. He comes in animal or vegetable shape; or perhaps he uses the agency of some inanimate object. In the Faroe Isles there is a story of a girl whose sister pushed her into the sea out of jealousy. The blue waves cast ashore her body, which was found by two pilgrims, who made the arms into a harp, and the flaxen locks into strings. Then they went and played the harp at the wedding feast of the murderess and the dead girl's betrothed. The first string said, "The bride is my sister." The second string said, "The bride caused my death." The third string said, "The bridegroom is my betrothed." The harp's notes swelled louder and louder, and the guilty bride fell sick unto death; before the pilgrims had done playing, her heart broke. This is much the same story as the "Twa Sisters of Binnorie." A Slovack legend describes two musicians who, as they were travelling together, noticed a fine plane tree; and one said to the other, "Let us cut it down, it is just the thing to make a violin of; the violin will be equally yours and mine; we will play on it by turn." At the first blow the tree sighed; at the second blow blood spurted out; at the third blow the tree began to talk. It said: "Musicians, fair youths, do not cut me down; I am not a tree, I am made of flesh and blood; I am a lovely girl of the neighbouring town; my mother cursed me while I drew water—while I drew water and chatted with my friend. 'Mayst thou change into a plane tree with broad leaves,' said

D

she. Go ye, musicians, and play before my mother."
So they betook themselves to the mother's door and
played a dirge over her child. "Play not, musicians,
fair youths," she entreated. "Rend not my heart by
your playing. I have enough of woe in having lost
my daughter. Hapless the mother who curses her
children!" The well-known German tale of the
juniper tree belongs to the same class. A beautiful
little boy is killed by his step-mother, who serves him
up as a dish of meat to his father. The father eats in
ignorance, and throws away the bones, which are
gathered up by the little half-sister, who puts them
into her best silk handkerchief and buries them under
a juniper tree. Presently a bird of gay plumage
perches on the tree, and whistles as it flits from branch
to branch—

> Min moder de mi slach't,
> Min fader de mi att,
> Min swester de Marleenken
> Söcht alle mine Beeniken,
> Und bindt sie in een syden Dook
> Legst unner den Machandelboom ;
> Ky witt! ky witt! Ach watt en schön vagel bin ich !

—a rhyme which Goethe puts into the mouth of
Gretchen in prison. In the German story the step-
mother's brains are knocked out by the fall of a mill-
stone, and the bird-boy is restored to human form;
but in a Scotch variant the last event does not take
place. It may have been thrown in by some narrator .
who had a weakness for a plot which ends well. All
these wonder-tales had probably an original connection with a belief in the transmigration of souls. In
truth, the people's *Märchen* are rooted nearly always

on some article of ancient faith : that is why they have
so long a life. Faith vitalizes poetry or legend or art ;
and what once lived takes a great time to die. Now
that the beliefs which fostered them have gone into
the lumber-room of disused religions, the old wonder-
tales still have a freshness and a horror which cannot
be found even in the best of brand-new "made-up"
stories.

Another reason why the dead come back is to fulfil
a promise. The Greek mother of the Kleft song has
nine sons and one only daughter. She bathes her in
the darkness, her hair she combs in the light, she
dresses her beneath the shining of the moon. A
stranger from Bagdad has asked her in marriage, and
Constantine, one of the sons, counsels his mother to
give her to the stranger. "Thou art wont to be prudent, but in this thou art senseless," says the mother.
"Who will bring her back to me if there be joy or
sorrow?" Constantine gives her God as surety, and
all the saints and martyrs, that if there be sorrow or
joy he will bring her back. In two years all the nine
sons die, and when it is Constantine's turn, the mother
leans over his body and tears her hair. Fain would
she have back her daughter Arete, and behold Constantine lies dead. At midnight Constantine gets up
and goes to where his sister dwells, and bids Arete to
follow him. She asks what has happened, but he tells
her nothing. While they journey along the birds
sing: "See you that lovely girl riding with the dead?"
Then Arete asks her brother if he heard what the
birds said. "They are only birds," he answers; "never
mind them." She says her brother has such an odour
of incense that it fills her with fear. "It is only," he

says, "because we passed the evening in the chapel of St John." When they reach their home, the mother opens the portal and sees the dead and the living come in together, and her soul leaves her body. The motive of a ride with the dead, made familiar by the "Erl König" and Burgher's "Lenore," can be traced through endless variations in folk-poesy.

In the Swedish ballad of "Little Christina," a lover rises from his grave, not to carry off his beloved, but simply to console her. One night Christina hears light fingers tapping at her door; she opens it, and her dead betrothed comes in. She washes his feet with pure wine, and for a long while they speak together. Then the cocks begin to crow, and the dead get them underground. The young girl puts on her shoes and follows her betrothed through the wide forest. When they reach the graveyard, the fair hair of the young man begins to disappear. "See, maiden," he says, "how the moon has reddened all at once; even so, in a moment, thy beloved will vanish." She sits down on the tomb and says : "I shall remain here till the Lord calls me." Then she hears the voice of her betrothed saying to her : "Little Christina, go back to thy dwelling-place. Every time a tear falls from thine eyes my shroud is full of blood. Every time thy heart is gay, my shroud is full of rose leaves."

If the display of excessive grief is thus shown to be only grievous to the dead, yet they are held to be keenly sensible of a lack of due and decorous respect. Such respect they generally get from rough or savage natures, unless it be denied out of intentional scorn or enmity. There is a factory in England where common men are employed to manipulate large importations of bones for agricultural uses. Each cargo contains a certain quantity of bones which are very obviously human. These the workmen sort out, and when they have got a heap they bury it, and ask the manager to read over it some passages from the Burial Service. They do it of their own free will and initiative; were they hindered, they would very likely leave the works. Shall it be called foolish or sublime? Another curious instance of respect to the dead comes to my mind. On board ship two cannon balls are ordinarily sewed up with a body to sink it. Once a negro died at sea, and his fellows, negroes also, took him in a boat and rowed a long way to a place where they were to commit him to the deep. After a while the boat returned to the ship, still with its burden. The explanation was soon made. The negroes discovered that they had only one cannon ball, they had rowed back for the other. One would have been quite enough to answer all purposes; but it seemed to them disrespectful to their comrade to cheat him out of half his due.

The dead particularly object to people treading carelessly on their graves. So we learn from one of the songs of Greek outlawry.

All Saturday we held carouse, and far through Sunday night,
And on the Monday morn we found our wine expended quite.
To seek for more without delay the captain made me go;
I ne'er had seen nor known the way, nor had a guide to show.
And so through solitary roads and secret paths I sped,
Which to a little ivied church long time deserted led.
This church was full of tombs, and all by gallant men possest;
One sepulchre stood all alone, apart from all the rest.

I did not see it, and I trod above the dead man's bones,
And as from out the nether world came up a sound of groans.
What ails thee, sepulchre? why thus so deeply groan and sigh?
Doth the earth press, or the black stone weigh on thee heavily?
"Neither the earth doth press me down, nor black stone do
    me. scath,
But I with bitter grief am wrung, and full of shame and wrath,
That thou dost trample on my head, and I am scorned in death.
Perhaps I was not also young, nor brave and stout in fight,
Nor wont as thou, beneath the moon, to wander through the
    night."

Egil Skallagrimson, after his son was drowned, resolved to let himself die of hunger. Thorgerd, his daughter, came to him and prayed hard of him that he would sing. Touched by her affection, he made an effort, gathered up his ideas, dressed them in images, expressed them in song ; and as he sang, his regrets softened, and in the end his soul became so calm that he was satisfied to live. In this beautiful saga lies the secret of folk-elegies. The people find comfort in singing. A Czech maiden asks of the dark woods how they can be as green in winter as in summer; as for her, she cannot help vexing her heart. "But who would not weep in my place? Where is my father, my beloved father? The sandy plain is his winding-sheet. Where is my mother, my good mother? The grass grows over her. I have no brother and no sister, and they have taken away my friend." Of a certainty when she had sung, her vexed heart was lighter. "Seul a un synonym: mort." Yes, but he who sings is scarcely alone, even though there be only the waving pine woods to answer with a sigh. The most passionate laments of the Sclavonic race are for father and mother. If a Little Russian

loses both his parents his despair is such that it often
drives him forth a wanderer on the face of the earth.
One so bereft cries out, " Dear mother, why didst
thou suffer me to see the day ? Why didst thou
bring me into the world without obtaining for me by
thy prayers a portion of its blessings ? My father
and my mother are dead, and with them my country.
Why was I left a wretched orphan ? Oh, could I
find a being miserable as myself that we might sym-
pathize one with the other !" The birth-ties of
kindred are reckoned the only strong ones. Some
Russian lines, translated by Mr Ralston, indicate the
degrees of mourning :

> There weeps his mother—as a river runs ;
> There weeps his sister—as a streamlet flows ;
> There weeps his youthful wife—as falls the dew ;
> The sun will rise and gather up the dew.

A Servian *pesma* illustrates the same idea. Young
Tövo has the misfortune to break his arm. A doctor
is fetched—no other than a Vila of the mountain.
The wily sprite demands in guerdon for the cure the
right hand of the mother, the sister's long hair, with
the ribbons that bind it, the pearl necklace of the
wife. Quickly the mother sacrifices her right hand,
quickly the sister cuts off her much-prized braid, but
the wife says, "Give up my white pearls that my
father gave me ? Not I !" The Vila waxes angry
and poisons Tövo's blood. When he is dead three
women fall "a-kookooing"—one groans without
ceasing ; one sobs at dawn and dusk ; one weeps just
now and then when it comes into her head so to do.
As the cuckoo is supposed to be a sister mourning

for her brother, kookooing has come to mean
lamenting. The Servian girl who has lately lost
her brother cannot hear the cuckoo's note without
weeping. In popular poetry the love of sister for
brother takes precedence even of the love of mother
for child. Not only does Gudrun in the Elder Edda
esteem the murder of her first lord, the god-like
Sigurd, to be of less importance than that of her
brothers, but also to avenge their deaths, she has no
scruple in slaying both her second husband and her
own sons. A Bulgarian ballad shows in still more
striking light the relative value set on the lives of
child and brother. There was a certain man named
Negul, whose head was in danger. The folk-poet is
careful to express no sort of censure upon his hero,
but the boasts he is made to utter are sufficient guides
to his character. Great numbers of Turks has he put
to flight, and yet more women has he killed of those
who would not follow him meekly as his wives.
"And now," he adds plaintively, "a misfortune has
befallen me which I have done nothing at all to
deserve." His sister Milenka hears him bemoaning
his fate, and at once she says to him, "Brother Negul,
Negul, my brother, do not disturb yourself; do not
distress yourself; I have nine sons, nine sons and one
daughter; the youngest of all is Lalo; him will I
sacrifice to save you; I will sacrifice him so that you
may remain to me." This was the promise of Milenka.
Then she hastened to her own home and prepared
hot meats and set flasks of golden wine wherewith to
feast her sons. "Eat and drink together," she said,
"and kiss one another's hands, for Lalo is going away
to be groomsman to his Uncle Negul. Let your

mother see you all assembled, and serve you each in turn with ruddy wine and with smoking viands." For the others she did not wholly fill the glass, but Lalo's glass she filled to the brim. Meanwhile Elka, Lalo's sister, made ready his clothes for the journey; and as she busied about it, the little girl cried because Lalo was going to be groomsman, and they had not asked her to be bridesmaid. Lalo said to Elka, "Elka, my little only sister, do not cry so, sister; do not be so vexed; we are nine brothers, and one of these days you will surely act as bridesmaid." The words were hardly spoken when the headsmen reached the door. They took Lalo, the groomsman, and they chopped off his head in place of his Uncle Negul's.

A new and different world is entered when we follow the folk-poet upon the wrestling-ground of Death and Love. If I have judged rightly, there were songs of death before there were any other love songs than those of the nightingale; but the folk-poet was still young when he learnt to sing of love, and the love poet found out early that his lyre was incomplete without the string of death. In all folk-poetry can be plainly heard that music of love and death which may be said almost to have been the dominant note that sounded through the literature of the ages of romance. Sometimes the victory is given to death, sometimes to love; in one song love, while yielding, conquers. Folk-poetry has not anything more instinct with the quality of intensity than is this "Last Request" of a Greek robber-lover—

> When thou shalt hear that I am ill,
> O my well-beloved! he said,
> O come to me, and quickly come,
> Or thou wilt find me dead.

And when that thou hast reached the house,
  And the great gates passed through,
Then, O my well-beloved, the braids
  Of thy bright hair undo.
And to my mother say straightway,
  Tell me, where is your son?
My son is lying on his bed
  In his chamber all alone.
Then mount the stairs, O my well-beloved,
  And come your lover anigh,
And smooth my pillow that I may
  Raise me a little high,
And hold my head up in thy hands
  Till flies away my soul.
And when thou seest the priest arrive,
  And dress him in his stole,   .
Then place, my well-beloved, a kiss
  On my lips pale and cold ;
And when four youths shall lift me up,
  And on their shoulders hold,
Then shalt thou, O my well-beloved,
  Cast at them many a stone.
And when they reach thy neighbourhood
  And by thy house pass on,
Then, O my well-beloved, thy hair,
  Thy golden tresses cut ;
And when they reach the church's gate,
  And there my coffin put,
Then as the hen her feathers plucks,
  So pluck thy hair for me.
And when my dirges all are done,
  And lights extinguished be,
Then shall my heart, O well-beloved,
  Still be possessed of thee.

We hardly notice the adventitious part of it—the
ancient custom of tearing off the hair, the strange
stone-casting at the youths who represent Charon ;
our attention is absorbed by what is the essence of

the song : passion which has burned itself into pure
fire. Greek folk-poetry shows a blending together of
southern emotions with an imaginative fervour, a
prophetic power that is rather of the East than of the
South. No Tuscan ploughman, for instance, could
·seize the idea of the Greek folk-poet of possessing his
living love in death. If the Tuscan thinks of a union
in the grave, it can only be attained by the one who
remains joining the one who is gone—

> O friendly soil,
> Soil that doth hold my love in thine embrace,
> Soon as for me shall end life's war and toil
> Beneath thy sod I too would have a place ;
> Where my love is, there do I long to be,
> Where now my heart is buried far from me—
> Yes, where my love is gone I long to go,
> Robbed of my heart I bear too deep a woe.

This stringer of pretty conceits fails to convince us
that he is very much in earnest in his wish to die.
Speaking in the sincerity of prose, the Tuscan says,
"Ogni cosa è meglio che la morte." He does not
believe in the nothingness of life. In his worst
troubles he still feels that all his faculties, all his
senses, are made for pleasure. Death is to him the
affair of a not cheerful religious ceremony—a cross
borne before a black draped bier, and bells tolling
dolefully:

> I hear Death's step, I see him at my side,
> I feel his bony fingers clasp me round ;
> I see the church's door is open wide,
> And for the dead I hear the knell resound.
> I see the cross and the black pall outspread ;
> Love, thou dost lead me whither lie the dead !
> I see the cross, the winding-sheet I see ;
> Love, to the graveyard thou art leading me !

Going further south, a stage further is reached in crude externality of vision. People of the South are the only born realists. To them that comes natural which in others is either affectation or the fruits of what the French call *l'amour du laid*—a morbid love of the hideous, such as marred the fine genius of Baudelaire. At Naples death is a matter of corruption naked in the sunlight. When the Neapolitan takes his mandoline amongst the tombs he unveils their sorry secrets, not because he gloats over them, but because the habit of a reserve of speech is entirely undeveloped in him. He dares to sing thus of his lost love—

> Her lattice ever lit no light displays.
> My Nella ! can it be that you are ill?
> Her sister from the window looks and says :
> "Your Nella in the grave lies cold and still.
> Ofttimes she wept to waste her life unwed,
> And now, poor child, she sleeps beside the dead."
> Go to the church and lift the winding-sheet,
> Gaze on my Nella's face—how changed, alas !
> See 'twixt those lips whence issued flowers so sweet
> Now loathsome worms (ah! piteous sight!) do pass.
> Priest, let it be your care, and promise me,
> That evermore her lamp shall lighted be.

The song beats with the pulses of the people's life— the life of a people swift in gesture, in action, in living, in dying : always in a hurry, as if one must be quick for the catastrophe is coming. They are all here : the lover waiting in the street for some sign or word ; the girl leaning out of window to tell her piece of news ; the "poor child" who had drunk of the lava stream of love ; the dead lying uncoffined in the church to be gazed upon by who will ; the priest to

whom are given those final instructions: pious, and
yet how uncomforting, how unilluminated by hope or
even aspiration ! Here there is no thought of reunion.
A kind-hearted German woman once tried to console a young Neapolitan whose lover was dead, by
saying that they might meet in Paradise. " In Paradise ? " she answered, opening her large black eyes ;
" Ah ! signora, in Paradise people do not marry."

The coming back or reappearance of a lover, in
whose absence his beloved has died, is a subject that
has been made use of by the folk-poets of every
country, and nothing can be more characteristic of the
nationalities to which they belong than the diver-
gences which mark their treatment of it. Northern
singers turn the narrative of the event into half a fairy
tale. On the banks of the Moldau we are introduced
to a joyous youth, returning with glad steps to his
native village. " My pretty girls, my doves, is my
friend cutting oats with you ? " he asks of a group of
girls working in the fields near his home. " Only
yesterday," they reply, " his friend was buried." He
begs them to tell him by which path they bore her
away. It is a road edged with rosemary ; everybody
knows it—it leads to the new cemetery. Thither he
goes, thrice he wanders round the place, the third
time he hears a voice crying, " Who is it treads on
my grave and breaks the rest of the dead ? " " It
is I, thy friend," he says, and he bids her rise up
and look on him. She says she cannot, she is too
weak, her heart is lifeless, her hands and feet are like
stones. But the gravedigger has left his spade hard
by ; with it her friend can shovel away the earth
that holds her down. He does what she tells him ;

when the earth is lifted he beholds her stretched out
at full length, a frozen maiden crowned with rosemary. He asks to whom has she bequeathed his gifts.
She answers that her mother has them ; he must
go and beg them of her. Then shall he throw the
little scarf upon a bush, and there will be an end to
his love. And the silver ring he shall cast into the
sea, and there will be an end to his grief. On the
shores of the Wener it is Lord Malmstein who wakes
before dawn from a dream that his beloved's heart is
breaking. " Up, up, my little page, saddle the grey ;
I must know how it fares with my love." He mounts
the horse and gallops into the forests. Of a sudden
two little maids stand in his path ; one wears a dress
of blue, and hails him with the words : " God keep
you, Lord Malmstein ; what bale awaits you ! " The
other is dight in red, and of her Lord Malmstein asks,
" Who is ill, and who is dead ? " " No one is ill, no
one is dead, save only the betrothed of Malmstein."
He makes haste to reach the village ; on the way he
meets the bier of his betrothed. Swiftly he leaps
from the saddle ; he pulls from off his finger rings of
fine gold, and throws them to the gravedigger—
" Delve a grave deep and wide, for therein we will
walk together." His face turns red and white, and he
deals a mortal blow at his heart. This Swedish
Malmstein not only figures as the reappearing lover ;
he is also one of that familiar pair whom death
unites. In an ancient Romansch ballad the story is
simply an episode of peasant life. A young Enga-
diner girl is forced by her father to marry a man of the
village of Surselva, but all the while her troth is
plighted to a youth from the village of Schams. On

the road to Surselva the lover joins the bride and
bridegroom unknown to the latter. When they reach
the place the people declare that they have never
seen so fair a woman as the youthful bride. Her
husband's father and mother greet her saying,
"Daughter, be thou welcome to our house!" But
she answers, "No, I have never been your daughter,
nor do I hope ever to be; for the time is near when
I must die." Then her brothers and sisters greet her
saying, "O sister, be thou welcome to our house!"
"No," she says, "I have never been your sister, nor
do I ever hope to be; for the time comes when I
must die. Only one kindness I ask of you, give me
a room where I may rest." They lead her to her
chamber, they try to comfort her with sweet words;
but the more they would befriend her, the more does
the young bride turn her mind away from this world.
Her lover is by her side, and to him she says, "O my
beloved, greet my father and my mother; tell them
that perhaps they have rejoiced their hearts, but sure
it is they have broken mine." She turns her face to
the wall and her soul returns to God. "O my
beloved," cries the lover, "as thou diest, and diest for
me, for thee will I gladly die." He throws himself
upon the bed, and his soul follows hers. As the clock
struck two they carried her to the grave, as the clock
struck three they came for him; the marriage bells
rang them to their rest; the chimes of Schams
answering back the chimes of Surselva. From the
grave mound of the girl grew a camomile plant, from
the grave mound of the youth a plant of musk; and
for the great love they bore one another even the
flowers twined together and embraced.

Uoi, i sül tömbel da quella bella
Craschiva sü üna flur da chiaminella ;
Uoi, i sül tömbel da que bel mat
Craschiva sü üna flur nusch muschiat ;
Per tant grond bain cha queus dus as leivan,
Parfin las fluors insemmel as brancleivan.

It is a sign of a natural talent for democracy when the people like better to tell stories about themselves than to discuss the fortunes of prince or princess. The devoted lovers are more often to be looked for in the immediate neighbourhood of a court. So it is in the ballad of Count Nello of Portugal. Count Nello brings his horse to bathe ; while the horse drinks, the Count sings. It was already very dark—the King could not recognise him. The poor Infanta knew not whether to laugh or to cry. " Be quiet, my daughter ; listen and thou wilt hear a beautiful song. It is an angel singing, or the siren in the sea." " No, it is no angel in heaven, nor is it the siren of the sea ; it is Count Nello, my father, he who fain would wed me." "Who speaks of Count Nella ? who dare name him, the rebel vassal whom I have exiled ? " " My Lord, mine only is the fault ; you should punish me alone ; I cannot live without him ; it is I who have made him come." " Hold thy peace, traitress ; before day dawns thou shalt see his head cut off." " The headsman who slays him may prepare for me too ; there where you dig his grave dig mine also." For whom are the bells tolling ? Count Nello is dead ; the Infanta is like to die. The two graves are open ; behold ! they lay the Count near the porch of the church and the Infanta at the foot of the altar. On one grave grows a cypress, on the other an orange

tree; one grows, the other grows; their branches join
and kiss. The king, when he hears of it, orders them
both to be cut down. From the cypress flows noble
blood, from the orange tree blood royal; from one
flies forth a dove, from the other a wood-pigeon.
When the king sits at table the birds perch before
him. "Ill luck upon their fondness," he cries, "ill
luck upon their love! Neither in life nor in death
have I been able to divide them." The musk and
the camomile of Switzerland, the cypress and the
orange tree of Portugal, are the cypress and the reed
of the Greek folk-song, the thorn and olive of the
Norman *chanson*, the rose and the briar of the English
ballad, the vine and the rose of the Tristram and
Iseult story. Through the world they tell their
tale—

> Amor condusse noi ad una morte.

The death of heroes has provided an inexhaustible
theme for folk-poets. The chief or partisan leader
had his complement in the skald· or bard or roving
ballad-singer; if the one acted, turned tribes into
nations, cut out history, the other sang, published his
fame, gave his exploits to the future, preserved to his
people the remembrance of his dying words. The
poetry of hero-worship, beginning on Homeric heights,
descends to the "lytell gestes" of all sorts and conditions of more or less respectable and patriotic outlaws and *condottieri*, whose "passing" is often the
most honourable point in their career. On the principle which has been followed—that of letting the
folk-poet speak for himself, and show what are his
ideas and his impressions after his own manner and

in his own language—I will take three death scenes from amongst the less known of those recorded in popular verse. The first is Scandinavian. What ails Hjalmar the Icelander? Why is his face so pale? The Norse Warrior answers : "Sixteen wounds have I, and my armour is shattered. All things grow black in my sight; I reel in walking; the bloody sword of Agantyr has pierced my heart. Had I five houses in the fields I could not dwell in one of them ; I must abide at Samsa, hopeless and mortally wounded. At Upsal, in the halls of Josur, many Jarls quaff joyously the foaming ale, many Jarls exchange hot words ; but as for me, I am here in this island, struck down by the point of the sword. The white daughter of Hilmer accompanied my steps to Aganfik beyond the reefs ; her words are come true, for she said I should return no more. Draw off my finger the ring of ruddy gold, bear it to my youthful Inge-brog, it will remind her that she will see me never more. In the east upsoars the raven; after him the mightier eagle wings his way. I will be meat for the eagle and my heart's blood his drink." One backward look to all that was the joy of his life—the feast, the fight, the woman he loved—and then a calm facing of the end. This is how the Norseman died. The Greek hero, who dies peaceably in the ripeness of old age, meets his doom with even less trouble of spirit—

> The sun sank down behind the hill,
>   And Dimos faintly said,
> ‘ Go, children, fetch your evening meal—
>   The water and the bread.

Thou, Lamprakis, my brother's son,
  Come hither, by me stand,
And arm me with my weapons,
  And be captain of the band.
And, children, take my dear old sword
  That I no more shall sway,
And cut the green boughs from the trees
  And there my body lay ;
And hither bring a priestly man
  To whom I may confess,
That I may tell him all my sins,
  And he forgive and bless. .
For thirty years a soldier,
  Twenty years a kleft was I;
Now death o'ertakes and seizes me,
  'Tis finished, I must die.
And be ye sure ye make my grave
  Of ample height and large,
That in it I may stand upright,
  Or lie my gun to charge.
And to the right a lattice make,
  A passage for the day,
Where the swallow, bringing springtide,
  May dart about and play,
And the nightingale, sweet singer,
  Tell the happy month of May.

The slight natural touches—the eagle soaring against
the sunrise, the nightingale singing through the May
nights—suggest an intuition of the will-of-the-wisp
affinity between nature and human chances which
seems for ever on the point of being seized, but which
for ever eludes the mental grasp. We think of the
"brown bird" in the noble "Funeral Song" of one
who would have been a magnificent folk-poet, had he
not learnt to write and read—Walt Whitman.

My third specimen is a Piedmontese ballad composed probably about a hundred and fifty years ago,

and still very popular. Count Nigra ascertained the
existence of eight or more variants. A German
soldier, known in Italy as the Baron Lodrone, took
arms under the house of Savoy, in whose service he
presently died. "In Turin," begins the ballad,
"counts and barons and noble dames mourn for the
death of the Baron Lodrone." The king went to
Cuneo to visit his dying soldier ; drums and cannons
greeted his approach. He spoke kind words to the
sick man : "Courage, thou wilt not die, and I will
give thee the supreme command." "There is no
commander who can stand against death," answered
the baron. Now Lodrone was a Protestant, and
when the king was convinced that he must die, he
exhorted him to conversion, saying that he himself
would stand his sponsor. Lodrone replied that that
could not be. The king did not insist ; he only
asked him where he would be buried, and promised
him a sepulchre of gold. He answered—

> Mi lasserü për testament
> Ch 'a mi sotero an val d' Lüserna,
> An val d' Lüserna a m sotraran
> Dova l me cör s'arposa tan !

He does not care for a golden sepulchre, but he
"leaves for testament" that his body may lie in Val
Luserna, "where my heart rests so well !" The valley
of Luserna was the seat of the Vaudois faith in the
"alpine mountains cold," watered with martyr blood
only a little while before Lodrone lived. To read
these four simple lines after the fantasia of wild or
whimsical guesses, passionate longing, unresisted
despair, insatiable curiosity, that death has been seen

to create or inspire, is like going out of a public place with its multiform and voluble presentment of men and things into the aisles of a small church which would lie silent but that unseen hands pass over the organ keys.

NATURE IN FOLK-SONGS.

NATURE, like music, does not initially make us think, it makes us feel. A midnight scene in the Alps, a sunrise on the Mediterranean, suspends at the moment of contemplating it all thought in pure emotion. Afterwards, however, thought comes back and asks for a reason for the emotion that has been felt. Man at an early age began to try and explain, or give a tangible shape, to the feelings wrought in him by Nature. In the first place he called the things that he saw gods, "because the things are beautiful that are seen." Later on, seers and myth-makers resigned their birthright into the hands of poets, who became henceforth the interpreters between nature and man. A small piece of this succession fell away from the great masters of the world's song, and was picked up almost unconsciously by the obscure and nameless folk-singer. Comparative folk-lore has shown that men have everywhere the same customs, the same superstitions, the same games. The study of folk-songs will go far to show that if they have not likewise a complete community of taste and sentiment, yet even in these, the finer fibres of their being, there is less of difference and more of analogy than has been hitherto supposed. Folk-songs prove, for instance, that the modern unschooled man is not so utterly ignorant of natural beauty as many of us have imagined him to be. Only we must not go from the extreme of expecting nothing to the extreme of ex-·pecting too much ; it has to be borne in mind that at best folk-poesy is rather the stammering speech of children than a mature eloquence.

It is a common idea that, until the other day, mountains were looked upon with positive aversion. Still we know that there were always men who felt the power of the hills : the men who lived in the hills. When they were kept too long in the plain without hope of return they sickened and died ; when a vivid picture of their mountains was of a sudden brought up before them, they lost control over their actions. By force of association the sound of the *Kuhreihen* could doubtless give the Switzer a vision of the white peak, the milky torrent, the chalet with slanting roof, the cows tripping down the green Alp to their night quarters. It is disappointing to find that the words accompanying the famous cow-call are as a rule mere nonsense. The first observation which the genuine folk-poet makes about mountains is the sufficiently self-evident one, that they form a wall between him-self and the people on the further side. The old Pyrenean balladist seized the political significance of this : "When God created those mountains," he said, "He did not mean that men should cross them." Very often the mountain wall is spoken of as a barrier which separates lovers. The Gascon peasants have an adaptation of Gaston Phœbus' romance :—

> Aqueros mountines
> Qui ta haoutes soun,
> M'empechen de bede
> Mas amous oun soun.

In Bohemia the simple countryman poetises after

much the same fashion as the Gascon cavalier:
"Mountain, mountain, thou art very high! My
friend, thou art far off, far beyond the mountains.
Our love will fade yet more and yet more; there is
nothing left for me; in this world no pleasantness
remains." Another Czech singer laments that he is
not where his thought is; if only the mountains did
not stand between them, he would see his beloved
walking in the garden and plucking blue. flowers. He
tries what a prayer will do: "Mountains, black
mountains, step aside, so I may get my good friend
for wife." In similar terms the native of Friuli begs
the dividing range to stoop so he may look upon his
love. Among Italian folk-poets the Friulian is foremost as a lover of the greater heights; he turns to
them habitually in his moments of poetic inspiration,
and, as he says, their echoes repeat his sighs. It
must be admitted that the Tuscan, on the contrary,
feels small sympathy with high mountains; if he
speaks of one he is careful to call it *aspra*, or rough
and bitter. But he yields to no man in his delight
in the lesser hills, the *be' poggioli* of his fair birthland.
Even if an intervening hillock divides him from his
beloved he speaks of the barrier tenderly rather than
sadly: "O sun, thou that goest over the hill-top, do
me a kindness if thou canst—greet my love whom I
have not seen to-day. O sun, thou that goest over
the pear-trees, greet those black eyes. O sun, thou
that goest over the small ash-trees, greet those beautiful eyes!" A maiden sings to herself, "I see what I
see and I see not what I would; I see the leaves
flying in the air and I do not see my love turn back
from the hill-top. I do not see him turn back . . .

that beautiful face has gone óver the hill." A youth tells all his story in these few words : "As I passed over the mountain-crest thy beautiful name came into my mind ; I fell upon my knees and I joined my hands, and to have left thee seemed a sin. I fell upon my knees on the hard stones ; may our love come back as of yore !" These are pure love-songs ; not by any means descriptions of scenery, and yet how much of the Tuscan landscape lives in them !

Almost the only folk-song which is avowedly descriptive of a mountain, comes from South Greenland :—

The great Koonak Mount yonder south I do behold it. The great Koonak Mount yonder south I regard it. The shining brightness yonder south I contemplate. Outside of Koonak it is expanding ; the same that Koonak towards the sea-side doth encompass. Behold how yonder south they tend to beautify each other ; while from the sea-side it is enveloped in sheets still changing ; from the sea-side it is enveloped to mutual embellishment.

At the first reading all this may seem incoherent ; at the second or third we begin to see the scene gradually rising before us ; the masses of sea-born cloud sweeping on and up at dawn or sunset, till, finding their passage barred, they enwrap the obstacle in folds of golden vapour. It is singular that the Eskimo is incessantly gazing southwards ; can it be that he, too, is dimly sensible of what a great writer has called "*la fatigue du Nord*" ?

Incidental mention of the varying aspects of peak and upland is common enough in popular songs. The Bavarian peasant notices the clearness of the heights while mist hangs over the valley :—

Im Thal ist der Nebel
Auf der Alm is schon klar . . .

The Basque observes the "misty summits;" the Greek sees the cloud hurrying to the heights "like winged messengers." There is the closest intimacy between the Greek and his mountains. When he has won a victory for freedom, they cry aloud, "God is great!" When he is in sorrow he pines for them as for the society of friends: "Why am I not near the hills? Why have I not the mountains to keep me company?" A sick Kleft cries to the birds, "Birds, shall I ever be cured? Birds, shall I recover my strength?" To which the birds reply just as might a fashionable physician who recommends his patient to try Pontresina: "If thou wouldst be cured, if thou wouldst have thy wounds close up, go thou to the heights of Olympus, to the beautiful uplands where the strong man never suffers, where the suffering regain their strength." This fine figure of speech also occurs in a Kleft song: "The plains thirst for water, the mountains thirst for snow."

The effect of light on his native ice-fields has not escaped the Switzer: "The sun shines on the glacier, and in the heavens shine the stars; O thou, my chiefest joy, how I love thee!" A Czech balladist describes two chieftains travelling towards the sunrise, with mountains to the right and to the left, on whose summit stands the dawn. Again, he represents a band of warriors halting on the spurs of the forest, while before them lies Prague, silent and asleep, with the Veltava shrouded in morning mist; beyond, the mountains turn blue; beyond the mountains the east is illuminated. In Bohemia mountains are spoken of as blue or grey or shadowy; in Servia they are invariably called green. Servians and Bul-

garians cannot conceive a mountain that is not a
wood or a wood that is not a mountain ; with them
the two words mean one and the same thing. The
charm and beauty of the combination of hill and
forest are often dwelt upon in the Balkan brigand
songs; outlaws and their poets have been among the
keenest appreciators of nature. Who thinks of Robin
Hood apart from the greenwood tree ? Who but has
smelt the very fragrance of the woods as he said over
the lines ?—

> " In somer when the shawes be sheyn
> And leves be large and long,
> Hit is full merry in feyre foreste
> To here the foulys song."

The Sclav or semi-Sclav bandit has not got the
high moral qualities of our "most gentle theefe," but,
like him, he has suffered the heat, the cold, the
hunger, the fatigue of a life in the good greenwood,
and, like him, he has tasted its joys. Take the ballad
called the "Wintering of the Heidukes." Three
friends sit drinking together in the mountains under
the trees ; they sip the ruddy wine, and discuss what
they shall do in the coming winter, when the leaves
have fallen and only the naked forest is left. Each
decides where he will go, and the last one says : " So
soon as the sad winter is passed, when the forest is
clad again in leaves and the earth in grass and flowers,
when the birds sing in the bushes on the banks of the
Save and the wolves are heard in the hills—then shall
we meet as to-day." Spring returns, the forest is
decked again with leaves, the black earth with flowers
and grass, the bird sings in the bush, the wolves howl

on the rocky heights; two of the friends meet at the
trysting place—the third comes not; he has been
slain. This is only one *Pesma* out of a hundred in
which the mountain background is faithfully sketched.
Sometimes the forest figures as a personage. The
Balkan mountaineer more than half believes that as
he loves it, so does it love him. The instinct which
insists that "love exempteth nothing loved from love"
has been a great myth-germinator, and when myths
die out, it still finds some niche in the mind of man
wherein to abide. It may seem foolish when applied
to inanimate objects; it must seem false in its human
application : but reasoning will not kill it. Is there
some truth unperceived behind the apparent fallacy?
The Balkan brigand cares little for such speculations;
all that he tells us is that when he speaks to the
greenwood, it most surely answers him in a soft low
voice. The Bulgarian " Farewell of Liben the brave "
is a good specimen of the dialogues between the
forest and its wild denizens. Standing on the top of
the Hodja Balkan, Liben cries aloud, " Forest, O
green forest, and ye cool waters ! dost thou remember,
O forest, how often I have roamed about thee with
my following of young comrades bearing aloft my red
banner ? " Many are the mothers, the wives, and the
little orphans whom Liben has made desolate so that
they curse him. Now must he bid farewell to the
mountain, for he is going home to his mother who
will affiance him to the daughter of the Pope Nicholas.
"The forest speaks to no one, yet to Liben she
replies." Enough has he roamed with his braves;
enough has he borne his red banner along the summit
of the old mountain, and under fresh and tufted shade.

and over moist green moss. Many are the mothers, the wives, and the little orphans, who curse the forest for his sake. Till now he has had the old mountain for mother; for love, the greenwood clothed in tufted foliage and freshened by the cool breeze. The grass was his bed, the leaves of the trees his coverlet; his drink came from the pure brook, for him the wood-birds sang. "Rejoice," sang the wood-birds, "for thee the wood is gay; the mountain and the cool brook!" But now Liben bids farewell to the forest; he is going home that his mother may affiance and wed him to the daughter of the Pope Nicholas.

Sea-views of the sea, rare in poetry of any sort, can scarcely be said to exist in folk-poesy. Sailors' songs have generally not much to do with the wonders of the deep; the larger part of them are known to be picked up on land, and the few exceptions to the rule are mostly kept from the ken of the outer and pro-fane public. The Basque sailors have certain songs of their own, but only a solitary fragment of one of them has ever been set on record. Once when a Basque was asked to repeat a song he had been heard singing, he quietly said that he only taught it to those who sailed with him. The fragment just mentioned speaks of the silver trumpet (the master's whistle?) sounding over the waters at break of day, while the coast of Holland trembles in the distance. The first glimpse of a level reach of land in the morning haze could hardly be better described.

The sea impresses the dwellers on its shores chiefly by its depth and vastness. In folk-songs there is a frequent recurrence of phrases such as "the waters of the sea are vast, you cannot discern the bottom"

(Basque); "High is the starry sky, profound the abyss of ocean" (Russian). The Greek calls the sea wicked, and watches the whitening waves which roll over drowned sailors. For the Southern Sclav it is simply a grey expanse. The Norseman calls it old, and blue—nature having for him one sole chord of colour—blue sea, white sands and snows, green pines. With Italian folk-singers it is a pretty point of dispute whether the blue sea-and-sky colour is to be preferred to the colour of the leaves and the grass. "Can you wear a lovelier hue than azure?" asks one; "the waves of the sea are clothed therein and the heavens when they are clear." The answer is that if the sky is clad in a blue garment, green is the vesture of the earth, "E foro del verde nasse ogni bel frutto." The arguments of the rival partisans remind one of an amusing scene in a play of Calderon's; one character is made to say, "Green is the earth's primal hue, the many-coloured flowers are born out of a green cradle." "In short," says another, "it is a mere earth-tint, while heaven is dressed in blue." "As to that," comes the retort, "it is all an azure fiction; far to be preferred is the veracious verdancy of the earth."

The Italian folk-poets' "castle in the air" is a castle in the sea. From Alp to Ætna the love-sick rhymers are fain to go and dwell with their heart's adoration "in mezzo al mar." But though agreed on the locality where they intend setting up in life, they differ considerably as to the manner of "castle" to be inhabited. The Sicilian, who makes a point of wishing for something worth having while he is about it, will only be satisfied with a palace built of peacock's plumes, a stair of gold, and a balcony inlaid with gems. A more modest minstrel, from the hither side of the straits of Messina, gives no thought at all to house-keeping; a little wave-lapped garden, full of pretty flowers, is all his desire. The Italian folk-poet sets afloat an astonishing number of things for no particular reason; one has planted a pear-tree, a second has heard a little wood-lark, a third has seen a green laurel, a fourth has found a small altar " in the sea-midst," a fifth discovers his own name " scritto all 'onne de lu mar."

The Greek lover has no wish to leave the mainland, but he is fond of picturing his beloved wandering by the shore at dawn to breathe the morning air, or reclining on a little stone bench at the foot of a hill, in the silence of solitude and the calm of the sea. For the rest, he knows too well " the wicked sea " for it to suggest to him none but pleasant images. If he is in despair, he likens himself to the waves, which follow one another to their inevitable grave. If he grows weary of waiting, he exclaims: " The sea darkens, the waves beat back on the beach; ah! how long have I loved thee!" One or two specimens have been already given of this particular kind of song; the recollection of a passing moment in nature is placed text-wise to a cry of human pain or love. A happy lover remembers in his transport the glacier glistening in the sunshine; he who languishes from the sickness of hope deferred, sees an affinity to his own mood in the lowering storm.

In the South, light is loved for its own sake. " Il lume è mezza compagnia," runs a Tuscan proverb : " Light is half company." In a memorable passage, St Augustine unfolds and elaborates the same idea of the companionship of light. A Tuscan countryman vows that if his love to fly from him becomes the light, he, to be near her, will become a butterfly. Perhaps so radiant an hyperbole would only have occurred to one who had grown up in the air of the Tuscan hills ; the air to whose purity Michael Angelo ascribed all that his mind was worth. Anyway, a keen poetic sensibility is argued by the mere fact of thus joining, in a symbol of the indivisible, the least earth-clogged of sentient things with the most impersonal of natural phenomena. It is the more remarkable because, generally speaking, butterflies do not attract the notice of the unlettered people, even as they did not attract the notice of the objective and practical Greeks. It may be that were spirits to be seen flitting noiselessly about the haunts of men, they would, in time, be equally disregarded. To so few has it happened to know a butterfly, to watch closely its living beauty, to feel day by day the light feet or fluttering wings upon the hands which minister to its unsubstantial wants. Butterflies, to most of us, are but ethereal strangers ; so by the masses they are not valued—at least, not in Europe. A tribe of West African negroes have this beautiful saying : " The Butterfly praises God within and without."

The folk-poet lives out of doors ; he is acquainted with the home life of the sun and stars, and day-break is his daily luxury. The Eskimo tell a story of a stay-at-home man who dwelt in an island near the coast of East Greenland. It was his chief joy to see the sun rising in the morning, out of the sea, and with that he was content. But when his son had come to years of discretion, he persuaded his father to set out

in a boat, so that he might see a little of the world.
The man started from the island ; no sooner, however,
had he passed Cape Farewell than he saw the sun
beginning to rise behind the land. It was more than
he could bear ; and he set off at once for his home.
Next morning very early he went out of his tent ; he
did not come back. When he was sought after, he
was found quite dead. The joy of seeing the sun
rising again out of the sea had killed him. Most
likely the story is based on a real incident. The
Aztec goes out upon his roof to see the sunrise ; it is
his one religious observance. But of the cult of the
sun I must not begin to speak. It belongs to an
immense subject that cannot be touched here : the
wide range of the unconscious appreciation of nature
which was worship.

There is nothing more graceful in · all folk-poesy
than a little Czech star-poem :—

> Star, pale star,
> Didst thou know love,
> Hadst thou a heart, my golden star,
> Thou wouldst weep sparks.

Further north men do not willingly stay out abroad
at night, but those whose calling obliges them to do
so are looked upon as wise in strange lore. The first
tidings of war coming reached the Esthonian shepherd boy, the keeper of the lambs, "who knew the
sun, and knew the moon, and knew the stars in the
sky." In Neo-Sanskrit speaking Lithuania there
abound star-legends which differ from the southern
tales of the same order, by reason of the pagan good
faith that clings to them. The Italian is aware that

F

he is romancing when he speaks of the moon travelling through the night to meet the morning star, or
when he describes her anger at the loss of one of her
stars; the Lithuanian has a suspicion that there may
be a good deal of truth in his poets' account of the
sun's domestic arrangements—how the morning star
lights the fire for him to get up by, and the evening
star makes his bed. He will tell you that once
there was a time when sun and moon journeyed together, but the moon fell in love with the morning
star, which brought about sad mischief. " The moon
went with the sun in the early spring ; the sun got up
early; the moon went away from him. The moon
walked alone, fell in love with the morning star.
Perkun, greatly angered, stabbed her with a sword.
'Why wentest thou away from the sun ? Why
walk alone in the night ? Why fall in love with the
morning star ? Your heart is full of sorrow.'" The
Lithuanians have not wholly left that stage in man's
development when what is imagined seems *primâ
facie* quite as likely to be real as what is seen. The
supernatural does not strike them as either mysterious
or terrifying. It is otherwise with the Teuton. His
night phantasms treat of what is, to man, of all things
the most genuinely alarming — his own shadow.
Ghosts, wild huntsmen, erl-kings take the place of an
innocuous un-mortal race. No starry radiance can
rob the night of its terrors. " The stars shine in the
sky, bright shine the rays of the moon, fast ride the
dead." Such is the wailing burden to the ballad
which Burgher imitated in his *Lenore*. There is a
wide gulf between this and the tender star-idylls of
Lithuania, and a gulf still wider divides it from the

neighbourly familiarity with which the southerner addresses the heavenly bodies. We go from one world to another when we turn back to Italy and hear the country lads singing, " La buona sera, O stella mattutina ! " " Good evening to you, O matutinal star."

The West African negroes call the sky the king of sheds, and the sun the king of torches ; the twinkling stars are the little chickens, and the meteor is the thief-star. " When day dawns, you rejoice," say the Yorubas ; " do you not know that the day of death is so much the nearer ? " The same tribe give this vivid description of a day-break scene : " The trader betakes himself to his trade, the spinner takes his distaff, the warrior takes his shield, the weaver bends over his sley, the farmer awakes, he and his hoe-handle, the hunter awakes, with his quiver and bow." Thoughtless of toil, the Tuscan joyfully cries, " Dawn is about to appear, bells chime, windows open, heaven and earth sing." The Greek holds that he who has not journeyed with the moon by night, or at dawn with the dew, has not tasted the world. Folk-poets have widely recognised the mysterious confusion between summer nights and days. The dispute at Juliet's window is recalled by the Venetian's chiding of the " Rondinella Traditora ; " by the Berry peasants' vexation at the "vilaine alouette ; " by the reproach of the Navarrese lover, " You say it is day, it is not yet midnight ; " and most of all by the Servian dialogue : " Dawn whitens, the cock crows : It is not the dawn, but the moon. The cows low round the house : It is not the cows, it is the call to prayer. The Turks call to the mosque : It is not the Turks, it is the wolves." The observation of the swallow's morning song is another point at which the master poet and the obscure folk-singer meet. This time both are natives of sunny lands ; there is a clear reason why it should be so—in the north the swallow passes almost for a dumb bird. Very rarely in England do we hear her notes, soft yet penetrating, like the high-pitched whisper of the Æolian harp. Some of us may, indeed, have first got acquainted with them in Dante's beautiful lines :—

> Nell' ora che comincia i tristi lai
> La Rondinella presso alla mattina . . .

Little suspecting that he is committing the sin of plagiarism, the Greek begins one of his songs, " In the hour when the swallows, twittering, awake the dawn."

The ancient swallow myth does not seem to have anywhere crept into folk-lore ; nor is there much trace of the old Scandinavian delusion that swallows spent the winter under the ice on lakes, or hanging up in caves like bunches of grapes. The swallow is taken simply as the typical bird of passage, the spring-bringer, the messenger, the traveller *outre mer.* She is the picked bird of countries, the African explorer, the Indian pioneer. A Servian story reports of her in the latter capacity. The small-leafed Sweet Basil complains, " Silent dew, why fallest thou not on me ? " " For two mornings," answers the dew, " I fell on thee ; this morning I amused myself by watching a great marvel. A vila (a mountain spirit) quarrelled with an eagle over yonder mountain. Said the vila, ' The mountain is mine.' ' No,' said the

eagle, 'it is mine.' The vila broke the eagle's wing,
and the young eaglets moaned bitterly, for great was
their peril. Then a swallow comforted them : 'Make
no moan, young eaglets, I will carry you to the land
of Ind, where the amaranth grows up to the horses'
knees, where the clover reaches their shoulders, where
the sun never sets.'" How, it may be asked, did the
poet come by that notion of an Asiatic Eden ? The
folk-singer seldom paints foreign scenery in these
glowing tints. There may be something of a south-
ward longing in the boast—

> I'll show ye how the lilies grow
> On the banks o' Italie.

But this is cold and colourless beside the empire of
the unsetting sun.

Next to the swallow, the grey gull has the reputation of being the greatest traveller. Till lately the
women of Croisic met on Assumption Day and sang
a song to the gulls, imploring them to bring back
their husbands and their lovers who were out at sea.
Larks are often chosen as letter-carriers for short dis-
tances. The Greek knows that it is spring when pair
by pair the turtle-doves swoop down to the brooks.
He is an accurate observer; in April or May any
retired English pool will be found flecked over with
the down of the wood-pigeons that come to drink and
bathe in it. The cooing of doves is by general consent associated with constancy and requited love. It
is not always, however, that nations are agreed as to
the sense of a bird's song. The "merrie cuckoo" is
supposed by the Sclavs to be rehearsing an endless
dirge for a murdered brother. A Czech poet lays

down yet another cause for its conjectured melancholy: "Perched upon an oak tree, a cuckoo weeps
because it is not always spring. How could the rye
ripen in the fields if it were always spring? How
could the apples ripen in the orchard if it were always
summer? How could the corn harden in the rick if
it were always autumn?" In spite of the sagacious
content shown by these inquiries, it is probable that
the sadness which the Sclav attributes to the cuckoo-
cry is but an echo of the sadness, deep and wide, of
his own race.

Of the nightingale the Tuscan sings, in the spirit of
one greater than he,—

> Vedete là quel rusignol che canta
> Col suo bel canto lamentar si vuole,—

which is not, by the by, his only Miltonic inspiration ;
there is a rustling of Vallombrosian leaves through
the couplet, composed perhaps in Vallombrosia :

> E quante primavera foglie adorna
> Che sì vaga e gentile a noi ritorna.

The Bulgarian sees a mountain *trembling* to the
song of three nightingales. Like his Servian neighbours, he must always have a story, and here is his
nightingale story. Marika went into the garden ; she
passed the pomegranate-tree and the apple-tree, and
sat her down under the red rose-tree to embroider a
white handkerchief. In the rose-tree was a nightingale,
and the nightingale said : "Let us sing, Marika ; if
you sing better than I, you shall cut off my wings at
the shoulders and my feet at the knee; if I sing
better than you, I will cut off your hair at the roots."
They sang for two days, for three days ; Marika sang

the best. Then the nightingale pleaded, " Marika, fair young girl, do not cut off my feet, let me keep my wings, for I have three little nightingales to rear, and of one of them I will make you a gift." " Nightingale, sweet singer," said Marika, " I will give thee grace of thy wings, and even of thy feet ; go, tend thy little ones, make me a gift of one to lull me to sleep, and of one to awake me."

We may take leave of bird-lays with the pretty old Bourbonnaise *chanson :*—

> Derrier' chez nous, il y a-t-un vert bocage,
> Le rossignol y chant' tous les jours ;
> Là il y dit en son charmant langage :
> Les amoreux sont malheureux toujours !

Flowers, the green leaves and the grass, are suggestive of two kinds of pathos. The individual flower, the grass or leaf of any one day or spring-tide, becomes the type of the transitoriness of beauty and youth and life. " Sing whilst ye are young and fair, soon you will be slighted, as are sere lilies," is the song even of happy Tuscany. To the Sclav it seems a question whether it be worth while that there should be any flowers or morning gladness, since they must be gone so soon. " O my garden," sings the Ruthenian, " O my little garden, my garden and my green vine, why bloomest thou in the morning ? Hardly bloomed, thou art withered, and the earth is strewn with thy leaves." The other kind of pathos springs from a deeper well. Man passes by, each one hurries to his tragedy ; Nature smiles tranquilly on. This moving force of contrast was known to Lywarch Hen, and to those Keltic bards who dived so deep into

Nature's secrets that scarcely a greater depth has been fathomed by any after-comers. It was perceived involuntarily by the English ballad-singers, who strung a burden of "Fine flowers" upon a tale of infanticide, and bade blackbird and mavis sing their sweetest between a murder and an execution. And it is this that gives its key-note to an Armenian popular song of singular power. A bishop tells how he has made himself a vineyard; he has brought stones from the valleys and raised a wall around it; he has planted young vines and plentifully has he watered their roots. Every morning the nightingale sings sweetly to the rose. Every morning Gabriel says to his soul: "Rise and come forth from this vineyard, from this newly-built vineyard." He has not eaten the fruit of the vine; he has built a wine-vat, but the wine he has not tasted; he has brought cool streams from the hills, but he has not drunk the water thereof; he has planted red and white roses, but he has not smelt their fragrance. The turtle-dove sings to the birds, and the spring is come. Gabriel calls to his soul, the light of his eyes grows dim; "It is time I leave my vineyard, my beautiful vineyard." There is hardly another poem treating of death which is so un-illuminated by one ray from a future dawn.

In the great mass of folk-songs flowers are dealt with simply as the accessories to all beautiful things. The folk-poet learns from them his alphabet of beauty. Go into any English cornfield after harvest; whilst the elder children glean wheat ears, the children of two and three years glean small yellow hearts-cases, vervaine, and blue scabious. They are as surely

learning to distinguish the Beautiful as the student in
the courts of the Vatican. Through life, when these
children think of a beautiful thing, the thought of a
flower will not be far off. Religion and love, after all
the two chief embellishments of the life of the poor,
have been hung about with flowers from the past of
Persephone and Freya till to-day. Even in England
the common people are glad if they can find a lily of
the valley to carry to church at Whitsuntide, and the
first sign that a country girl has got a sweetheart is
often to be read in the transformation of the garden-
plot before her door. In Italy you will not walk far
among the vineyards and maize-fields without coming
upon a shrine which bears traces of floral decoration.
Some Italian villages and country towns have their
special flower festival, or *Infiorata;* Genzano, for
instance, where, on the eighth day after Corpus
Domini, innumerable flowers are stripped of their
petals, which are sorted out according to colour and
then arranged in patterns on the way to the church,
the magnificence of the effect going far to make one
condone the heartlessness of immolating so many
victims to achieve an hour's triumph. A charge of
stupid indifference to beauty has been brought against
the Italian peasant—it would seem partly on the score
that he has been known to root up his anemones in
order to put a stop to the inroads of foreign marauders.
There are certain persons, law-abiding in the land
which gave them birth, who when abroad, adopt the
ethics of our tribal ancestors. A piece of ground, a
tree, or a plant not enclosed by a wall, is turned by this
strange public to its own uses. A walnut tree by the
wayside has a stick thrown among its branches to

fetch down the walnuts. The peasant does what he can to protect himself. He observes that flowers attract trespassers, and so he roots up the flowers. There are Italian folk-songs which show a delight in flowers not to be surpassed anywhere. Flower-loving beyond all the rest are the Tuscan poets, whose love-lyrics have been truly described as " tutti seminati di fiori "—all sown with lilies, clove pinks, and jessamine. The fact fits in pleasantly with the legend of the first Florentines, who are said to have called their city after " the great basket of flowers " in which it was built. It fits in, too, with the sentiment attached even now to the very name of Florence. The old *Floraja* in the overgrown straw hat at the railway station can reckon on something more abiding than her long-lost charms to find her patrons ; and it is curious to note how few of the passengers reject the proffered emblems of the flower town, or fail to earn the parting wish " Felice ritorno ! "

One point may be granted ; in Italy and elsewhere the common people do not highly or permanently value scentless flowers. A flower without fragrance is to them almost a dead flower. I put the question to a troop of English children coming from a wood laden with spoils, " What makes you like primroses ? " " The scent of them," was the answer. A little further along the lane came another troop, and the question was repeated. This time the answer was, " Because they smell so nice." No flower has been more widely reverenced than the unassuming sweet basil, the *Basilico odorato* of Sicilian songs, the Tulasi plant of India, where it is well-nigh worshipped in the house of every pious Hindu. The scale is grad-

uated thus: the flower which has no smell is plucked
in play, but left remorselessly to wither as children
leave their daisy chains ; the flower which has a purely
sweet and fresh perfume is arranged in nosegays, set
in water, praised and enjoyed for the day ; the flower
which has a scent of spice and incense and aromatic
gums bears off honours scarcely less than divine.

The folk-poet sings because heaven has given him
a sweet voice and a fair mistress ; because the earth
brings forth her increase and the sun shines, and the
spring comes back, and rest at noontide and at evening is lovely, and work in the oil-mill and in the vineyard is lovely too : he sings to embellish his labour
and to enhance his repose. He lives on the shield of
Achilles, singing, accompanied by a viol, to the grape-
pickers ; he is crowned with flowers in the golden
age of Lucretius as he raises his sweet song at the
festa. We have seen a little of what he says about
Nature, but, in truth, he is still her interpreter when
he says nothing. All folk-poesy is sung and folk-
songs are as much one of Nature's voices as the song
of the birds, the song of the brooks, the song of the
wind in the pine-tops. So it is likewise with the rude
musical instruments which the exigencies of his life
have taught the peasant how to make ; they utter
tones more closely in harmony with nature than those
of the finest Stradivarius. The Greeks were right
when they made Pan with his reed-pipe rather than
Apollo with his lyre the typical Nature-god. Anyone
to whom it has chanced to hear a folk-song sung in
its own home will understand what is meant. You
may travel a good deal and not have that chance.
The songs, the customs, the traditions of the people

form an arcanum of which they are not always ready to lift the veil. To those, of course, whose lives are cast among a people that still sings, the opportunity comes oftener. But if the song be sung consciously for your pleasure its soul will hardly remain in it. I shall always vividly remember two occasions of hearing a folk-song sung. Once, long ago, on the Bidassoa. The day was closing in; the bell was tolling in the little chapel on the heathery mountain-side, where mass is said for the peace of the brave men who fell there. Fontarabia stood bathed in orange light. It was low water, and the boat got almost stranded; then the boatmen, an older and a younger man, both built like athletes, began to sing in low, wild snatches for the tide. Once, not very long since, at the marble quarry of Sant' Ambrogio. Here also it was towards evening and in the autumn. The vintage was half over; all day the sweet "Prenda! Prenda!" of the grape-gatherers had invited the stranger to share in its purple magnificence. The blue of the more distant Veronese hills deepened against a coralline sky; not a dark thing was in sight except here or there the silhouette of a cypress. Only a few workmen were employed in the quarry; one, a tall, slight lad, sang in the intervals from labour an air full of passion and tenderness. The marble amphitheatre gave sonority to his high voice. Each time Nature would have seemed incomplete had it lacked the human song.

ARMENIAN FOLK-SONGS.

OBSCURE in their origin, and for the most part having at first had no such auxiliary as written record to aid · their preservation, the single fact of the existence of folk-songs may in general suffice to proclaim them the true articulate voice of some sentiment or feeling, common to the large bulk of the people whence they emanate. It is plain that the fittest only can survive —only such as are truly germane to those who say or sing them. A herdsman or tiller of the soil strings together a few verses embodying some simple thought which came into his head whilst he looked at the green fields or the blue skies, or it may be as he acted in a humble way as village poet-laureate. One or two friends get them by heart, and possibly sing them at the fair in the next hamlet: if they hit, others catch them up, and so the song travels for miles and miles, and may live out generations. If not, the effusion of our poetical cowherd dies away quite silently—not much to his distress, for had its fate been more propitious its author would probably have been very little the wiser. One celebrated poet, and I think but one, has in our own times begun his career in like manner with the unknown folk-singer. The songs of Sandor Petöfi were popular over the breadth of the Hungarian Puszta before ever they appeared in print; and those who know him, know how faithfully he breathes forth the soul of the Magyar race. In a certain sense it is true that every real poet is the spokesman of his people. No two works, for instance, are so characteristic of their respective countries as the *Divina Commedia* and *Faust.* Still, the hands of genius idealise what they touch ; the great poet personifies rather than reflects his people, and if he serves them as representative, it is in an august, imperial fashion within the Senate House of Fame, outside whose doors the multitude hustles and seethes. When we want to see this multitude as in a mirror, to judge its common instincts and impulses that go very far to cast the nation in the type which makes it what it is, it is a safer and surer plan to search out its own spontaneous and untutored songs than to consult the master work attached to immortal names.

How far the individuality of a race is decided or modified by the natural phenomena in which it is placed is a nice point for discussion, and one not to be disposed of by off-hand generalities. In what consists the sympathetic link, sometimes weak and scarcely perceptible, at others visibly strong, between man and nature ? Why does the emigrated mountaineer, settled in comfort, ease, and prosperity in some great metropolis, wake up one day with the knowledge that he must begone to the wooden chalet with the threat of the avalanche above and the menace of the flood below—or he must die ? Is it force of early association, habit, or fancy ? Why is the wearied town-tied brain-worker sensible of a nostalgia hardly less poignant when he calls to mind how the fires of day kindled across some scene of snow or sea with which his eyes were once familiar ? Is it

nothing more than the return of a long ago experienced admiration? I think that neither physicist
nor psychologist—and both have a right to be heard
in the matter—would answer that the cause of these
sensations was to be thus shortly defined. Again
ask the artist what the Athenian owed to the purity
and proportion of the lines of Grecian landscape,
what the Italian stole from the glow and glory of
meridional light and colour—what the Teuton learnt
from the ascending spires of Alpine ice? Was it that
they saw and copied? Or rather, that Nature's spirit,
vibrating through the pulses of their being, moulded
into form the half-divine visions of master-sculptor,
painter, architect?

It does not, however, require to go deeper than the
surface of things in order to understand that a
peoples' songs must be largely influenced by the
accidents of natural phenomena, and especially where
climate and physical conformation are such as must
perforce stir and stimulate the imaginative faculties of
the masses. We have an instance to the point in the
ballads of the "mountainous island" bounded by
seas and plains, which the natives call Hayasdan and
we Armenia. The wondering emotion aroused by a
first descent from the Alps into Italy is well known ;
to not a few of the mightiest of northern poets this journey has acted like a charm, a revelation, an awakening
to fuller consciousness. In Armenia, the incantation
of a like natural antithesis is worked by the advent of
its every returning spring: a sluggard of a season that
sleeps on soundly till near midsummer, but comes
forth at last fully clothed in the gorgeous raiment of
a king. In days gone by the Armenian spring was

dedicated to the goddess Anahid, and as it broke over the land the whole people joined in joyful celebration of the feast of Varthavar or " Rose-blossoms," which since Christian times has been transformed into the three days' festival of the Transfiguration. Beautiful is the face of the country when the tardy sun begins to make up for lost time, as though his very life depended on it ; shooting down his beams with fiery force through the rarefied ether, melting away the snows, and ripening all at once the grain and grapes, the wild fig, apricot and olive, mulberry and pomegranate. What wonder that the Armenian loves the revivifying lamp of day, that he turns the dying man towards it, and will not willingly commit his dead to the earth if some bright rays do not fall into the open grave ! At the sun's reveille there is a general resurrection of all the buried winter population — women and children, cows and sheep, pinkeyed lemmings, black-eyed caraguz, and little kangaroo-shaped jerboas. Out, too, from their winter lairs come wolf and bear, hyena and tiger, leopard and wild boar. The stork returns to his nest on the broad chimney-pot, and this is what the peasant tells him of all that has happened in his absence :

> Welcome, Stork !
>   Thou Stork, welcome ;
>   Thou hast brought us the sign of spring,
>   Thou hast made our heart gay.
> Descend, O Stork !
>   Descend, O Stork, upon our roof,
>   Make thy nest upon our ash-tree.
>   I will tell thee my thousand sorrows,
>   The sorrows of my heart, the thousand sorrows,

Stork, when thou didst go away,
    When thou didst go away from our tree,
    Withering winds did blow,
    They dried up our smiling flowers.
The brilliant sky was obscured,
    That brilliant sky was cloudy :
    From above they were breaking the snow in pieces :
    Winter approached, the destroyer of flowers.
Beginning from the rock of Varac,
Beginning from that rock of Varac,
    The snow descended and covered all ;
    In our green meadow it was cold.
Stork, our little garden,
    Our little garden was surrounded with snow ;
    Our green rose trees
    Withered with the snow and the cold.

But now the rose trees in the garden are green
again, and out abroad wild flowers enamel the earth.
Down pour the torrents of melted snow off Mount
Ararat, down crash the avalanches of ice and stones
let loose by the sun's might ; wherever an inch of
soil or rock is uncovered it becomes a carpet of
blossom. High up, even to 13,000 feet above the sea-
level, the deep violet aster, the saxifrage, and crocus,
and ranunculus, and all our old Alpine acquaintances,
form a dainty morsel for the teeth, or a carpet for
the foot, of swift capricorn or not less agile wild
sheep. A little lower, amidst patches of yet frozen
snow, hyacinths scent the air, yellow squills and blue
anemones peep out, clumps of golden iris cluster
between the rocks. There, too, is the "Fountain's
Blood," or "Blood of the Seven Brothers," as the
Turk would say, with its crimson, leafless stalk and
lily-like bloom, the reddest of all red flowers. Upon
the trees comes the sweet white *kasbé*, a kind of

G

manna much relished by the inhabitants. Amongst
the grass grow the Stars of Bethlehem, to remind us,
as tradition has it, that hard by on Ararat—beyond
question the great centre of Chaldean Star-worship—
the wise men were appointed to watch for the appearance of a sign in the heavens, and that thence they
started in quest of the place "where the young child
lay." Tulips also abound ; if we may credit the
legend, they had their origin in the Armenian town
of Erzeroom, springing from the life-blood of Ferdad
when he threw himself from the rocks in despair at a
false alarm of the death of his beloved Shireen.

Erzeroom is by common consent in these parts the
very site of the Garden of Eden. For many centuries,
affirms the Moslem, the flowers of Paradise might yet
be seen blossoming round the source of the Euphrates
not far from the town. But, alas! when the great
Persian King Khosref Purveez, the rival of the above-
mentioned Ferdad, was encamped in that neighbourhood, he was rash enough to spurn a message from
the young Prophet Mohammed, offering him protection if he would embrace the faith of Islâm. What
booted the protection of an insignificant sectary to
him ? thought the Shah-in-Shah, and tossed the letter
into the Euphrates. But Nature, horrified at the sac-
rilegious deed, dried up her flowers and fruits, and
even parched the sources of the river itself; the last
relic of Eden became a waste. There is a plaintive
Armenian elegy composed in the person of Adam
sitting at the gate of Paradise, and beholding Cheru-
bim and Seraphim entering the Garden of which he
once was king, "yea, like unto a powerful king!"
The poet puts into Adam's mouth a new line of

defence ; he did not eat of the fruit, he says, until after
he had witnessed its fatal effects upon Eve, when,
seeing her despoiled of all her glory, he was touched
with pity, and tasted the immortal fruit in the hope
that the Creator contemplating them both in the same
wretched plight might with paternal love take compassion on both.   But vain was the hope ; "the Lord
cursed the serpent and Eve, and I was enslaved between them."   " O Seraphim!" cries the exiled father
of mankind :

When ye enter Eden, shut not the gate of Paradise; place me
    standing at the gate; I will look in a moment, and then
    bring me back.
Ah! I remember ye, O flowers and sweet-swelling fountains.
    Ah! I remember ye O birds, sweet-singing—and ye, O
    beasts :
Ye who enjoy Paradise, come and weep over your king ; ye who
    are in Paradise planted by God, elected from the earth of
    every kind and sort.

High above the hardiest saxifrage tower the three
thousand feet of everlasting snows that crown Mount
Ararat.   The Armenians call it Massis or "Mother of
the World," and old geographers held that it was the
centre of the earth, an hypothesis supported by various
ingenious calculations.   The Persians have their own
set of legends about it ; they say that Ararat was
the cradle of the human race, and that at one time it
afforded pasture up to the apex of its dome ; but upon
man's expulsion from Eden, Ahriman the serpent
doomed the whole country to a ten months' winter.
As to the semi-scriptural traditions gathered round
the mountain, there is no end to them.   "And the
ark rested in the seventh month, on the seventeenth

day of the month, upon the mountains of Ararat,"
so says the Bible, and it is an article of faith with the
Armenian peasant that it is still somewhere up at the
top, only not visible. He is extremely loth to believe
that anybody has actually attained the summit. Parrot's famous ascent was long regarded as the merest
fable. At the foot of Ararat was a village named
Argoory, or "he planted the vine," where Noah's
vineyard is pointed out to this day, though the village
itself was destroyed in 1840, when the mountain woke
up from its long slumbers and rolled down its side a
stream of boiling lava; but we are told that, owing
to the sins of the world, the vines no longer bear fruit.
Close at hand is Manard, "the mother lies here,"
alluding to the burial-place of Noah's wife, and yonder
is Eravan or "Visible," the first dry land which Noah
perceived as the waters receded. Armenian choniclers
relate that when after leaving the ark the descendants
of Noah dispersed to different quarters, one amongst
them, by name Haig, the great-grandson of Japhet,
settled with his family in Mesopotamia, where he probably took part in the building of the Tower of Babel.
Later, however, upon Belus acquiring dominion over
the land, Haig found his rule so irksome to himself
and his clan that they migrated back in a body of 300
persons to Armenia, much to the displeasure of Belus,
who summoned them to return, and when they refused,
despatched a large army to coerce them into obedience.
Haig collected his men on the shores of Van, and thus
sagaciously addressed them:

When we meet with the army of Belus, let us attempt to draw
near where he lies surrounded by his warriors; either we shall
be killed, and our camp equipments and baggage will fall into

his hands, or, making a show of the strength of our arm, we shall defeat his army, and victory will be ours.

These tactics proved completely successful, and Belus fell mortally wounded by an arrow from Haig's bow. Having in this way disposed of his enemies, the patriarch was able before he died to consolidate Hayasdan into a goodly kingdom, which he left to the authority of his son Armenag.

After the reign of Haig the thread of Armenian annals continues without break or hitch ; it must be admitted that no people, not even the Jews, boast a history which " begins with the beginning " in a more thorough way, nor does the work of any chronicler proceed in a more methodical and circumstantial manner than that of Moses of Khoren, the Herodotus of Armenia. As is well known, Moses, writing in the fifth century, founded his chronicle upon a work undertaken about five hundred years before by one Marabas Cattina, a Syrian, at the request of the great Armenian monarch Vagshaishag. Marabas stated that his record was based upon a manuscript he had discovered in the archives of Nineveh which bore the indorsement, " This book, containing the annals of ancient history, was translated from the Chaldean into Greek, by order of Alexander the Great." Whatever may be the precise amount of credence to which the Chronicle of Moses is entitled, all will agree that it narrates the story of a high-spirited and intelligent people whom the alternating domination of Greek and Persian could not cower into relinquishing the substance of their liberties, and whose efforts, in the main successful, on behalf of their cherished independence, were never more vigorous than at times when their triumph seemed farthest off. For nearly a thousand years after the date of Moses of Khoren, his people maintained their autonomy, and whether we look before or after the flight of the last Armenian king before the soldiers of the Crescent, we must acknowledge that few nations have fought more valiantly for their political rights, whilst yet fewer have suffered more severely for their fidelity to their faith. It is the pride of the Armenians that theirs was the first country which adopted the Christian religion; it may well be their pride also, that they kept their Christianity in the teeth of persecutions which can only find a parallel in those undergone by the Hebrew race.

Armenia is naturally rich in early Christian legends, of which the most curious is perhaps that of the correspondence alleged to have occurred between Our . Lord and Abgar, king of Hayasdan. The latter, it is said, having sent messengers to transact some business with the Roman generals quartered in Palestine, received on their return such accounts of the miracles performed by Jesus of Nazareth as convinced him either that Christ was God come down upon the earth, or that he was the son of God. Suffering from a grave malady, and hearing, moreover, that the Jews had set their hearts on doing despite to the Prophet who had risen in their midst, Abgar wrote a letter beseeching Christ to come to his capital and cure him of his sickness. " My city is indeed small," this letter naïvely concludes, " but it is sufficient to contain us both." The king also sent a painter to Jerusalem, so that if Our Lord could not come to Edessa he might at least possess his portait. The painter was one day

endeavouring to fulfil his mission when he was observed by Christ, who passing a handkerchief over
his face, gave it to the Armenian impressed with the
likeness of his features. The response to Abgar's
letter was written by St Thomas, who said, on behalf
of his Divine Master, that his work lay elsewhere
than in Armenia, but that after his Ascension he
would send an Apostle to enlighten the people of
that country. This correspondence, though now not
accepted as authentic out of Armenia, was mentioned
by some of the earliest Church historians, and it is
asserted that one of the letters has been found written
on papyrus in an Egyptian tomb.

Christianity seems to have made some way in
Armenia in the second century, but to what extent
is unknown. What is certain is, that in the third
century, St Gregory the Illuminator, after having
been tortured in twelve different ways by King
Tiridates for refusing to worship the goddess Anahid,
and kept at the bottom of a well for fourteen years,
was taken out of it in consequence of a vision of the
king's sister, and converted that monarch and all his
subjects along with him. St Gregory is held in
boundless reverence by the Armenians; he is almost
looked upon as a divine viceroy, as will be seen from
the following canzonette which Armenian children
are taught to sing :

> The light appears, the light appears !
> The light is good :
> The sparrow is on the tree,
> The hen is on the perch,
> The sleep of lazy men is a year,
> Workman, rise and begin thy work !

> The gates of heaven are opened,
> The throne of gold is erected,
> Christ is sitting on it ;
> The Illuminator is standing,
> He has taken the golden pen,
> He has written great and small.
> Sinners are weeping,
> The just are rejoicing.

The poet of the people nowhere occupies himself with casting about for a fine subject; he writes of what he feels and of what he sees. The Armenian peasant sees the snow in winter ; in summer he sees the flowers and the birds—only birds and flowers are to him the pleasanter sight, so he sings more about them. He rarely composes any verse without a flower or a bird being mentioned in it ; all his similes are ornithological or botanical, and by them he expresses the tenderest emotions of his heart. There is a pathos, a simplicity really exquisite in the conception of some of these little bird-and-flower pieces, as, for example, in the subjoined " Lament of a Mother" over her dead babe :

> I gaze and weep, mother of my boy,
>   I say alas and woe is me wretched !
>   What will become of wretched me,
>   I have seen my golden son dead !
> They seized that fragrant rose
>   Of my breast, and my soul fainted away ;
>   They let my beautiful golden dove
>   Fly away, and my heart was wounded.
> That falcon Death seized
>   My dear and sweet-voiced turtle dove and wounded me.
>   They took my sweet-toned little lark
>   And flew away through the skies !

Before my eyes they sent the hail
  On my flowering green pomegranate,
  My rosy apple on the tree,
  Which gave fragrance among the leaves.
They shook my flourishing beautiful almond tree,
  And left me without fruit ;
  Beating it they threw it on the ground
  And trod it under foot into the earth of the grave.
What will become of wretched me !
  Many sorrows surrounded me.
  O, my God, receive the soul of my little one
  And place him at rest in the bright heaven !

The birds of Armenia are countless in their number
and variety, from vulture to wren ; there are so many
of them that a man (it is said poetically) may ride for
miles and miles and never see the ground, which they
entirely cover, except over the small space from
which they fly up with a deafening whizz to make a
passage for his horse. At times the plains have the
appearance of being dyed rose-colour through the
swarms of the gorgeous red goose which congregate
upon them, whilst here and there a whitish spot is
formed by a troop of his grey-coated relatives. It
seems that the Armenian has found out why it was
the wild goose and the tame one separated from each
other. Once upon a time, when all were wild and
free, one goose said to another on the eve of a journey,
" Mind you are ready, my friend, for, Inshallah (please
God), I set out to-morrow morning." " And so will
I," he profanely replied, " whether it pleases God or
not." Sure enough next morning both geese were
up betimes, and the religious one spread out his wings
and sailed off lightly towards the distant land. But,
lo ! when the impious goose tried to do likewise, he

flapped and flapped and could not stir from the ground. So a countryman caught him, and he and his children for ever fell into slavery.

The partridge is a great favourite of the Armenian, who does not tire of inventing lyrics in its honour. Here is a specimen :

> The sun beats from the mountain's top,
> Pretty, pretty :
> The partridge comes from her nest ;
> She was saluted by the flowers,
> She flew and came from the mountain's top.
> Ah ! pretty, pretty,
> Ah ! dear little partridge !

> When I hear the voice of the partridge
> I break my fast on the house-top :
> The partridge comes chirping
> And swinging from the mountain's side.
> Ah ! pretty, pretty,
> Ah ! dear little partridge !

> Thy nest is enamelled with flowers,
> With basilico, narcissus, and water-lily :
> Thy place is full of dew,
> Thou delightest in the fragrant odour.
> Ah ! pretty, pretty,
> Ah ! dear little partridge !

> Thy feathers are soft,
> Thy neck is long, thy beak little,
> The colour of thy wing is variegated :
> Thou art sweeter than the dove.
> Ah ! pretty, pretty,
> Ah ! dear little partridge !

> When the little partridge descends from the tree,
> And with his sweet voice chirps,
> He cheers all the world,
> He draws the heart from the sea of blood.
> Ah ! pretty, pretty,
> Ah ! dear little partridge.

All the birds call thee blessed,
They come with thee in flocks,
They come around thee chirping :
In truth there is not one like thee.
Ah ! pretty, pretty,
Ah ! beautiful little partridge !

Another song gives the piteous plaint of an unhappy partridge who was snared and eaten. " Like St Gregory, they let me down into a deep well; then they took me up and sat round a table, and they cut me into little pieces, like St James the Intercised." The crane, who, with the stork, brings the promise of summer on his wing, receives a warm welcome, and when the Armenian sees a crane in some foreign country he will say to him :—

Crane, whence dost thou come? I am the servant of thy voice. Crane, hast thou not news from our country? Hasten not to thy flock ; thou wilt arrive soon enough ! Crane, hast thou not news from our country?

I have left my possessions and vineyard and come hither. How often do I sigh ; it seems that my soul is taken from me. Crane, stay a little, thy voice is in my soul. Crane, hast thou not news from our country? My God, I ask of thee grace and favour, the heart of the pilgrim is wounded, his lungs are consumed ; the bread he eats is bitter, the water he drinks is tasteless. Crane, hast thou not news from our country?

Thou comest from Bagdad, and goest to the frontiers. I will write a little letter and give it to thee. God will be the witness over thee ; thou wilt carry it and give it to my dear ones.

I have put in my letter that I am here, that I have never even for a single day been happy. O, my dear ones, I am always anxious for you ! Crane, hast thou not news from our country?

The autumn is near, and thou art ready to go : thou hast joined a large flock : thou hast not answered me, and thou art flown ! Crane, go from our country and fly far away !

The nameless author of these lines has had Dante's thought :

> Tu proverai sì come sa di sale
> Lo pane altrui . . .

It is strange that the Armenians should be at once one of the most scattered peoples on the face of the earth, and one of the most passionately devoted to their fatherland.

It should not be forgotten, when reading these Armenian bird-lays, that an old belief yet survives in that country that the souls of the blessed dead fly down from heaven, in the shape of beautiful birds, and perching in the branches of the trees, look fondly at their dear ones on earth as they pass beneath. When the peasant sees the birds fluttering above overhead in the wood he will on no account molest them, but says to his boy, " That is your dear mother, your little brother, your sister—be a good child, or it will fly away and never look at you again with its sweet little eyes."

The clear cool streams and vast treacherous salt lakes of Armenia are not without their laureates. Thus sings the bard of a mountain rivulet :

> " Down from yon distant mountain
>   The water flows through the village, Ha !
>   A dark boy comes forth,
>   And washing his hands and face,
>   Washing, yes washing,
>   And turning to the water, asked, Ha !
>   Water, from what mountain dost thou come?
>   O my cool and sweet water ! Ha !
>   I came from that mountain,
>   · Where the old and new snow lie one on the other.

Water, to what river dost thou go?
  O my cool and sweet water! Ha!
I go to that river
  Where the bunches of violets abound. Ha!
Water, to what vineyard dost thou go?
  O my cool and sweet water! Ha!
I go to that vineyard
  Where the vine-dresser is within! Ha!
Water, what plant dost thou water?
  O my cool and sweet water! Ha!
I water that plant
  Whose roots give food to the lamb,
  The roots give food to the lamb,
  Where there are the apple tree and the anemone.
Water, to what garden dost thou go?
  O my cool and sweet water! Ha!
I go into that garden
  Where there is the sweet song of the nightingale! Ha!
Water, into what fountain dost thou go?
  O my cool and sweet little water!
I go to that fountain
  Where thy love comes and drinks.
  I go to meet her and kiss her chin,
  And satiate myself with her love.

The dwellers on the shores of Van—the largest lake in Armenia, which is situated between 5000 and 6000 feet above the sea, and covers more than 400 square miles—are celebrated for possessing the poetic gift in a pre-eminent degree. Their district is fertile and picturesque, so picturesque that when Semiramis passed that way she employed 12,000 workmen and 600 architects to build her a city on the banks of the lake, which was named Aghthamar, and which she thereafter made her summer residence. The business that brought Semiramis into Armenia was a strange romance. Ara, eighth patriarch of Hayasdan, was famed through all the East for his surpassing beauty, and the Assyrian queen hearing that he was the fairest to look upon of all mortal men, sent him a proposal of marriage; but he, staunch to the faith in the one true God, which he believed had been transmitted to him from Noah, would have nothing to say to the offer of the idolatrous ruler. Semiramis, greatly incensed, advanced with her army into the heart of Armenia, and defeated the forces of the Patriarch; but bitter were the fruits of the victory, for Ara, instead of being taken alive, as she had commanded, was struck down at the head of his men, and his beautiful form, stiffened by death, was laid at the queen's feet. Semiramis was plunged in the wildest despair; she endeavoured to bring him to life by magic; that failing, she had his body embalmed and placed in a golden coffin, which was set in her chamber; no one was allowed to call him dead, and she spoke of him as her beloved consort. A spot is pointed out to the traveller bearing the name of Ara Seni, "Ara is sacrificed."

The favourite theme of the men of Van is, of course, the treacherous element on which the lot of most of them is cast. One of their songs gives the legend of the "Old Man and the Ship." Our Lord, as an old man with a white beard, cried sweetly to the sailors to take him into the ship. The sailors answer that the ship is freighted by a merchant, and the passage-money is great. "Go away, white-bearded old man," they say. But our Lord pays the money and comes into the ship. Presently a gale blows up and the sailors are exceeding wroth, for they imagine the strange passenger has brought them ill-luck. They ask, "Whence didst thou come, O sinful man ? Thou art lost, and thou hast lost us !" "I a sinner !" replies the Lord, "give me the ship, and go you to sweet sleep." He made the sign of the cross with his right hand, with his left he steered the helm. It was not yet mid-day when the ship safely reached the shore.

Brothers, arise from your sweet sleep, from your sweet sleep and your sad dreams. Fall at the feet of Jesus ; here is our Lord, here is our ship.

"Sweet sleep and sad dreams"—he must have been a true poet who thus crystallised the sense of poor humanity's unrest, even in its profoundest repose. The whole little story strikes one as full of delicate suggestiveness.

One more sample of the style of the Armenian "Lake-school."

ON ONE WHO WAS SHIPWRECKED ON THE LAKE OF VAN.

We sailed in the ship from Aghthamar,
  We directed our ship towards Avan ;
  When we arrived before Vosdan
  We saw the dark sun of the dark day.

Dull clouds covered the sky,
  Obscuring at once stars and moon ;
  The winds blew fiercely,
  And took from my eyes land and shore.

Thundered the heaven, thundered the earth,
  The waters of the blue sea arose ;
  On every side the heavens shot forth fire ;
  Black terror invaded my heart.

There is the sky, but the earth is not seen,
  There is the earth, but the sun is not seen ;
  The waves come like mountains
  And open before me a deep abyss.

O sea, if thou lovest thy God,
Have pity on me, forlorn and wretched ;
Take not from me my sweet sun,
And betray me not to flinty-hearted Death.

Pity, O sea, O terrible sea !
Give me not up to the cold winds ;
My tears implore thee
And the thousand sorrows of my heart. . .

The savage sea has no pity!
It hears not the plaintive voice of my broken heart ;
The blood freezes in my veins,
Black night descends upon my eyes. . . .

Go tell to my mother
To sit and weep for her darkened son ;
That John was the prey of the sea,
The sun of the young man is set !

Summer, with its flowers, and warmth, and wealth, never stays long enough in Armenia for it to become a common ordinary thing. It is a beautiful wonder-time, a brief, splendid nature-fair, which vanishes like a dream before the first astonishment and delight are worn into indifference. The season when "the nightingale sings to the rose at dewy dawn" departs swiftly, and envious winter strangles autumn in its birth.

What a winter, too! a winter which despotically governs the complete economy of the people's system of life. Let us take a peep into an Armenian interior on a December evening. Three months the snow has been in possession of mountain and valley ; for more than four months more it will remain. Abroad it is light enough, though night has fallen ; for the moon shines down in wonderful brightness upon the ice-

bound earth. On the hill-slope various little uneven-
nesses are discernible, jutting out from the snow like
mushrooms. In one part the ground is cut away
perpendicularly for a few feet; this is the front of the
homestead, the body of which lies burrowed in the
slope of the hill. When the house was made the
floor was dug out some five feet underground, while
the ceiling beams rose three or four feet above it; but
all the dug-out soil was thrown about the roof and
back and side walls, and thus the whole is now
embedded in the hillock. The roof was neatly turfed
over when the house was finished, so that in summer
the lambs and children play upon it, and not unfrequently, in the great heats, the family sleep there—
"at the moon's inn." What look like mushrooms are
in reality the broad-topped chimneys, on which the
summer storks build their nests. The homestead has
but one entrance; a large front door which leads
through a long dark passage to a second door that
swings-to after you, and is hung with a rough red-
dyed sheepskin. This door opens upon the entrance-
hall, whence you mount half-a-dozen steps to a raised
platform, under which the house dogs are located.
On two sides the platform is bounded by solid stone
walls, from which are suspended saddles, guns, pistols,
and one or two pictures representing the deeds of
some Persian hero, and bought of Persian hawkers.
On the other two sides an open woodwork fence
divides it from a vast stable. Nearest the grating
are fastened the horses of the clan-chief; next are the
donkeys, then the cows; sheep and chickens find
places where they can. The breath of these animals
materially contributes to the warmth of the house,

which is at times almost like an oven, even in the coldest weather. A clear hot fire burns on the hearth; the fuel used is tezek, a preparation of cow-dung pressed into a substance resembling peat turf. By day the habitation is obscurely lighted through a small aperture in the roof glazed with oiled silk, and supplemented by a sort of funnel, the wide opening downwards. Now, in the evening, the oil burning in a simple iron lamp over the hearth, affords a dim illumination.

The platform above described is the salemlik, or hall of reception. It contains no chairs, but divans richly draped with Koordish stuffs; the floor is carpeted with tekeke, a kind of grey felt. To the right of the hearth sits the head of the family, a venerable old man, whose word is incontrovertible law to every member of his house. He is also Al Sakal, or "white beard" of the village, a dignity conferred on him by the unanimous voice of his neighbours, and constituting him intermediary in all transactions with government. When important matters are at stake, he meets the elders of the surrounding hamlets, who, resolved into committee, form the Commune. This ancient usage bears witness to the essentially patriarchal and democratic basis of Armenian society.

Our family party consists of three dozen persons, the representatives of four generations. The young married women come in and out from directing the preparations of the supper. Nothing is to be seen of their faces except their lustrous eyes (Armenian eyes are famous for their brilliancy), a tightly-fitting veil enclosing the rest of their features. Without this covering they do not by any chance appear even in the house ; it is said they wear it also at night. One of them is a bride ; her dress is rich and striking—a close-fitting bodice, fastening at the neck with silver clasps, full trousers of rose-coloured silk gathered in at the ankles by a fillet of silver, the feet bare, a silver girdle of curious workmanship loosely encircling the waist, and a long padded garment open down the front which hangs from the shoulders. Poor little bride! She has not uttered a single word save when alone with her husband since she pronounced the marriage vow. She may not hope to do so till after the birth of her first-born child ; then she will talk to her nursling, after a while to her mother-in-law, some-time later she may converse with her own mother, and by-and-by, in a subdued whisper, with the young girls of the house. During the first year of her married life she may not go out of the house except twice to church. Her disciplinary education will not be complete for six years, after which she will enjoy comparative liberty, but never in her life must she open her lips to a person of the stronger sex not related to her. Turn from the silent little bride to that bevy of young girls, merry and playful as the kittens they are fondling—silky-haired snowballs, of a breed peculiar to the neighbourhood of Van, their tails dyed pink with henna like the tail of the Shah's steed. The girls are laughing and chatting together without restraint—most probably about their love affairs, for they are free to dispose of their hands as they choose. And they may walk about unveiled, and show off their pretty faces and long raven plaits to the fullest advantage.

Suddenly a knocking is heard outside; the dogs yell from under the platform; the Whitebeard says whoever be the wanderer he shall have bed and board, and he orders fresh tezek to be thrown on the fire; for to-night it is bitter cold out abroad—were a man to stand still five minutes, he would freeze in his shoes. One of the sons descends the steps, pushes aside the sheep-skin, and leads the traveller in. This one says he is the minstrel. What joy in the family! The blind minstrel, who will sing the most exciting ballads and tell the most marvellous tales. He is welcomed by all; only the young bride steals out of the room—she may not remain in a stranger's presence. The lively girls want to hear a story at once; but the Whitebeard says the guest must first have rest and refreshment. But while they are waiting for the meal to be laid out, the blind minstrel relates something of his recent travels, which in itself is almost as good as a fairy tale. He has just arrived from Persia, whither he will soon return; for he has only come back to the snows of Armenia to breathe the air of home for a little. Did he go to Teheran? No; to say the truth, he deemed it wiser to keep at a discreet distance from that capital. Such a thing had been heard of ere now as the Shah putting under requisition any skilful musicians who came in his way to teach their art to the fair ones of the harem; so that occasionally it was unpleasantly difficult to get out of Teheran when once you were in it. Still he was by no means without interesting news. In a certain part of Persia he had met another blind master-singer, with whom he strove for the prize of minstrelsy. Both were entertained by a great Persian prince. When the day came they were led out upon an open grass-plot and seated one facing the other. The prince took up his position, and five thousand people made a circle round the competitors. Then the grand brain-fight began ; the rivals contended in song and verse, riddle and repartee. Now one starts an acrostic on the prince's name, in which each side takes alternate letters ; then the other versifies some sacred passage, which his opponent must catch up when he breaks off. The ball is kept flying to and fro with unflagging zeal ; the crowd is rapturous in its plaudits. But at length our minstrel's adversary pauses, hesitates, fails to seize the drift of his rival's latest sally, and answers at random. A shout proclaims him beaten. The triumphant bard is led to where he stands, and taking his lyre from him breaks it into atoms. The vanquished retires discomfited to the obscurity of his native village, where haply his humble talents will not be despised. The victor is robed in the prince's mantle, and taken to the highest seat in the banqueting-hall.

This is what the minstrel has to tell as he warms his hands over the fire while the young married women serve the supper. A rush-mat is placed upon the low round board, over that the table-cloth ; then a large tray is set in the middle, with the viands arranged on it in metal dishes : onion soup, salted salmon-trout from the blue Gokschai, hard-boiled eggs shelled and sliced, oil made from Kunjut seeds, which does instead of butter ; pilau, a dish resembling porridge ; mutton stewed with quinces, leeks, and various raw and preserved roots, cream cheese, sour milk, dried apricots, and stoned raisins, form the bill of fair. A can of

golden wine is set out: there is plenty more in the
goatskins should it be wanted. The provisions are
completed by an item more important in Armenia
than with us—bread. The flour-cake or *losh*, a yard
long and thin as paper, which is placed before each
guest, answers for plate, knives, forks, napkin, all of
which are absent. The Whitebeard says grace and
the Lord's Prayer, everyone crossing himself. The
company wipe their mouths with a *losh*, and proceed
to help themselves with it to anything that tempts
their fancy on the middle tray. Some make a promiscuous sandwich of fish, mutton, and leeks wrapped
up in a piece of *losh;* others twist the *losh* into the
shape of a spoon and ladle out the sour milk, swal-
lowing both together. The members of the family
watch the minstrel's least gesture, so as to anticipate
his wishes ; one after the other they claim the privilege
of waiting on him. When the meal is done, a young
housewife gently washes the guest's head and feet,
and the whole party adjourn to the chimney-corner.
The evening flies mirthfully away, listening to the
minstrel's tales and ballads, these latter being mostly
in Tartar, the Provençal of the eastern troubadour.
Finally, the honoured visitor is conducted to his room,
the " minstrel's chamber," which, in every well-ordered
Armenian household, is always kept ready.

Our little picture may be taken as the faithful
reproduction of no very extraordinary scene. Of
ballad-singers such as the one here introduced
there are numbers in Armenia, where that "sixth
sense," music, is the recognised vocation of the blind.
Those who are proficient travel within a very wide
area, and are everywhere received with the highest
consideration.

In the East, the ballad-singer and the story-teller are just where they were centuries ago. At Constantinople, the story-teller sits down on his mat in the public place or at the *café;* listeners gather round ; he begins his story in a conversational tone, varying his voice according to the characters ; and soon both himself and his hearers are as far away in the wondrous mazes of the "Arabian Nights" as if Europe were still trembling before the sword of the Caliph.

With regard to the unique marriage customs of Armenia, I ought to say that they are asserted to result in the happiest unions. The general idea upon which they rest seems to be derived from a series of conclusions logical enough if you grant the premisses —indeed, curiously more like some pen and paper scheme evolved out of the inner consciousness of a German professor than a working system of actual life. The prevailing custom in the East, as in some European countries, is for the young girl to know nothing whatever of her intended husband ; only in the one case this is followed by total seclusion after marriage, and in the other by complete emancipation. In Armenia, on the contrary, the young girl makes her own choice, and love-matches are not uncommon ; but the choice once made and ratified by the priest, the order of things is so arranged as to cause her husband to become the woman's absorbing thought, his society her sole solace, his pleasure the whole business of her life. For the rest she is treated with much solicitude ; even the peasant will not let his wife do out-door work.

Moses of Khoren gives the history of a wedding that took place about one hundred years after Christ.

In those days the tribes of the Alans, in league with the mountaineers of the Caucasus and a part of the people of Georgia, descended upon Armenia in considerable numbers. Ardashes, the Armenian king, assembled his troops and advanced against them. In a battle fought upon the confines of the two nations, the Alans gave way, and having crossed the Cyrus, encamped on the northern bank, the river dividing the contending forces. The son of the King of the Alans had been taken prisoner and was conducted to Ardashes. His father offered to conclude a peace on such conditions as Ardashes might exact and under promise, guaranteed by a solemn oath, that the Alans would attempt no further incursions on Armenian territory. As Ardashes refused to surrender the young prince, the sister of the youth ran to the edge of the river and climbing upon a lofty hillock, caused these words to be addressed to the enemy's camp by the mouth of interpreters: " Hear me, valorous Ardashes, conqueror of the brave Alans ; grant unto me the surrender of this young man—unto me, the maiden with beautiful eyes. It is not worthy of a hero in order to satisfy a desire for vengeance, to take the life of the sons of heroes or to hold them in bondage and keep up an endless feud between two nations." Ardashes, having heard these words, approached the river. He saw the beautiful Sathinig, listened to her wise counsels, and fell in love with her. Then, having called Sumpad, an aged warrior who had watched over his childhood, he laid bare the wish of his heart to marry the princess, make a treaty of amity with her nation and send back the prince in peace. Sumpad, having approved of these projects,

sent to ask the King of the Alans for the hand of
Sathinig. "What!" replied her father, "will the
valorous King Ardashes have ever treasure enough
to offer me in return for the noble damsel of the
Alans?"

A popular song, carefully preserved by Moses,
celebrates the marriage of Ardashes and Sathinig :—

> The valiant King Ardashes, astride of a sable charger,
> Drew forth a thong of leather, garnished with golden rings :
> And quick as fast-flying eagle he crossed the flowing river
> And the crimson leather thong, garnished with rings of gold,
> Cast he about the body of the Virgin of the Alans,
> Clasping in painful embrace the maiden's tender form :
> Even so he drew her swiftly to his encampment.

Once again Ardashes appears in the people's
poetry. He is no longer the triumphant victor in
love and war; the hour of his death draws near.
"Oh!" says the dying king, "who will give me back
the smoke of my hearth, and the joyous New Year's
morning, and the spring of the deer, and the light-
ness of the roe?" Then his mind wanders away to
, the ruling passion : "We sounded the trumpets ;
after the manner of kings we beat the drums."

The Armenian princes were in the habit, when
they married, of throwing pieces of money from the
threshold of their palace, whilst the royal brides
scattered pearls about the nuptial chamber. To this
custom allusion is made in two lines which used to be
sung as a sort of marriage chaunt :—

> A rain of gold fell at the wedding of Ardashes,
> A rain of pearls fell on the nuptials of Sathinig.

Armenian nuptial songs, like all other folk-

epithalamiums, so far as I am aware, seem to point
to an early state of society when the girl was simply
carried off by her marauding lover by fraud or force.
Exulting in what relates to the bridegroom, the
favourite song on this subject is profoundly melancholy as concerns the bride. The mother was
cajoled with a pack of linen, the father with a cup of
wine, the brother with a pair of boots, the little
sister with a finger of antimony—so complains the
dismal ditty of a new bride. There is great
pathos in the words in which she begs her mother
not to sweep the sand off the little plank, so that
the slight trace of her girl's footsteps may not be
effaced.

Marriage is called in Armenian, "The Imposition
of the Crown," from the practice of crowning bride
and bridegroom with fresh, white flowers. I remember how, in one of the last marriages celebrated in
the little Armenian church in the Rue Monsieur
(which was closed a few years ago, when the Mekhitarist property in Paris was sold), this ceremony
was omitted by particular request of the bridegroom,
a rising French Diplomatist, who did not wish to
wear a wreath of roses. The Armenian marriage
formulæ are extremely explicit. The priest, taking
the right hand of the bride, and placing it in that of
the bridegroom, says : "According to the Divine
order God gave to our ancestors, I give thee now this
wife in subjection. Wilt thou be her master ?" To
which the answer is, "Through the help of God, I
will." The priest then asks the woman : "Wilt thou
be obedient to him ?" She answers: "I am obedient according to the order of God." The inter-

rogations are repeated three times, and three times responded to.

An Armenian author, M. Ermine, published at Moscow in 1850 a treatise on the historical and popular songs of ancient Armenia.

Of popular songs current in more recent times there was not, till lately, a single specimen within reach of the public, though it was confidently surmised that such must exist. The Mekhitarist monks have taken the lead in this as in every other branch of Armenian research, and my examples are quoted from a small collection issued by their press at Venice. I am not sure that I have chosen those that are intrinsically the best, but think that those which figure in these pages are amongst the most characteristic of their authors and origin. The larger portion of these songs are printed from manuscripts in the library of San Lazzaro ; the date of their composition is thought to vary from the end of the thirteenth to the end of the eighteenth century. The language in which they are written is the vulgar tongue of Armenia, but in several instances it attains a very close · approximation to the classical Armenian.

It may not be amiss if I conclude this sketch with a brief account of the remarkable order of the Mekhitarists, which is so intimately related with all that bears on the subject of Armenian literature. Those who are well acquainted with it will not object to hear the history of this order recapitulated ; while I believe that many who have visited the Convent of San Lazzaro have yet but vague notions regarding the work and aims of its inmates. It is to be conjectured that, as a matter of fact, the majority of Englishmen go to San Lazzaro rather in the spirit of a Byron-pilgrimage than from any definite interest in the convent ; and without doubt were its only attraction its association with the English poet it would still be worth a visit. Byron's connection with San Lazzaro was not one of the least interesting episodes of his life ; and it is pleasant to remember the tranquil hours he spent in the society of the learned monks, and the fascination exercised over him by their sterling and unpretentious merit. " The neatness, the comfort, the gentleness, the unaffected devotion of the brethren of the order," he wrote, "are well fitted to strike the man of the world with the conviction that there is 'Another and a better even in this life.'" The desire to present himself with an excuse for frequent intercourse with the brothers was probably at the bottom of Byron's sudden discovery that his mind " wanted something craggy to break upon, and that Armenian was just the thing to torture it into attention." He says it was the most difficult thing to be found in Venice by way of an amusement, and describes the Armenian character as a very " Waterloo of an alphabet." The origin of this character is exceedingly curious, it being the only alphabet known to have been the work of a single man, with the exception of the Georgian, and now obsolete Caucasian Albanian. St Mesrop, an Armenian, invented all the three about A.D. 406. Byron informs Moore, with some elation, of the fate that befel a French professorship of Armenian, which had then been recently instituted : " Twenty pupils presented themselves on Monday morning, full of noble ardour, ingenuous youth, and impregnable industry. They persevered with a courage worthy of the nation, and of universal conquest till Thursday, then *fifteen* out of the *twenty* succumbed to the six-and-twentieth letter of the alphabet." The poet himself mastered all thirty-three letters, and a good deal more besides, under the superintendence of the librarian, Padre Paschal Aucher, a man who combined great learning with much knowledge of the world. As the result of these studies we have a translation into Scriptural English of two apocryphal epistles of St Paul, and an Anglo-Armenian grammar, of which, with characteristic liberality, Byron defrayed the cost of publication.

The order was founded by Varthabed Mekhitar, who was born at Sebaste, in Asia Minor, in 1676. Mekhitar was one of those men to whom it comes quite naturally to go forth with David's sling and stone against the Philistine and his host. He could have been scarcely more than twenty years of age when fearlessly and steadfastly he set himself to the gigantic task of raising his country out of the stagnant slough of ignorance in which he saw it sunk. He was then a candidate for holy orders, studying in an Armenian convent.

The monks he found no less ignorant than the rest of the population; those to whom he broached his ideas greeted them with derision, and this did not fail to turn to cruel persecution when he began to preach against certain prejudices which appeared to him to keep the Armenians from conforming with the Latin Church—a union he earnestly desired. Mekhitar now went to Constantinople, where he set on foot a small monastic society; presently he moved to

Modon, in the Morea, then under the rule of Venice, but before he had been there long, the place was seized by the Turks. A few of the monks, with their head, managed to escape to Venice ; the others were taken prisoners, and sold into a temporary slavery. At Venice, in 1717, the Signory made over to the fugitives in perpetuity a small barren island in the Lagune, once tenanted by the Benedictines, who had there established a hospital for lepers, but which, since the disappearance of that disease, had been entirely uninhabited. Mekhitar immediately organised a printing press, and began making translations of standard works, which were disseminated wherever Armenians were to be found, that is to say, all over the East. When he died in 1747, the work of the society was already placed on a solid foundation ; but it received considerable development and extension from the hands of the third abbot-general, Count Stephen Aconzkover, Archbishop of Sinnia, by birth a member of an Armenian colony in Hungary, who sought admittance into the order, and lived in the retirement of San Lazzaro for sixty-seven years. He was a poet, a scholar of no mean attainments, and the author of a universal geography in twelve volumes. The Society is now self-supporting, large numbers of its publications being sold in Persia, and India, and at Constantinople. These publications consist of numerous translations and of reproductions of the great part of Armenian literature. Many works have been printed from MSS. which are collected by emissaries sent out from San Lazzaro to travel over the plains and valleys of Armenia for the purpose of rescuing the literary relics which are widely scattered, and are in constant danger of loss or destruction, and

at the same time to distribute Armenian versions of
the Bible. Another of the undertakings of the convent is a school exclusively for the education of
Armenian boys. About one hundred boys receive
free instruction in the two colleges at Venice. What
this order have effected, both towards the enlighten-
ment of their country and in keeping alive the sentiment of Armenian nationality, is simply incalculable.
In their self-imposed exile they have nobly carried out
the precept of an Armenian folk-poet :

> Forget not our Armenian nation,
> And always assist and protect it.
> Always keep in thy mind
> To be useful to thy fatherland.

On my first visit I passed a long summer morning in
examining all the points of interest about the monas-
tery—the house and printing presses, the library with
its beautiful Pali papyrus of the Buddhist ordination
service, and its illuminated manuscripts, the mina-
retted chapel, and the silent little Campo Santo, under
the direction of the most courteous and accomplished
of cicerones, Padre Giacomo, Dr Issaverdenz : a name
signifying " Jesus-given." I saw the bright, intelligent band of scholars : " of these," said my conductor,
" five or six will remain with us." I was shown the
page of the visitor's book inscribed with Byron's sig-
nature in English and in Armenian. Later entries
form a long roll of royal and notable names. The
little museum contains Daniel Manin's tricolor scarf
of office, given to the monks by the son of that
devoted patriot. Queen Margherita does not fail to
pay San Lazzaro a yearly visit, and has lately
accepted the dedication of a book of Armenian church
music.

During this tour of inspection, various topics were
discussed: the tendencies of modern thought, the
future of the church, with other matters of a more
personal nature—and upon each my guide's observations displayed a singularly intellectual and tolerant
attitude of mind, together with a way of looking at
things and speaking of people in which "sweetness
and light" were felicitously apparent. It was difficult
to tear oneself away from the open window in Byron's
little study. The day was one of those matchless
Venetian days, when the heat is tempered by a breeze
just fresh enough to agitate the awning of your gon-
dola ; and the Molo and Riva, and Fortune's golden
ball on the Dogana, the white San Giorgio Maggiore,
the ships eastward bound, the billowy line of the
mountains of Vicenza against the horizon, lie steeped
in a bath of sunshine. But the outlook from the convent window is not upon these. Beneath are the
green berceaux of a small vineyard, a little garden
gay in its tangle of purple convolvulus, a pomegranate
lifting its laden boughs towards us—to remind the
Armenians of the "flowering pomegranates" of their
beloved country. Beyond the vineyard stretches the
aquamarine surface of the lagune—then the interminable reach of Lido—after that the ethereal blue of the
Adriatic melting away into the sky. Such is the
scene which till they die the good monks will have
under their eyes. Perhaps they are rather to be
envied than compassionated ; for it is manifest that
for them, duty—to use the eloquent expression of an
English divine—has become transfigured into happiness. " I shall stay here whilst I live," Dr Issaverdenz
said, "and I am happy—quite happy !"

VENETIAN FOLK-SONGS.

To the idealised vision that goes along with hereditary culture a large town may seem an impressive
spectacle. For Wordsworth, worshipper of nature
though he was, earth had not anything to show more
fair than London from Westminster Bridge, and
Victor Hugo found endless inspiration on the top of
a Parisian omnibus. As shrines of art, as foci of
historic memories, even simply as vast aggregates of
human beings working out the tragi-comedy of life,
great cities have furnished the key-note to much fine
poetry. But it is different with the letterless masses.
The student of literature, who turns to folk-songs in
search of a new enjoyment, will meet with little to
attract him in urban rhymes; if there are many that
present points of antiquarian interest, there are few
that have any kind of poetic worth. The people's
poetry grows not out of an ideal world of association
and aspiration, but from the springs of their life.
They cannot see with their minds as well as with
their eyes. What they do see in most great towns is
the monotonous ugliness which surrounds their homes
and their labour. Then again, it is a well-known fact
that with the people loss of individuality means loss
of the power of song; and where there is density of
population there is generally a uniformity as feature-
less as that of pebbles on the sea beach. Still to the

1

rule that folk-poesy is not a thing of town growth one exception has to be made. Venice, unique under every aspect, has songs which, if not of the highest, are unquestionably of a high order. The generalising influences at play in great political centres have hardly affected the inhabitants of the city which for a thousand years of independence was a body politic complete in itself. Nor has Venetian common life lacked those elements of beauty without whose presence the popular muse is dumb. The very industries of the Venetians were arts, and when they were young and spiritually teachable, their chief bread-winning work of every day was Venice—her ducal chapel, her campanile, her palaces of marble and porphyry. In the process of making her the delight of after ages, they attended an excellent school of poetry.

The gondolier contemporary with Byron was correctly described as songless. At a date closely coinciding with the overthrow of Venetian freedom, the boatmen left off waking the echoes of the Grand Canal, except by those cries of warning which, no one can quite say why, so thrill and move the hearer. It was no rare thing to find among the Italians of the Lombardo-Venetian provinces the old pathetic instinct of keeping silence before the stranger. I recollect a story told me by one of them. When he was a boy, Antonio—that was his name—had to make a journey with two young Austrian officers. They took notice of the lad, who was sprightly and good-looking, and by and by they asked him to sing. "Canta, canta, il piccolo," said they ; "sing us the songs of Italy." He refused. They insisted, and, coming to a tavern, they gave him wine, which sent the blood to his head. So

at last he said, "Very well, I will sing you the songs
of Italy." What he sang was one of the most furi-
ously anti-Austrian songs of '48. "Ah! taci, taci il
piccolo!" cried the officers, but the "piccolo" would
not be quiet until he had sung the whole revolutionary
repertory. The Austrians knew how to appreciate
the boy's spirit, for they pressed on him a ten franc
piece at parting.

To return to Venice. In the year 1819 an English
traveller asked for a song of a man who was reported
to have once chanted Tasso *alla barcaruolo;* the old
gondolier shook his head. "In times like these," he
said, "he had no heart to sing." Foreign visitors had
to fall back on the beautiful German music, at the
sound of which Venetians ran out of the Piazza, lest
they might be seduced by its hated sweetness.
Meanwhile the people went on singing in their own
quarters, and away from the chance of ministering to
their masters' amusement. It is even probable that
the moral casemate to which they fled favoured the
preservation of their old ways, that of poetising in-
cluded. Instead of aiming at something novel and
modern, the Venetian wished to be like what his
fathers were when the flags on St Mark's staffs were
not yellow and black. So, like his fathers, he made
songs and sang songs, of which a good collection has
been formed, partly in past years, and partly since
the black-and-yellow standard has given place, not,
indeed, to the conquered emblems of the Greek isles,
but to the colours of Italy, reconquered for herself.

Venetian folk-poesy begins at the cradle. The
baby Venetian, like most other babies, is assured that
he is the most perfect of created beings. Here and

there, underlying the baby nonsense, is a dash of pathos. "Would you weep if I were dead?" a mother asks, and the child is made to answer, "How could I help weeping for my own mamma, who loves me so in her heart?" A child is told that if he asks his mother, who is standing by the door, "What are you doing there?" she will reply, "I am waiting for thy father; I wait and wait, and do not see him coming; I think I shall die thus waiting." The little Venetian has the failings of baby-kind all the world over; he cries and he laughs when he ought to be fast asleep. His mother tells him that he was born to live in Paradise; she is sure that the angels would rejoice in her darling's beauty. "Sleep well, for thy mother sits near thee," she sings, "and if by chance I go away, God will watch thee when I am gone."

A christening is regarded in Venice as an event of much social as well as religious importance. By canon law the bonds of relationship established by god-fatherhood count for the same as those of blood, for which reason the Venetian nobles used to choose a person of inferior rank to stand sponsor for their children, thus escaping the creation of ties prohibitive of marriage between persons of their own class. In this case the material responsibilities of the sponsor were slight—it was his part to take presents, and not to make them. By way of acknowledging the new connection, the child's father sent the godfather a marchpane, that cake of mystic origin which is still honoured and eaten from Nuremberg to Malaga. With the poor, another order of things is in force. The *compare de l'anelo*—the person who acted as groomsman at the marriage—is chosen as sponsor to the first-born child. His duties begin even before the christening. When he hears of the child's birth, he gets a piece of meat, a fowl, and two new-laid eggs, packs them in a basket, and despatches them to the young mother. Eight days after the birth comes the baptism. On returning from the church, the sponsor, now called *compare de San Zuane*, visits the mother, before whom he displays his presents—twelve or fifteen lire for herself; for the baby a pair of earrings, if it be a girl; and if a boy, a pair of boy's earrings, or a single ornament to be worn in the right ear. Henceforth the godfather is the child's natural guardian next to its parents; and should they die, he is expected to provide for it. Should the child die, he must buy the *sogia* (the "joy"), a wreath of flowers now set on the coffins of dead infants, but formerly placed on their heads when they were carried to the grave-isle in full sight of the people. This last custom led to even more care being given to the toilet of dead children than what might seem required by decency and affection. To dress a dead child badly was considered shameful. Tradition tells of what happened to a woman who was so miserly that she made her little girl a winding-sheet of rags and tatters. When the night of the dead came round and all the ghosts went in procession, the injured babe, instead of going with the rest, tapped at its mother's door and cried, "Mamma, do you see me? I cannot go in procession because I am all ragged." Every year on the night of the dead the baby girl returned to make the same reproach.

Venetian children say before they go to bed :

> Bona sera ai vivi,
>   E riposo ai poveri morti ;
> Bon viagio ai naveganti   ·
>   E bona note ai tuti quanti.

There is a sort of touching simplicity in this ; and somehow the wish of peace to the "poor dead" recalls a line of Baudelaire's—

> Les morts, les pauvres morts, ont de grandes douleurs.

But as a whole, the rhymes of the Venetian nursery are not interesting, save from their extreme resemblance to the nursery rhymes of England, France, or any other European country. They need not, therefore, detain us.

Twilight is of an Eastern brevity on the Adriatic shore, both in nature and in life. The child of yesterday is the man of to-day, and as soon as the young Venetian discovers that he has a heart, he takes pains to lose it to a *Tosa* proportionately youthful. The Venetian and Provençal word *Tosa* signifies maiden, though whether the famous Cima Tosa is thus a sister to the Jungfrau is not sure, some authorities believing it to bear the more prosaic designation of baldheaded ("Tonsurata"). Our young Venetian may perhaps be unacquainted with the girl he has marked out for preference. In any case he walks up and down or rows up and down assiduously under her window. One night he will sing to a slow, languorous air—possibly an operatic air, but so altered as to be not easy of recognition—" I wish all good to all in this house, to father and to mother and as many as there be ; and to Marieta who is my beloved, she whom you have in your house." The name of the singer is most likely Nane, for Nane and Marieta are the commonest names in Venice, which is explained by the impression that persons so called cannot be bewitched, a serious advantage in a place where the Black Art is by no means extinct. The maiden long remembers the night when first her rest was disturbed by some such greeting as the above. . She has rendered account of her feelings :

> Ah ! how mine eyes are weighed in slumber deep !
> Now all my life it seems has gone to sleep ;
> But if a lover passes by the door,
> Then seems it this my life will sleep no more.

It does not do to appropriate a serenade with too much precipitation. Don Quixote gave it as his experience that no woman would believe that a poem was written expressly for her unless it made an acrostic on her name spelt out in full. Venetian damsels proceed with less caution: hence now and then a sad disappointment. A girl who starts up all pit-a-pat at the twanging of a guitar may be doomed to hear the cruel sentence pronounced in Lord Houghton's pretty lyric :

> " I am passing—Premé—but I stay not for you !
>   Premé—not for you !

Even more unkind are the literal words of the Venetian : " If I pass this way and sing as I pass, think not, fair one, that it is for you—it is for another love, whose beauty surpasses yours !"

A brother or a friend occasionally undertakes the

serenading. He is not paid like the professional
Trovador whom the Valencian lover engages to act as
his interpreter. He has no reward in view but empty
thanks, and it is scarcely surprising if on damp nights
he is inclined to fall into a rather querulous vein.
"My song is meant for the *Morosa* of my companion,"
says one of these accommodating minstrels. "If
only I knew where she was! But he told me that
she was somewhere in here. The rain is wetting me
to the skin!" Another exclaims more cheerfully,
"Beautiful angel, if it pleases God, you will become
my sister-in-law!"

After the singing of the preliminary songs, Nane
seeks a hint of the effect produced on the beloved
Marieta. As she comes out of church, he makes her
a most respectful bow, and if it be returned ever so
slightly, he musters up courage, and asks in so many
words whether she will have him. Marieta reflects
for about three days; then she communicates her
answer by sign or song. If she does not want him,
she shuts herself up in the house and will not look
out for a moment. Nane begs her to show her face
at the window: "Come, oh! come! If thou comest
not 'tis a sign that thou lovest me not; draw my
heart out of all these pangs." Marieta, if she is quite
decided, sings back from behind the half-closed
shutters, "You pass this way, and you pass in vain :
in vain you wear out shoes and soles ; expect no fair
words from me." It may be that she confesses to
not knowing her own mind: "I should like to be
married, but I know not to whom : when Nane passes,
I long to say 'Yes ;' when Toni passes, I am fain to
look kindly at him ; when Bepi passes, I wish to cry,

God bless you!" Or again, it may be that her heart
is not hers to give:

> Wouldst thou my love? For love I have no heart;
> I had it once, and gave it once away;
> To my first love I gave it on a day . . .
> Wouldst thou my love? For love I have no heart.

In the event of the girl intimating that she is disposed
to listen to her *Moroso* if all goes well, he turns to
her parents and formally asks permission to pay his
addresses to their daughter. That permission is, of
course, not always granted. If the parents have
thoughts of a wealthier match, the poor serenader
finds himself unceremoniously sent about his business.
A sad state of things ensues. Marieta steals many a
sorrowful glance at the despised Nane, who, on his
side, vents his indignation on the authors of her being
in terms much wanting in respect. "When I behold
thee so impassioned," he cries, "I curse those who
have caused this grief; I curse thy papa and thy
mamma, who will not let us make love." No idea is
here implied of dispensing with the parental fiat; the
same cannot be said of the following observations:
"When I pass this house, my heart aches. The girl
wills me well, her people will me ill; her people will
not hear of it, nor, indeed, will mine. So we have to
make love secretly. But that cannot really be done.
He who wishes for a girl, goes and asks for her—out
of politeness. He who wants to have her, carries her
off." It would seem that the maiden has been known
to be the first to incite rebellion:

> Do, my beloved, as other lovers do,
> Go to my father, and ask leave to woo;
> And if my father to reply is loth,
> Come back to me, for thou hast got my troth.

When the parents have no *primâ facie* objection to the youth, they set about inquiring whether he bears a good character, and whether the girl has a real liking for him. These two points cleared up satisfactorily, they still defer their final answer for some weeks or months, to make a trial of the suitor and to let the young people get better acquainted. The lover, borne up by hope, but not yet sure of his prize, calls to his aid the most effective songs in his repertory. The last thing at night Marieta hears :—

> Sleep thou, most fair, in all security,
> For I have made me guardian of thy gate,
> Safe shalt thou be, for I will watch and wait ;
> Sleep thou, most fair, in all security.

The first thing in the morning she is greeted thus :

> ' Art thou awake, O fairest, dearest, best ?
> Raise thy blond head and bid thy slumbers fly ;
> This is the hour thy lover passes by,
> Throw him a kiss, and then return to rest.

If she has any lurking doubts of Nane's constancy she receives the assurance, "One of these days I will surely make thee my bride—be not so pensive, fairest angel !" If, on the other hand, Nane lacks complete confidence in her affection, he appeals to her in words resembling I know not what Eastern love-song : "Oh, how many steps I have taken to have thee, and how many more I would take to gain thee! I have taken so many, many steps that I think thou wilt not forsake me."

The time of probation over, the girl's parents give a feast, to which the youth and his parents are invited. He brings with him, as a first offering, a small ring ornamented with a turquoise or a cornelian. Being now the acknowledged lover, he may come and openly pay his court every Sunday. On Saturday Marieta says to herself, "*Ancuo xe sabo, doman xe festa*—to-morrow is fête day, and to-morrow I expect Nane!" Then she pictures how he will come "dressed for the *festa* with a little flower in his hand;" and her heart beats with impatience. If, after all, by some chance—who knows? by some faithlessness perhaps—he fails to appear, what grief, what tears! Marieta's first thought when she rises on Sunday morning is this : "No one works to-day for it is *festa;* I pray you come betimes, dearest love!" Then comes the second thought : "If he does not come betimes, it is a sign that he is near to death; if later I do not see him, it is a sign that he is dead." The day passes, evening is here—no Nane! "Vespers sound and my love comes not; either he is dead, or" (the third and bitterest thought of all) "a love-thief has stolen him from me!"

Some little while after the lover has been formally accepted, he presents the maiden with a plain gold ring called *el segno*, and a second dinner or supper takes place at her parent's house, answering to the German betrothal feast; henceforth he is the *sposo* and she the *novizza*, and, as in Germany, people look on the pair as very little less than wedded. The new bride gives the bridegroom a silk handkerchief, to which allusion is made in a verse running, "What is that handkerchief you are wearing? Did you steal it or borrow it? I neither stole it nor borrowed it; my *Morosa* tied it round my neck." At Easter the *sposo* gives a cake and a couple of bottles of Cyprus or

Malaga ; at Christmas a box of almond sweetmeats and a little jug of *mostarda* (a Venetian *spécialité* composed of quinces dressed in honey and mustard) ; at the feast of St Martin, sweet chestnuts ; at the feast of St Mark, *el bocolo*—that is, a rosebud, emblematical of the opening year. The lover may also employ his generosity on New Year's day, on the girl's name-day, and on other days not specified, taking in the whole 365. Some maidens show a decided taste for homage in kind. "My lover bids me sing, and to please him I will do it," observes one girl, thus far displaying only the most disinterested amiability. But presently she reveals her motives : "He has a ring with a white stone ; when I have sung he will give it to me." A less sordid damsel asks only for a bunch of flowers ; it shall be paid for with a kiss, she says. Certain things there are which may be neither given nor taken by lovers who would not recklessly tempt fate. Combs are placed under the ban, for they may be made to serve the purposes of witchcraft ; saintly images and church-books, for they have to do with trouble and repentance ; scissors, for scissors stand for evil speaking ; and needles, for it is the nature of needles to prick.

Whether through the unwise exchange of these prohibited articles, or from other causes, it does sometimes happen that the betrothed lovers who have been hailed by everybody as *novizza* and *sposo* yet manage to fall out beyond any hopes of falling in again. If it is the youth's fault that the match is broken off, all his presents remain in the girl's undisputed possession ; if the girl is to blame, she must send back the *segno* and all else that she has received.

It is said that in some districts of Venetia the young man keeps an accurate account of whatever he spends on behalf of his betrothed, and in the case of her growing tired of him, she has to pay double the sum total, besides defraying the loss incurred by the hours he has sacrificed to her, and the boots he has worn out in the course of his visits.

It is more usual, as well as more satisfactory, for the betrothal to be followed in due time by marriage. After the *segno* has been " passed," the *sposo* sings a new song. "When," asks he, "will be the day whereon to thy mamma I shall say ' Madona ; ' to thy papa 'Missier ;' and to thee, darling, 'Wife'?" "Madona " is still the ordinary term for mother-in-law at Venice ; in Tuscan songs the word is also used in that sense, though it has fallen out of common parlance. Wherever it is to be found, it points to the days when the house-mother exercised an un-challenged authority over all members of the family. Even now the mother-in-law of Italian folk-songs is a formidable personage ; to say the truth, there is no scant measure of self-congratulation when she happens not to exist. "Oh ! Dio del siel, mandeme un ziovenin senza madona !" is the heartfelt prayer of the Venetian girl.

If the youth thinks of the wedding day as the occasion of forming new ties—above all that dearest tie which will give him his *anzola bela* for his own—the maiden dreams of it as the *zornada santa ;* the day when she will kneel at the altar and receive the solemn benediction of the church upon entering into a new station of life. "Ah ! when shall come to pass that holy day, when the priest will say to me, ' Are you content ?' when he shall bless me with the holy water—ah! when shall it come to pass?"

It has been noticed that the institution of marriage is not regarded in a very favourable light by the majority of folk-poets, but Venetian rhymers as a rule take an encouraging view of it. " He who has a wife," sings a poet of Chioggia, " lives right merrily *co la sua cara sposa in compagnia.*" Warning voices are not, however, wanting to tell the maiden that wedded life is not all roses : " You would never want to be married, my dear, if you knew what it was like," says one such ; while another mutters, " Reflect, girls, reflect, before ye wed these gallants ; on the Ponte di Rialto bird cages are sold."

The marriage generally comes off on a Sunday. Who weds on Monday goes mad ; Tuesday will bring a bad end ; Wednesday is a day good for nothing ; Thursday all manner of witches are abroad ; Friday leads to early death ; and, as to Saturday, you must not choose that, *parchè de sabo piove*, " because on Saturday it rains!"

The bride has two toilets—one for the church, one for the wedding dinner. At the church she wears a black veil, at the feast she appears crowned with flowers. After she is dressed and before the bridegroom arrives, the young girl goes to her father's room and kneeling down before him, she prays with tears in her eyes to be forgiven whatever grief she may have caused him. He grants her his pardon and gives her his blessing. In the early dawn the wedding party go to church either on foot or in gondolas, for it is customary for the marriage knot to be tied at the conclusion of the first mass. When the right

moment comes the priest puts the *vera*, or wedding
ring, on the tip of the bride's finger, and the bridegroom pushes it down into its proper place. If the
vera hitches, it is a frightfully bad omen. When once
it is safely adjusted, the best man steps forward and
restores to the bride's middle finger the little ring
which formed the lover's earliest gift; for this reason
he is called *compare de l'anelo*, a style and title he
will one day exchange for that of *compare de San
Zuane.*

At the end of the service the bride returns to her
father's house, where she remains quietly till it is time
to get ready for dinner. As the clock strikes four,
the entire wedding party, with the parents of bride
and bridegroom and a host of friends and relations,
start in gondolas for the inn at which the repast is to
take place. The whole population of the *calle* or
campo is there to see their departure, and to admire
or criticise, as the case may be. After dinner, when
everyone has tasted the good wine and enjoyed the
good fare, the feast breaks up with cries of *Viva
la novizza!* followed by songs, stories, laughter, and
much flirtation between the girls and boys, who make
the most of the freedom of intercourse conceded to
them in honour of the day. Then the music begins,
the table is whisked away, and the assembled guests
join lustily in the dance; the women perhaps, singing
at intervals, "Enôta, enôta, enlo!" a burden borne
over to Venice from the Grecian shore. The romance
is finished; Marieta and Nane are married, the
zornada santa wanes to its close, the tired dancers
accompany the bride to the threshold of her new
home, and so adieu!

Before leaving the subject of Venetian love-songs it may be as well to glance at a few points characteristic of the popular mind which it has not been convenient to touch upon in following the Venetian youth and maiden from the *prima radice* of their love to its consecration at the altar. What, for instance, does the Venetian singer say of poverty and riches? —for there is no surer test of character than the way of regarding money and the lack of it. It is taken pretty well for granted at Venice as elsewhere, that inequality of fortune is a bar to matrimony. The poor girl says to her better-to-do lover, "Thou passest this way sad and grieving, thou thinkest to speak to my father, and on thy finger thou dost carry a little ring. But thy thought does not fall in with my thought, and thy thought is not worth a gazette. Thou art rich and I am a poor little one!" Here the girl puts all faith in the good intentions of her suitor: it is not his fault if her poverty divides them; it is the nature of things, against which there is no appeal. But there is more than one song that betrays the suspicion that if a girl grows poor her lover will be only too eager and ready to desert her. "My lady mother has always told me that she who falls into poverty loses her lover; loses friend and loses hope. The purse does not sing when there is no coin in it." Still, on the whole, a more high-minded view prevails. "Do not look to my being a poor man," says one lover,

Che povatà no guasta gentilissa,

—"for poverty does not spoil or prevent gentle manners." A girl sings, "All tell me that I am poor, the world's honour is my riches; I am poor, I am of

fair fame ; poor both of us, let us make love." One
is reminded of "how the good wife taught her
daughter" in the old English poem of the fifteenth
century :

> I pray the, my dere childe, loke thou bere the so well
> That alle men may seyen thou art so trewe as stele;
> Gode name is golde worth, my leve childe !

A brave little Venetian maiden cries : " How many
there are who desire fortune ! and I, poor little thing,
desire it not. This is the fortune I desire, to wed a
youth of twenty-one years." One lover pines for
riches, but only that he may offer them to his beloved :
"Fair Marieta, I wish to make my fortune, to go
where the Turk has his cradle, and work myself
nearly to death, so that afterwards I may come back
to thee, my fair one, and marry thee." Finally, a
town youth says that if his country love has but a
milk-pail for her dowry, what matters ?

> De dota la me dà quel viso belo !

The Venetian displays no marked enthusiasm for
fair hair, notwithstanding the fame of Giorgione's
sunset heads and the traditional expedients by which
Venetian ladies of past times sought to bring their
dark locks into conformity with that painter's favourite
hue. In Venetian songs there is nothing about the
"golden spun silk" of Sicily ; if a Venetian folk-poet
does speak of fair hair, he calls it by the common-
place generic term of blond. The available evidence
goes rather to show that in his own heart he prefers a
brunette. "My lady mother always told me that I
should never be enamoured of white roses," says a

K

sententious young man ; "she told me that I should
love the little mulberries, which are sweeter than
honey." "Cara mora," *mora*, or mulberry, meaning
brunette, is an ordinary caressing term. Two frank
young people carry on this dialogue : "Will you come
to me, fair maid ?" "No ; I will not come, for I am
fair." "If you are fair, I am no less so ; if you are
the rose, I am the spotless lily." Beauty, therefore,
is valued, especially by the possessors of it. But the
Venetian admits the possibility of that which Keats
found so hard to comprehend—the love of the plain.
A girl says, and it is a pretty saying, "Se no so bela,
ghe piaso al mio amore" ("If I am not fair, I please
my beloved "). A soldier, whose *morosa* dies, does not
weep for her beauty, for she was not beautiful ; nor
for her riches, for she was not rich ; he weeps for her
sweet manners and conversation—it was that that
made him love her. The universal weakness for a
little flattery from the hand of the portrait-painter is
expressed in a sprightly little song :

> What does it matter if I am not fair,
> Who have a lover, who a painter is ?
> He will portray me like a star, I wis ;
> What does it matter if I am not fair?

We hear a good deal of lovers' quarrels, and of the
transitoriness of love. "Oh! God! how the sky is
overcast! It seems about to rain, and then it passes
so is it with a man in love ; he loves a fair woman
and then he leaves her." That is her version of the
affair. He has not anything complimentary to say: "I
I get out of this squall alive, never more shall woma
in the world befool me. I have been befooled upo

a pledge of sacred faith: mad is the man who believes in women." Another man says, with more serious bitterness : "What time have I not lost in loving you! Had I lost it in saying so many prayers, I should have found favour before God, and my mother would have blessed me." A matter-of-fact girl remarks, ". No one will grow thin on your account, nor will any one die on mine." When her lover says that he has sent her his heart in a basket, she replies that she sends back both basket and heart, being in want of neither; and if he should really happen to die, she unfeelingly meditates, "My love is dead, and I have not wept; I had thought to suffer more torment. A Pope dies, another is made; not otherwise do I weep for my love."

Certain vocations are looked upon with suspicion:

> Sailor's trade—at sea to die !
> Merchant's trade—that's bankruptcy ;
> Gambler's trade in cursing ends,
> Thief's trade to the gallows sends.

But in spite of the second line about "l'arte del mercante," a girl does not much mind marrying a merchant or shopkeeper; nay, it is sometimes her avowed ambition :

> I want no fisher with a fishy smell,
> A market gardener would not suit me well ;
> Nor yet a mariner who sails the sea :
> A fine flour-merchant is the man for me.

A miller seems to think that he stands a good chance: "Come to the window, Columbine! I am that miller who brought thee, the other evening, the pure white flour." Shoemakers are in very bad odour: "I cale-

gheri ga na trista fama." Fishermen are considered
poor penniless folk, and she who weds a sailor, does
so at her peril :

> L'amor del mariner no dura un 'ora,
> La dove che lu el và, lu s' inamora.

And even if the sailor's troth can be trusted, is it not
his trade "at sea to die"? But the young girl will
not be persuaded. "All say to me, 'Beauty, do not
take the mariner, for he will make thee die;' if he make
me die, so must it be; I will wed him, for he is
my soul." And when he is gone, she sings: "My
soul, as thou art beyond the port, send me word if
thou art alive or dead, if the waters of the sea have
taken thee?" She returns sadly ·to her work, the
work of all Venetian maidens :

> My love is far and far away from me,
> I am at home, and he has gone to sea ;
> He is at sea, and he has sails to spread,
> I am at home, and I have beads to thread.

The boatman's love can afford to sing in a lighter
strain; there is not the shadow of interminable
voyages upon her. "I go out on the balcony, I see
Venice, and I see my joy, who starts; I go out on
the balcony, I see the sea, and I see my love, who
rows." Another song is perhaps a statement of fact,
though it sounds like a poetic fancy :

> To-night their boats must seek the sea,
>   One night his boat will linger yet ;
> They bear a freight of wood, and he
>   A freight of rose and violet.

Who forgets the coming into Venice in the earl·

morning light of the boats laden with fresh flowers and fruit?

Isaac d'Israeli states that 'the fishermen's wives of the Lido, particularly those of the districts of Mala-mocca and Pelestrina (its extreme end), sat along the shore in the evenings while the men were out fishing, and sang stanzas from Tasso and other songs at the pitch of their voices, going on till each one could distinguish the responses of her own husband in the distance.

At first sight the songs of the various Italian pro-vinces appear to be greatly alike, but at first sight only. Under further examination they display essential differences, and even the songs which travel all over Italy almost always receive some distinctive touch of local colour in the districts where they obtain naturalisation. The Venetian poet has as strongly marked an identity as any of·his fellows. Not to speak of his having invented the four-lined song known as the "Vilota," the quality of his work unmistakably reflects his peculiar idiosyncrasies. An Italian writer has said, "nella parola e nello scritto ognuno imita sè stesso ;" and the Venetian "imitates himself" faithfully enough in his verses. He has a well-developed sense of humour, and his finer wit discerns less objectionable paths than those of parody and burlesque, for which the Sicilian shows so fatal a leaning. He is often in a mood of half-playful cyni-cism ; if his paramount theme is love, he is yet fully inclined to have a laugh at the expense of the whole race of lovers :

> A feast I will prepare for love to eat,
> Non-suited suitors I will ask to dine ;

> They shall have pain and sorrow for their meat,
>   They shall have tears and sobs to drink for wine;
> And sighs shall be the servitors most fit
> To wait at table where the lovers sit. .

As compared with the Tuscan, the Venetian is a confirmed egotist. While the former well-nigh effaces
his individual personality out of his hymns of adoration, the latter is apt to talk so much of his private
feelings, his wishes, his disappointments, that the
idol stands in danger of being forgotten. There is,
indeed, a single song—the song of one of the despised mariners—which combines the sweet humility
of Tuscan lyrics with a glow and fervour truly
Venetian—possibly its author was in reality some
Istriot seaman, for the *canti popolari* of Istria are
known to partake of both styles. Anyhow, it may
figure here, justified by what seems to me its own
excellence of conception :

> Fair art thou born, but love is not for me;
> A sailor's calling sends me forth to sea.
> I do desire to paint thee on my sail,
> And o'er the briny deep I'd carry thee.
> They ask, What ensign ? when the boat they hail—
> For woman's love I bear this effigy;
> For woman's love, for love of maiden fair;
> If her I may not love, I love forswear !

When he is most in earnest and most excited, the
Venetian is still homely—he has none of the Sicilian's
luxuriant imagination. I may call to mind
remark of Edgar Poe's to the effect that passion
demands a homeliness of expression. Passionate th
Venetian poet certainly is. Never a man was readic
to "dare e'en death " at the behest of his mistress—

Wouldst have me die ?   Then I'll no longer live.
Grant unto me for sepulchre thy bed,
Make me straightway a pillow of thy head,
And with thy mouth one kiss, beloved one, give.

At Chioggia, where still in the summer evenings
Orlando Furioso is read in the public places, and
where artists go in quest of the old Venetian type,
they sing a yet more impassioned little song.

Oh, Morning Star, I ask of thee this grace,
   This only grace I ask of thee, and pray :
The water where thou hast washed thy breast and face,
   In kindly pity throw it not away.
Give it to me for medicine ; I will take
A draught before I sleep and when I wake ;
And if this medicine shall not make me whole,
To earth my body, and to hell my soul !

It must be added that Venetian folk-poesy lacks the
innate sympathy with all beautiful natural things
which pervades the poesy of the Apennines.   This
is in part the result of outward conditions: nature,
though splendid, is unvaried at Venice.   The
temperament of the Venetian poet explains the rest.
If he alludes to the *bel seren con tante stelle*, it is only
to say that " it would be just the night to run away
with somebody " — to which assertion he tacks the
disreputable rider, " he who carries off girls is not
called a thief, he is called an enamoured young man."
Even in the most lovely and the most poetic of
cities you cannot breathe the pure air of the hills.
The Venetian is without the intense refinement of the
Tuscan mountaineer, as he is without his love of
natural beauty.   The Tuscan but rarely mentions the

beloved one's name—he respects it as the Eastern mystic respects the name of the Deity; the Venetian sings it out for the edification of all the boatmen of the canal. The Tuscan has come to regard a kiss as a thing too sacred to talk about; the Venetian has as few scruples on the subject as the poet of Sirmio. Nevertheless, it should be recognised that a not very blameable unreservedness of speech is the most serious charge to be brought against all save a small minority of Venetian singers. I believe that the able and conscientious collector, Signor Bernoni, has exercised but slight censorship over the mass of songs he has placed on record, notwithstanding which the number of those that can be accused of an immoral tendency is extremely limited. Whence it is to be inferred that the looseness of manners prevailing amongst the higher classes at Venice in the decadence of the Republic at no time became general in the lower and sounder strata of society.

At the beginning of this century, songs that were called Venetian ballads were very popular in London drawing-rooms. That they were sung with more effect before those who had never heard them in their own country than before those who had, will be easily believed. A charming letter-writer of that time described the contrast made by the gay or impassioned strain of the poetry to "the stucco face of the statue who doles it forth;" whilst in Venice, he added, it seconded by all the nice inflections of voice, grace, gesture, play of features, that distinguish Venetian women. One of the Venetian songs which gained most popularity abroad was the story of the dame who drops her ring into the sea, and of the fisherman who fishes it up, refusing all other reward than a kiss :

> Oh ! pescator dell 'onda,
>   Findelin,
> Vieni pescar in qua !
> Colla bella sua barca
> Colla bella se ne va
>   Findelin ! lin, la !

But this song is not peculiarly Venetian; it is sung everywhere on the Adriatic and Mediterranean coasts. And the version used was in pure Italian. Judged as poetry, the existing Venetian ballads take a lower place than the *Vilote*. They are often not much removed from doggerel, as may be shown by a lamentable history which confusedly suggests Enoch Arden with the moral of " Tuc-la :"

> " Who is that knocking at my gates ?
>   Who is that knocking at my door ? "
> " A London captain 'tis who waits,
>   Your very humble servitor."
> In deshabille the fair one ran,
>   Straightway the door she opened wide :
> " Tell me, my fair one, if you can,
>   Where does your husband now abide ? "
> " My husband he has gone to France,
>   Pray heaven that back he may not come ; "
> —Just then the fair one gave a glance,
>   It was her spouse arrived at home !
> " Forgive, forgive," the fair one cried,
>   " Forgive if I have done amiss ; "
> " There is no pardon," he replied,
>   For women who have sinned like this."
> Her head fell off at the first blow,
>   The first blow wielded by his sword ;
> So does just Heaven its anger show
>   Against the wife who wrongs her lord.

Venetian songs will serve as a guide to the character, but scarcely to the opinions, of the Venetians. The long struggle with Austria has left no other trace than a handful of rough verses dating from the Siege —mere strings of *Evvivas* to the dictator and the army. It may be argued that the fact is not exceptional, that like the *Fratelli d'Italia* of Goffredo Mameli, the war-songs of the Italian movement were all composed for the people and not by them. Still there have been genuine folk-poets who have discoursed after their fashion of *Italia libera*. The Tuscan peasants sang as they stored the olives of 1859—

L'amore l'ho in Piamonte,
Bandiera tricolor!

There is not in Venetian songs an allusion to the national cause so naïvely, so caressingly expressive as this. It cannot be that the Venetian *popolano* did not care; whenever his love of country was put to the test, it was found in no way wanting. Was it that to his positive turn of mind there appeared to be an absence of connection between politics and poetry? Looking back to the songs of an earlier period, we find the same habit of ignoring public events. A rhyme, answering the purpose of our "Ride a cock horse," contains the sole reference to the wars of Venice with the Porte—

Andemo a la guera
Per mare e per tera,
E cataremo i Turchi,
Li mazzaremo tuti, &c.

In the proverbs, if not in the songs, a somewhat stronger impress remains of the independent attitude assumed by the Republic in its dealings with the Vatican. The Venetians denied Papal Infallibility by anticipation in the saying, "The Pope and the countryman know more than the Pope alone;" and in one line of a nursery ditty, "El Papa no xè Rè," they quietly abolished the temporal power. When Paul V. laid the city under an interdict, the citizens made answer, "Prima Veneziani e poi cristiani," a proverb that survives to this day. "Venetians first" was the first article of faith of these men, or rather it was to them a vital instinct. Their patriotism was a kind of magnificent *amour propre*. No modern nation has felt a pride of state so absorbing, so convinced, so transcendent: a pride which lives incarnate in the forms and faces of the Venetian senators who look serenely down on us from the walls of the Art Gallery out of the company of kings, of saints, of angels, and of such as are higher than the angels.

A chance word or phrase now and then accidentally carries us back to Republican times and institutions. The expression, "Thy thought is not worth a *gazeta*," occurring in a love-song cited above, reminds us that the term gazette is derived from a Venetian coin of that name, value three-quarters of a farthing, which was the fee charged for the privilege of hearing read aloud the earliest venture in journalism, a manuscript news-sheet issued once a month at Venice in the sixteenth century. The figure of speech, "We must have fifty-seven," meaning, "we are entering on a serious business," has its origin in the fifty-seven votes necessary to the passing of any weighty measure in the Venetian Senate. The Venetian adapter of Molière's favourite ditty, in lieu of preferring his

sweetheart to the "bonne ville de Paris," prefers her
to "the Mint, the Arsenal, and the Bucentaur."
Every one is familiar with the quaint description of
the outward glories of St Mark's Square :

> In St Mark's Place three standards you descry,
> And chargers four that seem about to fly ;
> There is a time-piece which appears a tower,
> And there are twelve black men who strike the hour.

Social prejudices creep in where politics are almost
excluded. A group of *Vilote* relates to the feud—
old as Venice—between the islanders of San Nicol
and the islanders of Castello, the two sections of th
town east of the Grand Canal, in the first of whic
stands St Mark's, in the last the arsenal. The bes
account of the two factions is embodied in an ancien
poem celebrating the fight that rendered memorabl
St Simon's Day, 1521. The anonymous writer tell
his tale with an impartiality that might be envied b
greater historians, and he ends by putting a canto (
peaceable advice into the mouth of a dying champion
who urges his countrymen to dwell in harmony an
love one another as brothers. Are they not made (
the same flesh and bone, children alike of St Ma
and his State?

> Tuti a la fin no semio patrioti,
> Cresciu in sti campi, ste cale e cantoni ?

The counsel was not taken, and the old rivalry co
tinued unabated, fostered up to a certain point by t
Republic, which saw in it, amongst other things,
check on the power of the patricians. The two si
represented the aristocratic and democratic eleme

of the population: the Castellani had wealth and
birth and fine palaces, their upper classes monopolised
the high offices of State, their lower classes worked in
the arsenal, served as pilots to the men-of-war, and
acted as rowers in the Bucentaur. The better-to-do
Nicoloti came off with a share of the secondary
employs, whilst the larger portion of the San Nicolo
folk were poor fishermen. But their sense of personal
dignity was intense. They had a doge of their own,
usually an old sailor, who on high days and holidays
sat beside the "renowned prince, the Duke of Venice."
This doge, or *Gastaldo dei Nicoloti*, was answerable
for the conduct of his people, of whom he was at once
superior and equal. "Ti voghi el dose et mi vogo col
dose" ("You row the doge, I row with the doge"), a
Nicoloto would say to his rival. It is easy to see how
the party spirit engendered by the old feud produced
a sentiment of independence in even the poorest
members of the community, and how it thus became
of great service to the Republic. Its principal draw-
back was that of leading to hard blows, the last occasion of its doing so being St Simon's Day, 1817, when
a fierce local outbreak was severely suppressed by the
Austrians. Since then the contending forces have
agreed to dwell in harmony; whether they love one
another as brothers is not so clear. There are songs
still sung in which mutual recrimination takes the
form of too strong language for ears polite. "If a
Nicoloto is born, a Count is born; if a Castellan is
born—set up the gallows," is the mildest dictum of a
son of San Nicolo, to which his neighbour replies,
"When a Castellan is born, a god is born; when a
Nicoloto is born, a brigand is born." The feud lingers

on even in the matter of love. "Who is that yout who passes so often?" inquires a girl; "if it be Castellan, bid him be off; if it be a Nicoloto, bid hi: come in."

On the night of the Redeemer (in July) still take place what was perhaps one of the most ancient (Venetian customs. A fantastic illumination, a brid; of boats, a people's ball, a prize-giving to the be gondolas, a promiscuous wandering about the pub! gardens, these form some of the features of the fes: val. But its most remarkable point is the expediti to the Lido at three o'clock in the morning to see t dawn. As the sun rises from his cradle of easte: gold, he is greeted by the shout of thousands. Ma: of the youths leap into the water and disport the: selves like wild creatures of the sea.

A word in conclusion as to the dialect in whi Venetian songs are composed. The earliest specim extant consists in the distich—

Lom po far e die in pensar
E vega quelo che li po inchiontrar,

which is to be read on the façade of St Mark's, op; site the ducal palace. The meaning is, Look befo you leap—an adage well suited to the people w! had the reputation of being the most prudent in t world. This inscription belongs to the twelfth ce tury. There used to be a song sung at Ascension-ti on the occasion of the marriage of the doge with t. Adriatic, of which the signification of the words w lost and only the sound preserved. It is a pity th it was never written out phonetically; for mode: scholars would probably have proved equal to t

task of interpreting it, even as they have given us the
secret of the runes on the neck of the Greek lion at
the arsenal. We owe to Dante a line of early Venetian—one of those tantalising fragments of dialect
poems in his posthumous work, *De Vulgari Eloquen-
tia*—fragments perhaps jotted down with the intention
of copying the full stanzas had he lived to finish the
treatise. Students have long been puzzled by Dante's
judgment on the Venetian dialect, which he said was
so harsh that it made the conversation of a woman
resemble that of a man. The greatest master of the
Italian tongue was ruthless in his condemnation of its
less perfect forms, to the knowledge of which he was
all the same indebted in no slight degree. But it
must not be overlooked that the question in Dante's
day was whether Italy should have a language or
whether the nation should go on oscillating between
Latin and *patois*. For reasons patriotic and political
quite as much as literary, Dante's heart was set on
the adoption of one "illustrious, cardinal, aulic and
polite" speech by the country at large, and to that
end he contributed incalculably, though less by his
treatise than by his poem. The involuntary hatred
of *patois* as an outward sign of disunion has reap-
peared again in some of those who in our own time
have done and suffered most for united Italy. Thus I
once heard Signor Benedetto Cairoli say: "When we
were children, our mother would on no account let us
speak anything but good Italian." It is possible that
Dante's strong feeling on the subject made him un-
just. It is also possible that the Venetian and the
other dialects have undergone a radical change, though
this is not so likely as may at first be supposed. A

piece of nonsense written in the seventeenth century
gives an admirable idea of what the popular idiom
was then and is now :

> Mi son tanto inamorao
> In dona Nina mia vesina
> Che me dà gran disciplina,
> Che me vedo desparao.
>> Gnao bao, bao gnao,
>> Mi son tanto inamorao !

> Mi me sento tanti afani
> (Tuti i porto per so amore !)
> Che par proprio che sia cani
> Ch'al mi cor fazza brusore ;
> Che da tute quante l'ore
> Mi me sento passionao.
>> Gnao bao, bao gnao,
>> Mi son tanto inamorao !

In most respects Venetian would approach closely
to standard Italian were it not for the pronunciation
yet to the uneducated Venetian, Italian sounds very
strange. A maid-servant who had picked up a few
purely Italian words, was found to be under the
delusion that she had been learning English. The
Venetian is unable to detect a foreigner by his accent.
An English traveller had been talking for some
while to a woman of Burano, when she asked in
all seriousness, "Are you a Roman ? " A deficiency
of grammar, a richness in expressive colloquialisms
and the possession of certain terms of Greek origin
constitute the main features of the Venetian dialect
as it is known to us. It was used by the Republic
in the affairs of state, and it was generally understood throughout Italy, because, as Evelyn records

all the world repaired to Venice "to see the folly
and madnesse of the Carnevall." With the exception
of Dante, every one seems to have been struck by
its merits, of which the chief, to modern ears, are
vivacity and an exceeding softness. It can boast of
much elegant lettered poetry, as well as of Goldoni's
best comedies. To the reading of the latter when a
child, Alfieri traced his particular partiality for "the
jargon of the lagunes." Byron declared that its
naïveté was always pleasant in the mouth of a woman,
and George Sand mentions it approvingly as "ce
gentil parler Vénitien, fait à ce qu'il me semble pour
la bouche des enfants."

SICILIAN FOLK-SONG.

L'ISOLA DEL FUOCO—the Isle of Fire, as Dante named it—is singularly rich in poetic associations. Acis, the sweet wood-born stream, Galatea, the calm of the summer sea, and how many more flower-children of a world which had not learned to " look before and after," of a people who deified nature and naturalised deity, and felt at one with both, send us thence across the ages the fragrance of their immortal youth. Our mind's magic lantern shows us Sappho and Alcæus welcomed in Sicily as guests, Pindar writing his Sicilian Odes, the mighty Æschylus, burdened always perhaps with a sorrow—untainted by fretful anger—because of that slight, sprung from the enthusiasm for the younger poet, the heat of politics, we know not what, which drove him forth from Athens : yet withal solaced by the homage paid to his grey hairs, and not ill-content to die

On the bank of Gela productive of corn.

To Sicily we trace the germs of Greek comedy, and the addition of the epode to the strophe and anti-strophe. We remember the story of how, when the greatness of Athens had gone to wreck off Syracuse, a few of the starving slaves in the *latomiæ* were told they were free men, thanks to their ability to recite passages from Euripides ; we remember also that

new story, narrated in English verse, of the adventure
which befell the Rhodian maid Balaustion, on these
Sicilian shores, and of the good stead stood her by
the knowledge of *Alcestis.* We think of Sicily as
the birth-place of the Idyllists, the soil which bore
through them an aftermath of Grecian song thick
with blossom as the last autumn yield of Alpine
meads. Then by a strange transformation scene we
get a glimpse of Arabian Kasîdes hymning the
beauties of the Conca d'Oro, and as these disappear,
arise the forms of the poets of whom Petrarch says—

> . . . i Siciliani
> Che fur già primi

—those wonderful poet discoverers, more wonderful
as discoverers than as poets, who found out that a
new music was to be made in a tongue, not Latin,
nor yet Provençal—a tongue which had grown into
life under the double foster-fathership of Arabian
culture and Norman rule, the *lingua cortigiana* of the
palaces of Palermo, the " common speech " of Dante.
When we recollect how the earliest written essays
in Italian were composed in what once was styled
Sicilian, it seems a trifle unfair for the practical
adaptator—in this case as often happens in the case
of individuals—to have so completely borne away the
glory from the original inventor as to cause the latter
to be all but forgotten. We now hear only of the
" sweet Tuscan tongue," and even the pure pronunciation of educated Sicilians is not admitted without a
comment of surprise. But whilst the people of
Tuscany quickly assimilated the *lingua cortigiana*
and made it their own, the people of Sicily stuck fast

to their old wild-flower language, and left ungathered
the gigantic lily nurtured in Palermitan hot-houses
and carried by the great Florentine into heaven and
hell.   They continued speaking, not the Sicilian we
call Italian, but the Sicilian we call patois—the
Sicilian of the folk-songs. The study of Italic dialects
is one by no means ill-calculated to repay the trouble
bestowed upon it, and that from a point of view not
connected with their philological aspect.   How far,
or it may be I should say, how soon they will die out,
in presence of the political unity of the country, and
of the general modern tendency towards the adoption
of standard forms of language, it is not quite easy
to decide.   Were we not aware of the astonishing
rapidity with which dialects, like some other things,
may give way when once the least breach is opened,
we might suppose that those of Italy were good for
many hundred years.   Even the upper classes have
not yet abandoned them: it is said that there are
deputies at Monte Citorio who find the flow of their
ideas sadly baulked by the parliamentary etiquette
which expects them to be delivered in Italian.   And
the country-people are still so strongly attached to
their respective idioms as to incline them to believe
that they are the "real right thing," to the disadvan-
tage of all competitors.   Not long ago, a Lombard
peasant-woman employed as nurse to a neuralgic
Sicilian gentleman who spoke as correctly as any
Tuscan, assured a third person with whom she chatted
in her own dialect—it was at a bath establishment—
that her patient did not know a single word of Italian!
But it is reported that in some parts of Italy the
peasants are beginning to forget their songs; and

when a generation or two has lived through the æra of facile inter-communication that makes Reggio but two or three days' journey from Turin, when every full-grown man has served his term of military service in districts far removed from his home, the vitality of the various dialects will be put to a severe test. Come when it may, the change will have in it much that is desirable for Italy: of this there can be no question; nor can it be disputed that as a whole standard Italian offers a more complete and plastic medium of expression than Venetian, or Neapolitan, or Sicilian. Nevertheless, in the mouth of the people the local dialects have a charm which standard Italian has not — a charm that consists in clothing their thought after a fashion which, like the national peasant costumes, has an essential suitability to the purpose it is used for, and while wanting neither grace nor richness, suggests no comparisons that can reflect upon it unfavourably. The naïve ditty of a poet of Termini or Partinico is too much a thing *sui generis* for it to suffer by contrast with the faultless finish of a sonnet in *Vita di Madonna Laura.*

Sicily is notoriously richer in songs than any province of the mainland; Vigo collected 5000, and the number of those since written down seems almost incredible. It has even been conjectured that Sicily was the original fountain-head of Italian popular poetry, and that it is still the source of the greater part of the songs which circulate through Italy.[*]

* "Noi crediamo . . . . che il Canto popolare italiano sia nativo di Sicilia. Nè con questo intendiamo asserire che le plebi delle altre provincie sieno prive di poetica facoltà, e che non vi sieno poesie popolari sorte in altre regioni italiane, ed

Songs that rhyme imperfectly in the Tuscan version
have been found correct when put into Sicilian, a fact
which points to the island as their first home. Dr
Pitrè, however, deprecates such speculations as pre-
mature, and when so distinguished and so conscientious an investigator bids us suspend our judgment,
we can do no better than to obey. What can be
stated with confidence is, that popular songs are
inveterate travellers, and fly from place to place, no
one knows how, at much the same electrical rate as
news spreads amongst the people—a phenomenon
of which the more we convince ourselves that the
only explanation is the commonplace one that lies on
the surface, the more amazing and even mysterious
does it appear.

As regards the date of the origin of folk-songs in
Sicily, the boldest guess possibly comes nearest the
truth, and this takes us back to a time before Theocritus. Cautious students rest satisfied with adducing
undoubted evidence of their existence as early as the
twelfth century, in the reign of William II., whose
court was famed for "good speakers in rhyme of
every condition." Moreover, it is certain that Sicilian
songs had begun to travel orally and in writing
to the Continent considerably before the invention
of printing; and it is not unlikely that many

ivi cresciute e di là diramate attorno. Ma crediamo che, nella
maggior parte des casi, il Canto abbia per patria di origine
l'Isola, e per patria di adozione la Toscana : che, nato con veste
di dialetto in Sicilia, in Toscana abbia assunto forma illustre e
comune, e con siffatta veste novella sia migrato nelle altre
provincie."—*La Poesia Popolare Italiana : Studj di Alessandro
d'Ancona*, p. 285.

canzuni now current in the island could lay claim
to an antiquity of at least six or seven hundred
years. Folk-songs change much less than might
at first sight be expected in the course of their
transmission from father to son, from century to
century ; and some among the songs still popular
in Sicily have been discovered written down in
old manuscripts in a form almost identical to that
in which they are sung to-day. Although the
methodical collection of folk-songs is a thing but
recently undertaken, the fact of there being such
songs in Sicily was long ago perfectly well known.
An English traveller writing in the last century
remarks, that "the whole nation are poets, even the
peasants, and a man stands a poor chance for a
mistress that is not capable of celebrating her." He
goes on to say, that happily in the matter of serenades
the obligations of a chivalrous lover are not so onerous
as they were in the days of the Spaniards, when a fair
dame would frown upon the most devoted swain who
had not a cold in his head—the presumed proof of his
having dutifully spent the night "with the heavens for
his house, the stars for his shelter, the damp earth for
his mattress, and for pillow a harsh thistle"—to
borrow the exact words of a folk-poet.

One class of folk-songs may be fairly trusted to
speak for themselves as to the date of their composition, namely, that which deals with historical facts
and personages. Until lately the songs of Italy were
believed, with the exception of Piedmont, to be of an
exclusively lyrical character ; but fresh researches,
and, above all, the unremitting and enthusiastic efforts
of Signor Salvatore Salomone-Marino, have brought

to light a goodly quantity of Sicilian songs in which the Greek, Arabian, Norman, and Angevin denominations all come in for their share of commemoration. And that the authors of these songs spoke of the present, not of the past, is a natural inference, when actual observation certifies that such is the invariable custom of living folk-poets. For the people events soon pass into a misty perspective, and the folk-poet is a sort of people's journalist ; he makes his song as the contributor to a newspaper writes his leading article, about the matter uppermost for the moment in men's minds, whether it be important or trivial. In 1860 he sang of "the bringers of the tricolor," the "milli famusi guirreri," and "Aribaldi lu libiraturi." In 1868 he joked over the grand innovation by which "the poor folk of the piazza were sent to Paradise in a fine coach," *i.e.*, the substitution, by order of the municipality of Palermo, of first, second, and third class funeral cars in lieu of the old system of bearers. In 1870 he was very curious about the eclipse which had been predicted. "We shall see if God confirms this news that the learned tell us, of the war there is going to be between the moon and the sun," says he, discreetly careful not to tie himself down to too much faith or too much distrust. Then, when the eclipse has duly taken place, his admiration knows no bounds. " What heads—what beautiful minds God gives these learned men !" he cries ; "what grace is granted to man that he can read even the thoughts of God ! " The Franco-German war inspired a great many poets, who displayed, at all events in the first stages of the struggle, a strong predilection for the German side. All these songs long survive the period of the events they allude to, and help materially to keep their memory alive ; but for a new song to be composed on an incident ten years old, would simply argue that its author was not a folk-poet at all, in the strict sense of the word. The great majority of the historical songs are short, detached pieces, bearing no relation to each other ; but now and then we come upon a group of stanzas which suggest the idea of their having once formed part of a consecutive whole ; and in one instance, that of the historical legend of the Baronessa di Carini, the assembled fragments approach the proportions of a popular epic. But it is doubtful whether this poem — for so we may call it — is thoroughly popular in origin, though the people have completely adopted it, and account it "the most beautiful and most dolorous of all the histories and songs," thinking all the more of it in consequence of the profound secrecy with which it has been preserved out of fear of provoking the wrath of a powerful Sicilian family, very roughly handled by its author.

Of religious songs there are a vast number in Sicily, and the stock is perpetually fed by the pious rhyme tournaments held in celebration of notable saints' days at the village fairs. On such occasions the image or relics of the saints are exhibited in the public square, and the competitors, the assembled poetic talent of the neighbourhood, proceed, one after the other, to improvise verses in his honour. If they succeed in gaining the suffrage of their audience, which may amount to five or six thousand persons, they go home liberally rewarded. Along with these saintly eulogiums may be mentioned a style of composition more ancient than edifying — the Sicilian

parodies. A pious or complimentary song is traves-
tied into a piece of coarse abuse, or a sample of that
unblushing, astounding irreverence which sometimes
startles the most hardened sceptic, travelling in countries where the empire of Catholicism has been least
shaken—in Tyrol, for instance, and in Spain. We
cannot be sure whether the Sicilian parodist deliber-
ately intends to be profane, or is only indifferent as
to what weapons he uses in his eagerness to cast ridicule upon a rival versifier—the last hypothesis seems
to me to be the most plausible ; but it takes nothing
from the significance of his profanity as it stands. It
is pleasant to turn. from these several sections of
Sicilian verse, which, though valuable in helping us to
know the people from whom they spring, for the most
part have but small merits when judged as poetry, to
the stream of genuine song which flows side by side
with them : a stream, fresh, clear, pure : a poesy
always true in its artless art, generally bright and
ingenious in its imagery, sometimes tersely felici-
tous in its expression. In his love lyrics, and but
rarely save in them, the Sicilian *popolano* rises from
the rhymester to the poet.

The most characteristic forms of the love-songs of
Sicily are those of the *ciuri*, called in Tuscany *stor-
nelli*, and the *cancuni*, called in Tuscany *rispetti*.
The *ciuri* (flowers) are couplets or triplets beginning
with the name of a flower, with which the other line
or lines should rhyme. They abound throughout the
island, and notwithstanding the poor estimation in
which the peasants hold them, and the difficulty of
persuading them that they are worth putting on
record, a very dainty compliment—just the thing to

figure on a valentine—may often be found compressed into their diminutive compass. To turn such airy nothings into a language foreign and uncongenial to them, is like manipulating a soap-bubble: the bubble vanishes, and we have only a little soapy water left in the hollow of our hand: a simile which unhappily is not far from holding good of attempts at translating any species of Italian popular poetry. It is true that in *Fra Lippo Lippi* there are two or three charming imitations of the *stornello;* but, then, Mr Browning is the poet who, of all others, has got most inside of the Italian mind. Here is an *aubade*, which will give a notion of the unsubstantial stuff the *ciuri* are made of:

> Rosa marina,
> Lucinu l'alba e la stidda Diana:
> Lu cantu è fattu, addui, duci Rusina.

"Rose of the sea, the dawn and the star Diana are shining: the song is done, farewell sweet Rosina."

One of these flower-poets, invoking the Violet by way of heading, tells his love that "all men who look on her forget their sorrows;" another takes his oath that she outrivals sun, and moon, and stars. "Jasmine of Araby," cries a third, "when thou art not near, I am consumed by rage." A fourth says, "White floweret, before thy door I make a great weeping." A fifth, night and day, bewails his evil fate. A sixth observes that he has been singing for five hours, but that he might just as well sing to the wind. A seventh feels the thorns of jealousy. An eighth asks, "Who knows if Rosa will not listen to another lover?" A ninth exclaims,

Flower of the night,
Whoever wills me ill shall die to-night !

With which ominous sentiment I will leave the *ciuri*,
and pass on to the yet more interesting *canzuni :*
little poems, usually in eight lines, of which there are
so many thousand graceful specimens that it is embarrassing to have to make a selection.

Despite the wide gulf which separates lettered from
illiterate poetry, it is curious to note the not unfre-
quent coincidence between the thought of the ignorant
peasant bard and that of cultured poets.   In particular, we are now and then reminded of the pretty
conceits of Herrick, and also of the blithe paganism,
the happy unconsciousness that " Pan is dead," which
lay in the nature of that most incongruous of country
parsons.   Thus we find a parallel to " Gather ye
Rosebuds :"

> Sweet, let us pick the fresh and opening rose,
>   Which doth each charm of form and hue display :
> Hard by the margent of yon font it blows,
>   Mid guarding thorns and many a tufted spray ;
> And in yourself while springtide freshly glows,
>   Dear heart, with some sweet bloom my love repay :
> Soon winter comes, all flowers to nip and close,
>   Nor love itself can hinder time's decay.

No poet is more determined to deal out his compliments in a liberal, open-handed way than is the
Sicilian.   While the Venetians and the Tuscans are
content with claiming seven distinctive beauties for
the object of their affection, the Sicilian boldly asserts
that his *bedda* possesses no less than thirty-three
biddizzi.   In the same manner, when he is about

sending his salutations, he sends them without stint :

Many the stars that sparkle in the sky,
Many the grains of sand and pebbles small;
And in the ocean's plains the finny fry
And leaves that flourish in the woods and fall,
Countless earth's human hordes that live and die,
The flowers that wake to life at April's call,
And all the fruits the summer heats supply—
My greetings sent to thee out-number all.

On some rare occasions the incident which suggested the song may be gathered from the lips of the person who recites it. In one case we are told that a certain sailor, on his return from a long voyage, hastened to the house of his betrothed, to bid her prepare for the wedding. But he was met by the mother-in-law elect, who told him to go his way, for his love was dead— the truth being that she had meanwhile married a shoemaker. One fine day the disconsolate sailor had the not unmixed gratification of seeing her alive and well, looking out of her husband's house, and that night he sang her a reproachful serenade, inquiring wherefore she had hidden from him, that though dead to him she lived for another? This deceived mariner must have been a rather exceptional individual, for although there are baker-poets, carpenter-poets, waggoner-poets, poets in short of almost every branch of labour and humble trade, a sailor-poet is not often to be heard of. Dr Pitrè remarks that sailors pick up foreign songs in their voyages, mostly English and American, and come home inclined to look down upon the folk-songs and singers of their native land.

The serenades and aubades are among the most

delicate and elegant of all the *cansuni d'amuri;* this is one, which contains a favourite fancy of peasant lovers :

> Life of my life, who art my spirit and soul,
>   By no suspicions be nor doubts oppressed,
> Love me, and scorn false jealousy's control—
>   I not a thousand hearts have in my breast,
> I had but one, and gave to thee the whole.
>   Come then and see, if thou the truth wouldst test,
> Instead of my own heart, my love, my soul,
>   Thou wilt thine image find within my breast !

Another poet treats somewhat the same idea in a drolly realistic way—

> Last night I dreamt we both were dead,
> And, love ! beside each other laid.
> Doctors and Surgeons filled the place
> To make autopsy of the case—
> Knives, scissors, saws, with eager zest
> Of each laid open wide the breast :—
> Dumfounded then was every one,
> Yours held two hearts, but mine had none !

The *cansuni* differ very much as to adherence to the strict laws of rhyme and metre ; more often than not assonants are readily accepted in place of rhymes, and their entire absence has been thought to cast a suspicion of education on the author of a song. One truly illiterate living folk-poet was, however, heard severely to criticise some of the printed *cansuni* which were read aloud to him, on just this ground of irregularity of metre and rhyme. His name is Salvatore Calafiore, and he was employed a few years ago in a foundry at Palermo, where he was known among the workmen as "the poet." Being very poor, and having a young wife and family to support, he bethought himself of appealing to the proprietor of the foundry for a rise of wages, but the expedient was hazardous: those who made complaints ran a great chance of getting nothing by it save dismissal. So he offered up his petition in a little poem to this effect: "As the poor little hungry serpent comes out of its hole in search of food, heeding not the risk of being crushed, thus Calafiore, timorous and hard-pressed, O most just sir, asks of you help!" Calafiore was once asked what he knew about the classical characters whose names he introduced into his poems: he answered that some one had told him of them who knew little more of them than he did. He added that "Jove was God of heaven, Apollo god of music, Venus the planet of love, Cicero a good orator." On the whole, the folk-poets are not very lavish in mythological allusion; when they do make it, it is ordinarily fairly appropriate. "Wherever thou dost place thy feet," runs a Borgetto *canzuna*, "carnations and roses, and a thousand divers flowers, are born. My beautiful one, the goddess Venus has promised thee seven and twenty things—new gardens, new heavens, new songs of birds in the spot where thou dost take thy rest." The Siren is one of the ancient myths most in favour: at Partinico they sing:

> Within her sea-girt home the Siren dwells
>   And lures the spell-bound sailor with her lay,
> Amid the shoals the fated bark compels
>   Or holds upon the reef a willing prey,
> None ever 'scape her toils, while sinks and swells
>   Her rhythmic chant at close and break of day—
> Thou, Maiden, art the Siren of the sea,
> Who with thy songs dost hold and fetter me.

It is rarely indeed that we can trace a couple
these lyrics to the same brain—we may not say "
the same hand," for the folk-poet's hand is taken
with striking the anvil or guiding the plough;
more intellectual uses he does not put it—yet c
pressing as they do emotions which are not only t
same at bottom, but are here felt and regarded
precisely the same way, there results so much un
of design and execution, that, as we read, unawa
the songs weave themselves into slight pastoral idy
—typical peasant romances in which real *contad*
speak to us of the new life wrought in them by lo
Even the repeated mention of the Sicilian diminuti
of the names of Salvatore and Rosina helps the il
sion that a thread of personal identity conne
together many of the fugitive *canzuni.* Thus we
tempted to imagine Turiddu and Rusidda as a pair
lovers dwelling in the sunny Conca d'Oro—he "
sweet and beautiful a youth, that God himself m
surely have fashioned him"— a youth with "bl
and laughing eyes, and a little mouth from whe
drops honey:" she a maiden of

> . . . quattordicianni,
> L'occhi cilestri e li capiddi biunni—

"fourteen years, celestial eyes, blonde hair;" to
her long tresses "shining like gold spun by
angels," one would think "that she had just fa'
out of Paradise." "She is fairer than the foam of
sea "—

> "My little Rose in January born,
> Born in the month of cold and drifted snow,

Its whiteness stays thy beauty to adorn,
   Nought than thy velvet skin more white can show.
Thou art the star that shines, tho' bright the morn,
   And casts on all around a silver glow."

But Rusidda's mother will have nothing to say to poor Turiddu ; he complains, "Ah! God, what grief to have a tongue and not to be able to speak; to see her and dare not make any sign! Ah, God in heaven, and Virgin Mary, tell me what I am to do? I look at her, she looks at me, neither I nor she can say a word!" Then an idea strikes him ; he gets a friend to take her a message: "When we pass each other in the street, we must not let the folk see that we are in love, but you will lower your eyes and I will lower my head ; this shall be our way of saluting one another. Every saint has his day, we must await ours." Encouraged by this stratagem, Turiddu grows bold, and one dark night, when none can see who it is, he serenades his "little Rose:"

"Sleep, sleep, my hope, yea sleep, nor be afraid,
   Sleep, sleep, my hope, in confidence serene,   .
For if we both in the same scales be weighed,
   But little difference will be found between.
Have you for me unfeignèd love displayed,
   My love for you shall greater still be seen.
If we could both in the same scales be weighed,
   But small the difference would be found between."

He does not think the song nearly good enough for her : "I know not what song I can sing that is worthy of you," he says : he wishes he were "a goldfinch or a nightingale, and had no equal for singing ;" or, better still, he would fain "have an angel come and sing her a song that had never before been heard of out

M

Paradise," for in Paradise alone can a song be found appropriate to her. One day (it is Rusidda's fête-day), Turiddu makes a little poem, and says in it : "All in roses would I be clad, for I am in love with roses; I would have palaces and little houses of roses, and a ship with roses decked, and a little staircase all of roses, which I the fortunate one would ascend; but ere I go up it, I wish to say to you, my darling, that for you I languish." He watches her go to church : "how beautiful she is! Her air is that of a noble lady!" The mother lingers behind with her gossips, and Turiddu whispers to Rusidda, "All but the crown you look like a queen." She answers : "If there rode hither a king with his crown who said, 'I should like to place it on your head,' I should say this little word, 'I want Turiddu, I want no crown.'" Turiddu tells her he is sick from melancholy : "it is a sickness which the doctors cannot cure, and you and I both suffer from it. It will only go away the day we go to church together."

But there seems no prospect of their getting married; Turiddu sends his love four sighs, "e tutti quattru suspiri d'amuri :"

> " Four sighs I breathe and send thee,
>   Which from my heart love forces ;
> Health with the first attend thee,
>   The next our love discourses ;
> The third a kiss comes stealing ;
>   The fourth before thee kneeling ;
> And all hard fate accusing
>   Thee to my sight refusing."

And now he has to go upon a long journey; but before he starts he contrives one meeting with Rusidda

"Though I shall no longer see you, we yet may hope, for death is the only real parting," he says. "I would have you constant, firm, and faithful; I would have you faithful even unto death." She answers, "If I should die, still would my spirit stay with you." A year passes; on Rusidda's *festa* a letter arrives from Turiddu: "Go, letter mine, written in my blood, go to my dear delight; happy paper! you will touch the white hand of my love. I am far away, and cannot speak to her; paper, do you speak for me."

At last Turiddu returns—but where is Rusidda? "Ye stars that are in the infinite heavens, give me news of my love!"

Through the night "he wanders like the moon," he wanders seeking his love. In his path he encounters Brown Death. "Seek her no more," says this one; "I have her under the sod. If you do not believe me, my fine fellow, go to San Francesco, and take up the stone of the sepulchre: there you will find her." . . . Alas! "love begins with sweetness and ends in bitterness."

The Sicilian's "Beautiful ideal" would seem to be the white rose rather than the red, in accordance, perhaps, with the rule that makes the uncommon always the most prized; or it may be, from a perception of that touch of the unearthly, that pale radiance which gives the fair Southerner a look of closer kinship with the pensive Madonna gazing out of her aureole in the wayside shrine, than with the dark damsels of the more predominant type. Some such angelical association attached to golden heads has possibly disposed the Sicilian folk-poet towards thinking too little of the national black eyes and

olive-carnation colouring. Not that brunettes are
wholly without their singers; one of these has even
the courage to say that since his *bedda* is brown and
the moon is white, it is plain that the moon must
leave the field vanquished. One dark beauty of Termini shows that she is quite equal to standing up for
herself. " You say that I am black ?" she cries, " and
what of that ? Black writing looks well on white
paper, black spices are worth more than white curds,
and while dusky wine is drunk in a glass goblet, the
snow melts away unregarded in the ditch." [1]   But the
apologetic, albeit spirited tone of this protest, indicates
pretty clearly that the popular voice gives the palm
to milk-white and snowy faced maidens; the possessors of *capiddi biunni* and *capidduzzi d'oru* have no
need to defend their charms, a hundred canzuni proclaim them irresistible. " Before everything I am enamoured of thy blonde tresses," says one lyrist. The
luxuriant hair of the Sicilian women is proverbial.
A story is told how, when once Palermo was about to
surrender to the Saracens because there were no more
bowstrings in the town, an abundant supply was suddenly produced by the patriotic dames cutting off
their long locks and turning them to this purpose.
The deed so inspired the Palermitan warriors that
they speedily drove the enemy back, and the siege
was raised. A gallant poet adds : " The hair of our
ladies is still employed in the same office, but now it
discharges no other shafts but those of Cupid, and the
only cords it forms are cords of love."

[1] So Virgil :

" Alba ligustra cadunt, vaccinia nigra leguntur."

In the early morning, almost all the year round the women may be seen sitting before their doors undoing and doing up again this long abundant hair. The chief part of their domestic work they perform out in the sunshine; one thing only, but that the most important of all, has to be done in the house— the never finished task of weaving the clothes of the family. From earliest girlhood to past middle age the Sicilian women spend many hours every day at the loom. A woman of eighty, Rosa Cataldi of Borgetto, made the noble boast to Salomone-Marino: " I have clothed with stuff woven by my hands from fourteen to fifty years, myself, my brothers, my children, and their children." A girl who cannot, or will not, weave is not likely to find a husband. As they ply the shuttle, the women hardly cease from singing, and many, and excellent also, are the songs composed in praise of the active workers. The girl, not yet affianced, who is weaving perhaps her modest marriage clothes, may hear, coming up from the street, the first avowal of love:

Ciuri d'aranci.
Bedda, tu tessi e tessennu mi vinci ;
Bedda, tu canti, e lu me' cori chianci.

It has been said that love begins with sweetness and ends in bitterness. What a fine world it would be were Brown Death the only agent in the bitter end of love! It is not so. Rusidda, who dies, is possibly more fortunate than Rusidda who is married. When bride and bridegroom return from the marriage rite, the husband sometimes solemnly strikes his wife in presence of the assembled guests as a sign of his

henceforth unlimited authority. The symbol has but
too great appropriateness. Even in what may be
called a happy marriage, there is a formality akin
to estrangement, once the knot is tied. Husband and
wife say "voi" to each other, talking to a third
person, they speak of one another as "he" and "she,"
as "mio cristiano," and "mia cristiana," never as
"my husband" and "my wife." The wife sits down
to table with the husband, but she scrupulously waits
for him to begin first, and takes tiny mouthfuls as if
she were ashamed of eating before him. Then, if the
husband be out of humour, or if he thinks that the
wife does not work hard enough (an "enough" which
can never be reached), the nuptial blow is repeated in
sad and miserable earnest. The woman will not even
weep ; she bears all in silence, saying meekly afterwards, "We women are always in the wrong, the
husband is the husband, he has a right even to kill
us since we live by him." These things have been
recorded by one who loves the Sicilian peasant, and
who has defended him against many unfounded
charges. A hard case it would be for wedded
Rusidda if she had not her songs and the sun to
console her.

All the *canzuni* that have been quoted are, so far
as can be judged, of strictly popular origin, nor is
there any sign of continental derivation in their
wording or shape. Several, however, are the common
property of most of the Italian provinces. There is
a charming Vicentine version of "The Siren," and
the "Four Sighs" makes its appearance in Tuscany
under a dress of pure Italian. Has Sicily, then, a
right to the honour of their invention ? There is a

strong presumption that it has. On the other hand, there are some Sicilianized songs of plainly foreign birth, which shows that if the island gave much to the peninsula, it has had at least something back in return. There is a third category, comprising the songs of the Lombard colonies of Piazza and San Fratello, which have a purely accidental connection with Sicily. The founders of this community were Lombards or Longobards, who were attracted to Sicily somewhere in the eleventh century, either by the fine climate and the demand for soldiers of fortune, or by the marriage of Adelaide of Monferrato with Count Roger of Hauteville. But what is far more curious than how or why they came, is the circumstance of the extraordinary isolation in which they seem to have lived, and their preservation to this day of a dialect analogous with that spoken at Monferrato. In this dialect there exist a good many songs, but a full collection of them has yet to be made.

Besides the *ciuri* and *canzuni*, there is another style of love-song, very highly esteemed by the Sicilian peasantry, and that is the *aria*. When a peasant youth serenades his *'nnamurata* with an *aria*, he pays her by common consent the most consummate compliment that lies in his power. The *arii* are songs of four or more stanzas—a form which is not so germane to the Sicilian folk-poet as that of the *canzuna;* and, although he does use it occasionally, it may be suspected that he more often adapts a lettered or foreign *aria* than composes a new one. An aria is nothing unless sung to a guitar accompaniment, and is heard to great advantage when performed by the barbers, who are in the habit of whiling away their idle hours with that instrument. The Sicilian (lettered) poet, Giovanni Meli, has written some admirable *arii*, many of which have become popular songs.

Meli's name is as oddly yoked with the title of *abate* as Herrick's with the designation of clergyman. He does not seem, as a matter of fact, to have ever been an *abate* at all. Once, when dining with a person influential at court, his host inquired why he did not ask to be appointed to a rich benefice then vacant. "Because," he replied, " I am not a priest." And it appeared that when a young man he had adopted the clerical habit for no other reason than that he intended to practise medicine, and wished to gain access to convents, and to make himself acceptable to the nuns. It was not an uncommon thing to do. The public generally dubbed him with the ecclesiastical title. Not long before his death, in 1815, he actually assumed the lesser orders, and in true Sicilian fashion, wrote some verses to his powerful friend to beg him to get him preferment, but he died too soon after to profit by the result. The Sicilians are very proud of Meli. It is for them alone probably to find much pleasure in his occasional odes—to others their noble sentiments will be rather suggestive of the *sinfonia eroica* played on a flute; but the charm and light-ness of his Anacreontic poems must be recognised by all who care for poetry. He had a nice feeling for nature too, as is shown in a sonnet of rare beauty:

> Ye gentle hills, with intercepting vales,
> Ye rocks with musk and clinging ivy dight ;
> Ye sparkling falls of water, silvery pale,
> Still meres, and brooks that babble in the light ;

Deep chasms, wooded steeps that heaven assail,
　　Unfruitful rushes, broom with blossoms bright,
And ancient trunks, encased in gnarled mail,
　　And caves adorned with crystal stalactite ;
Thou solitary bird of plaintive song,
　　Echo that all dost hear, and then repeat,
Frail vines upheld by stately elms and strong,
　　And silent mist, and shade, and dim retreat ;
Welcome me ! tranquil scenes for which I long—
　　The friend of haunts where peace and quiet meet.

I must not omit to say a word about a class of songs which, in Sicily as elsewhere, affords the most curious illustration of the universality of certain branches of folk-lore—I mean the nursery rhymes. One instance of this will serve for all. Sicilian nurses play a sort of game on the babies' features, which consists in lightly touching nose, mouth, eyes, &c., giving a caressing slap to the chin, and repeating at the same time—

　　　　Varvaruttedu,
　　　　Vucca d'aneddu,
　　　　Nasu affilatu,
　　　　Occhi di stiddi,
　　　　Frunti quatrata,
　　　　E te' ccà 'na timpulata !

Now this rhyme has not only its counterpart in the local dialect of every Italian province, but also in most European languages. In France they have it :

　　　　Beau front,
　　　　Petits yeux,
　　　　Nez cancan,
　　　　Bouche d'argent,
　　　　Menton fleuri.
　　　　Chichirichi.

We find a similar doggerel in Germany, and in England, as most people know, there are at least two versions, one being—

> Eye winker,
> Tom Tinker,
>   Nose dropper.
> Mouth eater,
>   Chinchopper,
>   Chinchopper.

Of more intrinsic interest than this ubiquitous old nurse's nonsense are the Sicilian cradle songs, in some of which there may also be traced a family likeness with the corresponding songs of other nations. As soon as the little Sicilian gets up in the morning he is made to say—

> While I lay in my bed five saints stood by ;
> Three at the head, two at the foot—in the midst was Jesus Christ.

The Greek-speaking peasants of Terra d'Otranto have a song somewhat after the same plan :

> I lay me down to sleep in my little bed ; I lay me down to sleep with my Mamma Mary : the Mamma Mary goes hence and leaves me Christ to keep me company.

Very tender is the four-line Sicilian hushaby, in which the proud mother says—

> How beautiful my son is in his swaddling clothes ; just think what he will be when he is big ! Sleep, my babe, for the angel passes : he takes from thee heaviness, and he leaves thee slumber.

There is in Vigo's collection a lullaby so exquisite in its blended echoes from the cradle and the grave that it makes one wish for two great masters in the pathos of childish things, such as Blake and Schumann, to translate and set it to music. It is called "The Widow."

> Sweet, my child, in slumber lie,
> Father's dead, is dead and gone.
> Sleep then, sleep, my little son,
> Sleep, my son, and lullaby.
>
> Thou for kisses dost not cry,
> Which thy cheeks he heaped upon.
> Sleep then, sleep, my pretty one,
> Sleep, my child, and lullaby.
>
> We are lonely, thou and I,
> And with grief and fear I faint.
> Sleep then, sleep, my little saint,
> Sleep, my child, and lullaby.
>
> Why dost weep? No father nigh.
> Ah, my God! tears break his rest.
> Darling, nestle to my breast,
> Sleep, my child, and lullaby.

Very scant information is to be had regarding the Sicilian folk-poets of the past; with one exception their names and personalities have almost wholly slipped out of the memory of the people, and that exception is full three parts a myth. If you ask a Sicilian popolano who was the chief and master of all rustic poets, he will promptly answer, "Pietro Fullone;" and he will tell you a string of stories about the poetic quarry-workman, dissolute in youth, devout in old age, whose fame was as great as his fortune was small, and who addressed a troop of admiring strangers who had travelled to Palermo to visit him, and were surprised to find him in rags, in the following dignified strain :

Beneath these pilgrim weeds so coarse and worn
A heart may still be found of priceless worth.
The rose is ever coupled to the thorn.
The spotless lily springs from blackest earth.
Rubies and precious stones are only born
   Amidst the rugged rocks, uncouth and swarth.
Then wonder not though till the end I wear
Nought but this pilgrim raiment poor and bare.

Unfortunately nothing is more sure than that the
real Pietro Fullone, who lived in the 17th century, and
published some volumes of poetry, mostly religious,
had as little to do with this legendary Fullone as can
well be imagined. It is credible that he may have
begun life as a quarry workman and ignorant poet,
as tradition reports; but it is neither credible that a
tithe of the *canzuna* attributed to him are by the
same author as the writer of the printed and distinctly lettered poems which bear his name, nor that
the bulk of the anecdotes which profess to relate to
him have any other foundation than that of popular
fiction. But though we hear but little, and cannot
trust the little we hear, of the folk-poet of times gone
by, for us to become intimately acquainted with him,
we have only to go to his representative, who lives
and poetizes at the present moment. In this or that
Sicilian hamlet there is a man known by the name of
"the Poet," or perhaps "the Goldfinch." He is completely illiterate and belongs to the poorest class;
he is a blacksmith, a fisherman, or a tiller of the soil.
If he has the gift of improvisation, his fellow-villagers
have the satisfaction of hearing him applauded by
the Great Public—the dwellers in all the surrounding
hamlets assembled at the fair on St John's Eve. Or
it may be he is of a meditative turn of mind, and

makes his poetry leisurely as he lies full length under the lemon-trees taking his noontide rest. Should you pass by, it is unlikely he will give himself the trouble of lifting his eyes: He could not say the alphabet to save his life ; but the beautiful earth and skies and sea which he has looked on every day since he was born have taught him some things not learnt in school. The little poem he has made in his head is indeed a humble sort of poetry, but it is not unworthy of the praise it gets from the neighbours who come dropping into his cottage door, uninvited, but sure of a friendly welcome next Sunday after mass, their errand being to find out if the rumour is true that "the Goldfinch" has invented a fresh *canzuna ?*

Such is the peasant poet of to-day; such he was five hundred or a thousand years ago. He presents a not unlovely picture of a stage in civilisation which is not ours. To-morrow it will not be his either ; he will learn to read and write ; he will taste the fruit of the Tree of the Knowledge of Good and Evil as it grows in our great centres of intellectual activity; he will begin to "look before and after." Still, he will do all this in his own way, not in our way, and so much of his childhood having clung to him in youth, it follows that his youth will not wholly depart from him in manhood. Through all the wonderfully mixed vicissitudes of his country the Sicilian has preserved an unique continuity of spiritual life ; Christianity itself brought him to the brink of no moral cataclysm like that which engulfed the Norseman when he forsook Odin and Thor for the White Christ. It may therefore be anticipated that the new epoch he is entering upon will modify, not change his character.

That he has remained outside of it so long, is due rather to the conditions under which he has lived than to the man ; for the Sicilian grasps new ideas with an almost alarming rapidity when once he gets hold of them ; of all quick Italians he is the quickest of apprehension. This very intelligence of his, called into action by the lawlessness of his rulers and by ages of political tyranny and social oppression, has enabled him to accomplish that systemization of crime which at one time bred the Society of the Blessed Pauls, and now is manifested in the Mafia. You cannot do any business harmless or harmful, you cannot buy or sell, beg or steal, without feeling the hand of an unacknowledged but ever present power which decides for you what you are to do, and levies a tax on whatever profit you may get out of the transaction. If a costermonger sells a melon for less than the established price, his fellows consider that they are only executing the laws of their real masters when they make him pay for his temerity with his life. The wife of an English naval officer went with her maid to the market at Palermo, and asked the price of a fish which, it was stated, cost two francs. She passed on to another stall where a fish of the same sort was offered her for 1.50. She said she would buy it, and took out of her purse a note for five *lire*, which she gave the vendor to change. Meanwhile, unobserved, the first man had come up behind them, and no sooner was the bargain concluded, than he whipped a knife out of his pocket, and in a moment more would have plunged it in the second man's breast, had not the lady pushed back his arm, and cried by some sudden inspiration,

"Wait, he has not given me my change!" No imaginable words would have served their purpose so well; the man dropped the knife, burst out laughing, and exclaimed : "Che coraggio!" The brave Englishwoman nearly fainted when she returned home. Her husband asked what was the matter, to which she answered : " I have saved a man's life, and I have no idea how I did it."

Something has been done to lessen the hereditary evil, but the cure has yet to come. It behoves the Sicilians of a near future to stamp out this plague spot on the face of their beautiful island, and thus allow it to garner the full harvest of prosperity lying in its mineral wealth and in the incomparable fertility of its soil. That it is only too probable that the people will lose their lyre in proportion as they learn their letters is a poor reason for us to bid them stand still while the world moves on ; human progress is rarely achieved without some sacrifices—the one sacrifice we may not make, whatever be the apparent gain, is that of truth and the pursuit of it.

GREEK SONGS OF CALABRIA.

THAT the connecting link between Calabria and Greece was at one time completely cut in two, is an assumption which is commonly made, but it is scarcely a proved fact. What happened to the Italian Greeks on their surrender to Rome?. In a few instances they certainly disappeared with extreme rapidity. Aristoxenus, the peripatetic musician, relates of the Poseidonians — "whose fate it was, having been originally Greek, to be barbarised, becoming Tuscans or Romans," that they still met to keep one annual festival, at which, after commemorating their ancient customs, they wept together over their lost nationality. This is the pathetic record of men who could not hope. In a little while, Poseidonia was an obscure Roman town famous only for its beautiful roses. But the process of "barbarisation" was not everywhere so swift. Along the coast-line from Rhegium to Tarentum, Magna Græcia, in the strict use of the term, the people are known to have clung so long to their old language and their old conditions of life that it is at least open to doubt if they were not clinging to them still when it came to be again a habit with Greeks to seek an Italian home. In the ninth and tenth centuries the tide of Byzantine supremacy swept into Calabria from Constantinople, only, however, to subside almost as suddenly as it advanced. Once more history well-nigh loses sight of the Greeks of Italy. Yet at a moment of critical importance to modern learning their existence was honourably felt. Petrarch's friend and master, Barlaam, who carried the forgotten knowledge of Homer across the Alps, was by birth a Calabrian. In Barlaam's day there were large communities of Greeks both in Calabria and in Terra d'Otranto. A steady decrease from then till now has brought their numbers down to about 22,800 souls in all. These few survivors speak a language which is substantially the same as modern Greek, with the exceptions that it is naturally affected by the surrounding Italic dialects and that it contains hardly a Turkish or a Sclavonic word. Their precise origin is still a subject of conjecture. Soon after Niebuhr had hailed them as Magna Græcians pure and simple, they were pronounced offhand to be quite recent immigrants; then the date of their arrival was assigned to the reign of the first or second Basil; and lastly there is a growing tendency to push it back still further and even to admit that some strain of the blood of the original colonists may have entered into the elements of their descent. On the whole, it seems easier to believe that though their idiom was divided from the Romaic, it yet underwent much the same series of modifications, than to suppose them to have been in Greece when the language of that country was saturated with Sclavonic phrases, which have only been partly weeded out within the last thirty years.

Henry Swinburne visited the Greek settlements in 1780 or thereabouts, but like most of his contemporaries he mixes up the Greek with the Albanians,

of whom there are considerable colonies in Calabria,
dating from the death of Skanderbeg. Even in this
century a German savant was assured at Naples that
the so-called Greeks were one and all Albanians.
The confusion is not taken as a compliment. No one
has stayed in the Hellenic kingdom without noticing
the pride that goes along with the name of Greek—
a pride which it is excusable to smile at, but which
yet has both its touching and its practical aspect, for
it has remade a nation. The Greeks of Southern
Italy have always had their share of a like feeling.
"We are not ashamed of our race, Greeks we are,
and we glory in it," wrote De Ferraris, a Greek born
at Galatone in 1444, and the words would be warmly
endorsed by the enlightened citizens of Bova and
Ammendolea, who quarrel as to which of the two
places gave birth to Praxiteles. The letterless
classes do not understand the grounds of the Magna
Græcian pretensions, but they too have a vague
pleasure in calling themselves Greek and a vague
idea of superiority over their " Latin " fellow-country-
men. "Wake up," sings the peasant of Martignano
in Terra d'Otranto, " wake up early to hear a Grecian
lay, so that the Latins may not learn it."

> Fsunna, fsunna, na cusi ena sonetto
> Grico, na mi to matun i Latini.

Bova is the chief place in Calabria where Greek sur-
vives. The inhabitants call it "Vua," or simply
"Hora." The word "hora," *the city*, is applied by the
Greeks of Terra d'Otranto to that part of their ham-
lets which an Englishman would call "the old village."
It is not generally known that "city" is used in an

identical sense by old country-folks in the English Eastern counties. The Bovesi make a third of the whole Greek-speaking population of Calabria, and Bova has the dignity of being an episcopal seat, though its bishop has moved his residence to the Marina, a sort of seaside suburb, five miles distant from the town. Thirty years ago the ecclesiastical authorities were already agitating for the transfer, but the people opposed it till the completion of the railway to Reggio and the opening of a station at the Marina di Bova settled the case against them. The cathedral, the four or five lesser churches, the citadel, even the Ghetto, all tell of the unwritten age of Bova's prosperity. Old street-names perpetuate the memory of the familiar spirits of the place ; the Lamiæ who lived in a particular quarter, the *Fullitto* who frequented the lane under the cathedral wall. Ignoring Praxiteles, the poorer Bovesi set faith in a tradition that their ancestors dwelt on the coast, and that it was in consequence of Saracenic incursions that they abandoned their homes and built a town on the crags of Aspromonte near the lofty pastures to which herds of cattle (*bovi*) were driven in the summer. The name of Bova would thus be accounted for, and its site bears out the idea that it was chosen as a refuge. The little Greek city hangs in air. To more than one traveller toiling up to it by the old Reggio route it has seemed suggestive of an optical delusion. There is refreshment to be had on the way : a feast for the sight in pink and white flowers of gigantic oleanders ; a feast for the taste in the sweet and perfumed fruit of the wild vine. Still it is disturbing to see your destination suspended above your head at a distance that seems to get longer instead of shorter. Some comfort may be got from hearing Greek spoken at Ammendolea, itself an eyrie, and again at Condufuri. A last, long, resolute effort brings you, in spite of your forebodings, to Bova, real as far as stones and fountains, men and women, and lightly-clothed children can make it; yet still half a dream, you think, when you sit on the terrace at sunset and look across the blue Ionian to the outline, unbroken from base to crown, of " Snowy Ætna, nurse of endless frost, the prop of heaven."

There is plenty of activity among the Greeks of Calabria Ultra. Many of them contrive to get a livelihood out of the chase; game of every sort abounds, and wolves are not extinct. In the mountaineers' cottages, which shelter a remarkable range of animals, an infant wolf sometimes lies down with a tame sheep; whilst on the table hops a domesticated eagle, taken when young from its nest in defiance of the stones dropped upon the robber by the outraged parent-birds. The peasants till the soil, sow corn, plant vegetables, harvest the olives and grapes, gather the prickly pears, make cheese, tend cattle, and are wise in the care of hives. It is a kind of wisdom of which their race has ever had the secret. The Greek Calabrians love bees as they were loved by the idyllic poets. " Ehi tin cardia to melissa " (" he has the heart of a bee "), is said of a kindly and helpful man. Sicilian Hybla cannot have yielded more excellent honey than Bova and Ammendolea. It is sad to think of, but it is stated on good authority that the people of those lofty cities quarrel over their honey as much as about Praxiteles. Somehow envy, hatred, and all uncharit-

ableness find a way into the best of real idylls. You
may live at the top of a mountain and cordially detest
your neighbour. The folk of Condufuri greet the folk
of Bova as Vutáni dogs, which is answered by the
epithet of Spesi-spásu, all the more disagreeable
because nobody knows what it means. In Terra
d'Otranto the dwellers in the various Greek hamlets
call each other thieves, asses, simpletons, and necromancers. The Italian peasants are inclined to class
Greeks and Albanians alike in the category of
" Turchi," and though the word Turk, as used by
Italians, in some cases simply means foreign, it is a
questionable term to apply to individuals. The
Greeks, with curious scorn, are content to fling back
the charge of Latin blood.

When the day's work is done, comes the frugal
evening meal ; a dish of *ricotta*, a glass of wine and
snow. Wine is cheap in Calabria, where the finest
variety is of a white sweet kind called *Greco ;* and
the heights of Aspromonte provide a supply of frozen
snow, which is a necessary rather than a luxury in
this climate. About the hour of Avemmaria the bag-
pipers approach. In the mountains the flocks follow
the wild notes of the " Zampogna " or " Ceramedda,"
unerringly distinguishing the music of their own shepherd. A visit from the Zampognari to hill-town, or
village sets all the world on the alert. There is gossiping, and dancing, and the singing of songs, in
which expression takes the place of air. Two young
men sing together, without accompaniment, or one
sings alone, accompanied by bagpipe, violin, and
guitar. So the evening passes by, till the moon rises
and turns the brief, early darkness into a more glori-

fied day. The little hum of human sound dies in the silence of the hills ; only perhaps a single clear, sweet voice prolongs the monotone of love.

The Italian complimentary alphabet is unknown to the Greek poets. The person whom they address is not apostrophised as Beauty or Beloved, or star, or angel, or *Fior eterno,* or *Delicatella mia.* They do not carry about ready for use a pocketful of poetic-sugared rose-leaves, nor have they the art of making each word serve as an act of homage or a caress. It is true that " caxedda," a word that occurs frequently in their songs, has been resolved by etymologists into " pupil of my eye ; " but for the people it means simply " maiden." The Greek Calabrian gives one the impression of rarely saying a thing because it is a pretty thing to say. If he treats a fanciful idea, he presents it, as it were, in the rough. Take for instance the following :—

> Oh ! were I earth, and thou didst tread on me,
>   Or of thy shoe the sole, this too were sweet !
> Or were I just the dress that covers thee,
>   So might I fall entangling round thy feet.
> Were I the crock, and thou didst strike on me,
>   And we two stooped to catch the waters fleet ;
> Or were I just the dress that covers thee,
>   So without me thou couldst not cross the street.

Here the fancy is the mere servant of the thought behind it. The lover does not figure himself as the fly on the cheek of his mistress, or the flower on her breast. There is no intrinsic prettiness in the common earth or the common water-vessel, in the sole of a worn shoe, or in a workaday gown.

It cannot be pretended that the Greek is so advanced in untaught culture as some of his Italian brothers; in fact there are specimens of the *Sonetto Grico* which are so bald and prosaic that the "Latins" might not be at much pains to learn them even were they sung at noonday. The Titianesque glow which illuminates the plain materials of Venetian song must not be looked for. What will be found in Græco-Calabrian poesy is a strong appearance of sincerity, supplemented at times by an almost startling revelation of tender and chivalrous feeling. To these Greek poets of Calabria love is another name for self-sacrifice. "I marvel how so fair a face can have a heart so tyrannous, in that thou bearest thyself so haughtily towards me, while for thee I take no rest; and thou dost as thou wilt, because I love thee—if needs be that I should pour out my blood with all my heart for thee, I will do it." This is love which discerns in its own depths the cause of its defeat. A reproach suggestive of Heine in its mocking bitterness changes in less than a moment to a cry of despairing entreaty—

> I know you love me not, say what you may,
>   I'll not believe, no, no, my faithless one ;
> With all the rest I see you laugh and play,
>   'Tis only I, I only whom you shun.
> Ah, could I follow where you lead the way :
>   The obstinate thoughts upon your traces run
> Make me a feint of love, though you have none,
> For I must think upon you night and day.

The scene is easily pictured : the bravery of words at meeting, all the just displeasure of many a day bursting forth; then the cessation of anger in the beloved presence and the final unconditional surrender. A lighter mood succeeds, but love's royal clemency is still the text :

> Say, little girl, what have I done to thee,
>   What have I done to thee that thou art dumb?
> Oft wouldst thou seek me once, such friends were we,
>   But now thou goest away whene'er I come.
> If thou hast missed in aught, why quick, confess it,
>   For thee this heart will all, yes all, forgive ;
> If miss be mine, contrive that I should guess it ;
>   And soon the thing shall finish, as I live !

The dutiful lover rings all the changes on humble remonstrance :

> I go where I may see thee all alone,
>   So I may kneel before thee on the ground,
> And ask of thee how is it that unknown
>   Unto thy heart is every prick and wound ?
> Canst thou not see that e'en my breath is flown,
>   Thinking of thee while still the days go round?
> If thou wouldst not that I should quickly die,
>   Love only me and bid the rest good-bye.

He might as well speak to the winds or to the stones, and he admits as much. "Whensoever I pass I sing to make thee glad ; if I do not come for a few hours I send thee a greeting with my eyes. But thou dost act the deaf and likewise the dumb : pity thou hast none for my tears." If he fails to fulfil his prophecy of dying outright, at any rate he falls into the old age of youth, which arrives as soon as the bank of hope breaks :

> Come night, come day, one only thought have I,
>   Which graven on my heart must ever stay ;
> Grey grows my hair and dismal age draws nigh,
>   Wilt thou not cease the tyrant's part to play ?
> Thou seem'st a very Turk for cruelty,
>   Of Barbary a very Turk I say ;
> I know not why thy love thou dost deny,
>   Or why with hate my love thou dost repay.

This may be compared with a song taken down
from the mouth of a peasant near Reggio, an amusing
illustration of the kind of thing in favour with Calabrian herdsmen :—

> Angelical thou art and not terrene,
>   Who dost kings' wives excel in loveliness !
> Thou art a pearl, or Grecian Helen, I ween,
>   For whom Troy town was brought to sore distress ;
> Thine are the locks which graced the Magdalene,
>   Lucrece of Rome did scarce thy worth possess :
> If thou art pitiless to me, oh, my Queen,
>   No Christian thou, a Turk, and nothing less !

A glance at the daughter of Greek Calabria will
throw some light on the plaints of her devoted suitors.
The name she bears = *Dihatera*, brings directly to
mind the Sanskrit *Duhita ;* and the vocation of the
Græco-Calabrian girl is often as purely pastoral as
that of the Aryan milkmaid who stood sponsor for so
large a part of maidenhood in Asia and in Europe.
She is sent out into the hills to keep sheep ; a circumstance not ignored by the shepherd lad who sits
in the shade and trills on his treble reed.   Ewe's milk
is as much esteemed as in the days of Theocritus ; it
forms the staple of the inevitable *ricotta*.   In the
house the Greek damsel never has her hands idle.
She knows how to make the mysterious cakes and
comfits, for which the stranger is bound to have as
large an appetite in Calabria as in the isles of Greece.
A light heart lightens her work, whatever it be.
"You sit on the doorstep and laugh as you wind the
reels, then you go to the loom, *e cchuda magna travudia travudia*" ("and sing those beautiful songs").
So says the ill-starred poet, who discovers to his cost

that it is just this inexhaustible merriment that lends a sharp edge to maiden cruelty. "I have loved you since you were a little thing, never can you leave my heart; you bound me with a light chain; my mind and your mind were one. Now,"—such is the melancholy outcome of it all—" now you are a perfect little fox to me, while you will join in any frolic with the others." The fair tyrant develops an originality of thought which surprises her best friends : " Ever since you were beloved, you have always an idea and an opinion ! " It is beyond human power to account for her caprices : " You are like a fay in the rainbow, showing not one colour, but a thousand." When trouble comes to her as it comes to all—when she has a slight experience of the pain she is so ready to inflict—she does not meekly bow her head and suffer. " Manamu," cries a girl who seems to have been neglected for some one of higher stature. " Mother mine, I have got a little letter, and all sorts of despair. *She* is tall, and *I* am little, and I have not the power to tear her in pieces ! "—as she has probably torn the sheet of paper which brought the unwelcome intelligence. She goes on to say that she will put up a vow in a chapel, so as to be enabled to do some personal, but not clearly explained damage to the cause of her misfortunes. There is nothing new under the sun; the word "anathema" originally meant a votive offering : one of those execratory tablets, deposited in the sacred places, by means of which the ancient Greeks committed their enemies to the wrath of the Infernal Goddesses. Mr Newton has shown that it was the gentler sex which availed itself, by far the most earnestly, of the privilege. Most likely our Lady of Hate in Brittany would have the same tale to tell. Impotence seeks strange ways to compass its revenge.

In some extremities the lover has recourse, not indeed to anathemas, but to irony. "I am not a reed," he protests, "that where you bend me I should go; nor am I a leaf, that you should move me with a breath." Then, after observing that poison has been poured on his fevered vitals, he exclaims, "Give your love to others, and just see if they will love you as I do!" One poet has arrived at the conclusion that all the women of a particular street in Bova are hopelessly false : "Did you ever see a shepherd wolf, or a fox minding chickens, or a pig planting lettuces, or an ox, as sacristan, snuffing out tapers with his horns? As soon will you find a woman of Cuveddi who keeps her faith." Another begins his song with sympathy, but ends by uttering a somewhat severe warning :

> Alas, alas ! my heart it bleeds to see
>   How now thou goest along disconsolate ;
> And in thy sorrow I no help can be—
>   My own poor heart is in a piteous state.
> Come with sweet words—ah ! come and doctor me,
>   And lift from off my heart this dolorous weight.
> If thou come not, then none can pardon thee :
>   Go not to Rome for shrift ; it is too late.

The Calabrian Greek has more than his share of the pangs of unrequited love ; that it is so he assures us with an iteration that must prove convincing. Still, some balm is left in Gilead. Even at Bova there are maidens who do not think it essential to their dignity to act the *rôle* of Eunica. The poorest

herdsman, the humblest shepherd, has a chance of
getting listened to ; a poor, bare chance perhaps, but
one which unlocks the door to as much of happiness
as there is in the world.   At least the accepted lover
in the mountains of Calabria would be unwilling to
admit that there exists a greater felicity than his.   If
he goes without shoes, still "love is enough :"

> Little I murmur against my load of woe—
>   Our love will never fail, nor yet decline ;
> For to behold thy form contents me so,
>   To see thee laugh with those red lips of thine.
> Dost thou say not a word when past I go ?
>   This of thy love for me is most sure sign ;
> Our love will no decline or failing know
>   Till in the sky the sun shall cease to shine.

Karro, the day-labourer (to whom we will give the
credit of inventing this song), would not, if he could,
put one jot of his burden on Filomena of the Red
Lips.   Provided she laughs, he is sufficiently blest.
It so happens that Filomena is his master's grand-
daughter ; hence, alas ! the need of silence as the sign
of love.   The wealthy old peasant has sworn that the
child of his dead son shall never wed a penniless lad,
who might have starved last winter if he had not
given him work to do, out of sheer charity.   Karro
comes to a desperate resolution : he will go down to
Reggio and make his fortune.   When he thinks it
over, he feels quite confident of success : other folks
have brought back lots of money to Bova out of the
great world, and why should not he ?   In the early
morning he calls Filomena to bid her a cheerful
farewell :

Come hither ! run ! thy friend must go away ;
Come with a kiss—the time is flying fast.
Sure am I thou thy word wilt not betray,
And for remembrance' sake my heart thou hast.
Weep not because I leave thee for a day—
Nay, do not weep, for it will soon be past ;
And, I advise thee, heed not if they say,
" Journeys like this long years are wont to last."

Down at Reggio, Karro makes much poetry, and,
were it not for his defective education, one might
think that he had been studying Byron :

If I am forced far from thine eyes to go,
Doubt not, ah ! never doubt my constancy ;
The very truth I tell, if thou wouldst know—
Distance makes stronger my fidelity.
On my sure faith how shouldst thou not rely ?
How think through distance I can faithless grow ?
Remember how I loved thee, and reply
If distance love like mine can overthrow.

The fact is that he has not found fortune-making
quite so quick a business as he had hoped. To the
sun he says, when it rises, " O Sun ! thou that
travellest from east to west, if thou shouldst see her
whom I love, greet her from me, and see if she shall
laugh. If she asks how I fare, tell her that many are
my ills ; if she asks not this of thee, never can I be
consoled." One day, in the market place, he meets a
friend of his, Toto Sgrò, who has come from Bova
with wine to sell. Here is an opportunity of safely
sending a *sonetto* to the red-lipped Filomena. The
public letter-writer is resorted to. This functionary
gets out the stock of deep pink paper which is kept
expressly in the intention of enamoured clients, and
says gravely "Proceed." "An ímme lárga an' du

lúcchiu tu dicússu," begins Karro. "Pray use a tongue known to Christians," interposes the scribe. Toto Sgrò, who is present, remarks in Greek that such insolence should be punished; but Karro counsels peace, and racks his brains for a poem in the Calabrese dialect. ·Most of the men of Bova can poetize in two languages. The poem, which is produced after a moderate amount of labour, turns chiefly on the idle talk of mischief-makers, who are sure to insinuate that the absent are in the wrong. "The tongue of people is evil speaking; it murmurs more than the water of the stream; it babbles more than the water of the sea. But what ill can folks say of us if we love each other? I love thee eternally. Love me, Filomena, and think nothing about it."

Amame, Filomena, e nu' pensare !

Towards spring-time, Karro goes to Scilla to help in the sword-fish taking; it is a bad year, and the venture does not succeed. He nearly loses courage—fate seems so thoroughly against him. Just then he hears a piece of news : at the *osteria* there is an *Inglese* who has set his mind on the possession of a live wolf cub. "Mad, quite mad, like all *Inglesi,*" is the comment of the inhabitants of Scilla. "Who ever heard of taking a live wolf?" Karro, as a mountaineer, sees matters in a different light. Forthwith he has an interview with the Englishman; then he vanishes from the scene for two months. "Poveru giuvinetto," says the host at the inn, "he has been caught by an old wolf instead of catching a young one!" At the end of the time, however, Karro limps up to the door with an injured leg, and hardly a rag

left to cover him; but carrying on his back a sack
holding two wolf cubs, unhurt and tame as kittens.
The gratified *Inglese* gives a bountiful reward; he is
not the first of his race who has acted as the *deus ex
machina* of a love-play on an Italian stage. Nothing
remains to be done but for Karro to hasten back to
Bova. Yet a kind of uneasiness mixes with his joy.
What has Filomena been doing and thinking all this
while! He holds his heart in suspense at the sight
of her beauty :

> In all the world fair women met my gaze,
>> But none I saw who could with thee compare ;
> I saw the dames whom most the Rhegians praise,
>> And by the thought of thee they seemed not fair.
> When thou art dressed to take the morning air
> The sun stands still in wonder and amaze ;
> If thou shouldst scorn thy love of other days,
>> I go a wanderer, I know not where.

The story ends well. Filomena proves as faithful
as she is fair; Karro's leg is quickly cured, and the
old man gives his consent to the marriage—nay more,
feeble as he is now, he is glad to hand over the whole
management of the farm to his son-in-law. Thus the
young couple start in life with the three inestimable
blessings which a Greek poet reckons as representing
the sum total of human prosperity : a full granary, a
dairy-house to make cheese in, and a fine pig.

In collections of Tuscan and Sicilian songs it is
common to find a goodly number placed under the
heading " Delle loro bellezze." The Greek songs of
Calabria that exactly answer to this description are
few. A new Zeuxis might successfully paint an
unseen Tuscan or Sicilian girl—local Anacreons by

the score would give him the needful details: the
colour of the hair and eyes, the height, complexion,
breadth of shoulders, smallness of waist; nor would
they forget to mention the nobility of pose and
carriage, *il leggiadro portamento altero*, which is the
crowning gift of women south of the Alps. It can
be recognized at once that the poets of Sicily and
Tuscany have not merely a vague admiration for
beauty in general; they have an innate artistic perception of what goes to constitute the particular form
of beauty before their eyes. Poorer in words and
ideas, the Greek Calabrian hardly knows what to say
of his beloved, except that she is *dulce ridentem*,
"sweetly-laughing," and that she has small red lips,
between which he is sure that she must carry honey—

> To meli ferri s' ettunda hilúcia . . .

He seems scarcely to notice whether she is fair or
dark. Fortunately it is not impossible to fill in the
blank spaces in the picture. The old Greek stamp
has left a deep impression at home and abroad.
Where there were Greeks there are still men and
women whose features are cut, not moulded, and who
have a peculiar symmetry of form, which is not less
characteristic though it has been less discussed. A
friend of mine, who accompanied the Expedition of
the Thousand, was struck by the conformity of the
standard of proportion to be observed in the women
of certain country districts in Sicily with the rule
followed in Greek sculpture; it is a pity that the
subject is not taken in hand by some one who has
more time to give to it than a volunteer on the march.
I have said "men *or* women," for it is a strange fact

that the heritage of Greek beauty seems to fall to
only one sex at a time. At Athens and in Cyprus
young men may be seen who would have done credit
to the gymnasia, but never a handsome girl; whilst
at Arles, in Sicily, and in Greek Calabria the women
are easily first in the race. The typical Græco-
Calabrian maiden has soft light hair, a fairness of skin
which no summer heats can stain, and the straight
outline of a statue. There is another pattern of beauty
in Calabria: low forehead, straight, strongly-marked
eyebrows, dark, blue, serious eyes, lithe figure, elastic
step. Place beside the women of the last type a
man dyed copper-colour, with black, lank locks, and
the startled look of a wild animal. The Greeks have
many dark faces, and many ugly faces, too; for that
matter, uncompromising plainness was always amongst
the possibilities of an Hellenic physiognomy. But
the beautiful dark girl and her lank-locked companion
do not belong to them. Whom they do belong to is
an open question; perhaps to those early Brettians
who dwelt in the forest of the Syla, despised by the
·Greeks as savages, and docketed by the Romans,
without rhyme or reason, as the descendants of
escaped criminals. Calabria offers an inviting field
to the ethnologist. It is probable that the juxtaposi-
tion of various races has not led in any commensurate
degree to a mixture of blood. Each commune is a
unit perpetually reformed out of the same constituents.
Till lately intermarriage was carried to such a pitch
that it was rare to meet with a man in a village who
was not closely related to every other-inhabitant
of it.

The Greeks of Terra d'Otranto bear a strong phy-

O

sical resemblance to the Greeks of Calabria Ultra. It is fifty or sixty years since the Hon. R. Keppel Craven remarked a "striking regularity of feature and beauty of complexion" in the women of Martano and Calimera. At Martano they have a pretty song in praise of some incomparable maid:

> My Sun, where art thou going? Stay to see
> How passing beautiful is she I love.
> My Sun, that round and round the world dost move,
> Hast thou seen any beautiful as she?
> My Sun, that hast the whole world travelled round,
> One beautiful as she thou hast not found!

Next to his lady's laughter, the South Italian Greek worships the sun. It is the only feature in nature to which he pays much heed. In common with other forms of modern Greek the Calabrian possesses the beautiful periphrase for sunset, *o íglio vasiléggui* (ὁ ἥλιος βασιλεύει). Language, which is altogether a kind of poetry, has not anything more profoundly poetic. There is a brisk, lively ring in the "Sun up!" of the American Far West; but an intellectual Atlantic flows between it and the Greek ascription of kingship, of heroship, to the Day-giver at the end of his course—

> Wie herrlich die Sonne dort untergeht,
> So stirbt ein Held! Anbetungswürdig!

When we were young, were not our hearts stirred to their inmost depths by this?

The love-songs of Bova include one composed by a young man who had the ill-luck to get into prison. "Remember," he says, "the words I spoke to thee when we were seated on the grass; for the love of

Christ, remember them, so as not to make my life a torment. Think not that I shall stay in here for ever; already I have completed one day. But if it should happen that thou art forgetful of my words, beyond a doubt this prison awaits me!" The singer seems to wish it to be inferred that his line of conduct in the given case will be such as to entitle him to board and lodging at the expense of the state for the rest of his days. In times still recent, prisoners at Bova could see and be seen, and hear and be heard, through the bars. Thus the incarcerated lover had not to wait long for an answer, which must have greatly relieved his mind: "The words that thou didst say to me on the tender grass, I remember them —I forget them not. I would not have thee say them over again; but be sure I love thee. Night and day I go to church, and of Christ I ask this grace: 'My Christ, make short the hours—bring to me him whom I love!'"

The Greeks have a crafty proverb, "If they see me I laugh; but if not, I rob and run." A Græco-Italic word,[1] *maheri,* or "poignard," has been suggested as the origin of *Mafia,* the name of one of the two great organisations for crime which poison the social atmosphere of southern Italy. The way of looking upon an experience of the penalties of the law, not as a retribution or a disgrace, but as a simple mischance, still prevails in the provinces of the ex-kingdom of Naples. "The prisons," says a Calabrian poet, "are made for honest men." Yet the people of Calabria are rather to be charged with a confusion of moral sense than with a completely debased morality. What

---

[1] In classical Greek, μάχαιρα.

has been said of the modern Greek could with equal truth be said of them, whether Greeks or otherwise : put them upon their point of honour and they may be highly trusted. At a date when, in Sicily, no one went unarmed, it was the habit in Calabria to leave doors and windows unfastened during an absence of weeks or months; and it is still remembered how, after the great earthquake of 1783, five Calabrians who happened to be at Naples brought back to the treasury 200 ducats (received by them out of the royal bounty) on learning, through private sources, that their homesteads were safe. The sort of honesty here involved is not so common as it might be, even under the best of social conditions.

In that year of catastrophe—1783—it is more than possible that some of the Greek-speaking communities were swallowed up, leaving no trace behind. Calabria was the theatre of a series of awful transformation scenes; heroism and depravity took strange forms, and men intent on pillage were as ready to rush into the tottering buildings as men intent on rescue. A horrid rejoicing kept pace with terror and despair. In contrast to all this was the surprising calmness with which in some cases the ordeal was faced. At Oppido, a place originally Greek, a pretty young woman, aged nineteen years, was immured for thirty hours, and shortly after her husband had extricated her she became a mother. Dolomieu asked what had been her thoughts in her living tomb; to which she simply answered, " I waited." The Prince of Scilla and four thousand people were swept into the sea by a single volcanic wave. Only the mountains stood firm. Bova, piled against the rock like a child's card-city,

suffered no harm, whilst the most solid structures on
the shore and in the plain were pitched about as ships
in a storm. Still, in the popular belief the whole mischief was brewed deep down in the innermost heart
of Aspromonte. It may be that the theory grew out
of the immemorial dread inspired by the Bitter Mount
—a dread which seems in a way prophetic of the dark
shadow it was fated to cast across the fair page of
Italian redemption.

A thousand years ago every nook and cranny in
the Calabrian mountains had its Greek hermit. Now
and then one of these anchorites descended to the
towns, and preached to flocks of penitents in the
Greek idiom, which was understood by all. Under
Byzantine rule the people generally adhered to the
Greek rite ; nor was it without the imposition of the
heavy hand of Rome that they were finally brought
to renounce it. As late as the sixteenth century the
liturgies were performed in Greek at Rossano, and
perhaps much later in the hill-towns, where there are
women who still treasure up scraps of Greek prayers.
Greek, in an older sense than any attached to the
ritual of the Eastern Church, is the train of thought
marked out in this line from a folk-song of Bova: "O
Juro pu en ehi jerusia" ("The Lord who hath not
age"). The Italian imagines the Creator as an old
man ; witness, to take only one example, the frescoes
on the walls of the Pisan Campo Santo. A Tuscan
proverb, which means no evil, though it would not
very well bear translating—" Lascia fare a Dio che è
Santo Vecchio"—shows how in this, as in other
respects, Italian art is but the concrete presentation
of Italian popular sentiment. The grander idea of

"a Divine power which grows not old" seems very like an exotic in Italy. Without yielding too much to the weakness of seeking analogies, one other coincidence may be mentioned in passing. The Greek mother soothes her crying child by telling him that "the wild doves drink at the *holy sea.*" This "ago Thalassia" recalls the ἅλς δῖα of the greatest folk-poet who ever lived. *Thalassia* is now replaced in ordinary conversation by the Italian *mare;* indeed, in Terra d'Otranto it is currently supposed to be the proper name of a saint. The next step would naturally lead to the establishment of a cult of St Thalassia ; and this may have been the kind of way in which were established a good many of those cults that pass for evidences of nature-worship.

The language of the Græco-Calabrian songs, mixed though it is with numberless Calabrese corruptions, is still far more Greek than the actual spoken tongue. So it always happens ; poetry, whether the highest or the lowest, is the shrine in which the purer forms of speech are preserved. The Greeks of Calabria are at present bi-lingual, reminding one of Horace's "Canusini more bilinguis." It is a comparatively new state of things. Henry Swinburne says that the women he saw knew only Greek or "Albanese," as he calls it, which, he adds, "they pronounce with great sweetness of accent." The advance of Calabrese is attended by the decline of Greek, and a systematic examination of the latter has not been undertaken a moment too soon. The good work, begun by Domenico Comparetti and Giuseppe Morosi, is being completed by professor Astorre Pellegrini, who has published one volume of *Studi sui dialetti Greco-Calabro di Bova*, which will be followed in due course by a second instalment. I am glad to be able to record my own debt to this excellent and most courteous scholar. He informs me that he hopes to finish his researches by a thorough inspection of the stones and mural tablets in Calabrian graveyards. The dead have elsewhere told so much about the living that the best results are to be anticipated.

It need scarcely be said that the leavings of the past in the southern extremity of Italy are not confined to the narrow space where a Greek idiom is spoken. There is not even warrant for supposing them to lie chiefly within that area. The talisman which the hunter or brigand wears next to his heart, believing that it renders him invulnerable ; the bagpipe which calls the sheep in the hills, and which the wild herds of swine follow docilely over the marshes ; the faggot which the youth throws upon his mother's threshold before he crosses it after the day's toil ; the kick, aimed against the house door, which signifies the last summons of the debtor ; the shout of "Barca!" raised by boys who lie in wait to get the first glimpse of the returning fishing fleet, expecting largess for the publication of the good news ; the chaff showered down by vine-dressers upon bashful maids and country lads going home from market ; the abuse of strangers who venture into the vineyards at the vintage season—these are among the things of the young world that may be sought in Calabria.

Other things there are to take the mind back to the time when the coins the peasant turns up with his hoe

were fresh from the mint at Locri, and when the
mildest of philosophies was first—

> .   .   .   .   dimly taught
> In old Crotona ;

wild flowers as sweet as those that made Persephone
forsake the plain of Enna ; maidens as fair as the five
beautiful virgins after whom Zeuxis painted his *Helen;*
grasshoppers as loudly chirping as the "cricket" that
saved the prize to Eunomus ; and, high in the trans-
parent air, the stars at which Pythagoras gazed
straining his ears to catch their eternal harmonies.

FOLK SONGS OF PROVENCE.

On a day in the late autumn it happened to me to
be standing at a window looking down into an untidy
back street at Avignon.   It was a way of getting
through the hours between a busy morning and a
busy evening—hours which did not seem inclined to
go.   If ever man be tempted to upbraid the slowness
of the flight of time, it is surely in the vacant intervals
of travel.   The prospect at the window could hardly
be called enlivening; by-and-by, however, the dulness
of the outlook was lessened a little.   The sounds of
a powerful and not unmusical voice came along the
street; people hastened to their doors, and in a
minute or so a young lame man made his appearance.
He was singing Provençal songs.   Here was the last
of the troubadours!

If it needed some imagination to see in this humble
minstrel the representative of the courtly adepts in
the gay science, still his relationship to them was not
purely fanciful.   The itinerant singer used to be the
troubadour of the poor.   No doubt his more illustrious
brother grudged him the name.   "I am astonished,"
said Giraud Riquier to Alfonso of Aragon, "that folks
confound the troubadours with those ignorant and
uncouth persons who, as soon as they can play some
screeching instrument, go through the streets asking
alms and singing before a vile rabble;" and Alfonso

answered that in future the noble appellation of
"joglaria" should be granted no longer to mounte-
banks who went about with dancing dogs, goats,
monkeys, or puppets, imitating the song of birds, or
for a meagre pittance singing before people of base
extraction, but that they should be called " bufos," as
in Lombardy. Giraud Riquier was not benevolently
inclined when he embodied in verse his protest and
the King's endorsement of it ; yet his words now lend
an ancient dignity to the class they were meant to
bring into contempt. The lame young man at
Avignon had no dancing dogs, nor did he mimic the
song of birds — an art still practised with ·wonder-
ful skill in Italy.[1] He helped out his entertainment
by another device, one suitable to an age which reads;
he sold printed songs, and he presented "letters." If
you bought two sous' worth of songs you were entitled
to a "letter." It has to be explained that " letters "
form a kind of fortune-telling, very popular in Provence.
A number of small scraps of paper are attached to a
ring ; you pull off one at hazard, and on it you find a
full account of the fate reserved to you. Nothing
more simple. As to the songs, loose sheets containing four or five of them are to be had for fifteen
centimes. I have seen on the quay at Marseilles an
open bookstall, where four thousand of these songs
are advertised for sale. Some are in Provençal, some
in French; many are interlarded with prose sentences,
in which case they are called "cansounetto émé parla."
Formerly the same style of composition bore the

---

[1] I am told that the peasants of the country round Moscow
have a natural gift for imitating birds, and that they intersperse
the singing of their own sad songs with this sweet carolling.

name of *cantefable.* The subjects chosen are comic,
or sentimental, or patriotic, or, again, simply local.
There is, for example, a dialogue between a proprietor
and a lodger. "Workman, why are you always
grumbling?" asks the "moussu," who speaks French,
as do angels and upper-class people generally in
Provençal songs. "If your old quarters are to be
pulled down, a fine new one will be built instead.
Ere long the town of Marseilles will become a paradise,
and the universe will exclaim, 'What a marvel! Fine
palaces replace miserable hovels!'" For all that,
replies the workman in Provençal patois, the abandon-
ment of his old quarter costs a pang to a child *deis
Carmes* (an old part of Marseilles, standing where the
Greek town stood). It was full of attraction to him.
There his father lived before him; there his friends
had grown with him to manhood; there he had
brought up his children, and lived content. The
proprietor argues that it was far less clean than could
be wished—there was too much insectivorous activity
in it. He tells the workman that he can find a lodging,
after all not very expensive, in some brand-new
building outside the town; the railway will bring
him to his work. Unconvinced, the workman returns
to his refrain, "Regreterai toujour moun vieil Marsîo."
If the rhymes are bad, if the subject is prosaic, we
have here at least the force of a fact pregnant with
social danger. Is it only at Marseilles that the
grand improvements of modern days mean, for the
man who lives by his labour, the break-up of his
home, the destruction of his household gods, the dis-
persion of all that sweetened and hallowed his poverty?
The songs usually bear an author's name; but the

authors of the original pieces, though they may enjoy a solid popularity in Provence, are rarely known to a wider fame.   One of them, M. Marius Féraud, whose address I hold in my hands, will be happy to compose songs or romances for marriages, baptisms, and other such events, either in Provençal or in French, introducing any surname and Christian name indicated, and arranging the metre so as to suit the favourite tune of the person who orders the poem.

Street ditties occupy an intermediate place between literate and illiterate poesy.   Once the repertory of the itinerant *bufo* was drawn from a source which might be called popular without qualifying the term. With the pilgrim and the roving apprentice he was a chief agent in the diffusion of ballads.   Even now he has a right to be remembered in any account of the songs of Provence ; but, having given him mention, we must leave the streets to go to the well-heads of popular inspiration—the straggling village, the isolated farm, the cottage alone on the byeway.

When in the present century there was a revival of Provençal literature, after a suspension of some five hundred years, the poets who devoted their not mean gifts to this labour of love discerned, with true insight, that the only Provençal who was still thoroughly alive was the peasant.   Through the long lapse of time in the progress of which Provence had lost its very name—becoming a thing of French departments —the peasant, it was discovered, had not changed much ; acting on which discovery, the new Provençal school produced two works of a value that could not have been reached had it been attempted either to give an archaic dress to the ideas and interests of the modern world, or to galvanise the dry bones of mediæval romance into a dubious animation. These works are *Mirèio* and *Margarido*. Mistral, with the idealising touch of the imaginative artist, paints the Provence of the valley of the Rhone, whilst Marius Trussy photographs the ruder and wilder Provence of mountain and torrent. Taken together, the two poems perfectly illustrate the *Wahrheit und Dichtung* of the life of the people whose songs we have to study.

Since there is record of them the Provençals have danced and sung. They may be said to have furnished songs and dances to all France, and even to lands far beyond the border of France. A French critic relates how, when he was young, he went night after night to a certain theatre in Paris to see a dance performed by a company of English pantomimists. The dancers gradually stripped a staff, or may-pole, of its many-coloured ribbons, which became in their hands a sort of moving kaleidoscope. This, that he thought at the time to be an exclusively English invention, was the old Provençal dance of the *olivette*. In the Carnival season dances of an analogous kind are still performed, here and there, by bands of young men, who march in appropriate costume from place to place, led by their harlequin and by a player on the *galooubé*, the little pipe which should be considered the national instrument of Provence. Harlequin improvises couplets in a sarcastic vein, and the crowd of spectators is not slow to apply each sally to some well-known person; whence it comes that Ash Wednesday carries a sense of relief to many worthy individuals. May brings with it more dances and milder songs. Young men plant a tree, with a nosegay atop, before their sweethearts' doors, and then go singing—

> Lou premier jour de mai,
> 　　O Diou d'eime !
> Quand tout se renouvelo
> 　　Rossignolet !
> Quand tout se renouvelo.

The great business of the month is sheep-shearing, a labour celebrated in a special song. "When the month of May comes, the shearers come : they shear by night, they shear by day ; for a month, and a fortnight, and three weeks they shear the wool of these white sheep." When the shearers go, the washers come ; when the washers go, the carders come ; then come the spinners, the weavers, the buyers, and the ragmen who gather up the bits. Across the nonsense of which it is composed the ditty reflects the old excitement caused in the lonely homesteads by the annual visit of the plyers of these several trades, who turned everything upside down and brought strange news of the world. At harvest there was, and there is yet, a great gathering at the larger farms. Troops of labourers assemble to do the needful work. Sometimes, after the evening meal, a curious song called the " Reapers' Grace " is sung before the men go to rest. It has two parts : the first is a variation on the first chapter of Genesis. Adam and *nouestro maire Evo* are put into the Garden of Eden. Adam is forbidden to eat of the fruit of life ; he eats thereof, and the day of his death is foretold him. He will be buried under a palm, a cypress, and an olive, and out of the wood of the olive the

Cross will be made. The second part, sung to a quick, lively air, is an expression of goodwill to the master and the mistress of the farm, every verse ending, "Adorem devotoment Jesù eme Mario." A few years ago the harvest led on naturally to the vintage. It is not so now. The vines of Provence, excellent in themselves, though never turned to the same account as those of Burgundy or Bordeaux, have been almost completely ruined by the phylloxera. The Provençal was satisfied if his wine was good enough to suit his own taste and that of his neighbours; thus he had not laid by wealth to support him in the evil day that has come. "Is there no help?" I asked of a man of the poorer class. "Only rain, much rain, can do good," he answered, "and," he added, "we have not had a drop for four months." The national disaster has been borne with the finest fortitude, but in Provence at least there seems to be small faith in any method of grappling with it. The vines, they say, are spoilt by the attempt to submit them to an artificial deluge; so one after the other, the peasant roots them up, and tries to plant cabbages or what not. Three hundred years back the Provençals would have known what measures to take : the offending insect would have been prosecuted. Between 1545 and 1596 there was a run of these remarkable trials at Arles. In 1565 the Arlesiens asked for the expulsion of the grasshoppers. The case came before the Tribunal de l'Officialité, and Maître Marin was assigned to the insects as counsel. He defended his clients with much zeal. Since the accused had been created, he argued that they were justified in eating what was necessary to them. The

opposite counsel cited the serpent in the Garden of
Eden, and sundry other animals mentioned in Scrip-
ture, as having incurred severe penalties. The grasshoppers got the worst of it, and were ordered to quit
the territory, with a threat of anathematizatiom from
the altar, to be repeated till the last of them had
obeyed the sentence of the honourable court.

One night in the winter of 1819 there was a frost
which, had it been a few times repeated, would have
done as final mischief to the olives as the phylloxera
has done to the vines. The terror of that night is
remembered still. Corn, vine, and olive—these were
the gifts of the Greek to Provence, and the third is
the most precious of all. The olive has here an
Eastern importance; the Provençals would see a
living truth in the story of how the trees said unto it,
" Reign thou over us." In the flowering season the
slightest sharpness in the air sends half the rural
population bare-foot upon a pilgrimage to the nearest
St Briggitte or St Rossoline. The olive harvest is
the supreme event of the year. It has its song too.
In the warm days of St Martin's summer, says the
late Damase Arbaud, some worker in the olive woods
will begin to sing of a sudden—

Ai rescountrat ma mio—diluns.

It is a mere nonsense song respecting the meeting of
a lover and his lass on every day of the week, she
being each day on her way to buy provisions, and he
giving her the invariable advice that she had better
come back, because it is raining. Were it the rarest
poetry the effect could be hardly more beautiful than
it is. When the first voice has sung, " I met my

love . . ." ascending slowly from a low note, the whole group of olive-gatherers take it up, then the next, and again the next, till the country-side is made all musical by the swell and fall of sound sent forth from every grey coppice; and even long after the nearer singers have ceased, others unseen in the distance still raise the high-pitched call, "Come back, my love, come back! . . . come back!"

On the first of November it is customary in Provence for families to meet and dine. The fruits of the earth are garnered, the year's business is over and done. The year has brought perhaps new faces into the family; very likely it has taken old faces away. Towards evening the bells begin to toll for the vigil of the feast of All Souls. Tears come into the eyes of the older guests, and the children are hurried off to bed. Why should they be present at this letting loose of grief? To induce them to retire with good grace, they are allowed to take with them what is left of the dessert—chestnuts, or grapes, or figs. The child puts a portion of his spoils at the bottom of his bed for the *armettes:* so are called the spirits of the dead who are still in a state of relation with the living, not being yet finally translated into their future abode. Children are told that if they are good the *armettes* will kiss them this night; if they are naughty, they will scratch their little feet.

The Provençal religious songs, poor though they are from a literary point of view, yet possess more points of interest than can be commonly looked for in folk-songs which treat of religion. They contain frequent allusions to beliefs that have to be sought either in the earliest apocryphal writings of the Chris-

P

tian æra, or in the lately unearthed records of rab-
binical tradition. Various of them have regard to
what is still, as M. Lenthéric says, "one of the great
popular emotions of the South of France"—the
reputed presence there of Mary Magdalene. M.
Lenthéric is convinced that certain Jewish Christians,
flying from persecution at home, did come to Provence (between the ports of which and the East there
was constant communication) a short time after the
Crucifixion. He is further inclined to give credit to
the impression that Mary Magdalene and her companions were among these fugitives. I will not go
into the reasons that have been urged against the
story by English and German scholars; it is enough
for us that it is a popular credence of very ancient
origin. One side issue of it is particularly worth
noting. A little servant girl named Sara is supposed
to have accompanied the Jewish emigrants, and her
the gypsies of Provence have adopted as their patroness. Once a year they pay their respects to her
tomb at Saintes Maries de la Mer. This is almost
the only case in which the gypsy race has shown any
disposition to identify itself with a religious cultus.
The fairy legend of Tarascon is another offshoot from
the main tradition. "Have you seen the Tarasque?"
I was asked in the course of a saunter through that
town one cold morning between the hours of seven
and eight. It seemed that the original animal was
kept in a stall. To stimulate my anxiety to make
its acquaintance I was handed the portrait of a beast,
half hedgehog, half hippopotamus, out of whose somewhat human jaw dangled the legs of a small boy.
Later I heard the story from the lips of the sister of

the landlord at the primitive little inn ; much did it
gain from the vivacious grace of the narrator, in whom
there is as surely proof positive of a Greek descent
as can be seen in any of the more famous daughters
of Arles. "When the friends of our Lord landed in
Provence, St Mary Magdalene went to Sainte Baume,
St Lazarus to Marseilles, and St Martha came here to
Tarascon. Now there was a terrible monster called
the Tarasque, which was desolating all the country
round and carrying off all the young children to eat.
When St Martha was told of the straits the folks
were in, she went out to meet the monster with a
piece of red ribbon in her hand. Soon it came, snort-
ing fire out of its nostrils ; but the saint threw the red
ribbon over its neck, and lo! it grew quite still and
quiet, and followed her back into the town as if it
had been a good dog. To keep the memory of this
marvel, we at Tarascon have a wooden Tarasque,
which we take round the town at Whitsuntide with
much rejoicing. About once in twenty years there is
a very grand *fête* indeed, and people come from far,
far off. I have—naturally—seen this grand celebration only once." A gleam of coquetry lit up the long
eyes : our friend clearly did not wish to be supposed
to have an experience ranging over too long a period.
Then she went on, "You must know that at Beaucaire,
just there across the Rhone, the folks have been always
ready to die of jealousy of our Tarasque. Once upon
a time they thought they would have one as well as
we ; so they made the biggest Tarasque that ever had
been dreamt of. How proud they were ! But, alas !
when the day came to take it round the town, it was
found that it would not come out of the door of the

workshop! Ah! those dear Beaucairos!" This I
believe to be a pure fable, like the rest; to the good
people of Tarascon it appears the most pleasing part
of the whole story.   My informant added, with a
merry laugh, "There came this way an Englishman—
a very sceptical Englishman.   When he heard about
the difficulty of the Beaucairos he asked, 'Why did
they not have recourse to St Martha?'"

As I have strayed into personal reminiscence, the
record of one other item of conversation will perhaps
be allowed.   That same morning I went to breakfast
at the house of a Provençal friend to meet the
ablest exponent of political positivism, the Radical
deputy for Montmartre.   Over our host's strawberries
(strawberries never end at Tarascon) I imparted my
newly acquired knowledge.   When it came to the
point of saying that certain elderly persons were
credibly stated to have preserved a lively faith in the
authenticity of the legend, M. Clémenceau listened
with a look of such unmistakable concern that I said,
half amused, "You do not believe much in poetry?"
The answer was characteristic.   "Yes, I believe in it
much; but is it necessary to poetry that the people
should credit such absurdities?"   Is it necessary?
Possibly Marius Trussy, who inveighs so passionately
against "lou progré," would say that it is.   Anyhow
the Tarasques of the world are doomed; whether
they will be without successors is a different question.
Some one has said that mankind has always lived
upon illusions, and always will, the essential thing
being to change the nature of these illusions from
time to time, so as to bring them into harmony with
the spirit of the age.

Provençal folk-songs have but few analogies with the literature which heedlessly, though beyond recall, has been named Provençal. The poetry of the Miejour was a literary orchid of the fabulous sort that has neither root nor fruit. A chance stanza, addressed to some high-born Blanco-flour, finds its way occasionally into the popular verse of Provence with the marks of lettered authorship still clinging to it; but further than this the resemblance does not go. The love poets of the people make use of a flower language, which is supposed to be a legacy of the Moors. Thyme accompanies a declaration; the violet means doubt or uneasiness; rosemary signifies complaint; nettles announce a quarrel. The course of true love nowhere flows less smoothly than in old Provence. As soon as a country girl is sus-pected of having a liking for some youth, she is set upon by her family as if she were guilty of a mon-strous crime. A microscopic distinction of rank, a divergence in politics, or a deficiency of money will be snatched as the excuse for putting the lover under the ban of absolute proscription. From the inexplic-able obstacles placed in the way of lovers it follows that a large proportion of Provençal marriages are the result of an elopement. The expedient never fails; Provençal parents do not lock up their runaway daughters in convents where no one can get at them. The delinquents are married as fast as possible. What is more, no evil is thought or spoken of them. To make assurance doubly sure, a curious formality is observed. The girl calls upon two persons, secretly convened for the purpose, to bear witness that she carries off her lover, who afterwards protests that his part in the comedy was purely passive. In less than twenty years the same drama is enacted with Margarido, the daughter, in the *rôle* of Mario the mother.

> L'herbo que grio
> Toujours reverdilho ;
> L'herbo d'amour
> Reverdilho toujours.

The plant of love grows where there are young hearts ; but how comes it that middle-aged hearts turn inevitably to cast iron? There is one song which has the right to be accepted as the typical love-song of Provence. Mistral adapted it to his own use, and it figures in his poem as the "Chanson de Majali." My translation follows as closely as may be after the popular version which is sung from the Comtat Venaissin to the Var :

> Margaret! my first love,
>   Do not say me nay !
> A morning music thou must have,
>   A waking roundelay.
> —Your waking music irks me,
>   And irk me all who play ;
> If this goes on much longer
>   I'll drown myself one day.
> —If this goes on much longer,
>   And thou wilt drown one day,
> Why, then a swimmer I will be,
>   And save thee sans delay.
> —If then a swimmer thou wilt be,
>   And save me sans delay,
> Then I will be an eel, and slip
>   From 'twixt thy hands away.
> —If thou wilt be an eel, and slip
>   From 'twixt my hands away,
> Why, I will be the fisherman
>   Whom all the fish obey.

— If thou wilt be the fisherman
    Whom all the fish obey,
  Then I will be the tender grass
    That yonder turns to hay.
—If thou wilt be the tender grass
    That yonder turns to hay,
  Why, then a mower I will be,
    And mow thee in the may.
— If thou a mower then wilt be,
    And mow me in the may,
  I, as a little hare, will go
    In yonder wood to stray.
—If thou a little hare wilt go
    In yonder wood to stray,
  Then will I come, a hunter bold,
    And have thee as my prey.
—If thou wilt come a hunter bold
    To have me as thy prey,
  Then I will be the endive small
    In yonder garden gay.
—If thou wilt be the endive small
    In yonder garden gay,
  Then I will be the falling dew,
    And fall on thee alway.
—If thou wilt be the falling dew,
    And fall on me alway,
  Then I will be the white, white rose
    On yonder thorny spray.
—If thou wilt be the white, white rose
    On yonder thorny spray,
  Then I will be the honey bee,
    And kiss thee all the day.
—If thou wilt be the honey bee,
    And kiss me all the day,
  Then I will be in yonder heaven
    The star of brightest ray.
—If thou wilt be in yonder heaven
    The star of brighest ray,
  Then I will be the dawn, and we
    Shall meet at break of day.

—If thou wilt be the dawn, so we
    May meet at break of day,
Then I will be a nun professed,
    A nun of orders grey.
—If thou wilt be a nun professed,
    A nun of orders grey,
Then I will be the prior, and thou
    To me thy sins must say.
—If thou wilt be the prior, and I
    To thee my sins must say,
Then will I sleep among the dead,
    While the sisters weep and pray.
—If thou wilt sleep among the dead,
    While the sisters weep and pray,
Then I will be the holy earth
    That on thee they shall lay.
—If thou wilt be the holy earth
    That on me they shall lay—
Well—since some gallant I must have,
    I will not say thee nay.

A distinguished French scholar thought that he heard in this an echo of Anacreon's ode κ' εὖς κόρην. The inference suggested is too hazardous for acceptance; yet that in some sort the song may date from Greek Provence would seem to be the opinion even of cautious critics. Thus we are led to look back to those associations which, without giving a personal or political splendour such as that attached to Magna Græcia, lend nevertheless to Provençal memories the exquisite charm, the "*bouquet*" (if the word does not sound absurd) of all things Greek. The legend of Greek beginnings in Provence will bear being once more told. Four hundred and ninety years before Christ a little fleet of Greek fortune-seekers left Phocæa, in Asia Minor, and put into a small creek on the Provençal coast, the port of the future Marseilles. As soon as they had disembarked, deeming it to be of importance to them to stand well with the people of the land, they sent to the king of the tribes inhabiting those shores an ambassador bearing gifts and overtures of friendly intercourse. When the ambassador reached Arles, Nann, the king, was giving a great feast to his warriors, from among whom his daughter Gyptis was that day to choose a husband. The young Greek entered the banqueting-hall and sat down at the king's board. When the feasting was over, fair-haired Gyptis, the royal maiden, rose from her seat and went straightway to the strange guest; then, lifting in her hands the cup of espousal, she offered it to his lips. He drank, and Provence became the bride of Greece.

The children of that marriage left behind them a graveyard to tell their history. Desecrated and despoiled though it is, still the great Arlesian ceme-tery bears unique witness as well to the civilised prosperity of the Provençal Greeks as to their decline under the influences which formed the modern Pro-vence. Irreverence towards the dead—a compara-tively new human characteristic—can nowhere be more fully observed than in the *Elysii Campi* of Arles. The love of destruction has been doing its worst there for some centuries. To any king coming to the town the townsfolk would make a gift of a price-less treasure stolen from their dead ancestors, while the peasant who wanted a cattle trough, or the mason in need of a door lintel, went unrebuked and carried off what thing suited him. Not even the halo of Christian romance could save the Alyscamps. The

legend is well known. St Trefume, man or myth,
summoned the bishops of Gaul and Provence to the
consecration of this burial-ground. When they were
assembled and the rite was to be performed, each one
shrank from taking on himself so high an office ; then
Christ appeared in their midst and made the sign of
the cross over the sleeping-place of the pagan dead.
Out of the countless stories of the meeting of the new
faith and the old—stories too often of a nascent or an
expiring fanaticism, there is not one which breathes a
gentler spirit. It was long believed, that the devil
had little power with the dead that lay in Arles.
Hence the multitude of sepulchres which Dante saw
ove 'l Rodano stagna. Princes and archbishops and
an innumerable host of minor folks left instructions
that they might be buried in the Alyscamps. A
simple mode of transport was adopted by the population of the higher Rhone valley. The body, bound
to a raft or bier, was committed to the current of the
river, with a sum of money called the "drue de
mourtalage" attached to it. These silent travellers
always reached their destination in safety, persons
appointed to the task being in readiness to receive
them. The sea water washed the limits of the
cemetery in the days of the Greeks, who looked
across the dark, calm surface of the immense lagune
and thought of dying as of embarkation upon a
voyage—not the last voyage of the body down the
river of life, but the first voyage of the soul over the
sea of death—and they wished their dead εὔπλοι.

The Greek traces that exist in the living people of
Provence are few, but distinct. There is, in the first
place, the type of beauty particularly associated with

the women of Arles. As a rule, the Provençal woman
is not beautiful ; nor is she very willing to admit that
her Arlesian sisters are one whit more beautiful than
she. The secret of their fame is interpreted by her in
the stereotyped remark, " C'est la coiffe ! " But the
coif of Arles, picturesque though it is in its stern
simplicity, could not change an ugly face into a
pretty one, and the wearers of it are well entitled to
the honour they claim as their birthright. Scarcely
due attention has been paid to the good looks of the
older and even of the aged women ; I have not seen
their equals save among a race of quite another type,
the Teutonic amazons of the Val Mastalone. In
countries where the sun is fire, if youth does not
always mean beauty, beauty means almost always
youth. M. Lenthéric thinks that he detects a second
clear trace of the Greeks in the horn wrestling practised all over the dried-up lagune which the fork of
the Rhone below Arles forms into an island. Astride
of their wild white steeds, the horsemen drive one of
the superb black bulls of the Camargue towards a
group of young men on foot, who, catching him by
his horns, wrestle with him till he is forced to bend
the knee and bite the dust. The amusement is dangerous, but it is not brutal. The horses escape unhurt,
so does the bull ; the risk is for the men alone, and it
is a risk voluntarily and eagerly run. So popular is
the sport that it is difficult to prevent children from
joining in it. In Thessaly it was called κεράτισις, and
the bull in the act of submission is represented on a
large number of Massaliote and other coins.

Marseilles, which has lost the art and the type of
Greece, has kept the Greek temperament. It is no

more French than Naples is Italian: both are Greek
towns, though the characteristics that prove them
such have been somewhat differentiated by unlike
external conditions. Still they have points in common which are many and strong. Marsalia can match
in *émeutes* the proverbial *quattordici rebellioni* of "loyal"
Parthenope; and quickness of intelligence, love of display, mobility of feeling, together with an astounding
vitality, belong as much to Marseillais as to Neapolitan. The people of Marseilles, the most thriftless in
France, have thriven three thousand years, and are
thriving now, in spite of the readiness of each small
middle-class family to lay out a half-year's savings on
a breakfast at Roubion's; in spite of the alacrity with
which each working man sacrifices a week's wages in
order to "demonstrate" in favour of, or still better
against, no matter whom or what. Nowhere is there
a more overweening local pride. "Paris," say the
Marseillais, "would be a fine town if it had our *Can-
nebière.*" Nowhere, as has been made lamentably
plain, are the hatreds of race and caste and politics
more fierce or more ruthless. Even with her own
citizens Marseilles is stern; only after protest does
she grant a monument to Adolphe Thiers—himself
just a Greek Massaliote thrown into the French political arena. There is reason to think that Greek was
a spoken tongue at Marseilles at least as late as the
sixth century A.D. The Sanjanen, the fisherman of
St John's Quarter, has still a whole vocabulary of
purely Greek terms incidental to his calling. The
Greek character of the speech of the Marseillais sailors
was noticed by the Abbé Papon, who attributed to
the same source the peculiar prosody and intonation

of the street cries of Marseilles. The Provençal historian remarks, with an acuteness rare in the age in
which he wrote (the early part of the last century),
"I draw my examples from the people, because it is
with them that we must seek the precious remains of
ancient manners and usages. Amongst the great,
amongst people of the world, one sees only the imprint of fashion, and fashion never stands still."

The Sanjanens are credited with the authorship of
this cynical little song :

> Fisher, fishing in the sea,
> Fish my mistress up for me.
>
> Fish her up before she drowns,
> Thou shalt have four hundred crowns.
>
> Fish her for me dead and cold,
> Thou shalt have my all in gold.

The romantic ballads of Provence are of an importance which demands, properly speaking, a separate
study. Provence was, beyond a doubt, one of the
main sources of the ballad literature of France, Spain,
and Italy. That certain still existing Provençal ballads passed over into Piedmont as early as the thirteenth century is the opinion of Count Nigra, the
Italian diplomatist, not the least of whose distinguished services to his country has been the support
he was one of the first to give to the cause of popular
research. In all these songs the plot goes for everything, the poetry for little or nothing; I shall therefore best economise my space by giving a rough
outline of the stories of two or three of them.
"Fluranço" is a characteristic specimen. Fluranço,
"la flour d'aquest pays," was married when she
was a little thing, and her husband at once

went away to the wars. Monday they were wed, Tuesday he was gone. At the end of seven years the knight comes back, knocks at the door, and asks for Fluranço. His mother says that she is no longer here; they sent her to fetch water, and the Moors, the Saracen Moors, carried her off. "Where did they take her to?" "They took her a hundred leagues away." The knight makes a ship of gold and silver; he sails and sails without seeing aught but the washerwomen washing fine linen. At last he asks of them : " Tell me whose tower is that, and to whom that castle belongs." "It is the castle of the Saracen Moor." "How can I get into it?" " Dress yourself as a poor pilgrim, and ask alms in Christ's name." In this way he gains admittance, and Fluranço (she it is) bids the servant set the table for the "poor pilgrim." When the knight is seated at table, Fluranço begins to laugh. "What are you laughing at, Madamo?" She confesses that she knows who he is. They collect a quantity of fine gold ; then they go the stable, and she mounts the russet horse and he mounts the grey. Just as they are crossing the bridge the Moor sees them. " Seven years," he cries, " I have clothed thee in fine damask, seven years I have given thee morocco shoes, seven years I have laid thee in fine linen, seven years I have kept thee—for one of my sons!" The carelessness or cruelty of a stepmother (the head-wife of Asiatic tales) is a prolific central idea in Provençal romance. While the husband was engaged in distant adventures—tournaments, feudal wars, or crusading expeditions—the wife, who was often little more than a child, remained at the mercy of the occasionally unamiable dowager who ruled the masterless *château.*

The case of cruelty is exemplified in the story of Guilhem de Beauvoire, who has to leave his child-wife five weeks after marriage. "I counsel you, mother," he says as he sets out, "to put her to do no kind of work: neither to fetch water, nor to spin, nor yet to knead bread. Send her to mass, and give her good dinners, and let her go out walking with other ladies." At the end of five weeks the mother put the young wife to keep swine. The swine girl went up to the mountain top and sang and sang. Guilhem de Beauvoire, who was beyond the sea, said to his page, "Does it not seem as though my wife were singing?" He travels at all speed over mountain and sea till he comes to his home, where no man knows him. On the way he meets the swine girl, and from her he hears that she has to eat only that which is rejected of the swine. At the house he is welcomed as an honoured guest; supper is laid for him, and he asks that the swine girl whom he has seen may come and sup with him. When she sits down beside him the swine girl bursts into tears. "Why do you weep, swine girl?" "For seven years I have not supped at table!" Then in the bitterness of yet another out--rage to which the vile woman subjects her, she cries aloud, "Oh! Guilhem de Beauvoire, who art beyond the sea, God help thee! Verily thy cruel mother has abandoned me!" Secretly Guilhem tells her who he is, and in proof of it shows her the ring she gave him. In the morning the mother calls the swine girl to go after her pigs. "If you were not my mother," says Guilhem, "I would have you hung; as you are my mother, I will wall you up between two walls."

The antiquity of the ballads of *Fluranco* and

Guilhem de Beauvoire is shown by the fact that they plainly belong to a time when such work as fetching water or making bread was regarded as amongst the likely employments of noble ladies—though, from excess of indulgence, Guilhem did not wish his wife to be set even to these light tasks. A ballad, probably of about the same date, treats the case of a man who, through the weakness which is the cause of half the crimes, becomes the agent of his mother's guilt. The tragedy is unfolded with almost the sublime laconicism of the *Divina Commedia*. Françoiso was married when she was so young that she did not know how to do the service, and the cruel mother was always saying to her son that Françoiso must die. One day, after the young wife had laid the table, and had set thereon the wine and the bread, and the fresh water, her husband said to her, "My Françoiso, is there not anyone, no friend, who shall protect thy life?" "I have my mother and my father, and you, who are my husband, very well will you protect my life." Then, as they sit at meat, he takes a knife and kills her; and he lifts her in his arms and kisses her, and lays her under the flower of the jessamine, and he goes to his mother and says, "My mother, your greatest wish is fulfilled : I have killed Françoiso."

The genuine Provençal does not shrink from violence. Old inhabitants still tell tales of the savage brigandage of the Estérel, of the horrors of the *Terreur blanche.* Mild manners and social amenities have never been characteristic of fair Provence. Even now the peasant cannot disentangle his thoughts without a volley of oaths—harmless indeed, for the most part (except those which are borrowed from the *franciots*), but in sound terrific. Yet if it be true that the character. of a nation is asserted in its songs, it must be owned that the songs of Provence speak favourably for the Provençal people. They say that they are a people who have a steady and abiding sympathy with honest men and virtuous women. They say further that rough and ruthless though they may be when their blood is stirred, yet have they a pitiful heart. The Provençal singer is slow to utterly condemn ; he grasps the saving inconsistencies of human nature ; he makes the murderer lay his victim "souto lou flour dou jaussemin :" under the white jessamine flower, cherished beyond all flowers in Provence, which has a strange passion for white things—white horses, white dogs, white sheep, white doves, and the fair white hand of woman. Many songs deal directly with almsgivings, the ritual of pity. To no part of the Bible is there more frequent reference than to the parable of the rich man and Lazarus ; no neocatholic legend has been more gladly accepted than the story in which some tattered beggar proves to be Christ—a story, by the by, that holds in it the essence of the Christian faith. If a Greek saw a beautiful unknown youth playing his pipe beside some babbling stream, he believed him to be a god ; the Christian of the early ages recognised Christ in each mendicant in loathsome rags, in each leper succoured at the risk of mortal infection.·

The Provençal tongue is not a mixture (as is too often said) of Italian and French ; nor is physical Provence a less fair Italy or a fairer France. A land

Q

wildly convulsed in its storms, mysteriously breathless in its calms; a garden here, a desert there; a
land of translucent inlets and red porphyry hills;
before all, a land of the illimitable grey of olive
and limestone—this is Provence. Anyone finding
himself of a sudden where the Provençal olives
raise their dwarf heads with a weary look of eternity
to the rainless heaven, would say that the dominant
feature in the landscape was its exceeding seriousness. Sometimes on the coast the prevailing note
changes from grey to blue; the blanched rocks catch
the colour of the sea, and not the sky only, but dry
fine air close around seems of a blueness so intense
as to make the senses swim. Better suited to a
Nature thus made up of crude discords and subtle
harmonies is the old Provençal speech, howsoever
corrupt, than the exquisite French of Parisian *salons.*
But the language goes and the songs go too. Damase
Arbaud relates how, when he went on a long journey
to speak with a man reported to have cognisance of
much traditional matter, he met, issuing from the
house door, not the man, but his coffin. The fact is
typical; the old order of things passes away : *nouastei
diou se'n van.*

THE WHITE PATERNOSTER.

IN a paper published under the head of "Chaucer's Night Spell" in the Folk-lore Record (part i. p. 145), Mr Thoms drew attention to four lines spoken by the carpenter in Chaucer's *Miller's Tale :*

> Lord Jhesu Crist, and seynte Benedyht
> Blesse this hous from every wikked wight,
> Fro nyghtes verray, the White Paternostre
> When wonestow now, seynte Petres soster.

("Verray" is commonly supposed to mean night-mare, but Mr Thoms referred it to "Werra," a Sclavonic deity.)

Mention of the White Paternoster occurs again in White's *Way to the True Church* (1624) :

> White Paternoster, Saint Peter's brother,
> What hast i' th t'one hand? white booke leaves,
> What hast i' th t'other hand? heaven gate keyes.
> Open heaven gates, and streike (shut) hell gates :
> And let every crysome child creepe to its own mother.
> > White Paternoster, Amen.

A reading of the formula is preserved in the *Enchiridion Papæ Leonis*, a book translated into French soon after its first appearance in Latin at Rome in 1502 :

Au soir, m'allant coucher, je trouvis trois anges à mon lit couchés, un aux pieds, deux au chevet, la bonne Vierge Marie du milieu, qui me dit que je me couchis, que rien ne doutis. Le bon Dieu est mon Père, la bonne Vierge est ma mère, les trois vierges sont mes sœurs. La chemise où Dieu fut né, mon corps en est enveloppé ; la croix Sainte Marguerite à ma poitrine est écrite ; madame d'en va sur les champs à Dieu pleurant, rencontrit Monsieur Saint Jean. Monsieur Saint Jean, d'où venez vous ? Je viens d' *Ave Salus.* Vous n'avez pas vu le bon Dieu ; si est, il est dans l'arbre de la croix, les pieds pendans, les mains clouans, un petit chapeau d'épine blanche sur la tête.

Qui la dira trois fois au soir, trois fois au matin, gagnera le Paradis à la fin.

Curious as are the above citations, they only go a little way towards filling up the blanks in the history of this waif from the fabric of early Christian popular lore. A search of some years has yielded evidence that the White Paternoster is still a part of the living traditional matter of at least five European countries. Most persons are familiar with the English version which runs thus :

> Four corners to my bed,
> Four angels round my head,
> One to watch, one to pray,
> And two to bear my soul away.

A second English variant was set on record by Aubrey, and may also be read in Ady's " Candle in the Dark " (1655) :

> Matthew, Mark, Luke, John,
> Bless the bed that I lye on ;
> And blessed guardian angel keep
> Me safe from danger while I sleep.

Halliwell suggests that the two last lines were imitate from the following in Bishop Ken's Evening Hymn :

> Let my blest guardian, while I sleep,
> His watchful station near me keep.

But if there was any imitation in the case, it was the bishop who copied from the folk-rhymer, not the folk-rhymer from the bishop.

The thought of the coming of death in sleep, is expressed in a prayer that may be sometimes seen inscribed at the head and foot of the bed in Norwegian homesteads :

HEAD.

Here is my bed and sleeping place ;
God, let me sleep in peace
And blithe open my eyes
And go to work.

FOOT.

Go into thy bed, take thee a slumber,
Reflect now on the last hour ;
Reflect now,
That thou mayest take thy last slumber.

Analogous in spirit is a quatrain that has been known to me since childhood, but which I do not remember to have seen in print :

I lay me down to rest me,
And pray the Lord to bless me.
If I should sleep no more to wake
I pray the Lord my soul to take.

The *Petite Patenôtre Blanche* lingers in France in a variety of shapes. One version was written down as late as 1872 from the mouth of an old woman named Cathérine Bastien, an inhabitant of the department of the Loire. It was afterwards communicated to *Mélusine*.

Jésu m'endort,
Si je trépasse, mande mon corps,
Si je trépasse, mande mon âme,

> Si je vis, mande mon esprit.
> (Je) prends les anges pour mes amis,
>   Le bon Dieu pour mon père,
>   La Sainte Vierge pour ma mère,
>   Saint Louis de Gonzague,
>   Aux quatre coins de ma chambre,
>   Aux quatre coins be mon lit ;
>   Preservez moi de l'ennemi,
>   Seigneur, a l'heure de ma mort.

Quenot, in his *Statistique de la Charante* (1818), gives the subjoined :

> Dieu l'a faite, je la dit ;
> J'ai trouvé quatre anges couchés dans mon lit ;
>   Deux à la tête, deux aux pieds,
>   Et le bon Dieu aux milieu.
>   De quoi puis-je avoir peur ?
>   Le bon Dieu est mon père,
>   La Vierge ma mère,
>   Les saints mes frères,
>   Les saints mes sœurs ;
>   Le bon Dieu m'a dit :
>   Lève-toi, couche-toi,
> Ne crains rien ; le feu, l'orage, et la tempête
>   Ne peuvent rien contre toi.
> Saint Jean, Saint Marc, Saint Luc, et St Matthieu,
>   Qui mettez les âmes en repos,
>   Mettez-y la mienne si Dieu veut.

In Provence many a worthy country woman repeats each night this *preiro doou soir :*—

> Au liech de Diou
> Me couche iou,
> Sept anges n'en trouve iou,
>   Tres es peds,
>   Quatre au capet (caput—head) ;
> La Buoeno Mero es au mitan
> Uno roso blanco à la man.

The white rose borne by the Good Mother is a pretty and characteristic interpolation peculiar to flower-loving Provence. In the conclusion of the prayer the *Boueno Mero* tells whosoever recites it to have no fear of dog or wolf, or wandering storm or running water, or shining fire, or any evil folk. M. Damase Arbaud got together a number of other devotional fragments that may be regarded as offshoots from the parent stem. St Joseph, "Nourricier de Diou," is asked to preserve the supplicant from sudden death, "et de l'infer et de ses flammos." St Ann, "mero-grand de Jésus Christ," is prayed to teach the way to Paradise. To St Denis a very practical petition is addressed :

> Grand Sant Danis de Franço,
> · Gardetz me moun bouen sens, ma boueno remembranço.

Another verse points distinctly to a desire for protection against witchcraft. The Provençals, by the bye, are of opinion that the *Angelus* was instituted to scare away any ill-conditioned spirits that might be tempted out by the approach of night.

In Germany the guardian saints are dispensed with, but the angels are retained in force. I am indebted to Mr C. G. Leland for a translation of the most popular German even-song :

> Fourteen angels in a band
> Every night around me stand.
> Two to my left hand,
> Two to my right,
> Who watch me ever
> · By day and night.
> Two at my head,
> Two at my feet,
> To guard my slumber
> Soft and sweet ;

> Two to wake me
>   At break of day,
> When night and darkness
>   Pass away ;
> Two to cover me
>   Warm and nice,
> And two to lead me
>   To Paradise.

Passing on to Italy we find an embarrassing abundance of folk-prayers framed after the self-same model.
The repose of the Venetian is under the charge of the
Perfect Angel, the Angel of God, St Bartholomew, the
Blessed Mother, St Elizabeth, the Four Evangelists,
and St John the Baptist. Venetian children are
taught to say: "I go to bed, I know not if I shall
arise. Thou, Lord, who knowest, keep good watch
over me. Before my soul separates from my body,
give me help and good comfort. In the name of the
Father, the Son, and the Holy Ghost, so be it. Bless
my heart and my soul!" The Venetians also have
a "Paternoster pichenin," and a "Paternoster grande,"
both of which are, in their existing form, little else
than nonsense. The native of the Marches goes to
his rest accompanied by our Lord, the Madonna, the
Four Evangelists, *l'Angelo perfetto*, four greater angels,
and three others—one at the foot, one at the head,
one in the middle. The Tuscan, like the German,
has only angels around him : of these he has seven—
one at the head, one at the foot, two at the sides, one
to cover him, one to watch him, and one to bear him
to Paradise. The Sicilian says : "I lay me down in
this bed, with Jesus on my breast. I sleep and he
watches. In this bed where I am laid, five saints I

find : two at the head, two at the feet, in the middle
is St Michael."

Perhaps the best expression of the belief in the
divine guardians of sleep is that given to it by an
ancient Sardinian poet :—

Su letto meo est de battor cantones,
Et battor anghelos si bie ponen ;
Duos in pes, et duos in cabitta,
Nostra Segnora a costazu m'ista.
E a me narat : Dormi e reposa,
No hapas paura de mala cosa,
No hapas paura de mala fine.
S' Anghelu Serafine,
S' Anghelu Biancu,
S' Ispiridu Santu,
Sa Vigine Maria,
Tote siant in cumpagnia mea.
Anghelu de Deu,
Custodio meo,
Custa nott' illuminame !
Guarda e difende a me
Ca eo mi incommando a tie.

My bed has four corners and four angels standing by it. Two
at the foot and two at the head ; our Lady is beside me. And
to me she says, " Sleep and repose ; have no fear of evil things ;
have no fear of an evil end." The angel Serafine, the angel
Blanche, the Holy Spirit, the Virgin Mary—all are here to keep
me company. Angel of God, thou my guardian, illuminate me
this night. Watch and defend me; for I commend myself to
thee.

A Spanish verse, so near to this that it would be
needless to give it a separate translation, was sent by
a friend who at that time was in the Royal College
of Santa Ysabel at Madrid :

Quatro pirondelitas
Tiene mi cama ;
Quatro angelitos
Me la acompaña.
La madre de dios
Esta enmedio,
Dicendome :
Duerme y reposa,
Que no te sucedera
Ninguna mala cosa.

Amen.

In harmony with the leading idea of the White
Paternoster, the recumbent figures of the Archbishops
in Canterbury Cathedral have angels kneeling at each
corner of their altar tombs. It is worth remarking,
too, how certain English lettered compositions have
become truly popular through the fact of their introducing the same idea. A former Dean of Canterbury
once asked an old woman, who lived alone without
chick or child, whether she said her prayers ? "Oh!
yes," was the reply, "I say every night of my life,

"Hush, my babe, lie still in slumber,
Holy angels guard thy bed !"

The White Paternoster itself, in the form of "Matthew,
Mark, Luke, John," was, till lately, a not uncommon
evening prayer in the agricultural parts of Kent. At
present the orthodox night and morning prayers of
the people in Catholic countries are the Lord's
Prayer, *Credo* and *Ave Maria*, but to these, as has
been seen, the White Paternoster is often added, and
at the date of the Reformation — when the "Hail
Mary" had scarcely come into general use—it is
probable that it was rarely omitted. Prayers that
partake of the nature of charms, have always been

popular, and people have ever indulged in odd, little roundabout devices to increase the efficacy of even the most sacred words. Boccaccio, for instance, speaks of "the Paternoster of San Giuliano," which seems to have been a Paternoster said for the repose of the souls of the father and mother of St Julian, in gratitude for which attention, the Saint was bound to give a good night's lodging. It remains to be asked, why the White Paternoster is called white? In the actual state of our knowledge, the reason is not apparent; but possibly the term is to be taken simply in an apologetic sense, as when applied to a stated form of dealing with the supernatural. White charms had a recognised place in popular extra-belief. It was sweet to be able to compel the invisible powers to do what you would, and yet to feel secure from uncomfortable consequences. Of course, in such a case, the thing willed must be of an innocent nature. The Breton who begs vengeance of St Yves, knows tolerably well that what he is doing is very black indeed, even though the saint were ten times a saint. Topsy-turvy as may be his moral perceptions, he would not call this procedure a "white charm." He has, however, white charms of his own, one of which was described with great spirit by Auguste Brizeux, the Breton poet who wove many of the wild superstitions of his country into picturesque verse. Brizeux' poems are not very well known either in France or out of it, but they should be dear to students of folk-lore. The following is a version of " La Poussière Sainte : "

> Sweeping an ancient chapel through the night
> (A ruin now), built 'neath a rocky height,
> The aged Coulm's old wife was muttering,
> As if some secret strange abroad to fling.

" I brave, thee tempest, and will do alone
What by my grand-dame in her youth was done,
When at her beck (of Leon's land, the pride),
The ocean, lion-headed, curbed its tide.

" Sweep, sweep, my broom, until my charm uprears
A force more strong than sighs, more strong than tears :
Charm loved of heaven, which forces wind and wave,
Though fierce and mad, our children's lives to save.

" My angel knows, a Christian true am I.;
No Pagan, nor in league with sorcery.
Hence I dispense to the four winds of God,
To quell their rage, dust from the holy sod.

" Sweep on my broom ; by virtues such as these
Oft through the air I scattered swarms of bees.
And you, old Coulm, to-morrow shall be prest,
You, and my children three, against my breast."

In Enn-Tell's port meanwhile, the pier along
Pressed forward, mute, dismayed, the anxious throng.
And as the billows howl, the lightnings flash,
And skies, lead-black, to earth seem like to dash :
Neighbours clasped hand to hand, and each one prayed,
Through superstition, speechless, while afraid.
Still as the port a sail did safely reach,
All shouting hurried forward to the beach :
" Father, is't you ?   Speak, father is it true ?"
Others, " Hast seen my son ?"   " My brother, you ?"
" Brave man, the truth, whate'er has happened, say,
Am I a widow?"   Night in such dismay
Dragged 'neath a sky without a moon or star.
Thank God !   Meanwhile all boats in safety are,
And every hearth is blazing—all save one,
The Columban's.   But that was void and lone.
But you, Coulm's wife, still battle with the storm,
Fixed on the rocks, your task you still perform,—
You cast, towards east, towards west, and towards the north,
And towards the south, your incantations forth.

The White Paternoster.

" Go, holy dust, 'gainst all the winds that fly.
No sorceress, but a Christian true am I.
By the lamp's light, when I the fire had lit,
In God's own house, my hands collected it.

" You from the statues of the saints I swept,
And silken flags, still on the pillars kept,
And the dark tombs, of those whose sons neglect,
But you, with your white winding-sheet protect.

" Go, holy dust !   To stem the winds depart !
Born beneath Christian feet, thou glorious art :
When from the porch, I to the altar sped,
I seemed upon some heavenly path to tread.

" On you the deacons and the priests have trod,
Pilgrims who live, forefathers 'neath the sod ;
Wood flowers, sweet grains of incense, saintly bones ;
By dawn you will restore my spouse and sons."

She ceased her charm ; and from the chapel then
She saw approach four bare-foot fishermen.
The aged dame in tears fell on her knees
And cried, " I knew they would escape the seas !"
Then cleansing sand and sea-weed o'er them spread,
With happy lips she kissed each cherished head.

THE DIFFUSION OF BALLADS.

I.—Lord Ronald in Italy.

SEVERAL causes have combined to give the professional minstrel a more tenacious hold on life in Italy , than in France or Germany or England. One of them is, that Italian culture has always been less· dependent on education—or what the English poor call "book-learning"—than the culture of those countries.

To this day you may count upon finding a blind ballad-singer in every Italian city. The connection of blindness with popular songs is a noteworthy thing. It is not, perhaps, a great exaggeration to say that, had there been no blind folks in the world, there would have been few ballads. Who knows, indeed, but that Homer would not have earned his bread by bread-making instead of by enchanting the children and wise men of all after-ages, had he not been "one who followed a guide"? Every one remembers how it was the singing of a "blinde crowder, with no rougher voice than rude style," that moved the heroic heart of Sidney more than the blare of trumpets. Every one may not know that in the East of Europe and in Armenia, "blinde crowders" still wander from village to village, carrying, wheresoever they go, the

songs of a former day and the news of the latest
hour ; acting, after a fashion, as professors of history
and " special correspondents," and keeping alive the
sentiment of nationality under circumstances in which,
except for their agency, it must almost without a
doubt have expired.

When the Austrians occupied Trebinje in the
Herzegovina, they forbade the playing of the " guzla,"
the little stringed instrument which accompanies the
ballads; but the ballads will not be forgotten. Proscription does not kill a song. What kills it sometimes, if it have a political sense, is the fulfilment of
the hopes it expresses ; then it may die a natural
death. I hunted all over Naples for some one who
could sing a song which every Neapolitan, man and
boy, hummed through the year when the Redshirts
brought freedom : *Camicia rossa, camicia ardente.* It
seemed that there was not one who still knew it.
Just as I was on the point of giving up the search, a
blind man was produced out of a tavern at Posilippo;
a poor creature in threadbare clothes, holding a
wretched violin. He sang the words with spirit and
pathos; he is old, however, and perhaps the knowledge of them will not survive him.

Our present business is not with songs of a national
or local interest, but with those which can hardly be
said to belong to any country in particular. And,
first of all, we have to go back to a certain *Camillo,
detto il Bianchino cieco fiorentino,* who sang ballads at
Verona in the year 1629, and who had printed for
the greater diffusion of his fame a sort of rhymed
advertisement containing the first few lines of some

twenty songs that belonged to his repertory. Last
but one of these samples stands the following :

> " Dov' andastú jersera,
> Figlioul mio ricco, savio e gentil ;
> Dov' andastú jersera?"

!'When I come to look at it," adds Camillo, "this is
too long; it ought to have been the first to be sung"
—alluding, of course, to the song, not to the sample.

Later in the same century, the ballad mentioned
above had the honour of being cited before a more
polite audience than that which was probably in the
habit of listening to the blind Florentine.   On the
24th of September 1656, Canon Lorenzo Panciatichi
reminded his fellow-academicians of the Crusca of
what he called "a fine observation" that had been
made regarding the song :

> " Dov' andastú a cena figlioul mio
> Ricco, savio, e gentile?

The observation (continued the Canon) turned on the
answer the son makes to the mother when she asks
him what his sweetheart gave him for supper.   "She
gave me," says the son, "*un' anguilla arrosto cotta nel
pentolin dell' olio.*"   The idea of a roasted eel cooked
in an oil pipkin offended the academical sense of the
fitness of things ; it had therefore been proposed to
say instead that the eel was hashed :

> " Madonna Madre,
> Il cuore stá male,
> Per un anguilla in guazzetto."

· Had we nothing to guide us beyond these fragments,

there could be no question but that in this Italian
ballad we might safely recognise one of the most
spirited pieces in the whole range of popular literature
—the song of Lord Ronald, otherwise Rowlande, or
Randal, or " Billy, my son :"

" O where hae ye been, Lord Ronald, my son?
O where hae ye been, my handsome young man?"
" I hae been to the wood ; mother, make my bed soon,
For I'm weary wi' hunting, and fain would lie down."

" Where gat ye your dinner, Lord Ronald, my son?
Where gat ye your dinner, my handsome young man?"
" I dined wi' my love ; mother, make my bed soon,
For I'm weary wi' hunting, and fain would lie down."

" What gat ye to dinner, Lord Ronald, my son?
What gat ye to dinner, my handsome young man?"
" I gat eels boil'd in broo ; mother, make my bed soon,
For I'm weary wi' hunting, and fain would lie down."

"And where are your bloodhounds, Lord Ronald, my son?
And where are your bloodhounds, my handsome young man?"
" O they swell'd and they died ; mother, make my bed soon,
For I'm weary wi' hunting, and fain would lie down."

" O I fear ye are poison'd, Lord Ronald, my son !
O I fear ye are poison'd, my handsome young man!"
" O yes, I am poison'd ! mother, make my bed soon,
For I'm sick at the heart, and I fain would lie down."

This version, which I quote from Mr Allingham's
Ballad Book (1864), ends here ; so does that given by
Sir Walter Scott in the *Border Minstrelsy.* There is,
however, another version which goes on :

" What will ye leave to your father, Lord Ronald, my son?
What will ye leave to your father, my handsome young man?"
" Baith my houses and land ; mither, mak' my bed sune
For I'm sick at the heart, and I fain wad lie doun."

R

" What will ye leave to your brither, Lord Ronald, my son?
What will ye leave to your brither, my handsome young man?" '
" My horse and my saddle·; mither, mak' my bed sune,
For I'm sick at the heart, and I fain wad lie doun."

" What will ye leave to your sister, Lord Ronald, my son?
What will ye leave to your sister, my handsome young man?"
" Baith my gold box and rings; mither, mak' my bed sune,
For I'm sick at the heart, and I fain wad lie doun."

" What will ye leave to your true love, Lord Ronald, my son?
What will ye leave to your true love, my handsome young man?"
" The tow and the halter, for to hang on yon tree,
And let her hang there for the poisoning o' me."

Lord Ronald has already been met with, though
somewhat disguised, both in Germany and in Sweden,
but his appearance two hundred and fifty years ago
at Verona has a peculiar interest attached to it. That
England shares most of her songs with the Northern
nations is a fact familiar to all; but, unless I am mistaken, this is almost the first time of discovering a
purely popular British ballad in an Italian dress.

It so happens that to the fragments quoted by
Camillo and the Canon can be added the complete
story as sung at the present date in Tuscany, Venetia,
and Lombardy. Professor d'Ancona has taken pains
to collate the slightly different texts, because few
Italian folk-songs now extant can be traced even as
far back as the seventeenth century. The learned
Professor, whose great antiquarian services are well
known, does not seem to be aware that the song has
currency out of Italy. The best version is one set
down from word of mouth in the district of Como,
and of this I subjoin a literal rendering:

" Where were you yester eve?
My son, beloved, blooming, and gentle bred,
    Where were you yester eve ? "
    " I with my love abode ;
O lady mother, my heart is very sick :
    I with my love abode ;
Alas, alas, that I should have to die."

"What supper gave she you ?
My son beloved, blooming, and gentle bred,
    What supper gave she you ? "
    " I supped on roasted eel ;
O lady mother, my heart is very sick :
    I supped on roasted eel ;
Alas, alas, that I should have to die."

" And did you eat it all ?
My son, beloved, blooming, and gentle bred,
    And did you eat it all ?"
    " Only the half I eat ;
O lady mother, my heart is very sick :
    Only the half I eat ;
Alas, alas, that I should have to die."

" Where went the other half?
My son beloved, blooming, and gentle bred,
    Where went the other half ? "
    " I gave it to the dog ;
O lady mother, my heart is very sick :
    I gave it to the dog ;
Alas, alas, that I should have to die?"

" What did you with the dog ?
My son beloved, blooming, and gentle bred,
    What did you with the dog ?"
    " It died upon the way ;
O lady mother, my heart is very sick :
    It died upon the way ;
Alas, alas, that I should have to die."

" Poisoned it must have been !
My son beloved, blooming, and gentle bred,
   Poisoned it must have been !"
  " Quick for the doctor send ;
O lady mother, my heart is very sick :
   Quick for the doctor send ;
Alas, alas, that I should have to die.

  " Wherefore the doctor call ?
My son beloved, blooming, and gentle bred,
   Wherefore the doctor call ?"
  " That he may visit me ;
O lady mother, my heart is very sick :
   That he may visit me ;
Alas, alas, that I should have to die."

    .   .   .   .   .

  " Quick for the parson send ;
O lady mother, my heart is very sick :
   Quick for the parson send ;
Alas, alas, that I should have to die."

  " Wherefore the parson call ?
My son beloved, blooming, and gentle bred,
   Wherefore the parson call ?"
  " So that I may confess ;
O lady mother, my heart is very sick :
   So that I may confess ;
Alas, alas, that I should have to die."

    .   .   .   .   .

  " Send for the notary;
O lady mother, my heart is very sick :
   Send for the notary;
Alas, alas, that I should have to die."

  " Why call the notary ?
My son beloved, blooming, and gentle bred,
   Why call the notary ?"
  " To make my testament ;
O lady mother, my heart is very sick :
   To make my testament ;
Alas, alas, that I should have to die."

" What to your mother leave ?
My son beloved, blooming, and gentle bred,
  What to your mother leave ?"
  " To her my palace goes ;
O lady mother, my heart is very sick :
  To her my palace goes ;
Alas, alas, that I should have to die."

" What to your brothers leave ?
My son beloved, blooming, and gentle bred,
  What to your brothers leave ?"
  " To them the coach and team ;
O lady mother, my heart is very sick :
  To them the coach and team ;
Alas, alas, that I should have to die."

" What to your sisters leave ?
My son beloved, blooming, and gentle bred,
  What to your sisters leave ?"
  " A dower to marry them ;
O lady mother, my heart is very sick :
  A dower to marry them ;
Alas, alas, that I should have to die."

  " What to your servants leave ?
My son beloved, blooming, and gentle bred,
  What to your servants leave ?"
  " The road to go to Mass ;
O lady mother, my heart is very sick :
  The road to go to Mass ;
Alas, alas, that I should have to die."

  " What leave you to your tomb ?
My son beloved, blooming, and gentle bred,
  What leave you to your tomb ?"
  " Masses seven score and ten ;
O lady mother, my heart is very sick :
  Masses seven score and ten ;
Alas, alas, that I should have to die."

" What leave you to your love ?
My son beloved, blooming, and gentle bred,
What leave you to your love ? "
" The tree to hang her on ;
O lady mother, my heart is very sick :
The tree to hang her on ;
Alas, alas, that I should have to die."

At first sight it would seem that the supreme dramatic element of the English song—the circumstance that the mother does not know, but only suspects, with increasing conviction, the presence of foul play —is weakened in the Lombard ballad by the refrain, " Alas, alas, that I should have to die." But a little more reflection will show that this is essentially of the nature of an *aside*. In many instances the office of the burden in old ballads resembles that of the chorus in a Greek play : it is designed to suggest to the audience a clue to the events enacting which is not possessed by the *dramatis personæ*—at least not by all of them.

In the northern songs, Lord Ronald is a murdered child : a character in which he likewise figures in the Scotch lay of " The Croodlin Doo." This is the Swedish variant :

" Where hast thou been so long, my little daughter ? "
" I have been to Bœnne to see my brother ;
                    Alas ! how I suffer."
" What gave they thee to eat, my little daughter ? "
" Roast eel and pepper, my step-mother.
                    Alas ! how I suffer."
" What didst thou do with the bones, my little daughter ? "
" I threw them to the dogs, my step-mother.
                    Alas ! how I suffer."
" What happened to the dogs, my little daughter ? "
" Their bodies went to pieces, my step-mother.
                    Alas ! how I suffer."

"What dost thou wish for thy father, my little daughter?"
"Good grain in the grange, my step-mother.

Alas! how I suffer."

"What dost thou wish for thy brother, my little daughter?"
"A big ship to sail in, my step-mother.

Alas! how I suffer."

"What dost thou wish for thy sister, my little daughter?"
"Coffers and caskets of gold, my step-mother.

Alas! how I suffer."

"What dost thou wish for thy step-mother, my little daughter?"
"The chains of hell, step-mother.

Alas! how I suffer."

"What dost thou wish for thy nurse, my little daughter?"
"The same hell, my nurse.

Alas! how I suffer."

A point connected with the diffusion of ballads is the extraordinarily wide adoption of certain conventional forms. One of these is the form of testamentary instructions by means of which the plot of a song is worked up to its climax. It reappears in the "Cruel Brother"—which, I suppose, is altogether to be regarded as of the Roland type:

"O what would ye leave to your father, dear?"
With a heigh-ho! and a lily gay.
"The milk-white steed that brought me here,"
As the primrose spreads so sweetly.

"What would ye give to your mother, dear?"
With a heigh-ho! and a lily gay.
"My wedding shift which I do wear,"
As the primrose spreads so sweetly.

"But she must wash it very clean,"
With a heigh-ho! and a lily gay,
"For my heart's blood sticks in every seam,"
As the primrose spreads so sweetly.

"What would ye give to your sister Anne?"
With a heigh-ho! and a lily gay.
" My gay gold ring and my feathered fan,"
As the primrose spreads so sweetly.

" What would ye give to your brother John?"
With a heigh-ho! and a lily gay.
" A rope and a gallows to hang him on!"
As the primrose spreads so sweetly.

"What would ye give to your brother John's wife?"
With a heigh-ho! and a lily gay.
" Grief and sorrow to end her life!"
As the primrose spreads so sweetly.

" What would ye give to your own true lover?"
With a heigh-ho! and a lily gay.
" My dying kiss, and my love for ever!"
As the primrose spreads so sweetly.

The Portuguese ballad of "Helena," which has not much in common with "Lord Roland"—except that it is a story of treachery—is brought into relation with it by its bequests. Helena is a blameless wife whom a cruel mother-in-law first encourages to pay a visit to her parents, and then represents to her husband as having run away from him in his absence. No sooner has he returned from his journey than he rides irate after his wife. When he arrives he is met by the news that a son is born to him, but unappeased he orders the young mother to rise from her bed and follow him. She obeys, saying that in a well-ordered marriage it is the husband who commands; only, before she goes, she kisses her son and bids her mother tell him of these kisses when he grows up. Then her husband takes her to a high mountain, where the agony of death comes upon her. The

husband asks: "To whom leavest thou thy jewels?"
She answers: "To my sister; if thou wilt permit it."
"To whom leavest thou thy cross and the stones of
thy necklace?" "The cross I leave to my mother;
surely she will pray for me; she will not care to
have the stones, thou canst keep them—if to another
thou givest them, better than I, let her adorn herself
with them." "Thy substance, to whom leavest thou?"
"To thee, my husband; God grant it may profit
thee." "To whom leavest thou thy son, that he may
be well brought up?" "To thy mother, and may it
please God that he should make himself loved of
her." "Not to that dog," cries the husband, his eyes
at last opened, "she might well kill him. Leave him
rather to thy mother, who will bring him up well;
she will know how to wash him with her tears, and
she will take the coif from her head to swaddle him."

A strange, wild Roumanian song, translated by Mr
C. F. Keary (*Nineteenth Century*, No. lxviii.), closes
with a list of "gifts" of the same character:

> "But mother, oh mother, say how
> Shall I speak, and what name call him now?"
> "My beloved, my step-son,
> My heart's love, my cherished one."
> "And her, O my mother, what word
> Shall I give her, what name?"
> "My step-daughter, abhorred,
> The whole world's shame."
> "Then, my mother, what shall I take him?
> What gift shall I make him?"
> "A handkerchief fine, little daughter,
> Bread of white wheat for thy loved one to eat,
> And a glass of wine, my daughter."
> "And what shall I take *her*, little mother,

What gift shall I make *her ?*"
"A kerchief of thorns, little daughter ;
A loaf of black bread for her whom he wed,
And a cup of poison, my daugher."

Before parting with "Lord Ronald" it should be noticed that the song clearly travelled in song-shape, not simply as a popular tradition ; and that its different adaptators have been still more faithful to the shape than to the substance. It is not so easy to decide whether the victim was originally a child or a lover, whether the north or the south has preserved the more correct version. Some crime of the middle ages may have been the foundation of the ballad ; on the other hand it is conceivable that it formed part of the enormous accumulation of literary odds and ends brought to Europe from the east, by pilgrims and crusaders. Stories that, as we know them, seem distinctly mediæval, such as Boccaccio's " Falcon," have been traced to India. If a collection were made of the ballads now sung by no more widely extended class than the three thousand ballad singers inscribed in the last census of the North-Western Provinces and Oude, what a priceless boon would not be conferred upon the student of comparative folk-lore ! We cannot arrive at a certainty even in regard to the minor question of whether Lord Ronald made his appearance first in England or in Italy. The English and Italian songs bear a closer affinity to each other than is possessed by either towards the Swedish variant. Supposing the one to be directly derived from the other—a supposition which in this case does not seem improbable—the Italian was most likely the original. There was a steady migration into England of Italian literature, literate and probably also illiterate, from the thirteenth to the sixteenth century, The English ballad-singers may have been as much on the look-out for a new, orally communicated song from foreign parts, as Chaucer was for a poem of Petrarch's or a tale of Boccaccio's.

II.—THE THEFT OF A SHROUD.

The ballad with which we have now to deal has had probably as wide a currency as that of " Lord Ronald." The student of folk-lore recognises at once, in its evident fitness for local adaptation, its simple yet terrifying motive, and the logical march of its events, the elements that give a popular song a free pass among the peoples.

M. Allègre took down from word of mouth and communicated to the late Damase Arbaud a Provençal version, which runs as follows :

> His scarlet cape the Prior donned,   .
>   Ding dong, dong ding dong !
> His scarlet cape the Prior donned,
>   And all the souls in Paradise
>   With joy and triumph fill the skies.

> His sable cape the Prior donned,
>   Ding dong, dong ding dong !
> His sable cape the Prior donned,
>   And all the spirits of the dead
>   Fast tears within the graveyard shed.

> Now, Ringer, to the belfry speed,
>   Ding dong, dong ding dong !
> Now, Ringer, to the belfry speed,
>   Ring loud, to-night thy ringing tolls
>   An office for the dead men's souls.

Ring loud the bell of good St John :
  Ding dong, dong ding dong !
Ring loud the bell of good St John :
    Pray all, for the poor dead ; aye pray,
    Kind folks, for spirits passed away.

Soon as the midnight hour strikes,
  Ding dong, dong ding dong !
Soon as the midnight hour strikes,
    The pale moon sheds around her light,
    And all the graveyard waxeth white.

What seest thou, Ringer, in the close ?
  Ding dong, dong ding dong !
What seest thou, Ringer, in the close ?
    " I see the dead men wake and sit
    Each one by his deserted pit."

Full thousands seven and hundreds five,
  Ding dong, dong ding dong !
Full thousands seven and hundreds five,
    Each on his grave's edge, yawning wide,
    His dead man's wrappings lays aside.

Then leave they their white winding-sheets,
  Ding dong, dong ding dong !
Then leave they their white winding-sheets,
    And walk, accomplishing their doom,
    In sad procession from the tomb.

Full one thousand and hundreds five,
  Ding dong, dong ding dong !
Full one thousand and hundreds five,
    And each one falls upon his knees
    Soon as the holy cross he sees.

Full one thousand and hundreds five,
  Ding dong, dong ding dong !
Full one thousand and hundreds five
    Arrest their footsteps, weeping sore
    When they have reached their children's door.

Full one thousand and hundreds five,
 Ding dong, dong ding dong !
Full one thousand and hundreds five
 · Turn them aside and, listening, stay
 Whene'er they hear some kind soul pray.

Full one thousand and hundreds five,
 Ding dong, dong ding dong !
Full one thousand and hundreds five,
 Who stand apart and groan bereft,
 Seeing for them no friends are left.

But soon as ever the white cock stirs,
 Ding dong, dong ding dong !
But soon as ever the white cock stirs,
 They take again their cerements white,
 And in their hands a torch alight.

But soon as ever the red cock crows,
 Ding dong, dong ding dong !
But soon as ever the red cock crows,
 All sing the Holy Passion song,
 And in procession march along.

But soon as the gilded cock doth shine,
 Ding dong, dong ding dong !
But soon as the gilded cock doth shine,
 Their hands and their two arms they cross,
 And each descends into his foss.

'Tis now the dead men's second night,
 Ding dong, dong ding dong !
Tis now the dead men's second night :
 Peter, go up to ring ; nor dread
 If thou shouldst chance to see the dead.

" The dead, the dead, they fright me not,"
 Ding dong, dong ding dong !
" The dead, the dead, they fright me not,
 —Yet prayers are due for the dead, I ween,
 And due respect should they be seen."

When next the midnight hour strikes,
   Ding dong, dong ding dong !
When next the midnight hour strikes,
    The graves gape wide and ghastly show
    The dead who issue from below.

Three diverse ways they pass along,
   Ding dong, dong ding dong !
Three diverse ways they pass along,
    Nought seen but wan white skeletons
    Weeping, nought heard but sighs and moans.

Down from the belfry Peter came,
   Ding dong, dong ding dong!
Down from the belfry Peter came,
    While still the bell of good St John
    Gave forth its sound : barin, baron.

He carried off a dead man's shroud,
   Ding dong, dong ding dong !
He carried off a dead man's shroud ;
    At once it seemed no longer night,
    The holy close was all alight.

The holy Cross that midmost stands,
   Ding dong, dong ding dong !
The holy Cross that midmost stands
    Grew red as though with blood 'twas dyed,
    And all the altars loudly sighed.

Now, when the dead regained the close,
   Ding dong, dong ding dong !
Now, when the dead regained the close
    —The Holy Passion sung again—
    They passed along in solemn train.

Then he who found his cerements gone,
   Ding dong, dong ding dong !
Then he who found his cerements gone,
    From out the graveyard gazed and signed
    His winding-sheet should be resigned.

But Peter every entrance closed,   .
Ding dong, dong ding dong !
But Peter every entrance closed
With locks and bolts, approach defies,
Then looks at him—but keeps the prize !

He with his arm, and with his hand,
Ding dong, dong ding dong !
He with his arm, and with his hand,
Made signs in vain, two times or three,
And then the belfry entered he.

A noise is mounting up the stair,
Ding dong, dong ding dong !
A noise is mounting up the stair,
The bolts are shattered, and the door
Is burst and dashed upon the floor.

The Ringer trembled with dismay,
Ding dong, dong ding dong !
The Ringer trembled with dismay,
And still the bell of good St John
For ever swung : barin, baron.

At the first stroke of Angelus,
Ding dong, dong ding dong !
At the first stroke of Angelus
The skeleton broke all his bones,
Falling to earth upon the stones.

Peter upon his bed was laid,
Ding dong, dong ding dong !
Peter upon his bed was laid,
Confessed his sin, repenting sore,
Lingered three days, then lived no more.

It will be seen that, in this ballad, which is locally
called " Lou Jour des Mouerts," the officiating priest
assumes red vestments in the morning, and changes
them in the course of the day for black. The vestments appropriate to the evening of All Saints' Day

are still black (it being the Vigil of All Souls'), but in the morning the colour worn is white or gold. An explanation, however, is at hand. The feast of All Saints had its beginning in the dedication of the Roman Pantheon by Boniface IV., in the year 607, to *S. Maria ad Martyres,* and red ornaments were naturally chosen for a day set apart especially to the commemoration of martyrdom. These were only discarded when the feast came to have a more general character, and there is evidence of their retention here and there in French churches till a date as advanced as the fifteenth century. Thus, we gain incidentally some notion of the age of the song.

Not long after giving a first reading to the Provençal ballad of the Shroud-theft, I became convinced of its substantial identity with a poem whose author holds quite another rank to that of the nameless folk-poet. Goethe's "Todten Tanz" tends less to edification than "Lou jour des Mouerts;" nor has it, I venture to think, an equal power. We miss the pathetic picture of the companies of sad ghosts; these kneeling before the wayside crosses; these lingering by their children's thresholds; these listening to the prayers of the pious on their behalf; these others weeping, *en vesent que n'ant plus d'amics.* But the divergence of treatment cannot hide the fact that the two ballads are made out of one tale.

THE DANCE OF DEATH.

The watcher looks down in the dead of the night
  On graves in trim order gleaming ;
The moon steeps the world all around in her light—
  'Tis clear as if noon were beaming.

One grave gaped apart, then another began ;
Here forth steps a woman, and there steps a man,
   White winding-sheets trailing behind them.

On sport they determine, nor pause they for long,
   All feel for the measure advancing ;
The rich and the poor, the old and the young ;
   But winding-sheets hinder the dancing.
Since sense of decorum no longer impedes,
They hasten to shake themselves free of their weeds,
   And tombstones are quickly beshrouded.

Then legs kick about and are lifted in air,
   Strange gesture and antic repeating ;
The bones crack and rattle, and crash here and there,
   As if to keep time they were beating.
The sight fills the watcher with mirth 'stead of fear,
And the sly one, the Tempter, speaks low in his ear :
   " Now go and a winding-sheet plunder ! "

The hint he soon followed, the deed it was done,
   Then behind the church-door he sought shelter ;
The moon in her splendour unceasingly shone,
   And still dance the dead helter-skelter.
At last, one by one, they all cease from the play,
And, wrapt in the winding-sheets, hasten away,
   Beneath the turf silently sinking.

One only still staggers and stumbles along,
   The grave edges groping and feeling ;
'Tis no brother ghost who has done him the wrong ;
   Now his scent shows the place of concealing.
The church-door he shakes, but his strength is represt ;
'Tis well for the watcher the portals are blest
   By crosses resplendent protected.

His shirt he must have, upon this he is bent,
   No time has he now for reflection ;
Each sculpture of Gothic some holding has lent,
   He scales and he climbs each projection.
Dread vengeance o'ertakes him, 'tis up with the spy !
From arch unto arch draws the skeleton nigh,
   Like lengthy-legged horrible spider.

S

The watcher turns pale, and he trembles full sore,
  The shroud to return he beseeches ;
. But a claw (it is done, he is living no more),
  A claw to the shroud barely reaches.
The moonlight grows faint; it strikes one by the clock ;
A thunderclap burst with a terrible shock ;
  To earth falls the skeleton shattered.

It needed but small penetration to guess that Goethe
had neither seen nor heard of the Provençal song. It
seemed, therefore, certain that a version of the Shroud-
theft must exist in Germany, or near it—an inference
I found to be correct on consulting that excellent
work, Goethe's *Gedichte erläutert von Heinrich Viehoff*
(Stuttgart, 1870). So far as the title and the incident
of the dancing are concerned, Goethe apparently had
recourse to a popular story given in Appel's *Book of
Spectres*, where it is related how, when the guards of
the tower looked out at midnight, they saw Master
Willibert rise from his grave in the moonshine, seat
himself on a high tombstone, and begin to perform
on his pocket pipe. Then several other tombs opened,
and the dead came forth and danced cheerily over
the mounds of the graves. The white shrouds flut-
tered round their dried-up limbs, and their bones
clattered and shook till the clock struck one, when
each returned into his narrow house, and the piper
put his pipe under his arm and followed their example.
The part of the ballad which has to do directly with
the Shroud-theft is based upon oral traditions collected by the poet during his sojourn at Teplitz, in
Bohemia, in the summer of 1813. Viehoff has ascertained that there are also traces of the legend in
Silesia, Moravia, and Tyrol. In these countries the

story would seem to be oftenest told in prose; but
Viehoff prints a rhymed rendering of the variant
localised in Tyrol, where the events are supposed to
have occurred at the village of Burgeis:

> The twelve night strokes have ceased to sound,
> The watchman of Burgeis looks around,
>   The country all in moonlight sleeps;
> Standing the belfry tower beneath
> The tombstones, with their wreaths of death,
>   The wan moon's ghastly pallor steeps.
>
> " Does the young mother in child-birth dead
> Rise in her shroud from her lonely bed,
>   For the sake of the child she has left behind ?
> To mock them (they say) makes the dead ones grieve,
> Let's see if I cannot her work relieve,
>   Or she no end to her toil may find."
>
> So spake he, when something, with movement slow,
> Stirs in the deep-dug grave below,
>   And in its trailing shroud comes out ;
> And the little garments that infants have
> It hangs and stretches on gate and grave,
>   On rail and trellis, the yard about.
>
> The rest of the buried in sleep repose,
> That nothing of waking or trouble knows,
>   For the woman the sleep of the grave is killed ;
> Her leaden sleep, each midnight hour,
> Flees, and her limbs regain their power,
>   And she hastes as to tend her new-born child.
>
> All with rash spite the watchman views,
> And with cruel laughter the form pursues,
>   As he leans from the belfrey's narrow height,
> And in sinful scorn on the tower rails
> Linen and sheets and bands he trails,
>   Mocking her acts in the moon's wan light.

Lo, with swift steps, foreboding doom,
From the churchyard's edge o'er grave and tomb
   The ghost to the tower wends its ways ;
And climbs and glides, ne'er fearing fall,
Up by the ledges, the lofty wall,
   Fixing the sinner with fearful gaze.

The watcher grows pale, and with hasty hand,
Tears from the tower the shrouds and bands ;
   Vainly !   That threatening grin draws nigh !
With a trembling hand he tolls the hour,
And the skeleton down from the belfry-tower,
   Shattered and crumbling, falls from high.

This story overlaps the great cycle of popular
belief which treats of the help given by a dead
mother to her bereaved child.   They say in Germany, when the sheets are ruffled in the bed of a
motherless infant, that the mother has lain beside it
and suckled it.   Kindred superstitions stretch through
the world.   The sin of the Burgeis watchman is that
of heartless malice, but it stops short of actual robbery,
which is perhaps the reason why he escapes with his
life, having the presence of mind to toll forth the first
hour of day, when—

   Whether in sea or fire, in earth or air,
   The extravagant and erring spirit hies
   To his confine.

The prose legends which bear upon one or another
point in the Shroud-theft, are both numerous and
important.   Joseph Macé, a cabin-boy of Saint Cast,
in Upper Brittany, related the following to the able
collector of Breton folk-lore, M. Paul Sébillot.   There
was a young man who went to see a young girl ; his
parents begged him not to go again to her, but he
replied : " Mind your own business and leave me to

mind mine." One evening he invited two or three of his comrades to accompany him, and as they passed by a stile they saw a woman standing there, dressed all in white. "I'll take off her coif," said the youth. "No," said the others, "let her alone." But he went straight up to her and carried off her coif—there only remained the little skullcap underneath, but he did not see her face. He went with the others to his sweetheart, and showed her the coif. ."Ah!" said he, "as I came here I met a woman all in white, and I carried off her coif." "Give me the coif," replied his sweetheart; "I will put it away in my wardrobe." Next evening he started again to see the girl, and on reaching the stile he saw a woman in white like the one of the day before, but this one had no head. "Dear me," he said to himself, "it is the same as yesterday; still I did not think I had pulled off her head." When he went in to his sweetheart, she said, "I wore to-day the coif you gave me; you can't think how nice I look in it!" "Give it back to me, I beg of you," said the young man. She gave it back, and when he got home he told his mother the whole story. "Ah, my poor lad," she said, "you have kept sorry company. I told you some ill would befall you." He went to bed, but in the night his mother heard sighs coming from the bed of her son. She woke her good man and said, "Listen; one would say someone was moaning." She went to her son's bed and found him bathed in sweat. "What is the matter with you?" she asked. "Ah, my mother, I had a weight of more than three hundred pounds on my body; it stifled me, I could bear it no longer." Next day the youth went to confession, and he told all to the curate. "My

boy," said the priest, "the person you saw was a
woman who came from the grave to do penance; it
was your dead sister." "What can I do?" asked the
young man. "You must go and take her back her
coif, and set it on the neck on the side to which it
leans." "Ah! sir, I should never dare, I should die
of fright!" Still he went that evening to the stile,
where he saw the woman who was dressed in white
and had no head; he set the coif just on the side
the neck leant to; all at once a head showed itself
inside it, and a voice said, "Ah! my brother, you
hindered me from doing penance; to-morrow you will
come and help me to finish it." The young man went
back to bed, but next day he did not get up when the
others did, and when they went to his bed he was
dead.

At Saint Suliac a young man saw three young girls
kneeling in the cemetery. He took the cap off one of
them, saying that he would not give it back till she
came to embrace him. Next day, instead of the cap
he found a death's head. At midnight he carried it
back, holding in his arms a new-born infant. The
death's head became once more a cap, the woman
disappeared, and the young man, thanks to the child,
suffered no harm.

In a third Breton legend a child commits the theft,
but without any consciousness of wrong-doing. A
little girl picked up a small bone in a graveyard and
took it away to amuse herself with it. In the evening,
when she returned home, she heard a voice saying:

> Give me back my bone!
> Give me back my bone!

"What's that?" asked the mother.

"Perhaps it is because of a bone I picked up in the cemetery."

"Well, it must be given back."

The little girl opened the door and threw the bone into the court, but the voice went on saying :

> Give me back my bone !
> Give me back my bone !

"Maybe it is the bone of a dead man ; take the candle, go into the court and give it back to him."

It is most unfortunate to possess a human bone, even by accident. It establishes unholy relations between the possessor and the spirit world which render him defenceless against spells and enchantments. A late chaplain to the forces in Mauritius told me that the witches, or rather wizards, who have it all their own way in that island, contrived, after a course of preparatory persecution, to surreptitiously introduce into his house the little finger of a child. He could not think what to do with it: at last he consulted a friend, a Catholic priest, who advised him to burn it, which was done. We all know "the finger of birth-strangled babe" in the witches' cauldron in *Macbeth;* but it is somewhat surprising to find a similar "charm for powerful trouble" in current use in a British colony.

A Corsican legend, reported by M. Frédéric Ortoli, should have a place here. On the Day of the Dead a certain man had to go to Sartena to sell chestnuts. Overnight he filled his panniers, so as to be ready to start with the first gleam of daylight. The only thing left for him to do was to go and get his horse, which

was out at pasture not far from the village. So he
went to bed, but hardly had he lain down when a
fearful storm broke over the house.   Cries and curses
echoed all round : "Cursed be thou! cursed be thy
wife! cursed be thy children!"   The wretched man
grew cold with fear ; he got quite close to his wife, who
asked : "Did you put the water outside the window?"
"Sangu di Cristu!" cried the man, "I forgot!"   He
rose at once to put vessels filled with water on the
balcony.   The dead—whose vigil it was—were in fact
come, and finding no water either to drink or to
wash and purify their sins in, they had made a frightful noise and hurled maledictions against him who
had forgotten their wants.   The poor man went to
bed again, but the storm continued, though the
cursing and blaspheming had ceased.

Towards three in the morning the man wished to
get up.   "Stay," said his wife, "do not go."

"No, go I must."

"The weather is so bad, the wind so high; some
mischief will come to you."

"Never mind ; keep me no more."

And so saying the husband went out to find his
horse.   He had barely reached the crossway when by
the path from Giufari, he saw, marching towards
him, the *squadra d'Arrozza*—the Dead Battalion.
Each dead man held a taper, and chanted the
Miserere.

The poor peasant was as if petrified ; his blood
stood still in his veins, and he could not utter a word.
Meanwhile the troop surrounded him, and he who
was at its head offered him the taper he was carrying.
"Take hold!" he said, and the poor wretch took it.

Then the most dreadful groans, and cries were heard. "Woe! woe! woe! Be accursed, be accursed, be accursed."

The villager soon came to himself, but oh! horrid sight! in his hand was the arm of a little child. It was that, and not a taper, that the dead had given him. He tried to get rid of it, but every effort proved fruitless. In despair, he went to the priest, and told him all about it. "Men should never take what spirits offer them," said the priest, "it is always a snare they set for us; but now that the mischief is done, let us see how best we can repair it."

"What must I do?"

"For three successive nights the Dead Battalion will come under your windows at the same hour as when you met it: some will cry, some will sob, others will curse you, and ask persistently for the little child's arm; the bells of all the churches will set to tolling the funeral knell, but have no fear. At first you must not throw them the arm—only on the third day may you get rid of it, and this is how. Get ready a lot of hot ashes; then when the dead come and begin to cry and groan, throw them a part. That will make them furious; they will wish to attack your house—you will let them in, but when all the spectres are inside, suddenly throw at them what is left of the hot ashes with the child's arm along with it. The dead will take it away, and you will be saved."

Everything happened just as the priest said; for three nights cries, groans, and imprecations surrounded the man's house, while the bells tolled the death-knell. It was only by throwing hot ashes on the ghosts that he got rid of the child's arm. Not long after, he died. "Woe be to him who forgets to give drink to the dead."

The Dead Battalion, or Confraternity of Ghosts, walk abroad dressed as penitents, with hoods over their heads. The solitary night traveller sees them from time to time, defiling down the mountain gorges ; they invariably try to make him accept some object, not to be recognised in the dark—but beware, lest you accept ! If some important person is about to die, they come out to receive his soul into their dread brotherhood.

Ghost stories are common in Corsica. What wilder tale could be desired than that of the girl, betrayed by her lover to wed a richer bride, who returns thrice, and lies down between man and wife—twice she vanishes at cock-crow, the third time she clasps her betrayer in her chilly arms, saying, "Thou art mine, O beloved ! mine thou wilt be forever, we part no more." While she speaks he breathes his last breath.

The dead, when assembled in numbers, and when not employed in rehearsing the business or calling of their former lives, are usually engaged either in dancing or in going through some sort of religious exercise. On this point there is a conformity of evidence. A spectre's mass is a very common superstition. On All Soul's Eve an old woman went to pray in the now ruined church of St Martin, at Bonn. Priests were performing the service, and there was a large congregation, but by and by the old woman became convinced that she was the only living mortal in the church. She wished to get away, but she could not ; just as Mass was ending, however, her deceased husband whispered to her that now was the time to fly for her life. She ran to the door, but she stopped for one moment at the spot in the aisle where two of her children were buried, just to say, "Peace be unto them." The door swung open and closed after her: a bit of her cloak was shut in, so that she had to leave it behind. Soon after she sickened and died ; the neighbours said it must be because a piece of her clothes had remained in the possession of the dead.

The dance of the dead sometimes takes the form not of an amusement but of a doom. One of the most curious instances of this is embodied in a Rhineland legend, which has the advantage of giving names, dates, and full particulars. In the 14th century, Freiherr von Metternich placed his daughter Ida in a convent on the island of Oberwörth, in order to separate her from her lover, one Gerbert, to whom she was secretly betrothed. A year later the maiden lay sick in the nunnery, attended by an aged lay sister. "Alas!" she said, "I die unwed though a betrothed wife." "Heaven forefend!" cried her companion, "then you would be doomed to dance the death-dance." The old sister went on to explain that betrothed maidens who die without having either married or taken religious vows, are condemned to dance on a grassless spot in the middle of the island, there being but one chance of escape—the coming of a lover, no matter whether the original betrothed or another, with whom the whole company dances round and round till he dies; then the youngest of the ghosts makes him her own, and may henceforth rest in her grave. The old nun's gossip does not delay (possibly it hastens) the hapless Ida's departure, and Gerbert, who hears of her illness on the shores of the Boden See, arrives at Coblentz only to have tidings

of her death.   He rows over to Oberwörth: it is
midnight in midwinter.   Under the moonlight dance
the unwed brides, veiled and in flowing robes; Gerbert thinks he sees Ida amongst them.   He joins in
the dance; fast and furious it becomes, to the sound
of a wild, unearthly music.   At last the clock strikes,
and the ghosts vanish—only one, as it goes, seems to
stoop and kiss the youth, who sinks to the ground.
There the gardener finds him on the morrow, and in
spite of all the care bestowed upon him by the sister-
hood he dies before sundown.

In China they are more practical.   In the natural
course of things the spirit of an engaged girl would
certainly haunt her lover, but there is a way to prevent it, and that way he takes.   He must go to the
house where she died, step over the coffin containing
her body, and carry home a pair of her shoes.   Then
he is safe.

A story may be added which comes from a Dutch
source.   The gravedigger happened to have a fever
on All Saints' Day.   "Is it not unlucky?" he said to
a friend who came to see him, "I am ill, and must go
to-night in the cold and snow to dig a grave."   "Oh,
I'll do that for you," said the gossip.   "That's a little
service."   So it was agreed.   The gossip took a spade
and a pick-axe, and cheered himself with a glass at
the alehouse; then, by half-past eleven, the work was
done.   As he was going away from the churchyard
he saw a procession of white friars—they went round
the close, each with a taper in his hand.   When they
passed the gossip, they threw down the tapers, and
the last flung him a big ball of wax with two wicks.
The gossip laughed quite loudly: all this wax would

sell for a pretty sum! He picked up the tapers and hid them under his bed. Next day was All Souls'. The gossip went to bed betimes, but he could not get to sleep, and as twelve struck he heard three knocks. He jumped up and opened the door—there stood all the white monks, only they had no tapers! The gossip fell back on his bed from fright, and the monks marched into the room and stood all round him. Then their white robes dropped off, and, only to think of it! they were all skeletons! But no skeleton was complete; one lacked an arm, another a leg, another a backbone, and one had no head. Some-how the cloth in which the gossip had wrapped the wax came out from under the bed and fell open; instead of tapers it was full of bones. The skeletons now called out for their missing members: "Give me my rib," "Give me my backbone," and so on. The gossip gave back all the pieces, and put the skull on the right shoulders—it was what he had mistaken for a ball of wax. The moment the owner of the head had got it back he snatched a violin which was hanging against the wall, and told the gossip to begin to play forthwith, he himself extending his arms in the right position to conduct the music. All the skeletons danced, making a fearful clatter, and the gossip dared not leave off fiddling till the morning came and the monks put on their clothes and went away. The gossip and his wife did not say one word of what had happened till their last hour, when they thought it wisest to tell their confessor.

Mr Benjamin Thorpe saw a link between the above legend, of which he gave a translation in his "Northern Mythology," and the Netherlandish proverb, " Let no

one take a bone from the churchyard : the dead will
torment him till he return it." Its general analogy
with our Shroud-theft does not admit of doubt, though
the proceedings of the expropriator of wax lights are
more easily accounted for than are those of the Shroud-
thief. Peter of Provence either stole the winding-
sheet out of sheer mischief, or he took it to enable
him to see sights not lawfully visible to mortal eyes.
In any case a well-worn shroud could scarcely enrich
the thief, while the wax used for ecclesiastical candles
was, and is still, a distinctly marketable commodity.
A stranger who goes into a church at Florence in the
dusk of the evening, when a funeral ceremony is in
the course of performance, is surprised to see men
and boys dodging the footsteps of the brethren of the
Misericordia, and stooping at every turn to the pavement ; if he asks what is the object of their peculiar
antics, he will hear that it is to collect

> The droppings of the wax to sell again.

The industry is time-honoured in Italy. At Naples
in the last century, the wax-men flourished exceedingly by reason of a usage described by Henry Swinburne. Candidates for holy orders who had not
money enough to pay the fees, were in the habit of
letting themselves out to attend funerals, so that they
might be able to lay by the sum needful. But as
they were often indisposed to fulfil the duties thus
undertaken, they dressed up the city vagrants in
their clothes and sent them to pray and sing instead
of them. These latter made their account out of the
transaction by having a friend near, who held a paper
bag, into which they made the tapers waste plen-

teously. Other devices for improving the trade were common at that date in the Neapolitan kingdom. Once, when an archbishop was to be buried, and four hundred genuine friars were in attendance, suddenly a mad bull was let loose amongst them, whereupon they dropped their wax lights, and the thieves, who had laid the plot, picked them up. At another great funeral, each assistant was respectfully asked for his taper by an individual dressed like a sacristan ; the tapers were then extinguished and quietly carried away—only afterwards it was discovered that the supposed sacristans belonged to a gang of thieves. The Shroud-theft is a product of the peculiar fascination exercised by the human skeleton upon the mediæval fancy. The part played by the skeleton in the early art and early fiction of the Christian æra is one of large importance ; the horrible, the grotesque, the pathetic, the humorous—all are grouped round the bare remnants of humanity. The skeleton, figuring as Death, still looks at you from the *façades* of the village churches in the north of Italy and the Trentino—sometimes alone, sometimes with other stray members of the *Danse Macabre;* carrying generally an inscription to this purport :

> Giunge la morte piena de egualeza,
> Sole ve voglio e non vostra richeza.
> Digna mi son de portar corona,
> E che signoresi ogni persona.

The *Danse Macabre* itself is a subject which is well nigh exhaustless. The secret of its immense popularity can be read in the lines just quoted : it proclaimed equality. " Nous mourrons tous," said the French preacher—then, catching the eye of the king,

he politely substituted "*presque* tous." Now there is
no "presque" in the Dance of Death. Whether
painted by Holbein's brush, or by that of any
humble artist of the Italian valleys, the moral is the
same: grand lady and milkmaid, monarch and herdsman, all have to go. Who shall ·fathom the grim
comfort there was in this vivid, this highly intelligible
showing forth of the indisputable fact? It was a
foretaste of the declaration of the rights of man.
Professor Pellegrini, who has added an instructive
monograph to the literature of the *Danse Macabre,*
mentions that on the way to the cemetery of Galliate
a wall bears the guiding inscription: "Via al vero
comunismo!"

The old custom of way-side ossuaries contributed
no doubt towards keeping strongly before the people
the symbol and image of the great King. I have
often reflected on the effect, certainly if unconsciously
felt, of the constant and unveiled presence of the
dead. I remember once passing one of the still
standing chapels through the gratings of which may
be seen neatly ranged rows of human bones, as I was
descending late one night a mountain in Lombardy.
The moon fell through the bars upon the village
ancestors; one old man went by along the narrow
way, and said gravely as he went the two words:
"È tardi!" It was a scene which always comes
back to me when I study the literature of the
skeleton.

SONGS FOR THE RITE OF MAY.

ONE of the first of living painters has pointed to the old English custom of carrying about flowers on May Day as a sign that, in the Middle Ages, artistic sensibility and a pleasure in natural beauty were not dead among the common people of England. Nothing can be truer than this way of judging the observance of the Rite of May. Whatever might be the foolishness that it led to here and there, its origin lay always in pure satisfaction at the returned glory of the earth; in the wish to establish a link that could be seen and felt—if only that of holding a green bough or of wearing a daffodil crown—between the children of men and the new and beautiful growth of nature. The sentiment is the same everywhere, but the manner of its expression varies. In warmer lands it finds a vent long before the coming of May. March, in fact, rather than May, seems to have been chosen as the typical spring month in ancient Greece and Rome; and when we see the almond-trees blooming down towards Ponte Molle in the earliest week in February, even March strikes us as a little late for the beginning of the spring festival. A few icicles next morning on the Trevi, act, however, as a corrective to our ideas. In a famous passage Ovid tells the reason why the Romans kept holiday on the first of March: "The ice being broken up, winter at last yields, and

T

the snow melts away, conquered by the sun's gentle
warmth; the leaves come back to the trees that were
stripped by the cold, the sap-filled bud swells with
the tender twig, and the fertile grass, that long lay
unseen, finds hidden passages and uplifts itself in the
air. Now is the field fruitful, now is the time of the
birth of cattle, now the bird prepares its house and
home in the bough." (*Fastorum*, lib. iii.)

March day is still kept in Greece by bands of
youngsters who go from house to house in the hopes
of getting little gifts of fruit or cheese. They take
with them a wooden swallow which they spin round
to the song:

> The swallow speeds her flight
> 　O'er the sea-foam white,
> And then a-singing she doth slake her wing.
> 　" March, March, my delight,
> 　And February wan and wet,
> 　For all thy snow and rain thou yet
> Hast a perfume of the spring."

Or perhaps to the following variant, given by Mr
Lewis Sergeant in *New Greece :*

> She is here, she is here,
> The swallow that brings us the beautiful year ;
> Open wide the door,
> We are children again, we are old no more.

These little swallow-songs are worth the attention
of the Folk-Lore student, since they are of a greater
antiquity than can be proved on written evidence in
the case, so far as I know, of any other folk-song
still current. More than two thousand years ago
they existed in the form quoted from Theognis by

Athenæus as "an excellent song sung by the children of Rhodes."

> The swallow comes ! She comes, she brings
> Glad days and hours upon her wings.
>> See on her back
>> Her plumes are black,
>> But all below
>> As white as snow.
> Then from your well-stored house with haste,
> Bring sweet cakes of dainty taste,
> Bring a flagon full of wine,
> Wheaten meal bring, white and fine ;
> And a platter load with cheese,
> Eggs and porridge add—for these
> Will the swallow not decline.
> Now shall we go, or gifts receive !
> Give, or ne'er your house we leave,
> Till we the door or lintel break,
> Or your little wife we take ;
> She so light, small toil will make.
>> But whate'er ye bring us forth,
>> Let the gift be one of worth.
> Ope, ope your door, to greet the swallow then,
> For we are only boys, not bearded men.

In Ægina the children's prattle runs : "March is come, sing, ye hills and ye flowers and little birds ! Say, say, little swallow, where hast thou passed ? where hast thou halted ? " And in Corfu : " Little swallow, my joyous one, joyous my swallow ; thou that comest from the desert, what good things bringest thou ? Health, joy, and red eggs." Yet another version of the swallow song deals in scant compliments to the month of March, which was welcomed so gladly at its first coming :

From the Black Sea the swallow comes,
> She o'er the waves has sped,
And she has built herself a nest
> And resting there she said :
" Thou February cold and wet,
> And snowy March and drear,
Soft April heralds its approach,
> And soon it will be here.
The little birds begin to sing,
> Trees don their green array,
Hens in the yard begin to cluck,
> And store of eggs to lay.
The herds their winter shelter leave
> For mountain-side and top ;
The goats begin to sport and skip,
> And early buds to crop ;
Beasts, birds, and men all give themselves
> To joy and merry heart,
And ice and snow and northern winds
> Are melted and depart.
Foul February, snowy March,
> Fair April will not tarry.
Hence, February ! March, begone !
> Away the winter carry ! "

When they leave off singing, the children cry " Pritz!
Pritz!" imitating the sound of the rapid flight of a
bird. Longfellow translated a curious Stork-carol
sung in spring-time by the Hungarian boys on the
islands of the Danube :

> Stork ! Stork ! Poor Stork !
> Why is thy foot so bloody ?
> A Turkish boy hath torn it,
> Hungarian boy will heal it,
> With fiddle, fife, and drum.

Before the sun was up on May-day morning, the
people of Edinburgh assembled at Arthur's Seat to

"meet the dew." May-dew was thought to possess all kinds of virtues. English girls went into the fields at dawn to wash their faces in it, in order to procure a good complexion. Pepys speaks of his wife going to Woolwich for a little change of air, and to gather the May-dew. In Croatia, the women get from the woods flowers and grasses which they throw into water taken from under a mill-wheel, and next morning they bathe in the water, imagining that thus the new strength of Nature enters into them. There is said to also exist a singular rain-custom in Croatia. When a drought threatens to injure the crops, a young girl, generally a gipsy, dresses herself entirely in flowers and grasses, in which primitive raiment she is conducted through the village by her companions, who sing to the skies for mercy. In Greece, too, there are many songs and ceremonies in connection with a desire for the rain, which never comes during the whole pitiless summer.

If there be a part of the world where spring plays the laggard, it is certainly the upper valley of the Inn. Nevertheless the children of the Engadine trudge forth bravely over the snow, shaking their cow-bells and singing lustily:

> Chalanda Mars, chaland'Avrigl
> Lasché las vachias our d'nuilg.

Were the cows to leave their stables as is here enjoined, they would not find a blade of grass to eat—but that does not matter. The children have probably sung that song ever since their forefathers came up to the mountains; came up in all likelihood from sunny Tuscany. The Engadine lads, after doing

justice to their March-day fare, set out for the boundaries of their commune, where they are met by
another band of boys, with whom they contend in
various trials of strength, which sometimes end in
hand-to-hand fights. This may be analogous to the
old English usage of beating the younger generation
once a year at the village boundaries in order to im·
press on them a lasting idea of local geography. By
the Lake of Poschiavo it is the custom to "call after
the grass "—" chiamar l'erba "—on March-day.

In the end, as has been seen, March gets an ill-word
from the Greek folk-singer, who is not more constant
in his praise of April. It is the old fatality which
makes the Better the Enemy of the Good.

May is coming, May is coming, comes the month so blithe and
    gay ;
April truly has its flowers, but all roses bloom in May ;
April, thou accurst one, vanish ! Sweet May-month I long to
    see ;
May fills all the world with flowers, May will give my love to me.

May is pre-eminently the bridal month in Greece ;
a strange contradiction to the prejudice against May
marriages that prevails in most parts of Europe.
"Marry in May, rue for aye." The Romans have
been held responsible for this superstition. They
kept their festival of the dead during May, and while
it lasted other forms of worship were suspended. To
contract marriage would have been to defy the fates.
Traces of a spring feast of souls survive in France,
where, on Palm Sunday, *Pâques fleuries* as it is called,
it is customary to set the first fresh flowers of the
year upon the graves. Nor is it by any means unin-

teresting to note that in one great empire far outside of the Roman world the *fête des morts* is assigned not to the quiet close of the year but to the delightful spring. The Chinese festival of Clear Weather which falls in April is the chosen time for worshipping at the family tombs.

· The marriage of Mary Queen of Scots and James Bothwell was celebrated on the 16th of May; an unknown hand wrote upon the gate of Holyrood Palace Ovid's warning :

> Si te proverbia tangunt,
> Mense malas Maio nubere vulgus ait.

Of English songs treating of that " observance " or " rite " of May to which Chaucer and Shakespeare bear witness, there are unfortunately few. The old nursery rhyme :

> Here we go a-piping,
> First in spring and then in May,

tells the usual story of house-to-house visiting and expected largess. In Devonshire, children used to take round a richly-dressed doll ; such a doll is still borne in triumph by the children of Great Missenden, Bucks, where a doggerel is sung, of which these are the concluding verses :

> · A branch of May I have you brought,
> And at your door I stand ;
> 'Tis but a spray that's well put out
> By the works of the mighty Lord's hand.
>
> If you have got no strong beer,
> We'll be content with small ;
> And take the goodwill of your house,
> And give good thanks for all.

God bless the master of this house,
The mistress also ;
Likewise the little children
That round the table go.

My song is done, I must be gone,
No longer can I stay ;
God bless you all, both great and small,
And send you a joyful May.

The poets of Great Missenden not being prolific, the
two middle stanzas are used at Christmas as well as
on May-day.

May-poles were prohibited by the Long Parliament
of 1644, being denounced as a "heathenish vanity
generally abused to superstition and wickedness." A
long while before, the Roman Floralia, the feast when
people carried green boughs and wore fresh garlands,
had been put down for somewhat the same reasons.
With regard to May-poles I am not inclined to think
too harshly of them. They died hard : an old Essex
man told me on his death-bed of how when he was a
lad the young folks danced regularly round the May-
pole on May-day, and in his opinion it was a good
time. It was a time, he went on to say, when the
country was a different thing ; twice a day the
postillion's horn sounded down the village street, the
Woolpack Inn was often full even to the attics in its
pretty gabled roof, all sorts of persons of quality fell
out of the clouds, or to speak exactly, emerged from
the London coach. The life of the place seemed to
be gone, said my friend, and yet "the place" is in the
very highest state of modern prosperity.

The parade of sweeps in bowers of greenery lingered
on rather longer in England than May-poles. It is

stated to have originated in this way. Edward
Wortley Montagu (born about 1714), who later was
destined to win celebrity by still stranger freaks,
escaped when a boy from Westminster School and .
borrowed the clothes of a chimney sweep, in whose
trade he became an adept. A long search resulted
in his discovery and restoration to his parents on
May 1 ; in recollection of which event Mrs Elizabeth
Montagu is said to have instituted the May-day feast
given by her for many years to the London chimney-
sweepers.

In the country west of Glasgow it is still remembered
how once the houses were adorned with flowers and
branches on the first of May, and in some parts of
Ireland they still plant a May-tree or May-bush before
the door of the farmhouse, throwing it at sundown
into a bonfire. The lighting of fires was not an
uncommon feature of May-day observance, but it is
a practice which seems to me to have strayed into
that connection from its proper place in the great
festival of the summer solstice on St John's Eve.
Among people of English speech, May-day customs
are little more than a cheerful memory. Herrick
wrote :

> Wash, dress, be brief in praying,
> Few beads are best when once we go a-maying.

People neglect their "beads" or the equivalents now
from other motives.

May night is the German Walpurgis-nacht. The
witches ride up to the Brocken on magpies' tails, not
a magpie can be seen for the next twenty-four hours
—they are all gone and they have not had time to

return.   The witches dance on the Brocken till they have danced away the winter's snow.   May-brides and May-kings are still to be heard of in Germany, and children run about on May-day with buttercups or with a twist of bread, a *Bretzel*, decked with ribbons, or holding imprisoned may-flies, which they let loose whilst they sing :   ·

> Maïkäferchen fliege,
> Dein Vater ist in kriege,
> Deine Mutter ist in Pommerland,
> Pommerland ist abgebrannt,
> Maïkäferchen fliege.

May chafer must fly away home, his father is at the wars, his mother is in Pomerania, Pomerania is all burnt.   May chafer in short is the brother of our lady-bird.   Dr Karl Blind is of opinion that " Pommer-land " is a later interpolation for " Holler-land "—the land of Freya—Holda, the Teutonic Aphrodite ; and he and other German students of mythology see in the conflagation an allusion to the final end and doom of the kingdom of the gods.   It is pointed out that the ladybird was Freya's messenger, whose business it was to call the unborn from their tranquil sojourn amongst celestial flowers, into the storms of human existence.   There is an airy May chafer song in Alsace — Teutonic in tradition, though French in tongue :

> Avril, tu t'en vas,
> Car Mai vient là-bas,
> Pour balayer ta figure
> De pluie, aussi de froidure.
>   Hanneton, vole !
>   Hanneton, vole !

Au firmament bleu
Ton nid est en feu,
Les Turcs avec leur épée
Viennent tuer ta couvée.
Hanneton, vole !
Hanneton, vole !

Dr Blind recollects taking part, as a boy, in an extremely curious children's drama, which is still played in some places in the open air. It is an allegory of the expulsion of winter, who is killed and burnt, and of the arrival of summer, who comes decked with flowers and garlands. The children repeat :

Now have we chased death away,
And we bring the summer weather ;
Summer dear and eke the May,
And the flowers all together :
Bringing summer we are come,
Summer tide and sunshine home.

With this may be compared an account given by Olaus Magnus, a Swedish writer of the fifteenth century, of how May Day was celebrated in his time. "A number of youths on horseback were drawn up in two lines facing each other, the one party representing 'Winter' and the other 'Summer.' The leader of the former was clad in wild beasts' skins, and he and his men were armed with snow-balls and pieces of ice. The commander of the latter—'Maj Greve,' or Count May—was, on the contrary, decorated with leaves and flowers, and his followers had for weapons branches of the birch or linden tree, which, having been previously steeped in water, were then in leaf. At a given signal, a sham fight ensued

between the opposing forces. If the season was cold
and backward, 'Winter' and his party were im-
petuous in their attack, and in the beginning the
advantage was supposed to rest with them ; but if
the weather was genial, and the spring had fairly set
in, 'Maj Greve' and his men carried all before them.
Under any circumstances, however, the umpire always
declared the victory to rest with 'Summer.'   The
winter party then strewed ashes on the ground, and a
joyous banquet terminated the game."   Mr L. Lloyd,
author of "Peasant Life in Sweden" (1870), records
some lines sung by Swedish children when collecting
provisions for the *Maj gille* or May feast, which recall
the "Swallow-song" :

> " Best loves from Mr and Mrs Magpie,
> From all their eggs and all their fry,
> O give them alms, if ever so small,
> Else hens and chickens and eggs and all,
> A prey to 'Piet' will surely fall."

The Swedes raise their *Maj stång* or May-pole, not
on May, but on St John's Eve, a change due, I suspect, to the exigencies of the climate.

German *Mailieder* are one very much like the
other ; they are full of the simple gladness of children
who have been shut up in houses, and who now can
run about in the sunny air.   I came across the following in Switzerland :

> " Alles neu macht der Mai,
> Macht die Seele frisch und frei.
> Lasst dans Haus !
> Kommt hinaus !
> Windet einen Strauss !

" Rings erglänzet Sonnenschein,
Dustend pranget Flur und Hain.
Vögel-sang,
Lust'ger Klang
Tönt den Wald entlang."

In Lorraine girls dressed in white go from village
to village stringing off couplets, in which the inhabitants are turned into somewhat unmerciful ridicule.
The girls of this place enlighten the people of that
as to their small failings, and so *vice versâ*. All the
winter the village poets harvest the jokes made by
one community at the expense of another, in order to
shape them into a consecutive whole for recital on
May Day. The girls are rewarded for their part in
the business by small coin, cakes and fruit. The
May-songs of Lorraine are termed " Trimazos," from
the fact that they are always sung to the refrain,

" O Trimazot, ç'at lo Maye ;
O mi-Maye !
Ç'at lo joli mois de Maye,
Ç'at lo Trimazot."

The derivation of *Trimazo* is uncertain ; someone
suggested that *Tri* stands for three, and *mazo* for
maidens ; but I think *mazo* is more likely to be connected with the Italian *mazzo*, " nosegay." The word
is known outside Lorraine : at Islettes children say :

" Trimazot ! en nous allant
Nous pormenés eddans les champs ·
Nous y ons trouvé les blés si grands
Les Aubépin' en fleurissant."

They beg for money to buy a taper for the Virgin's
altar ; for it must not be forgotten that the month of

May is the month of Mary. The villagers add a little flour to their pious offering, so that the children may make cakes. Elsewhere in Champagne young girls collect the taper money; they cunningly appeal to the tenderness of the young mother by bringing to her mind the hour "when she takes her pretty child up in the morning and lays him to sleep at night." There was a day on which the girls of the neighbourhood of Remiremont used to way-lay every youth they met on the road to the church of Dommartin and insist on sticking a sprig of rosemary or laurel in his cap, saying, "We have found a fine gentleman, God give him joy and health; take the May, the pretty May!" The fine gentleman was requested to give "what he liked" for the dear Virgin's sake. In the department of the Jura there are May-brides, and in Bresse they have a May-queen who is attended by a youth, selected for the purpose, and by a little boy who carries a green bough ornamented with ribands. She heads the village girls and boys, who walk as in a marriage procession, and who receive eggs, wine, or money. A song still sung in Burgundy recalls the præ-revolutionary æra and the respect inspired by the seigneurial woods :—

> " Le voilà venu le joli mois,
>   Laissez bourgeonner le bois ;
> Le voilà venu le joli mois,
>   Le joli bois bourgeonne.
> Il faut laisser bourgeonner le bois,
>   Le bois du gentilhomme."

The young peasants of Poitou betake themselves to the door of each homestead before the dawn of the

May morning and summon the mistress of the house
to waken her daughters.:—

> " For we are come before hath come the day
> To sing the coming of the month of May."

But they do not ask the damsels to stand there
listening to compliments ; "Go to the hen-roost,"
they say, "and get eighteen, or still better, twenty
new laid eggs." If the eggs cannot be had, they can
bring money, only let them make haste, as day-break
is near and the road is long. By way of acknowledg-
ment the spokesman adds a sort of "And your peti-
tioners will ever pray ;" they will pray for the purse
which held the money and for the hen that laid the
eggs. If St Nicholas only hears them that hen will
eat the fox, instead of the fox eating the hen. The
gift is seemly. Now the dwellers in the homestead
may go back to their beds and bar doors and windows ; "as for us, we go through all the night singing
at the arrival of sweet spring."

The antiquary in search of May-songs will turn to
the Motets and Pastorals of that six-hundred-year-old
Comic Opera "Li gieus de Robin et de Marion."
Its origin was not illiterate, but in Adam de la Halle's
time and country poets who had some letters and
poets who had none did not stand so widely apart.
The May month, the summer sweetness, the lilies of
the valley, the green meadows—these constituted
pretty well the whole idea which the French rustic
had formed to himself of what poetry was. It cannot
be denied that he came to use these things occasionally as mere commonplaces, a tendency which in-
creased as time wore on. But he has his better

moods, and some of his ditties are not wanting in elegance. Here is an old song preserved in Burgundy:

> Voici venu le mois des fleurs
> Des chansons et des senteurs ;
> Le mois qui tout enchante
> Le mois de douce attente.
> Le buisson reprend ses couleurs
> Au bois l'oiseau chante.
>
> Il est venu sans mes amours
> Que j'attends, hélas, toujours ;
> Tandis que l'oiseau chante
> Et que le mai l' on plante
> Seule en ces bois que je parcours
> Seule je me lamente.

In the France of the sixteenth century, the planting of the May took a literary turn. At Lyons, for instance, the printers were in the habit of setting up what was called "Le Mai des Imprimeurs" before the door of some distinguished person. The members of the illustrious Lombard house of Trivulzi, who between them held the government of Lyons for more than twenty-five years, were on several occasions chosen as recipients of the May-day compliment. "Le Grand Trivulce," marshal of France, was a great patron of literature, and the encouragement of the liberal arts grew to be a tradition in the family. In 1529 Theodore de Trivulce had a May planted in his honour bearing a poetical address from the pen of Clement Marot, and Pompone de Trivulce received a like distinction in 1535, when Etienne Dolet wrote for the occasion an ode in the purest Latin, which may be read in Mr R. C. Christie's biography of its author.

Giulio Cesare Croce, the famous ballad-singer of Bologna (born 1550), wrote a "Canzonetta vaga in lode del bel mese di maggio et delle regine o contesse che si fanno quel giorno in Bologna," and in 1622, a small book was published at Bologna, entitled: "Ragionamenti piacevoli intorno alle contesse di maggio; piantar il maggio; nozze che si fanno in maggio." The author, Vincenzo Giacchiroli, observes: "These countesses, according to what I have read, the Florentines call Dukes of May—perhaps because there they have real dukes." The first of May, he continues, the young girls select one from among them and set her on a high seat or throne in some public street, adorned and surrounded with greenery, and with such flowers as the season affords. To this maiden, in semblance like the goddess Flora, they compel every passer-by to give something, either by catching him by his clothes, or by holding a cord across the street to intercept him, singing at the same time, "Alla contessa, alla contessa!" They who pass, therefore, throw into a plate or receptacle prepared for the purpose, money, or flowers, or what not, for the new countess. In some places it was the custom to kiss the countess ; "neither," adds the author, "is this to be condemned, since so were wont to do the ancients as a sign of honour."

Regarding a similar usage at Mantua, Merlinus Coccaius (Folengo) wrote :

> " Accidit una dies qua Mantua tota bagordat
> Prima dies mensis Maii quo quisque piantat
> Per stradas ramos frondosos nomine mazzos." &c.

Exactly the same practice lingers in Spain. In the

U

town of Almeria, improvised temples are raised at the street corners and gateways, where, on an altar covered with damask or other rich stuff, a girl decked with flowers is seated, whilst around her in a circle stand other girls, also crowned with flowers, who hold hands, and intone, like a Greek chorus—

> "Un cuartito para la Maya,
> Que no tiene manto ni saya."

"A penny for the May who has neither mantle nor petticoat."

Lorenzo de' Medici says in one of his ballads:

> Se tu vuo' appiccare un maio.
> A qualcuna che tu ami. . . . . .

In his day "Singing the May" was almost a trade; the country folk flocked into Florence with their May trees and rustic instruments and took toll of the citizens. The custom continues along the Ligurian coast. At Spezia I saw the boys come round on May-day piping and singing, and led by one, taller than the rest, who carried an Italian flag covered with garlands. The name of the master of the house before which they halt is introduced into a song that begins:

> Siam venuti a cantar maggio,
> Al Signore ——
> Come ogn' anno usar si suole,
> Nella stagion di primavera.

Since Chaucer, who loved so dearly the "May Kalendes" and the "See of the day," no one has celebrated them with a more ingenuous charm than the country lads of the island of Sardinia, who sing "May, May, be thou welcome, with all Sun and Love; with the Flower and with the Soul, and with the Marguerite." A Tuscan and a Pisan *Rispetto* may be taken as representative of Italian May-song :

> 'Twas in the Calends of the month of May,
>   I went into the garden for a flower,
> A wild bird there I saw upon a spray,
>   Singing of love with skilled melodious power.
> O little bird, who dost from Florence speed
> Teach me whence loving doth at first proceed?
> Love has its birth in music and in songs
> Its end, alas! to tears and grief belongs.

> Era di maggio, se ben mi ricordo
>   Quando c'incominciammo a ben volere
> Eran fiorite le rose dell'orto,
>   E le ciliege diventavan nere;
>   Ciliege nere e pere moscatelle,
>   Siete il trionfo delle donne belle
>   Ciliege nere e pere moscatate.
>   Siete il trionfo delle innamorate
>   Ciliege nere e pere moscatine.
>   Siete il trionfo delle piu belline.

The child's or lover's play of words in this last baffles all attempt at translation : it is not sense but sweetness, not poetry but music. It is as much without rule or study or conventionality as the song of birds when in Italian phrase, *fanno primavera.*

In the Province of Brescia the Thursday of Mid-Lent is kept by what is called "Burning the old women." A doll made of straw or rags, representing the oldest woman, is hung outside the window; or, if in a street, suspended from a cord passed from one side to the other. Everyone makes the tour of town or village to see *le Vecchie* who at sundown are con-

signed to the flames, generally with a distaff placed
in their hands. It is a picturesque sight at Salò,
when the bonfires blaze at different heights up the
hills, casting long reflections across the clear lake-
water. The sacrifice is consummated—but what sacrifice? I was at first disposed to simply consider the
"old woman" as a type of winter, but I am informed
that by those who have studied relics of the same
usage in other lands, she is held to be a relative of the
"harvest-man" or growth-genius, who must be either
appeased or destroyed. Yet a third interpretation
occurs to me, which I offer for what it is worth.
Might not the *Vecchia* be the husk which must be
cast off before the miracle of new birth is accomplished? "The seed that thou sowest shall not
quicken unless it die." Hardly any idea has furnished
so much occasion for symbolism as this, that life is
death, and death is life.

Professor d'Ancona believes, that to the custom of
keeping May by singing from house to house and
collecting largess of eggs or fruit or cheese, may be
traced the dramatic representations, which, under the
name of *Maggi*, can still be witnessed in certain
districts of the Tuscan Hills and of the plain of Pisa.
These May-plays are performed any Sunday in
Spring, just after Mass; the men, women, and children, hastening from the church-door to the roughly-
built theatre which has the sky for roof, the grey
olives and purple hills for background. The verses
of the play (it is always in verse) are sung to a sort of
monotonous but elastic chant, in nearly every case
unaccompanied by instruments. No one can do more
than guess when that chant was composed; it may

have been five hundred years ago and it may have been much more. Grief or joy, love and hate, all are expressed upon the same notes. It is possible that some such recitative was used in the Greek drama. A play that was not sung would not seem a play to the Tuscan contadino. The characters are acted by men or boys, the peasants not liking their wives and daughters to perform in public. A considerable number of *Maggi* exist in print or in MS. carefully copied for the convenience of the actors. The subjects range from King David to Count Ugolino, from the siege of Troy to the French Revolution. They seem for most part modern compositions, cast in a form which was probably invented before the age of Dante.

THE IDEA OF FATE IN SOUTHERN TRADITIONS.

In the early world of Greece and Italy, the beliefs relating to Fate had a vital and penetrative force which belonged only to them. " Nothing," says Sophocles, " is so terrible to man as Fate." It was the shadow cast down the broad sunlight of the roofless Hellenic life. All Greece, its gods and men, bowed at that word which Victor Hugo saw, or imagined that he saw, graven on a pillar of Nôtre Dame : 'Aνάγκη. Necessity alone of the supernatural powers was not made by man in his own image. It had no sacred grove, for in the whole world there was no place where to escape from it, no peculiar sect of votaries, for all were bound equally to obey ; it could not be bought off with riches nor withstood by valour ; no man worshipped it, many groaned under its dispensation ; but by all it was vaguely felt to be the instrument of a pure justice. If they did not, with Herder, call Fate's law " Eternal Truth," yet their idea of necessity carried these men nearer than did any other of their speculative guesses to the idea of a morally-governed universe.

The belief in one Fate had its train of accessorial beliefs. The Parcae and the Erinnyes figured as dark angels of Destiny. Then, in response to the double needs of superstition and materialism, the impersonal

Fate itself took the form of the Greek Tyche, and of
that Fortuna, who, in Rome alone, had no less than
eight temples. There were some indeed who saw in
Fortune nothing else than the old *dira necessitas;* but
to the popular mind, she was nearer to chance than to
necessity; she dealt out the favourable accident
which goes further to secure success than do the
subtlest combinations of men. The Romans did not
only demand of a military leader that he should have
talent, foresight, energy; they asked, was he *felix*—
happy, fortunate? Since human life was seen to be,
on the whole, but a sorry business, and since it was
also seen that the prosperous were not always the
meritorious, the inference followed that Fortune was
capricious, changeable, and, if not immoral, at least
unmoral. With this character she came down to the
Middle Ages, having contrived to outlive the whole
Roman pantheon.

So Dante found her, and inquired of his guide who
and what she might really be?

> Maestro, dissi lui, or mi di' anche :
> Questa Fortuna di che tu mi tocche,
> Che è, che i ben del mondo ha sì tra branche?

Dante had no wish to level the spiritual windmills
that lay in his path : he left them standing, only
seeking a proper reason for their being there. Therefore he did not answer himself in the words of the
Tuscan proverb : "Chi crede in sorte, non crede in
Dio;" but, on the contrary, tried to prove that the
two beliefs might be perfectly reconciled. "He
whose knowledge transcends all things" (is the reply)
"fashioned the heavens, and gave unto them a control-

ling force in such wise that each part shines upon
each, distributing equally the light.   Also to worldly
splendours he ordained a general minister, and
captain, who should timely change the tide of vain
prosperity from race to race and from blood to
blood.   Why these prevail, and those languish, according to her ruling, is hidden, like the snake in
the grass ; your knowledge has in her no counterpart;
she provides, judges, and pursues her governance, as
do theirs the other gods.   Her permutations have no
truce, necessity makes her swift; for he is swift in
coming who would have his turn.   This is she who is
upbraided even by those who should praise her, giving
her blame wrongfully and ill-repute; but she continues blessed, and hearkens not; glad among the
other primal creatures, she revolves her sphere, and
being blessed, rejoices."

The peasants, the *pagani* of Italy, did not give
their name for nothing to the entire system of antiquity.   They were its last, its most faithful adherents,
and to this day their inmost being is watered from
the springs of the antique.   They have preserved old-
world thoughts as they have preserved old-world pots
and pans.   In the isolated Tuscan farm you will be
lighted to your bed by a woman carrying an oil lamp
identical in form with those buried in Etruscan
tombs ; on the Neapolitan hill-side a girl will give
you to drink out of a jar not to be distinguished from
the amphoræ of Pompeii.   A stranger hunting in the
campagna may often hear himself addressed with the
"Tu" of Roman simplicity.   The living Italian
people are the most interesting of classical remains.
Even their religion has helped to perpetuate practices

older than Italy. How is it possible, for instance, to see the humble shrine by vineyard or maize field, with its posy of flowers and its wreath of box hung before the mild countenance of some local saint, without remembering what the chorus says to Admetus : " Deem not, O king, of the tomb of thy wife as of the vulgar departed ; rather let it be kept in religious veneration, a cynosure for the way-faring man. And as one climbs the slanting pathway, these will be the words he utters : ' This was she who erewhile laid down her life for her husband ; now she is a saint for evermore. Hail, blessed spirit, befriend and aid us ! ' Such the words that will be spoken."

Can it be doubted that the Catholic honour of the dead—nay, even the cult of the Virgin, which crept so mysteriously into the exercise of Christian worship—had birth, not in the councils of priests and schoolmen, but in the all-unconscious grafting by the people of Italy of the new faith upon an older stock ?

With this persistency of thought, observable in outward trifles, as in the deepest yearnings of the soul, it would be strange if the Italian mind had ceased to occupy itself with the old wonder about fate. The folk-lore of the country will show the mould into which the ancient speculations have been cast, and in how far these have undergone change, whether in the sense of assimilating new theories or in that of reverting to a still earlier order of ideas.

They tell at Venice the story of a husbandman who had set his heart on finding *one who was just* to be sponsor to his new-born child. He took the babe in his arms and went forth into the public ways to seek *El Giusto.* He walked and walked and met a man (who was our Lord) and to him he said, "I have got this son to christen, but I do not wish to give him to any one who is not just. Are you just?" To him the Lord replied, "But I do not know if I am just." Then the husbandman went a little further and met a woman (who was the Madonna), and to her he said, "I have this son to christen, but I only wish to give him to one who is just. Are you just?" "I know not," said the Madonna; "but go a little further and you will meet one who is just." After that, he went a little further, and met another woman who was Death. "I have been sent to you," he said, "for they say you are just. I have a child to christen, and I do not wish to give him except to one who is just. Are you just?" "Why, yes; I think I am just," said Death; "but let us christen the babe and afterwards I will show you if I am just." So the boy was christened, and then this woman led the husbandman into a long, long room where there were an immense number of lighted lamps. "Gossip," said the man, who marvelled at seeing so many lamps, "what is the meaning of all these lights?" Said Death: "These are the lights of all the souls that are in the world. Would you like just to see, Gossip? That is yours, and that is your son's." And the husbandman, who saw that his lamp was going out, said, "And when there is no more oil, Gossip?" "Then," replied Death, "one has to come to me, for I am Death." "Oh! for charity," said the husbandman, "do let me pour a little of the oil out of my son's lamp into mine!" "No, no, Gossip," said Death, "I don't go in for that sort of thing. A just one you wished to meet, and a just one you have found.

And now, go you to your house and put your affairs in order, for I am waiting for you."[1]

In this parable, we see a severe fatalism, which is still more oriental than antique.

> . . . God gives each man one life, like a lamp, then gives
> That lamp due measure of oil. . . .

The Mahomedans say that there are trees in heaven on each of whose leaves is the name of a human being, and whenever one of these leaves withers and falls, the man whose name it bears dies with it. The conception of human life as of something bound up and incorporated with an object seemingly foreign, lies at the very root of elementary beliefs. In an Indian tale the life of a boy resides in a gold necklace which is in the heart of a fish ; in another a woman's life is contained in a bird : when the bird is killed, the woman must perish. In a third a prince plants a tree before he goes on a journey, saying as he does so, "This tree is my life. When you see the tree

---

[1] In a Breton variant the "Bon Dieu" is the first to offer himself as sponsor, but is refused by the peasant, "Because you are not just ; you slay the honest bread-winner and the mother whose children can scarce run alone, and you let folks live who never brought aught but shame and sorrow on their kindred." Death is accepted, "Because at least you take the rich as well as the poor, the young as well as the old." The German tale of "Godfather Death" begins in the same way, but ends rather differently, as it is the godson and not the father who is shown the many candles, and who vainly requests Death to give him a new one instead of his own which is nearly burnt out. A poem by Hans Sachs (1553) contains reference to the legend, of which there are also Provençal and Hungarian versions.

green and fresh, then know that it is well with me.
When you see the tree fade in some parts, then know
that I am in an ill case. When you see the whole
tree fade, then know that I am dead and gone."

According to a legend of wide extension—it is
known from Esthonia to the Pyrenees—all men were
once aware of the hour of their death. But one day
Christ went by and saw a man raising a hedge of
straw. "That hedge will last but for a short while,"
He said; to which the man answered, "It will be
good for as long as I live; that it should last longer,
matters not;" and forthwith Christ ordained that no
man should thereafter know when he should die.

The southern populations of Italy cling to the idea
that from the moment of a man's birth his future lot
is decided, whether for good or evil hap, and that he
has but little power of altering or modifying the
irrevocable sentence. There are lucky and unlucky
days to be born on ; lucky and unlucky circumstances
attendant on an entry into the world, which affect all
stages of the subsequent career. He who is born on
the last day of the year, will always arrive late. It
is very unfortunate to be born when there is no moon.
Anciently the moon was taken as symbol both of
Fortune, and of Hecate, goddess of Magic. The
Calabrian children have a song : "Moon, holy moon,
send me good fortune ; thou shining, and I content,
lustrous thou, I fortunate." Also at Cagliari, in
Sardinia, they sing: "Moon, my moon, give me
luck ; give me money, so I may amuse myself; give
it soon, so I may buy sweetmeats." The changing
phases of the moon doubtless contributed to its
identification with fortune ; "Wind, women, and for-

tune," runs the Basque proverb, "change like the moon." But yet more, its influence over terrestrial phenomena, always mysterious to the ignorant observer and by him readily magnified to any extent, served to connect it with whatever occult, unaccountable power was uppermost in people's minds.

In Italy, nothing is done without consulting the *Lunario*. All kinds of roots and seeds must be planted with the new moon, or they will bear no produce. Timber must be cut down with the old moon, or it will quickly rot. These rules and many more are usually followed; and it is reported as a matter of fact, that their infringement brings the looked-for results. In the Neapolitan province, old women go to the graveyards by night and count the tombs illuminated by the moonlight; the sum total gives them a "number" for the lottery. The extraordinary vagaries of superstition kept alive by the public lotteries are of almost endless variety and complexity. No well-known man dies without thousands of the poorest Neapolitans racking their brains with abtruse calculations on the dates of his birth, death, and so on, in the hope of discovering a lucky number. Fortune, chance (what, after all, shall it be called?) sometimes strangely favours these pagan devices. When Pio Nono died, the losses of the Italian exchequer were enormous; and in January 1884, the numbers staked on the occasion of the death of the patriot De Sanctis, produced winnings to the amount of over two million francs. During the last cholera epidemic, the daily rate of mortality was eagerly studied with a view to happy combinations. Even in North Italy such things are not unknown. At Venice, when a notable Englishman died some years ago in a hotel, the number of his room was played next day by half the population. Domestic servants are among the most inveterate gamblers ; they all have their cabalistic books, and a large part of their earnings goes to the insatiable "lotto."

The feeling of helplessness in the hands of Fate is strongest in those countries where there is the least control over Nature. The relations between man and Nature affect not only the social life, but also the theology and politics of whole races of men. A learned Armenian who lives at Venice, came to London for a week in June to see some English friends. It rained every day, and when he left Dover, the white cliffs were enveloped in impenetrable fog. "I asked myself" (he wrote, describing his experiences) "how it was possible that a great nation should exist behind all that vapour?" It was suggested to him that in the continual but, in the long run, victorious struggle with an ungenial climate might lie the secret of the development of that great nation. Different are the lands where the soil yields its increase almost without the labour of man, till one fine day the whole is swallowed up by flood or earthquake.

The songs of luck, or rather of ill-luck, nearly all come from the Calabrias. There are hundreds of variations upon the monotonous theme of predestined misery. "In my mother's womb I began to have no fortune ; my swaddling clothes were woven of melancholy ; when we went to church, the woman who carried me died upon the way, and the godfather who held me at the font said, 'Misfortunate art thou born, my daughter!'" Here is another: "Hapless was I

born, and with a darkened moon; never did a fair
day dawn for me. Habited in weeds, and attended
by cruel fortune, I sail upon a sea of grief and
trouble." Or this: "Wretched am I, for against me
conspired heaven and fortune and destiny; and the
four elements decreed that never should I prosper:
earth would engulf me; air took away my breath;
water flowed with my tears; fire burnt this poor
heart." Again: "I was created under an ill-star;
never had I an hour's content. By my friends I saw
myself forsaken, and chased away by my mistress.
The heavens moved against me, the stars, the planets,
and fortune; if there is no better lot for me, open
thou earth and give me sepulchre!" The luckless
wretch imagines that the sea, even where it was
deepest, dried up at his birth; and the spring dried
up for that year, and all the flowers that were in the
world dried up; and the birds went singing: "I am
the most luckless wight on earth!" Human friendship is a delusion: "I was the friend of all, and a true
friend—for my friends I reckoned life as little." But
he is not served so by others: "Wretched is he who
trusts in fortune; sad is he who hopes in human
friendship! Every friend abandons thee at need, and
walks afar from thy sorrow." No good can come to
him who is born for ill: "When I was born, it was at
sea, amongst Turks and Moors. A gipsy asked to
tell my fortune; 'Dig,' she said, 'and thou shalt find
a great treasure.' I took the spade in my hand to
dig, but I found neither silver nor gold. Traitress
gipsy who deceived me! Who is born afflicted, dies
disconsolate."

So continues the long tale of woe; childish in part,

but withal tragic by other force of iteration. This song of Nardò may be taken as its epitome :

> The heavens were overcast when I was born ;
> No luck for me, no, luckless and forlorn,
> E'en from my cradle, all forlorn was I ;
> No luck for me, no, grief for ever nigh.
> I loved—my love was paid by fraud and scorn ;
> No luck for me, no, luckless and forlorn.
> The stars and moon were darkened in the sky,
> No luck for me, no, naught but misery !

The Calabrians have a house-spirit called the *Auguriellu*, who appears generally dressed as a little monk, and who has his post especially by babies' cradles : he is thought to be one of the less erring fallen angels, and is harmless and even beneficent if kindly treated. The " house-women " (*Donne di casa*) of Sicily are also in the habit of watching the sleep of infants. But in no part of Italy does there seem to be any distinct recollection of the Parcae. In Greece, on the other hand, the three dread sisters are still honoured by propitiatory rites, and they figure frequently in the folk-lore of Bulgaria and Albania. A Bulgarian song shows them weaving the destiny of the infant Saviour. In M. Auguste Dozon's collection of Albanian stories, there is one called " The sold child," which bears directly on the survival of the Parcae. " There was an old man and woman who had no children " (so runs the tale). " At last at the end of I do not know how many years, God gave them a son, and their joy was without bounds that the Lord had thus remembered them. Two nights had passed since the birth, and the third drew nigh, when the Three Women would come to assign the child his destiny.

"That night it was raining so frightfully that nobody dared put his nose out of doors, lest he should be carried away by the waters and drowned. Nevertheless, who should arrive through the rain but a Pasha, who asked the old man for a night's lodging. The latter, seeing that it was a person of importance, was very glad; he put him in the place of honour at the hearth, lit a large fire, gave him to eat what he could find; and putting aside certain objects, which he set in a corner, he made room for the Pasha's horse—for this house was only half covered in, a part of the roof was missing.

"The Pasha, when he was warmed and refreshed, had nothing more to do but to go to sleep; but how can one let himself go to sleep when he has I know · not how many thousand piastres about him?

"That night, as we have said already, the Three Women were to come and apportion the child his destiny. They came, sure enough, and sat down by the fire. The Pasha, at the sight of that, was in a great fright, but he kept quiet, and did not make the least sound.

"Let us leave the Pasha and busy ourselves with these women. The first of the three said, ' This child will not live long; he will die early.' The second said, replying to her who had just spoken, ' This child will live many years, and then he will die by the hand of his father.' Finally the third spoke as follows: ' My friends, what are you talking about? This child will live sufficiently long to kill the Pasha you see there, rob him of his authority, and marry his daughter.'"

How the Pasha froze with fear when he heard that

X

sentence, how he persuaded the old man to let him have the child under pretence of adopting him, how he endeavoured by every means, but vainly, to put him out of the way, and how, in the end, he fell into an ambush he had prepared for his predestined successor, must be read in M. Dozon's entertaining pages. Though not precisely stated, it would seem that the mistaken predictions of the two first women arose rather from a misinterpretation of the future than from complete ignorance. The boy but narrowly escaped the evils they threatened. In Scandinavian traditions a disagreement among the Norns is not uncommon. In one case, two Norns assign to a new-born child long life and happiness, but the third and youngest decrees that he shall only live while a lighted taper burns. The eldest Norn snatches the taper, puts it out, and gives it to the child's mother, not to be kindled till the last day of his life.

In India it is the deity Bidhata-Purusha who forecasts the events of each man's life, writing them succinctly on the forehead of the child six days after birth. The apportionment of good and evil fortune belongs to Lakshmi and Sani. Once they fell out in heaven, and Sani, the giver of ill, said that he ranked higher than the beneficent Lakshmi. The gods and goddesses were equally ranged on either side, so the two disputants decided to refer the case to a just mortal. To which end they approached a wise and wealthy man called Sribatsa. Now Sribatsa means "the child of Fortune," Sri being one of the names of Lakshmi. Sribatsa did not know what to do lest he should give offence to one or the other of the celestial powers. At last he set out two stools

without saying a word; one was silver, and on that
he bade Sani sit; the other was gold, and to that he
conducted Lakshmi. But Sani was furious at having
only the silver stool, so he swore that he would cast
his evil eye upon Sribatsa for three years, "and I
should like to see how you fare at the end of that
time," he added. When he was gone, Lakshmi said:
"My child, do not fear; I'll befriend you." Needless
to say that after the three trial years were passed,
Sribatsa became far more prosperous than he had
ever been before.

Among the Parsis, a tray with writing materials
including a sheet of blank paper is placed by the
mother's bed on the night of the sixth day. The
goddess who rules human destiny traces upon the
paper the course of the child's future, which henceforth cannot be changed, though the writing is
invisible to mortal eyes.

In Calabria there is a plant called "Fortune's
Grass," which is suspended to the beams of the ceiling: if the leaves turn upwards, Fortune is sure to
follow; if downwards, things may be expected to go
wrong. The oracle is chiefly consulted on Ascension
Day, when it is asked to tell the secrets confided to
it by Christ when He walked upon the earth.

Auguries, portents, charms, waxen images, votive
offerings, the evil eye and its antidotes, happy "finds,"
such as horseshoes, four-leaved shamrocks, and two-
tailed lizards: these, and an infinite number of
kindred superstitions, are closely linked with what
may be called the Science of Luck. Fortune and
Hecate come into no mere chance contiguity when
they meet in the moon. For the rest, there is hardly

any popular belief that has not points of contact with magic, and that is not in some sort made the more comprehensible by looking at the premises on which magical rites rest. Magic is the power admitted to exist among all classes not so very long ago, of entering by certain processes into relation with invisible powers. For modern convenience it was distinguished into black magic, and natural, and white—the latter name being given when the intention of the operant was only good or allowable, and when the powers invoked were only such as might be supposed, whether great or small, to be working in good understanding with the Creator. The reason of existence of all magic, which runs up into unfathomable antiquity, lies in the maxim of the ancient sages, Egyptian, Hebrew, Platonist, that all things visible and sensible are but types of things or beings immediately above them, and have their origin in such. Hence, in magical rites, black or white, men used and offered to the unseen powers those words or actions or substances which were conceived to be in correspondence with their character or nature, employing withal certain secret traditional manœuvres. The lowest surviving form is fetish; sacrifice also had a similar source; so had the Mosaic prescriptions, in which only innocent rites and pure substances were to be employed. Whereas the most horrible practices and repulsive substances have always been associated with witches, necromancers, &c., who are reported to have put their wills at the absolute disposal of the infernal and malevolent powers who work in direct counter action of the decrees and providence of the Deity. Hence the renunciation of baptism, treading on holy things, the significant act of saying the Lord's Prayer backwards, *i.e.*, in the opposite intention to that of the author. This is the consummate sin of *pacti*, or, as it is said, "selling the soul," and is the very opposite of divine magic or the way of the typical saint: "Present yourselves a living sacrifice (not a dead carcase) in body, soul, and spirit." To persons in the last condition unusual effects have been ascribed, as it was believed that those who had put themselves at the absolute disposal of the malignant powers were also enabled to effect singular things, on the wrong side, indeed, and very inferior in order, so long as the agreement held good.

The most sensible definition of magic is "an effect sought to be produced by antecedents obviously inadequate in themselves." Certain words, gestures, practices, have been recognised on the tradition of ancient experience to have certain remedial or other properties or consequents, and they are used in all simplicity by persons who can find no other reason than that they are thought to succeed.

One of the most remarkable of early ideas still current about human destiny is that which pictures each man coupled with a personal and individualised fate. This fate may be beneficent or maleficent, a guardian angel or a possessive fiend; or it may, in appearance at least, combine both functions. The belief in a personal fate was deeply rooted among the Greeks and Romans, and proved especially acceptable to the Platonists. Socrates' dæmon comes to mind: but in that case the analogy is not clear, because the inward voice to which the name of dæmon was afterwards given, was rather a personal conscience than a

personal fate—a difference that involves the whole
question of the responsibility of man. But the evil
genii of Dion the Syracusan and of Brutus were
plainly "personal fates." Dion's evil genius appeared
to him when he was sitting alone in the portico before
his house one evening; it had the form of a gigantic
woman, like one of the furies as they were represented
on the stage, sweeping the floor with a broom. It
did not speak, but the apparition was followed by the
death of Dion's son, who jumped in a fit of childish
passion from the house-top, and soon after, Dion himself was assassinated. Brutus' dæmon was, as everyone knows, a monstrous spectre that seemed to be
standing beside him in his tent one night, a little
while before he left Asia, and which, on being questioned, said to him, "I am thy evil genius, Brutus,
thou wilt see me at Philippi."

We catch sight again of the personal fate in the
relations of Antony with the young Octavius. Antony had in his house an Egyptian astrologer, who
advised him by all means to keep away from the
young man, "for your genius," he said, "is in fear of
his; when it is alone its port is erect and fearless,
when his approaches it, it is dejected and depressed."
There were circumstances, says Plutarch, that carried
out this view, for in every kind of play, whether they
cast lots or cast the die, Antony was still the loser;
in their cock fights and quail fights, it was still
" Cæsar's cock and Cæsar's quail."

In ancient Norse and Teutonic traditions, where
Salida, or Frau Sælde, takes the place of Fortuna, we
find indications of the personal fate, both kindly and
unkindly. The fate appeared to its human turn

chiefly in the hour of death, that is, in the hour of parting company. Sometimes it was attached not to one person, but to a whole family, passing on from one to another, as in the case of the not yet extinct superstition of the White Lady of the Hohenzollerns.

In a very old German story, quoted by Jacob Grimm, a poor knight is shown, eating his frugal meal in a wood, who on looking up, sees a monstrous creature among the boughs which cries, "I am thy *ungelücke !*" The knight asks his "ill-luck" to share his meal, and when it comes down, catches it, and shuts it up in a hollow oak. Someone, who wishes to do him an ill-turn, lets out the *ungelücke ;* but instead of reverting to the knight, it jumps on the back of its evil-minded deliverer.

In the Sicilian story of "Feledico and Epomata," one of those collected by Fräulein Laura Gonzenbach,[1] a childless king and queen desire to have children. One day they see a soothsayer going by : they call him in, and he says that the queen will bear a son,

[1] Laura Gonzenbach was the daughter of the Swiss Consul at Messina, where she was born. At an early age she developed uncommon gifts, and she was hardly twenty when she made her collection of Sicilian stories, almost exclusively gathered from a young servant-girl who did not know how to write or read. It was with great difficulty that a publisher was found who would bring out the book. Fräulein Gonzenbach married Colonel La Racine, a Piedmontese officer, and died five or six years ago, being still quite young. A relation of hers, from whom I have these particulars, was much surprised to hear that the *Sicilianische Märchen* is widely known as one of the best works of its class. It is somewhat singular that the preservation of Italian folk-tales should have been so substantially aided by two ladies not of Italian origin : Fräulein Gonzenbach and Miss R. H. Busk, author of "The Folk-lore of Rome."

but that he will die when he is eighteen years of age. The grief of the royal pair is extreme, and they ask the soothsayer for advice what to do. He can only suggest that they should shut the child up in a tower till the unlucky hour be past, after which his fate will have no more power over him. This is accordingly done, and the child sees no one in the tower but the nurse and a lady of the court, whom he believes to be his mother. One day, when the lady has gone to make her report to the queen, the boy hears his fate crying to him in his sleep, and asking why he stays shut up there, when his real father and mother are king and queen and live in a fine castle? He makes inquiries, and at first is pacified by evasive answers, but after three visits of his fate, who always utters the same words, he insists on going to the castle and seeing his father and mother. "His fate has found him out, there is no good in resisting it," says the queen. However, by the agency of Epomata, the beautiful daughter of an enchantress, who had conveyed the prince to her castle, and had provided for his execution on the very day ordained by his fate, Feledico tides over the fatal moment and attains a good old age.

Hahn states that the Greek name of Μοῖραι is given by the Albanians to what I have called personal fates, as well as to the Parcae; but the Turkish designation of *Bakht,* meaning a sort of protecting spirit, seems to be in more common use. The Albanian story-teller mentions a negress who is in want of some sequins, and who says, "Go and find my fortune (*Bakht*), but first make her a cake, and when you offer it to her, ask her for a few gold pieces."

A like propitiatory offering of food to one's personal fate forms a feature of a second Sicilian story which is so important in all its bearings on the subject in hand, that it would not do to abridge it. Here it is, therefore, in its entirety.

There was a certain merchant who was so rich that he had treasures which not even the king possessed. In his audience chamber there were three beautiful arm-chairs, one of silver, one of gold, and one of diamonds. This merchant had an only daughter of the name of Caterina, who was fairer than the sun. One day Caterina sat alone in her room, when suddenly the door opened of itself, and there entered a tall and beautiful lady, who held a wheel in her hands.' "Caterina," said she, "when would you like best to enjoy your life? in youth, or in age?" Caterina gazed at her in amazement, and could not get over her stupor. The beautiful lady asked again, "Caterina, when do you wish to enjoy your life in youth or in age?" Then Caterina thought, "If I say in youth, I shall have to suffer in age; hence I prefer to enjoy my life in age, and in youth I must get on as the Lord wills." So she said, "In age." "Be it unto you according to your desire," said the beautiful lady, who gave a turn to her wheel, and disappeared. This tall and beautiful lady was poor Caterina's fate. After a few days her father received the sudden news that several of his ships had gone down in a storm; again, after a few days, other of his ships met with the same fate, and to make a long story short, a month had not gone by before he saw himself despoiled of all his wealth. He had to sell everything, and remained poor and miserable, and finally he fell ill and died. Thus poor Caterina was left alone in the world, and no one would give her a home. Then she thought, "I will go to another city and will seek a place as serving-maid." She wandered a long way till she reached another city. As she passed down the street, she saw at a window a worthy-looking lady, who questioned her. "Where are you going, all alone, fair girl?" "Oh! noble lady, I am a poor girl, and I would willingly go into service to earn my bread. Could you, by chance, employ me?" The worthy lady engaged her, and Caterina served her faithfully. After a few days the lady said one even-

ing, "Caterina, I am going out, and shall lock the house-door."
"Very well," said Caterina, and when her mistress was gone, she
took her work and began to sew. Suddenly the door opened,
and her fate came in. "So!" cried this one, "you are here,
Caterina, and you think that I shall leave you in peace!" With
these words, she ran to the cupboards and turned out the linen
and clothes of Caterina's mistress, and threw them all about the
room. Caterina thought, "When my mistress returns and finds
everything in such a state, she will kill me!" And out of fear
she broke open the door and fled. But her fate made all the
things right again, and gathered them up and put them in their
places. When the mistress came home, she called Caterina,
but she could not find her anywhere. She thought she must
have robbed her, but when she looked at her cupboards, she
saw that nothing was missing. She wondered greatly, but
Caterina never came back—she ran and ran till she reached
another city, when, as she passed along the street, she saw once
more a lady at a window, who asked her, "Where are you going,
all alone, fair girl?" "Ah! noble lady, I am a poor girl, and I
wish to find a place so as to earn my bread. Could you take
me?" The lady took her into her service, and Caterina thought
now to remain in peace. Only a few days had passed, when
one evening, when the lady was out, Caterina's fate appeared
again, and spoke hard words to her, saying, "So you are here,
are you? and you think to escape from me?" Then she
scattered whatever she could lay hands on, and poor Caterina
once more fled out of fright.

To be brief, poor Caterina had to lead this terrible life for
seven years, flying from city to city in search of a place.
Whenever she entered service, after a few days her fate always
appeared and disordered her mistress' things, and so the poor
girl had to fly. As soon as she was gone, however, her fate repaired all the damage that had been done. At last, after seven
years, it seemed as if the unhappy Caterina's fate was weary of
persecuting her. One day she arrived in a city where she saw
a lady at a window, who said, "Where go you, all alone, fair
girl?" "Ah! noble lady, I am a poor girl, and willingly would
I enter service to earn my bread; could you employ me?"
The lady replied, "I will take you, but every day you will have

to do me a certain service, and I am not sure that you have the strength." " Tell me what it is," said Caterina, " and if I can, I will do it." " Do you see that high mountain?" said the lady; " every morning you will have to carry up to the top a baker's tray of new bread, and then you must cry aloud, ' O fate of my mistress !' three times repeated. My fate will appear and will receive the bread." " I will do it willingly," said Caterina, and thereupon the lady engaged her. With this lady Caterina stayed many years, and every morning she carried the tray of fresh bread up the mountain, and after she had cried three times, " O fate of my mistress !" there appeared a beautiful, stately lady, who received the bread. Caterina often wept, thinking how she, who was once so rich, had now to work like any poor girl, and one day her mistress asked her, " Why are you always crying?" Caterina told her how ill things had gone with her, and her mistress said, " You know, Caterina, when you take the bread up the mountain to-morrow? Well, do you beg my fate to try and persuade yours to leave you in peace. Perhaps this may do some good." The advice pleased poor Caterina, and the following morning when she carried up the bread, she told her mistress' fate of the sore straits she was in, and said, " O fate of my mistress, pray ask my fate no longer to torment me." " Ah ! poor girl," the fate answered, " your fate is covered with a sevenfold covering, and that is why she cannot hear you. But to-morrow when you come, I will lead you to her." When Caterina had gone home, her mistress' fate went to her fate, and said, " Dear sister, why are you not tired of persecuting poor Caterina? Let her once again see happy days." The fate replied, " To-morrow bring her to me ; I will give her something that will supply all her needs." The next morning, when Caterina brought the bread, her mistress' fate conducted her to her own fate, who was covered with a sevenfold covering. The fate gave her a skein of silk, and said, " Take care of it, it will be of use to you." After she had returned home, Caterina said to her mistress, " My fate has made me a present of a skein of silk ; what ought I to do with it?" " It is not worth three grains of corn," said the mistress. " Keep it, all the same ; who knows what it may be good for?"

After some time, it happened that the young king was

about to take a wife, and, therefore, he had himself made some
new clothes. But when the tailor was going to make up one
fine piece of stuff, he could not anywhere find silk of the same
colour with which to sew it. The king had it cried through the
land, that whosoever had silk of the right colour was to bring it
to court, and would be well paid for his pains. " Caterina," said
her mistress, "your skein of silk is of that colour ; take it to the
king and he will make you a fine present." Caterina put on her
best gown, and went to court, and when she came before the
king, she was so beautiful that he could not take his eyes off her
" Royal Majesty," she said, " I have brought a skein of silk of th
colour you could not find." " Royal majesty," cried one of the
ministers, "we should give her the weight of her silk in gold.
The king agreed, and the scales were brought in. On one side
the king placed the skein of silk, and on the other a gold piece
Now, what do you think happened ? The silk was always th
heaviest, no matter how many gold pieces the king placed i
the balance. Then he ordered a larger pair of scales, and I
put all his treasure to the one side, but the silk remained th
heaviest. Then he took his gold crown off his head and set
with the other treasure, and upon that the two scales became
even.

"Where did you get this silk?" asked the king. "Roy
Majesty, my mistress gave it to me." "That is not possible
cried the king. "If you do not tell me the truth I will ha
your head cut off !" Caterina related all that had happen
to her since the time when she was a rich maiden. At Cou
there was a very wise lady, who said : "Caterina, you ha
suffered much, but now you will see happy days, and since t
gold crown made the balance even, it is a sign that you will li
to be a queen." " She shall be a queen," cried the king, " I w
make her a queen ! Caterina and no other shall be my bride
And so it was. The king sent to his bride to say that he
longer wanted her, and married the fair Caterina, who, aft
much suffering in youth, enjoyed her age in full prosperity, l
ing happy and content, whereof we have assured testimony.

The most suggestive passages in this ingenic
story are those which refer to the relative positions

a man and his fate, and of one fate to another. On
these points something further is to be gleaned from
an Indian, a Servian, and a Spanish tale, all having a
family likeness amongst themselves, and a strong
affinity with our story. The Indian variant is one of
the collection due to the youthful energies of Miss
Maive Stokes, whose book of "Indian Fairy Tales"
is a model of what such a book ought to be. The
Servian tale is to be found in Karadschitsch's
"Volksmaerschen der Serben;" the Spanish in Fernan
Caballero's "Cuentos y Poesias Populares Andaluses."
The chief characteristics of the personal fates, as they
appear in folk-lore, may be briefly summarised. In
the first place, they know each other, and are acquainted up to a given point with one another's
secrets. Thus, in the Servian story, a man who goes
to seek his fate is commissioned by persons he meets
on the road to ask it questions touching their own
private concerns. A rich householder wants to know
why his servants are always hungry, however much
food he gives them to eat, and why " his aged, miserable father and mother do not die?" A farmer
would have him ask why his cattle perish; and a
river, whose waters bear him across, is anxious to
know why no living thing dwells in it. The fate
gives a satisfactory answer to each inquiry.

The fates exercise a certain influence, one over the
other, and hence over the destinies of the people in
their charge. Caterina's mistress' fate intercedes for
her with her own fate. The attention of the fates is
not always fixed on the persons under them: they
may be prevented from hearing by fortuitous circumstances, such as the "seven coverings or veils" of

Caterina's fate, or they may be asleep, or absent from home. Their home, by the by, is invariably placed in a spot very difficult to get at. In the Spanish variant, the palace of Fortune is raised "where our Lord cried three times and was not heard"—it is up a rock so steep that not even a goat can climb it, and the sunbeams lose their footing when trying to reach the top. A personal fate is propitiated by suitable offerings, or, if obdurate, it may be brought to reason by a well-timed punishment. The Indian beats his fate-stone, just as the Ostyak beats his fetish if it does not behave well and bring him sport. The Sicilian story gives no hint of this alternative, but it is one strictly in harmony with the Italian way of thinking, whether ancient or modern. Statius' declaration :

> Fataque, et injustos rabidis pulsare querelis
> Cælicolas solamen erat   .   .   .

was frequently put into practice, as when, upon the death of Germanicus, the Roman populace cast stones at the temples, and the altars were levelled to the ground, and the Lares thrown into the street. Again. Augustus took revenge on Neptune for the loss of his fleet, by not allowing his image to be carried in the procession of the Circensian games. It is on record that at Florence, in 1498, a ruined gamester pelted the image of the Virgin with horse dung Luca Landucci, who tells the story, says that the Florentines were shocked ; but in the southern king dom the incident would have passed without much notice. The Neapolitans have hardly now left of heaping torrents of abuse on San Gennaro if he fail to perform the miracle of liquefaction quick enough. Probably every country could furnish an illustration. In the grand procession of St Leonhard, the Bavarians used from time to time to drop the Saint into the river, as a sort of gentle warning.

The physical presentment of the personal fate differs considerably. According to the Indian account, "the fates are stones, some standing, and others lying on the ground." It has been said that this looks like a relic of stock and stone worship: which is true if it can be said unreservedly that anyone ever worshipped a stock or a stone. The lowest stage of fetish worship only indicates a diseased spiritualism—a mental state in which there is no hedge between the real and the imagined. No savage ever supposed that his fetish was a simple three-cornered stone and nothing more. If one could guess the thoughts of the pigeon mentioned by Mr Romanes as worshipping a gingerbeer bottle, it would be surely seen that this pigeon believed his gingerbeer bottle to be other than a piece of unfeeling earthenware. It is, however, a sign of progress when man begins to picture the ruling powers not as stones, or even as animals, but as men. This point is reached in the Servian narrative, where the hero's fortune is a hag given to him as his luck by fate. In the Spanish tale, the aspect of the personal fate varies with its character: the fortunate man's fate is a lovely girl, the fate of the unfortunate man being a toothless old woman. In the *Pentamerone* of Giambattista Basile, Fortune is also spoken of as an old woman, but this seems a departure from the true Italian ideal, which is neither a stone nor a luck-hag, nor yet a varying fair-and-foul fortune, but a "bella, alta Signora:" the imposing figure that surmounts the wheel of fortune on the marble pavement of the Cathedral of Siena. It is a graver conception than the gracefully fickle goddess of Jean Cousin's " Liber Fortunæ ":

> .   .   .   On souloit la pourtraire,
> Tenant un voile afin d'aller au gré du vent
> Des aisles aux costez pour voler bien avant.

Shakespeare had the Emblematist's Fortune in his mind when he wrote : "Fortune is painted blind, with a muffler afore her eyes, to signify to you, which is the moral of it, that she is turning, and inconstant, and mutability, and variation : and her foot, look you, is fixed upon a spherical stone, which rolls, and rolls, and rolls."

In hands less light than Cousin's, it was easy for the Fortune of the emblem writers to become grotesque, and to lose all artistic merit. The Italian Fortuna does not in the least lend herself to carica-ture. In Italy, the objects of thought, even of the common people, have the tendency to assume con-crete and æsthetic forms—a fact of great significance in the history of a people destined to render essentia service to art.

The "tall, beautiful lady" of the Sicilian story reappears in a series of South Italian folk-song which contains further evidence of this unconsciousl artistic instinct. The Italian folk-poet, for the mo part, lets the lore of tradition altogether alone. I does not lie in his province, which is purely lyrica But he has seized upon Fortune as a myth very ca

able of lyrical treatment, and following the free bent
of his genius, he has woven out of his subject the
delicate fancies of these songs. A series in the sense
of being designed to form a consecutive whole, they,
of course, are not. No two, probably, had the same
author; the perfect individuality of the figure presented, only showing how a type may be so firmly
fixed that the many have no difficulty in describing
it with the consistency of one man who draws the
creation of his own brain.

I.

Once in the gloaming, Fortune met me here;
Fair did she seem, and Love was on me laid,
Her hair was raised, as were it half a sphere,
Flowered on her breast a rose that cannot fade.
Then said I, "Fortune, thou without a peer,
What rule shall tell the measure of thine aid?"
"The pathway of the moon through all the year,
The channel of the exhaustless sea," she said.

II.

One night, the while I slept, drew Fortune near,
At once I loved, such beauty she displayed;
A crescent moon did o'er her brows appear,
And in her hand a wheel that never stayed.
Then said I to her, "O my mistress dear,
Grant all my wishes, mine if thou wilt aid."
But she turned from me with dark sullen cheer
And "Never!" as she turned, was all she said.

III.

I saw my Fortune midst the sounding sea
Sit weeping on a rocky height and steep,
Said I to her, "Fortune, how is't with thee?"
"I cannot help thee, child" (so answered she),
"I cannot help thee more—so must I weep."
How sweet were those her tears, how sweet, ah me!
Even the fishes wept within the deep.

Y

IV.

One day did Fortune call me to her side,
"What are the things," she asked, "that thou hast done?"
Then answered I, "Dear mistress, I have tried
To grave them upon marble, every one."
"Ah! maddest of the mad!" so she replied,
"Better hadst writ on sand than wrought in stone;
He who to marble should his love confide,
Loves when he loves till all his wits are gone."

V.

There where I lay asleep came Fortune in,
She came the while I slept and bid me wake,
"What dost thou now?" she said, "companion mine?
What dost thou now? Wilt thou then love forsake?
Arise," she said, "and take this violin,
And play till every stone thereat shall wake."
I was asleep when Fortune came to me,
And bid me rise, and led me unto thee!

These songs come from different villages; from
Caballino and Morciano in Calabria, from Corigliano
and Calimera in Terra d'Otranto; the two last are in
the Greek dialect spoken in the latter district. There
are a great many more, in all of which the same sweet
and serious type is preserved; but the above quinte
suffices to give a notion of this modern Magna
Græcian Idyll of Fortune.

FOLK-LULLABIES.

. . . A nurse's song
Of lullaby, to bring her babe asleep.

INFANCY is a great mystery. We know that we each have gone over that stage in human life, though even this much is not always quite easy to realise. But what else do we know about it? Something by observation, something by intuition; by experience hardly anything at all. We have as much personal acquaintance with a lake-dwelling or stone age infant as with our proper selves at the time when we were passing through the "avatar" of babyhood. The recollections of our earliest years are at most only as the confused remembrance of a morning dream, which at one end fades into the unconsciousness of sleep, whilst at the other it mingles with the realities of awaking. And yet, as a fact, we did not sleep through all the dawn of our life, nor were we unconscious; only we were different from what we now are; the term "thinking animal" did not then fit us so well. We were less reasonable and less material. Babies have a way of looking at you that makes you half suspect that they belong to a separate order of beings. You speculate as to whether they have not invisible wings, which drop off afterwards as do the birth wings of the young ant. There is one thing, however, in which the baby is very human, very manlike. Of all new-born creatures he is the least happy. You may sometimes see a little child crying softly to himself with a look of world woe on his face that is positively appalling. Perhaps human existence, like a new pair of shoes, is very uncomfortable till one gets accustomed to it. Anyhow the child, being for some reason or reasons exceedingly disposed to vex its heart, needs much soothing. In one highly civilised country a good many mothers are in the habit of going to the nearest druggist for the means to tranquillise their offspring, with the result that these latter are not unfrequently rescued from the sea of sorrows in the most final and expeditious way. In less advanced states of society another expedient has been resorted to from time immemorial—to wit, the cradle song.

Babies show an early appreciation of rhythm. They rejoice in measured noise, whether it takes the form of words, music, or the jingle of a bunch of keys. In the way of poetry I am afraid they must be admitted to have a perverse preference for what goes by the name of sing-song. It will be a long time before the infantine public are brought round to Walt Whitman's views on versification. For the rest, they are not very severe critics. The small ancient Roman asked for nothing better than the song of his nurse—

Lalla, lalla, lalla,
Aut dormi, aut lacta.

This two-line lullaby constitutes one of the few but sufficing proofs which have come down to us of the existence among the people of old Rome of a sort of folk verse not by any means resembling the Latin classics, but bearing a considerable likeness to the

canti popolari of the modern Italian peasant. It may
be said parenthetically that the study of dialect tends
altogether to the conviction that there are country
people now living in Italy to whom, rather than to
Cicero, we should go if we want to know what style
of speech was in use among the humbler subjects of
the Cæsars. The lettered language of the cultivated
classes changes; the spoken tongue of the uneducated
remains the same; or, if it too undergoes a process of
change, the rate at which it moves is to the other
what the pace of a tortoise is to the speed of an
express train. About eight hundred years ago a
handful of Lombards went to Sicily, where they still
preserve the Lombard idiom. The Ober-Engadiner
could hold converse with his remote ancestors who
took refuge in the Alps three or four centuries before
Christ; the Aragonese colony at Alghero, in Sardinia,
yet discourses in Catalan; the Roumanian language
still contains terms and expressions which, though
dissimilar to both Latin and standard Italian, find
their analogues in the dialects of those eastward-
facing "Latin plains" whence, in all probability, the
people of Roumania sprang. But we must return to
our lullabies.

There exists another Latin cradle song, not indeed
springing from classical times, but which, were popular
tradition to be trusted, would have an origin greatly
more illustrious than that of the laconic effusion of
the Roman nurse. It is composed in the person of
the Virgin Mary, and was, in bygone days, believed
to have been actually sung by her. Authorities differ
as to its real age, some insisting that the peculiar
structure of the verse was unknown before the 12th

century.　There is, however, good reason to think
that the idea of composing lullabies for the Virgin
belongs to an early period.

> Dormi, fili, dormi ! mater
>   Cantat unigenito :
> Dormi puer, dormi ! pater
>   Nato clamat parvulo :
> Millies tibi laudes canimus
> Mille, mille, millies.
>
> Lectum stravi tibi soli,
>   Dormi, nate bellule !
> Stravi lectum foeno molli :
>   Dormi mi animule.
> Millies tibi laudes canimus
> Mille, mille, millies.
>
> Dormi, decus et corona !
>   Dormi, nectar lacteum !
> Dormi, mater dabo dona,
>   Dabo favum melleum.
> Millies tibi laudes canimus
> Mille, mille, millies.
>
> Dormi, nate mi mellite !
>   Dormi plene saccharo,
> Dormi, vita, meae vitae,
>   Casto natus utero.
> Millies tibi laudes canimus
> Mille, mille, millies.
>
> Quidquid optes, volo dare ;
>   Dormi, parve pupule
> Dormi, fili ! dormi carae,
>   Matris deliciolae !
> Millies tibi laudes canimus
> Mille, mille, millies.

Dormi cor, et meus thronus ;
 Dormi matris jubilum ;
Aurium caelestis sonus,
 Et suave sibilum !
Millies tibi laudes canimus
Mille, mille, millies.

Dormi fili ! dulce, mater
 Dulce melos concinam ;
Dormi, nate ! suave, pater,
 Suave carmen accinam.
Millies tibi laudes canimus
Mille, mille, millies.

Ne quid desit, sternam rosis,
 Sternam foenum violis,
Pavimentum hyacinthis
 Et praesepe liliis.
Millies tibi laudes canimus
Mille, mille, millies.

Si vis musicam, pastores
 Convocabo protinus ;
Illis nulli sunt priores ;
 Nemo canit castius.
Millies tibi laudes canimus
Mille, mille, millies.

Everybody who is in Rome at Christmas-tide makes a point of visiting Santa Maria in Ara Cœli, the church which stands to the right of the Capitol, where once the temple of Jupiter Feretrius is supposed to have stood. What is at that season to be seen in the Ara Cœli is well enough known—to one side a " presepio," or manger, with the ass, the ox, St Joseph, the Virgin, and the Child on her knee ; to the other side a throng of little Roman children rehearsing in their infantine voices the story that is pictured

opposite.[1] The scene may be taken as typical of the
cult of the Infant Saviour, which, under one form or
another, has existed distinct and separable from the
main stem of Christian worship ever since a Voice in
Judæa bade man seek after the Divine in the stable
of Bethlehem. It is almost a commonplace to say
that Christianity brought fresh and peculiar glory
alike to infancy and to motherhood. A new sense
came into the words of the oracle—

> Thee in all children, the eternal Child . . .

And the mother, sublimely though she appears
against the horizon of antiquity, yet rose to a higher
rank—because the highest—at the founding of the
new faith. Especially in art she left the second place
that she might take the first. The sentiment of
maternal love, as illustrated, as transfigured, in the
love of the Virgin for her Divine Child, furnished the
great Italian painters with their master motive, whilst
in his humble fashion the obscure folk-poet exempli-
fies the selfsame thought. I am not sure that the
rude rhymes of which the following is a rendering do
not convey, as well as can be conveyed in articulate
speech, the glory and the grief of the Dresden
Madonna:

> Sleep, oh sleep, dear Baby mine,
> King Divine ;
> Sleep, my Child, in sleep recline ;

[1] The " Preaching of the children " took place as usual in the
Christmas week of 1885, but as the convent in connection with
the church of Santa Maria is about to be pulled down, I cannot
tell whether the pretty custom will be adhered to in future
The church, however, which was also threatened with demoli-
tion, is now safe.

Lullaby, mine Infant fair,
          Heaven's King
          All glittering,
Full of grace as lilies rare.

Close thine eyelids, O my treasure,
          Loved past measure,
Of my soul, the Lord, the pleasure;
Lullaby, O regal Child,
          On the hay
          My joy I lay;
Love celestial, meek and mild.

Why dost weep, my Babe? alas!
          Cold winds that pass
Vex, or is 't the little ass?
Lullaby, O Paradise;
          Of my heart
          Though Saviour art;
On thy face I press a kiss.

Wouldst thou learn so speedily,
          Pain to try,
          To heave a sigh?
Sleep, for thou shalt see the day
          Of dire scath,
          Of dreadful death,
To bitter scorn and shame a prey.

Rays now round thy brow extend,
          But in the end
A crown of cruel thorns shall bend.
Lullaby, O little one,
          Gentle guest
          Who for thy rest
A manger hast, to lie upon.

Born in winter of the year,
          Jesu dear,
As the lost world's prisoner.

Lullaby (for thou art bound
       Pain to know,
       And want and woe),
Mid the cattle standing round.

Beauty mine, sleep peacefully;
       Heaven's monarch! see,
With my veil I cover thee.
Lullaby, my Spouse, my Lord,
       Fairest Child
       Pure, undefiled,
Thou by all my soul adored. .

Lo ! the shepherd band draws nigh ;
       Horns they ply
Thee their Lord to glorify.
Lullaby, my soul's delight,
       For Israel,
       Faithless and fell,
Thee with cruel death would smite.

Now the milk suck from my breast,
       Holiest, best,
Thy kind eyes thou openest.
Lullaby, the while I sing ;
       Holy Jesu
       Now sleep anew,
My mantle is thy sheltering.

Sleep, sleep, thou who dost heaven impart
       My Lord thou art ;
Sleep, as I press thee to my heart.
Poor the place where thou dost lie,
       Earth's loveliest !
       Yet take thy rest ;
  Sleep my Child, and lullaby.

It would be interesting to know if Mrs Browning
ever heard any one of the many variants of this lullaby before writing her poem "The Virgin Mary to

the Child Jesus." The version given above was communicated to me by a resident at Vallauria, in the
heart of the Ligurian Alps. In that district it is
sung in the churches on Christmas Eve, when out
abroad the mountains sleep soundly in their snows
and a stray wolf is not an impossible apparition,
nothing reminding you that you are within a day's
journey of the citron groves of Mentone.

There are several old English carols which bear a
strong resemblance to the Italian sacred lullabies.
One, current at least as far back as the time of Henry
IV., is preserved among the Sloane MSS. :

Lullay ! lullay ! lytel child, myn owyn dere fode,
How xalt thou sufferin be nayled on the rode.
        So blyssid be the tyme !

Lullay ! lullay ! lytel child, myn owyn dere smerte,
How xalt thou sufferin the scharp spere to Thi herte ?
        So blyssid be the tyme !

Lullay ! lullay ! lytel child, I synge all for Thi sake,
Many on is the scharpe schour to Thi body is schape.
        So blyssid be the tyme !

Lullay ! lullay ! lytel child, fayre happis the befalle,
How xalt thou sufferin to drynke ezyl and galle ?
        So blyssid be the tyme !

Lullay ! lullay ! lytel child, I synge al beforn
How xalt thou sufferin the scharp garlong of thorn ?
        So blyssid be the tyme !

Lullay ! lullay ! lytel child, gwy wepy Thou so sore,
Thou art bothin God and man, gwat woldyst Thou be more ?
        So blyssid be the tyme !

Here, as in the Piedmontese song, the "shadow of
the cross " makes its presence distinctly felt, whereas

in the Latin lullaby it is wholly absent. Nor are there any dark or sad forebodings in the fragment:

> Dormi Jesu, mater ridet,
> Quæ tam dulcem somnum videt,
> Dormi, Jesu blandule.
> Si non dormis, mater plorat,
> Inter fila cantans orat :
> Blande, veni Somnule.

Many Italian Christmas cradle songs are in this lighter strain. In Italy and Spain a *presepio* or *nacimento* is arranged in old-fashioned houses on the eve of Christmas, and all kinds of songs are sung or recited before the white image of the Child as it lies in its bower of greenery. "Flower of Nazareth sleep upon my breast, my heart is thy cradle," sing the Tuscans, who curiously call Christmas "the Yule-log Easter." In Sicily a thousand endearing epithets are applied to the Infant Saviour : "figghiu duci," "Gesiuzzi beddu," "Gesiuzzi picchiureddi." The Sicilian poet relates how once, when the Madunazza was mending St Joseph's clothes, the Bambineddu cried in His cradle because no one was attending to Him ; so the archangel Raphael came down and rocked Him, and said three sweet little words to Him, "Lullaby, Jesus, Son of Mary!" Another time, when the Child was older and the mother was going to visit St Anne, he wept because He wished to go too. The mother let Him accompany her on condition that He would not break St Anne's bobbins. Yet another time the Virgin went to the fair to buy flax, and the Child said that He too would like to have a fairing. The Virgin buys Him a tambourine, and angels descend to listen to His playing. Such stories are end-

less ; some, no doubt, are invented on the spur of the
moment, but the larger portion are scraps of old
legendary lore. Not a few of the popular beliefs, relating to the Infant Jesus may be traced to the apocryphal Gospels, which were extensively circulated
during the earlier Christian centuries. There is, for
instance, a Provençal song containing the legend of
an apple-tree that bowed its branches to the Virgin,
which is plainly derived from this source. Speaking
of Provence, one ought not to forget the famous
"Troubadour of Bethlehem," Saboly, who was born
in 1640, and who composed more than sixty *noëls.*
Five pretty lines of his form an epitome of sacred
lullabies :

> Faudra dire, faudra dire,
> Quauco cansoun,
> Au garçoun,
> A la façoun
> D'aquelo de *soum-soum.*

George Wither deserves remembrance here for
what he calls a "Rocking hymn," written about the
year of Saboly's birth. "Nurses," he says, "usually
sing their children asleep, and through want of perti-
nent matter they oft make use of unprofitable, if not
worse, songs ; this was therefore prepared that it
might help acquaint them and their nurse children
with the loving care and kindness of their Heavenly
Father." Consciously or unconsciously, Wither caught
the true spirit of the ancient carols in the verses—
charming in spite, or perhaps because of their demure
simplicity—which follow his little exordium :

> Sweet baby, sleep : what ails my dear ;
> What ails my darling thus to cry ?

Be still, my child, and lend thine ear,
To hear me sing thy lullaby.
    My pretty lamb, forbear to weep ;
    Be still, my dear ; sweet baby, sleep.

Thou blessed soul, what canst thou fear?
What thing to thee can mischief do?
Thy God is now thy Father dear,
His holy Spouse thy mother too.
    Sweet baby, then forbear to weep ;
    Be still, my babe ; sweet baby, sleep. . . .

Whilst thus thy lullaby I sing,
For thee great blessings ripening be ;
Thine eldest brother is a king,
And hath a kingdom bought for thee.
    Sweet baby, then forbear to weep ;
    Be still, my babe ; sweet baby, sleep. &c., &c.

Count Gubernatis, in his "Usi Natalizj," quotes a popular Spanish lullaby, addressed to any ordinary child, but having reference to the Holy Babe :

The Baby Child of Mary,
    Now cradle He has none ;
His father is a carpenter,
    And he shall make Him one.

The lady good St Anna,
    The lord St Joachim,
They rock the Baby's cradle,
    That sleep may come to Him.

Then sleep thou too, my baby,
    My little heart so dear ;
The Virgin is beside thee,
    The Son of God is near.

When they are old enough to understand the meaning of words, children are sure to be interested up to a certain point by these saintly fables, but, taken as a whole, the songs of the South give us the impression that the coming of Christmas kindles the imagination of the Southern mother rather than that of the Southern child. On the north side of the Alps it is otherwise; there is scarcely need to say that in the Vaterland, Christmas is before all the children's feast. We, who have borrowed many of the German yule-tide customs, have left out the "Christkind;" and it is well that we have done so. Transplanted to foreign soil, that poetic piece of extra-belief would have become a mockery. As soon try to naturalise Koly-ada, the Sclavonic white-robed New-year girl. The Christkind in His mythical attributes is nearer to Kolyada than to the Italian Bambinello. He belongs to the people, not to the Church. He is not swathed in jewelled swaddling clothes; His limbs are free, and He has wings that carry Him wheresoever good children abide. There is about Him all the dreamy charm of lands where twilight is long and shade and shine intermingle softly, and where the earth's wintry winding-sheet is more beautiful than her April bride gown. The most popular of German lullabies is a truly Teutonic mixture of piety, wonder-lore, and homeliness. Wagner has introduced the music to which it is sung into his "Siegfried-Idyl." I have to thank a Heidelberg friend for the text:

> Sleep, baby, sleep:
> Your father tends the sheep;
>> Your mother shakes the branches small,
>> Whence happy dreams in showers fall:
> Sleep, baby, sleep.

Sleep, baby, sleep:
The sky is full of sheep;
>   The stars the lambs of heaven are,
>   For whom the shepherd moon doth care:
Sleep, baby, sleep.

Sleep, baby, sleep:
The Christ Child owns a sheep;
>   He is Himself the Lamb of God;
>   The world to save, to death He trod:
Sleep, baby, sleep.

Sleep, baby, sleep:
I'll give you then a sheep
>   With pretty bells, and you shall play
>   And frolic with him all the day:
Sleep, baby, sleep.

Sleep, baby, sleep:
And do not bleat like sheep,
>   Or else the shepherd's dog will bite
>   My naughty, little, crying spright:
Sleep, baby, sleep.

Sleep, baby, sleep:
Begone, and watch the sheep,
>   You naughty little dog! Begone,
>   And do not wake my little one:
Sleep, baby, sleep.

In Denmark children are sung to sleep with a
cradle hymn which is believed (so I am informed by
a youthful correspondent) to be "very old." It has
seven stanzas, of which the first runs, "Sleep sweetly,
little child; lie quiet and still; as sweetly sleep as
the bird in the wood, as the flowers in the meadow.
God the Father has said, 'Angels stand on watch
where mine, the little ones, are in bed.'" A correspondent at Warsaw (still more youthful) sends me
the even-song of Polish children:

The stars shine forth from the blue sky ;
   How great and wondrous is God's might ;
Shine, stars, through all eternity,
   His witness in the night.

O Lord, Thy tired children keep :
   Keep us who know and feel Thy might ;
Turn Thine eye on us as we sleep,
   And give us all good-night.

Shine, stars, God's sentinels on high,
   Proclaimers of His power and might ;
May all things evil from us fly :
   O stars, good-night, good-night !

Is this "Dobra Noc" of strictly popular origin? From internal evidence I should say that it is not. It seems, however, to be extremely popular in the ordinary sense of the word. Before me lie two or three settings of it by Polish musicians.

The Italians call lullabies *ninne-nanne*, a term used by Dante when he makes Forese predict the ills which are to overtake the dames of Florence :

   E se l'anteveder qui non m' inganna,
      Prima fien triste che le guance impeli
      Colui che mo si consola con *nanna.*

Some etymologists have sought to connect "nanna" with *neniæ* or νήνιτος, but its most apparent relationship is with ναυναρισματα, the modern Greek name for cradle songs, which is derived from a root signifying the singing of a child to sleep. The *ninne-nanne* of the various Italian provinces are to be found scattered here and there through volumes of folk poesy, and no attempt has yet been made to collate and compare them. Signor Dal Medico did indeed publish, some

z

ten years ago, a separate collection of Venetian nursery rhymes, but his initiative has not been followed up. The difficulty I had in obtaining the little work just mentioned is characteristic of the way in which Italian printed matter vanishes out of all being; instead of passing into the obscure but secure limbo into which much of English literature enters, it attains nothing short of Nirvāna—a happy state of non-existence. The inquiries of several Italian booksellers led to no other conclusion than that the book in question was not to be had for love or money; and most likely I should still have been waiting for it were it not for the courtesy of the Baron Giovanni di Sardagna, who, on hearing that it was wanted by a student of folk-lore, borrowed from the author the only copy in his possession and made therefrom a verbatim transcript. The following is one of Signor Dal Medico's lullabies :

> Hush ! lulla, lullaby !　So mother sings;
> For hearken, 'tis the midnight bell that rings.
> But, darling, not thy mother's bell is this :
> St Lucy's priests it calls to prayer, I wis.
> St Lucy gave thee eyes—a matchless pair—
> And gave the Magdalen her golden hair ;
> Thy cheeks their hue from heaven's angels have ;
> Her little loving mouth St Martha gave.
> Love's mouth, sweet mouth, that Florence hath for home,
> Now tell me where love springs, and how doth come? . . .
> With music and with song doth love arise,
> And then its end it hath in tears and sighs.

The question and answer as to the beginning and end of love run through all the songs of Italy, and in nearly every case the reply proceeds from Florence.

The personality of the answerer changes : sometimes it is a little wild bird ; on one occasion it is a preacher. And the idea has been suggested that the last is the original form, and that the Preacher of Florence who preaches against love is none other than Jeronimo Savonarola.

In an Istriot variant of the above song, "Santa Luceia" is spoken of as the Madonna of the eyes ; "Santa Puluonia" as the Madonna of the teeth : we hear also something of the Magdalene's old shoes and of the white lilies she bears in her hands. It is not always quite clear upon what principle the folk-poet shapes his descriptions of religious personages ; if the gifts and belongings he attributes to them are at times purely conventional, at others they seem to rest on no authority, legendary or historic. Most likely his ideas as to the personal appearance of such or such a saint are formed by the paintings in the church where he is accustomed to go to mass ; it is probable, too, that he is fond of talking of the patrons of his village or of the next village, whose names are associated with the *feste*, which as long as he can recollect have constituted the great annual events of his life. But two or three saints have a popularity independent of local circumstance. One of these is Lucy, whom the people celebrate with equal enthusiasm from her native Syracuse to the port of Pola. Perhaps the maiden patroness of the blessed faculty of vision has come to be thought of as a sort of gracious embodiment of that which her name signifies : of the sweet light which to the southerner is not a mere helpmate in the performance of daily tasks, but a providential luxury. Concerning the earthly career of their favourite, her peasant votaries have vague notions : once when a French traveller in the Apennines suggested that St Januarius might be jealous of her praises, he received the answer, "*Ma che, excellenza,* St Lucy was St Januarius' wife !"

In Greece we find other saints invoked over the baby's cradle. The Greek of modern times has his face, his mind, his heart, set in an undeviating eastward position. To holy wisdom and to Marina, the Alexandrian martyr, the Greek mother confides her cradled darling :

> Put him to bed, St Marina ; send him to sleep, St Sophia ! Take him out abroad that he may see how the trees flower and how the birds sing ; then come back and bring him with you, that his father may not ask for him, may not beat his servants, that his mother may not seek him in vain, for she would weep and fall sick, and her milk would turn bitter.

At Gessopalena, in the province of Chieti (Abruzzo Citeriore) there would seem to be much faith in numbers. Luke and Andrew, Michael and Joseph, Hyacinth and Matthew are called in, and as if these were not enough to nurse one baby, a summons is sent to *Sant Giusaffat,* who, as is well known, is neither more nor less than Buddha introduced into the Catholic calendar.

Another of Signor Dal Medico's *ninne-nanne* presents several points of interest :

> O Sleep, O Sleep, O thou beguiler, Sleep,
> Beguile this child, and in beguilement keep,
> Keep him three hours, and keep him moments three ;
> Until I call beguile this child for me.
> And when I call I'll call :—My root, my heart,
> The people say my only wealth thou art.
> Thou art my only wealth ; I tell thee so.
> Now, bit by bit, this boy to sleep will go ;

He falls and falls to sleeping bit by bit,
Like the green wood what time the fire is lit,
Like to green wood that never flame 'can dart,
Heart of thy mother, of thy father heart !
Like to green wood, that never flame can shoot.
Sleep thou, my cradled hope, sleep thou, my root,
My cradled hope, my spirit's strength and stay ;
Mother, who bore thee, wears her life away ;
Her life she wears away, and all day long
She goes a-singing to her child this song.

Now, in the first place, the comparison of the child's gradual falling asleep with the slow ignition of fresh-cut wood is the common property of all the populations whose ethnical centre of gravity lies in Venice. I have seen an Istriot version of it, and I heard it sung by a countrywoman at San Martino di Castrozza in the Trentino ; so that, at all event, *Italia redenta* and *irredenta* has a community of song. The second thing that calls for remark is the direct invocation of sleep. A distinct little group of cradle ditties displays this characteristic. " Come, sleep," cries the Grecian mother, " come, sleep, take him away ; come sleep, and make him slumber. Carry him to the vineyard of the Aga, to the gardens of the Aga. The Aga will give him grapes ; his wife, roses ; his servant, pancakes." A second Greek lullaby must have sprung from a luxuriant imagination. It comes from Schio :

Sleep, carry off my son, o'er whom three sentinels do watch,
Three sentinels, three warders brave, three mates you cannot
    match.
These guards : the sun upon the hill, the eagle on the plain,
And Boreas, whose chilly blasts do hurry o'er the main.
—The sun went down into the west, the eagle sank to sleep,
Chill Boreas to his mother sped across the briny deep.

"My son, where were you yesterday? Where on the former
   night?
Or with the moon or with the stars did you contend in fight?
Or with Orion did you strive—though him I deem a friend?"
"Nor with the stars, nor with the moon, did I in strife contend,
Nor with Orion did I fight, whom for your friend I hold,
But guarded in a silver cot a child as bright as gold."

The Greeks have a curious way of looking at sleep:
they seem absorbed in the thought of what dreams
may come — if indeed the word dream rightly
describes their conception of that which happens to
the soul while the body takes its rest—if they do
not rather cling to some vague notion of a real
severance between matter and spirit during sleep.

The mothers of La Bresse (near Lyons) invoke
sleep under the name of "le souin-souin." I wish I
could give here the sweet, inedited melody which
accompanies these lines:

Le poupon voudrait bien domir ;
Le souin-souin ne veut pas venir.
Souin-souin, vené, vené, vené ;
Souin-souin, vené, vené, donc !

The Chippewaya Indians were in the habit of
personifying sleep as an immense insect called Weeng,
which someone once saw at the top of a tree engaged in making a buzzing noise with its wings.
Weeng produced sleep by sending fairies, who beat
the foreheads of tired mortals with very small clubs.

Sleep acts the part of questioner in the lullaby of
the Finland peasant woman, who sings to her child
in its bark cradle: "Sleep, little field bird; sleep
sweetly, pretty redbreast. God will wake thee when

it is time. Sleep is at the door, and says to me, ' Is
not there a sweet child here who fain would sleep?
a young child wrapped in swaddling clothes, a fair
child resting beneath his woollen coverlet?'" A
questioning sleep makes his appearance likewise in a
Sicilian *ninna :*—

My little son, I wish you well, your mother's comfort when in
grief.
My pretty boy, what can I do? Will you not give one hour's
relief?
Sleep has just past, and me he asked if this my son in slumber
lay.
Close, close your little eyes, my child ; send your sweet breath
far leagues away.
You are the fount of rose water ; you are with every beauty
fraught.
Sleep, darling son, my pretty one, my golden button richly
wrought.

A vein of tender reproach is sprung in that inquiry,
" Ca n' ura ri riposu 'un vuo rari?" The mother
appeals to the better feeling, to the Christian charity
as it were, of the small but implacable tyrant. Another time she waxes yet more eloquent. " Son, my
comfort, I am not happy. There are women who
laugh and enjoy themselves while I chafe my very
life out. Listen to me, child ; beautiful is the lullaby
and all the folk are asleep—but thou, no! My wise
little son, I look about for thy equal ; nowhere do I
find him. Thou art mamma's consolation. There,
do sleep just a little while." So pleads the Sicilian ;
her Venetian sister tries to soften the obduracy of
her infant by still more plaintive remonstrances.
" Hushaby ; but if thou dost not sleep, hear me. Thou

hast robbed me of my heart and of all my sentiments. I really do not know for what cause thou lamentest, and never will have done lamenting." On this occasion the appeal seems to be made to some purpose, for the song concludes, " The eyes of my joy are closing ; they open a little and then they shut. Now is my joy at peace with me and no longer at war." So happy an issue does not always arrive. It may happen that the perverse babe flatly refuses to listen to the mother's voice, sing she never so sweetly. Perhaps he might have something to say for himself could he but speak, at any rate in the matter of midday slumbers. It must no doubt be rather trying to be called upon to go straight to sleep just when the sunbeams are dancing round and round and wildly inviting you to make your first studies in optics. Most often the long-suffering mother, if she does not see things in this light, acts as though she did. Her patience has no limit ; her caresses are never done ; with untiring love she watches the little wakeful, wilful culprit—

> Chi piangendo e ridendo pargoleggia . . . .

But it is not always so ; there are times when she loses all patience, and temper into the bargain. Such a contingency is only too faithfully reflected in a Sicilian *ninna* which ends with the utterance of a horrible wish that Doctor Death would come and quiet the recalcitrant baby once for all. I ought to add that this same murderous lullaby is nevertheless brimful of protestations of affection and compliments ; the child is told that his eyes are the finest imaginable, his cheeks two roses, his countenance

like the moon's. The amount of incense which the
Sicilian mother burns before her offspring would
suffice to fill any number of cathedrals. Every
moment she breaks forth into words such as, " Hush !
child of my breath, bunch of jasmine, handful of
oranges and lemons ; go to sleep, my son, my beauty :
I have got to take thy portrait." It has been remarked that a person who resembled an orange
would scarcely be very attractive, whence it is inferred that the comparison came into fashion at the
date when the orange tree was first introduced into
Sicily and when its fruit was esteemed a rare novelty.
A little girl is described as a spray of lilies and a
bouquet of roses. A little boy is assured that his
mother prefers him to gold or fine silver. If she lost
him where would she find a beloved son like to him ?
A child dropped out of heaven, a laurel garland, one
under whose feet spring up flowers ? Here is a string
of blandishments prettily wound up in a prayer :

Hush, my little round-faced daughter ; thou art like the stormy
   sea.
Daughter mine of finest amber, godmother sends sleep to thee.
Fair thy name, and he who gave it was a gallant gentleman.
Mirror of my soul, I marvel when thy loveliness I scan.
Flame of love, be good. I love thee better far than life I love.
Now my child sleeps. Mother Mary, look upon her from
   above.

The form taken by parental flattery shows the
tastes of nations and of individuals. The other day
a young and successful English artist was heard to
exclaim with profound conviction, whilst contemplating his son and heir, twenty-four hours old, " There is
a great deal of *tone* about that baby ! "

The Hungarian nurse tells her charge that his cot must be of rosewood and his swaddling clothes of rainbow threads spun by angels. The evening breeze is to rock him, the kiss of the falling star to awake him; she would have the breath of the lily touch him gently, and the butterflies fan him with their brilliant wings. Like the Sicilian, the Magyar has an innate love of splendour.

Corsica has a *ninna-nanna* into which the whole genius of its people seems to have passed. The village *fêtes*, with dancing and music, the flocks and herds and sheep-dogs, even the mountains, stars, and sea, and the perfumed air off the *macchi*, come back to the traveller in that island as he reads—

> Hushaby, my darling boy;
> Hushaby, my hope and joy.
> You're my little ship so brave
> Sailing boldly o'er the wave ;
> One that tempests doth not fear,
> Nor the winds that blow from high.
> Sleep awhile, my baby dear ;
> Sleep, my child, and hushaby.
>
> Gold and pearls my vessel lade,
> Silk and cloth the cargo be,
> All the sails are of brocade
> Coming from beyond the sea ;
> And the helm of finest gold,
> Made a wonder to behold.
> Fast awhile in slumber lie ;
> Sleep, my child, and hushaby.
>
> After you were born full soon
> You were christened all aright ;
> Godmother she was the moon,
> Godfather the sun so bright ;

All the stars in heaven told
Wore their necklaces of gold.
Fast awhile in slumber lie ;
Sleep, my child, and hushaby.

Pure and balmy was the air,
Lustrous all the heavens were ;
And the seven planets shed
All their virtues on your head ;
And the shepherds made a feast
Lasting for a week at least.
Fast awhile in slumber lie ;
Sleep, my child, and hushaby.

Nought was heard but minstrelsy,
Nought but dancing met the eye,
In Cassoni's vale and wood
And in all the neighbourhood ;
Hawk and Blacklip, stanch and true,
Feasted in their fashion too.
Fast awhile in slumber lie ;
Sleep, my child, and hushaby.

Older years when you attain,
You will roam o'er field and plain ;
Meadows will with flowers be gay,
And with oil the fountains play,
And the salt and bitter sea
Into balsam changèd be.
Fast awhile in slumber lie ;
Sleep, my child, and hushaby.

And these mountains, wild and steep,
Will be crowded o'er with sheep,
And the wild goat and the deer
Will be tame and void of fear ;
Vulture, fox, and beast of prey,
From these bounds shall flee away.
Fast awhile in slumber lie ;
Sleep, my child, and hushaby.

You are savory, sweetly blowing,
You are thyme, of incense smelling,
Upon Mount Basella growing,
Upon Mount Cassoni dwelling;
You the hyacinth of the rocks
Which is pasture for the flocks.
Fast awhile in slumber lie ;
Sleep, my child, and hushaby.

At the sight of a new-born babe the Corsican involuntarily sets to work making auguries. The mountain shepherds place great faith in divination based on . the examination of the shoulder-blades of animals : according to the local tradition the famous prophecy of the greatness of Napoleon was drawn up after this method. The nomad tribes of Central Asia search the future in precisely the same way. Corsican lullabies are often prophetical. An old woman predicts a strange sort of millennium, to begin with the coming of age of her grandson :

"There grew a boy in Palneca of Pumonti, and his dear grandmother was always rocking his cradle, always wishing him this destiny :—

" Sleep, O little one, thy grandmother's joy and gladness, for I have to prepare the supper for thy dear little father, and thy elder brothers, and I have to make their clothes.

"When thou art older, thou wilt traverse the plains, the grass will turn to flowers, the sea-water will become sweet balm.

" We will make thee a jacket edged with red and turned up in points, and a little peaked hat, trimmed with gold braid.

" When thou art bigger, thou wilt carry arms ; neither soldier nor gendarme will frighten thee, and if thou art driven up into a corner, thou wilt make a famous bandit.

" Never did woman of our race pass thirteen years unwed, for when an impertinent fellow dared so much as look at her, he escaped not two weeks unless he gave her the ring.

" But that scoundrel of Morando surprised the kinsfolk, arrested them all in one day, and wrought their ruin. And the thieves of Palneca played the spy.

" Fifteen men were hung, all in the market-place : men of great worth, the flower of our race. Perhaps it will be thou, O dearest ! who shall accomplish the vendetta !"

An unexpected yet logical development leads from the peaceful household cares, the joyous images of the familiar song, the playful picture of the baby boy in jacket and pointed hat, to a terrible recollection of deeds of shame and blood, long past, and perhaps half-forgotten by the rest of the family, but at which the old dame's breast still burns as she rocks the sleeping babe on whom is fixed her last passionate hope of vengeance fulfilled.

In the mountain villages scattered about the borders of the vast Sila forest, Calabrian mothers whisper to their babes, " brigantiellu miu, brigantiellu della mamma." They tell the little ones gathered round their knees legends of Fra Diavolo and of Talarico, just as Sardinian mothers tell the legend of Tolu of Florinas. This last is a story of to-day. In 1850, Giovanni Tolu married the niece of the priest's house-keeper. The priest opposed the marriage, and soon after it had taken place, in the absence of Tolu, he persuaded the young wife to leave her husband's house, never to return. Tolu, meeting his enemy in a lonely path, fired his pistol, but by some accident it did not go off, and the priest escaped with his life. Arrest and certain conviction, however, awaited Tolu, who preferred to take to the woods, where he remained for thirty years, a prince among outlaws. He pro-tected the weak ; administered a rude but wise justice to the scattered peasants of the waste country between Sassari and the sea ; his swift horse was always ready to fly in search of their lost or stolen cattle ; his gun was the terror of the thieves who preyed upon these poor people. In Osilo lived two families, hereditary foes, the Stacca and the Achena. An Achena offered Tolu five hundred francs to kill the head of the Stacca family. Tolu not only refused, he did not rest till he had brought about a reconciliation between the two houses. At last, in the autumn of 1880, the gendarmes, after thirty years' failure, arrested Tolu without a struggle at a place where he had gone to take part in a country *festa*. For two years he was kept untried in prison. In September 1882 he was brought before the Court of Assize at Frosinone. Not a witness could be found to testify against him. "Tolu," they said, "è un Dio." When asked by the President what he had to say in his defence, he replied : "I never fired first. The carabineers hunted me like a wild beast, because a price was set on my head, and like a wild beast I defended myself." The jury brought in a verdict of acquittal ; and if any one wishes to make our hero's acquaintance, he has only to take ship for Sardinia and then find the way to the village of Florinas, where he is now peaceably living, beloved and respected by all who know him.

The Sardinian character has old-world virtues and old-world blemishes ; if you live in the wilder districts you may deem it advisable to keep a loaded pistol on the table at meal-time ; but then you may go all over the island without letters of introduction, sure of a hearty welcome, and an hospitality which gives to the stranger the best of everything that there is. If the

Sardinian has an imperfect apprehension of the sacredness of other laws, he is blindly obedient to that of custom; when some progressive measure is proposed, he does not argue—he says quietly: " Custu non est secundu la moda nostra." No man sweeps the dust on antique time less than he. One of his distinctive traits is an overweening fondness of his children; the ever-marvellous baby is represented not only as the glory of its mother, but also as the light even of its most distant connexions—

> Lullaby, sweet lullaby,
> You our happiness supply;
> Fair your face, and sweet your ways,
> You, your mother's pride and praise.
> As the coral, rare and bright,
> In your life does father live ;
> You, of all the dear delight,
> All around you pleasure give.
>
> All your ways, my pretty boy,
> Of your parents are the joy;
> You were born for good alone,
> Sunshine of the family !
> Wise, and kind to every one.
> Light of every kinsman's eye ;
> Light of all who hither come,
> And the gladness of our home.
>   Lullaby, sweet lullaby.

On the northern shore the people speak a tongue akin to that of the neighbouring isle, and the dialect of the south is semi-Spanish; but in the midland Logudoro the old Sard speech is spoken much as it is known to have been spoken a thousand years ago. It is simply a rustic Latin. Canon Spano's loving rather than critical labours have left Sardinia a fine field for some future folk-lore collector. The Sardinian is short in speech, copious in song. I asked a lad, just returned to Venetia from working in Sardinian quarries, if the people there had many songs? "Oh! tanti!" he answered, with a gesture more expressive than the words. He had brought back more than a touch of that malarious fever which is the scourge of the island and a blight upon all efforts to develop its rich resources. A Sardinian friend tells me that the Sard poet often shows a complete contempt for metrical rules; his poesy is apt to become a rhythmic chant of which the words and music cannot be dissevered. But the Logudorian lullabies are regular in form, their distinguishing feature being an interjection with an almost classical ring that replaces the *fa la nanna* of Italy—

> Oh! ninna and anninia !
>   Sleep, baby boy ;
> Oh! ninna and anninia !
>   God give thee joy.
> Oh! ninna and anninia !
>   Sweet joy be thine ;
> Oh! ninna and anninia !
>   Sleep, brother mine.
>
> Sleep, and do not cry,
>   Pretty, pretty one,
> Apple of mine eye,
>   Danger there is none ;
> Sleep, for I am by,
>   Mother's darling son.
>
> Oh! ninna and anninia !
>   Sleep, baby boy ;
> Oh! ninna and anninia !
>   God give thee joy.

Oh ! ninna and anninia !
Sweet joy be thine ;
Oh ! ninna and anninia !
. Sleep, brother mine.

The singer is the little mother-sister : the child who, while the mother works in the fields or goes to market, is left in charge of the last-come member of the family, and is bound to console it as best she may, for the absence of its natural guardian. The baby is to her somewhat of a doll, just as to the children of the rich the doll is somewhat of a baby. She may be met without going far afield ; anyone who has lived near an English village must know the curly-headed little girl who sits on the cottage door-step or among the meadow buttercups, her arms stretched at full length, round a soft, black-eyed creature, small indeed, yet not much smaller than herself. This, she solemnly informs you, is her baby. Not quite so often can she be seen now as before the passing of the Education Act, prior to which all truants fell back on the triumphant excuse, " I can't go to school because I have to mind my baby," some neighbouring infant brother, cousin, nephew, being producible at a moment's notice in support of the assertion. In those days the mere sight of a baby filled persons interested in the promotion of public instruction with wrath and suspicion. Yet woman-hood would lose a sweet and sympathetic phase were the little mother-sister to wholly disappear. The songs of the child-nurse are of the slenderest kind ; the tether of her imagination has not been cut by hope or memory. As a rule she dwells upon the important fact that mother will soon be here, and

when she has said that, she has not much more to
say. So it is in an Istriot song: "This is a child
who is always crying; be quiet, my soul, for mother
is coming back; she will bring thee nice milk, and
then she will put thee in the crib to hushaby." A
Tuscan correspondent sends me a sister-rhyme which
is introduced by a pretty description of the grave-eyed
little maiden, of twelve or thirteen years perhaps, responsible almost to sadness, who leans down her face
over the baby brother she is rocking in the cradle;
and when he stirs and begins to cry, sings softly the
oft-told tale of how the dear mamma will come
quickly and press him lovingly to her breast:

> Che fa mai col volto chino,
>   Quella tacita fanciulla?
> Sta vegliando il fratellino,
>   Adagiato nella culla.
>
> Ed il pargolo se desta,
>   E il meschino prorompe in pianto,
> La bambina, mesta, mesta,
>   Vuol chetarlo col suo canto:
>
> Bambolino mio, riposa,
>   Presto mamma tornerà;
> Cara mamma che amorosa
>   Al suo sen ti stringerà.

The little French girl turns her thoughts to the hot
milk and chocolate that are being prepared, and of
which she no doubt expects to have a share:—

> Fais dodo, Colin, mon p'tit frère,
> Fais dodo, t'auras du lolo.
>   Le papa est en haut, qui fait le lolo,
>   Le maman est en bas, qui fait le colo;
> Fais dodo, Colin, mon p'tit frère
>   Fais dodo

In enumerating the rewards for infantine virtue—which is sleep—I must not forget the celebrated hare's skin to be presented to Baby Bunting, and the "little fishy" that the English father, set to be nurse *ad interim*, promises his "babby" when the ship comes in ; nor should I pass over the hopes raised in an inedited cradle song of French Flanders, which opens, like the Tuscan lullaby, with a short narration :

> Un jour un' pauv' dentillière
> En amicliton ch'un petiot garchun,
> Qui d'puis le matin n'fesions que blaîre,
> Voulait l'endormir par une canchun.

In this barbarous *patios*, the poor lace-maker tells her "p'tit pocchin" (little chick) that to-morrow he shall have a cake made of honey, spices, and rye flour ; that he shall be dressed in his best clothes "com' un bieau milord ; " and that at "la Ducasse," a local *fête*, she will buy him a laughable Polchinello and a bird-organ playing the tune of the sugar-loaf hat. Toys are also promised in a Japanese lullaby, which the kindness of the late author of "Child-life in Japan" has enabled me to give in the original :

> Nén-ne ko yŏ—nén-né ko yŏ
> Nén-né no mori wa—doko ye yuta
> Ano yama koyété—sato ye yuta
> Sato no miyagé ni—nani morota
> Tén-tén taiko ni—shŏ no fuyé
> Oki-agari koboshima—ìnu hari-ko.

Signifying in English :

> Lullaby, baby, lullaby, baby
> Baby's nursey, where has she gone

Over those mountains she 's gone to her village ;　.
And from her village, what will she bring?
A tum-tum drum, and a bamboo flute,
A " daruma " (which will never turn over) and a paper dog.

Scope is allowed for unlimited extension, as the
singer can go on mentioning any number of toys.
The *Daruma* is what English children call a tumbler ;
a figure weighted at the bottom, so that turn it how
you will, it always regains its equilibrium.

More ethereal delights than chocolate, hare's skins,
bird-organs, or even paper dogs (though these last
sound irresistibly seductive), form the subject of a
beautiful little Greek song of consolation : " Lullaby,
lullaby, thy mother is coming back from the laurels
by the river, from the sweet banks she will bring thee
flowers ; all sorts of flowers, roses, and scented pinks."
When she does come back, the Greek mother makes
such promises as eclipse all the rest : " Sleep, my
child, and I will give thee Alexandria for thy sugar,
Cairo for thy rice, and Constantinople, there to reign
three years ! " Those who see deep meaning in
childish things will look with interest at the young
Greek woman, who sits vaguely dreaming of empire
while she rocks her babe. The song is particularly
popular in Cyprus ; the English residents there must
be familiar with the melody—an air constructed on
the Oriental scale, and only the other day set on
paper. The few bars of music are like a sigh of passionate longing.

From reward to punishment is but a step, and next
in order to the songs that refer to the recompense of
good, sleepy children, must be placed those hinting at
the serious consequences which will be the result of
unyielding wakefulness. It must be confessed that

retribution does not always assume a very awful form; in fact, in one German rhyme, it comes under so gracious a disguise, that a child might almost lie awake on purpose to look out for it :

> Sleep, baby, sleep,
> I can see two little sheep ;
> One is black and one is white,
> And, if you do not sleep to-night,
> First the black and then the white
> Will give your little toes a bite.

The translation is by " Hans Breitmann."

In the threatening style of lullaby, the bogey plays a considerable part. A history of the bogeys of all nations would be an instructive book. The hero of one people is the bogey of another. Wellington and Napoleon (or rather " Boney ") served to scare naughty babies long after the latter, at least, was laid to rest. French children still have songs about " le Prince Noir," and the nurses sang during the siege of Paris :

> As-tu vu Bismarck
> A la porte de Chatillon ?
> Il lance les obus
> Sur le Panthéon.

The Moor is the nursery terror of many parts of Southern Europe; not, however, it would seem of Sicily—a possible tribute to the enlightened rule of the Kalifs. The Greeks do not enjoy a like immunity : Signor Avolio mentions, in his " Canti popolari di Noto," that besides saying "the wolf is coming," it is common for mothers to frighten their little ones with, " Zittiti, ca viènunu i Riece ; Nu sciri ca 'ncianu

ci sù i Rieci" ("Hush, for the Greeks are coming':
don't go outside for the Greeks are there.") Noto
was the centre of the district where the ancient Sikeli
made their last stand against Greek supremacy: a
coincidence that opens the way to bold speculation,
though the originals of the bogey Greeks may have
been only pirates of times far less remote.

In Germany the same person distributes rewards
and punishments: St Nicholas in the Rhenish provinces, Knecht Ruprecht in Northern and Central
Germany, Julklapp in Pomerania.   On Christmas
eve, some one cries out "Julklapp!" from behind a
door, and throws the gift into the room with the
child's name pinned upon it. Even the gentle St
Lucy, the Santa Claus of Lombardy, withholds her
cakes from erring babes, and little Tuscans stand a
good deal in awe of their friend the Befana; delightful as are the treasures she puts in their shoes when
satisfied with their behaviour, she is credited with an
unpleasantly sharp eye for youthful transgressions.
She has a relative in Japan of the name of Hotii.
Once upon a time Hotii, who belongs to the sterner
sex, lived on earth in the garb of a priest. His birthland was China, and he had the happy fame of being
extremely kind to children. At present he walks
about Japan with a big sack full of good things for
young people, but the eyes with which the back of
his head is furnished, enable him to see in a second
if any child misconducts itself. Of more dubious
antecedents is another patron of the children of Japan,
Kishi Mojin, the mother of the child-demons. Once
Kishi Mojin had the depraved habit of stealing any
young child she could lay hands on and eating it. In

spite of this, she was sincerely attached to her own family, which numbered one thousand, and when the exalted Amida Niorai hid one of its members to punish her for her cruel practices, she grieved bitterly. Finally the child was given back on condition that Kishi Mojin would never more devour her neighbours' infants : she was advised to eat the fruit of the pomegranate whenever she had a craving for unnatural food. Apparently she took the advice and kept the compact, as she is honoured on the 28th day of every month, and little children are taught to solicit her protection. The kindness shown to children both in Japan and China is well known ; in China one baby is said to be of more service in insuring a safe journey than an armed escort.

"El coco," a Spanish bogey, figures in a sleep-song from Malaga : "Sleep, little child, sleep, my soul ; sleep, little star of the morning. My child sleeps with eyes open like the hares. Little baby girl, who has beaten thee that thine eyes look as if they had been crying ? Poor little girl ! who has made thy face red ? The rose on the rose-tree is going to sleep, and to sleep goes my child, for already it is late. Sleep little daughter for the *coco* comes."

The folk-poet in Spain reaps the advantage of a recognised freedom of versification ; with the great stress laid upon the vowels, a consonant more or less counts for nothing :

> A dormir va la rosa
> De los rosales ;
> A dormir va mi niña
> Porque ya es tarde.

All folk-poets, and notably the English, have recourse

to an occasional assonant, but the Spaniard can trust altogether to such. Verse-making is thus made easy, provided ideas do not fail, and up to to-day, they have not failed the Spanish peasant. He has not, like the Italian, begun to leave off composing songs. My correspondent at Malaga writes that at that place improvisation seems innate in the people: they go before a house and sing the commonest thing they wish to express. Love and hate they also turn into songs, to be rehearsed under the window of the individual loved or hated. There is even an old woman now living in Malaga who rhymes in Latin with extraordinary facility. To the present section falls one other lullaby—coo-aby, perhaps I ought to say, since the Spanish *arrullo* means the cooing of doves as well as the lulling of children. It is quoted by Count Gubernatis:

Isabellita, do not pine
  Because the flowers fade away;
  If flowers hasten to decay
Weep not, Isabellita mine.

Little one, now close thine eyes,
  Hark, the footsteps of the Moor!
  And she asks from door to door,
Who may be the child who cries?

When I was as small as thou
  And within my cradle lying,
  Angels came about me flying
And they kissed me on my brow.

Sleep, then, little baby, sleep:
  Sleep, nor cry again to-night,
  Lest the angels take to flight
So as not to see thee weep.

"The Moor" is in this instance a benignant kind of
bogey, not far removed from harmless "wee Willie
Winkile" who runs upstairs and downstairs in his
nightgown:

> Tapping at the window,
> Crying at the lock,
> "Are the babes in their beds?
> For it's now ten o'clock."

These myths have some analogy with a being known
as "La Dormette" who frequents the neighbourhood
of Poitou. She is a good old woman who throws
sand and sleep on children's eyes, and is hailed with
the words:

> Passez la Dormette,
> Passez par chez nous !
> Endormir gars et fillettes
> La nuit et le jou.

Now and then we hear of an angel who passes by at
nightfall; it is not clear what may be his mission,
but he is plainly too much occupied to linger with
his fellow seraphs, who have nothing to do but to kiss
the babe in its sleep. A little French song speaks of
this journeying angel:

> Il est tard, l'ange a passé,
> Le jour a déja baissé ;
> Et l'on n'entend pour tout bruit
> Que le ruisseau qui s'enfuit.
> Endors toi,
> Mon fils ! c'est moi.
> Il est tard et ton ami,
> L'oiseau blue, s'est endormi.

In Calabria, when a butterfly flits around a baby's
cradle, it is believed to be either an angel or a baby's
soul.

The pendulum of good and evil is set swinging from the moment that the infant draws its first breath. Angelical visitation has its complement in demonial influence; it is even difficult to resist the conclusion that the ministers of light are frequently outnumbered by the powers of darkness. In most Christian lands the unbaptised child is given over entirely to the latter. Sicilian women are loth to kiss a child before its christening, because they consider it a pagan or a Turk. In East Tyrol and Styria, persons who take a child to be baptised say on their return—"A Jew we took away, a Christian we bring back." Some Tyrolese mothers will not give any food to their babies till the rite has been performed. . The unbaptised Greek is thought to be simply a small demon, and is called by no other designation than ςρακος if a boy, and ςρακουλα if a girl. Once when a christening was unavoidably delayed, the parents got so accustomed to calling their little girl by the snake name, that they continued doing so even after she had been presented with one less equivocal. Dead unchristened babes float about on the wind; in Tyrol they are marshalled along by Berchte, the wife of Pontius Pilate; in Scotland they may be heard moaning on calm nights. The state to which their baby souls are relegated, is probably a lingering recollection of that into which, in pagan days, all innocent spirits were conceived to pass: an explanation that has also the merit of being as little offensive as any that can be offered. There is naturally a general wish to make baptism follow as soon as possible after birth—an end that is sometimes pursued regardless of the bodily risks it may involve. A poor

woman gave birth to a child at the mines of Vallauria; it was a bitterly cold winter; the snow lay
deep enough to efface the mountain tracks, and
all moisture froze the instant it was exposed to the
air. However, the grandmother of the new-born
babe carried it off immediately to Tenda—many
miles away—for the christening rite. As she had
been heard to remark that it was a useless encum-
brance, there were some who attributed her action to
other motives than religious zeal; but the child survived the ordeal and prospered. In several parts of the
Swiss mountains a baptism, like a funeral, is an event
for the whole community. I was present at a christening in a small village lying near the summit of the
Julier Pass. The bare, little church was crowded,
and the service was performed with a reverent care-
fulness contrasting sharply with the mechanical and
hurried performance of a baptism witnessed shortly
before in a very different place, the glorious baptistry
at Florence. It ended with a Lutheran hymn, sung
sweetly without accompaniment, by five or six young
girls. More than half of the congregation consisted
of men, whose weather-tried faces were wet with tears,
almost without exception. I could not find out that
there was anything particularly sad in the circumstances of the case; the women certainly wore black,
but then, the rule of attending the funerals even of
mere acquaintances, causes the best dress in Switzerland to be always one suggestive of mourning. It
seemed that the pathos of the dedication of a dawning
life to the Supreme Good was sufficient to touch the
hearts of these simple folk, starved from coarser
emotion.

In Calabria it is thought unlucky to be either born or christened on a Friday. Saturday is likewise esteemed an inauspicious day, which points to its association with the witches' Sabbath, once the subject of numerous superstitious beliefs throughout the southern provinces of Italy. Not far from the battle-field near Benevento where Charles of Anjou defeated Manfred, grew a walnut tree, which had an almost European fame as the scene of Sabbatical orgies. People used to hang upon its branches the figure of a two-headed viper coiled into a ring, a symbol of incalculable antiquity. St Barbatus had the tree cut down, but the devil raised new shoots from the root and so it was renewed. Shreds of snake-worship may be still collected. The Calabrians hold that the cast-off skin of a snake is an excellent thing to put under the pillow of a sick baby. Even after their christening, children are unfortunately most suscepti-ble to enchantment. When a beautiful and healthy child sickens and dies, the Irish peasant infers that the genuine baby has been stolen by fairies, and this miserable sprite left in its place. Two ancient anti-dotes have great power to counteract the effect of spells. One is the purifying Fire. In Scotland, as in Italy, bewitched children, within the memory of living men, have been set to rights by contact with its salutary heat. My relative, Count Belli of Viterbo, was "looked at" when an infant by a *Jettatrice*, and was in consequence put by his nurse into a mild oven for half-an-hour. One would think that the remedy was nearly as perilous as the practice of the lake-dwellers of cutting a little hole in their children's heads to let out the evil spirits, but in the case men-tioned it seems to have answered well.

The other important curative agent is the purifying
spittle. In Scotland and in Greece, any one who
should exclaim, "What a beautiful child !" is expected
to slightly spit upon the object of the remark, or
some misfortune will follow. Ladies in a high position at Athens have been observed to do this quite
lately. The Scotch and Greek uneasiness about the
"well-faured" is by no means confined to those
peoples ; the same anxiety reappears in Madagascar ;
and the Arab does not like you to praise the beauty
of his horse without adding the qualifying "an it
please God." Persius gives an account of the pre-
cautions adopted by the friends of the infant Roman :
"Look here—a grandmother or superstitious aunt
has taken baby from his cardle, and is charming his
forehead and his slavering lips against mischief by
the joint action of her middle finger and her purifying
spittle ; for she knows right well how to check the
evil eye. Then she dandles him in her arms, and
packs off the little pinched hope of the family, so far
as wishing can do it, to the domains of Licinus, or to
the palace of Crœsus. 'May he be a catch for my
lord and lady's daughter ! May the pretty ladies
scramble for him ! May the ground he walks on turn
to a rose-bed.'" (Prof. Conington's translation.)

One of the rare lullabies that contain allusion to
enchantment is the following. Roumanian "Nani-
nani" :

> Lullaby, my little one,
> Thou art mother's darling son ;
> Loving mother will defend thee,
> Mother she will rock and tend thee,
> Like a flower of delight,
> Or an angel swathed in white.

Sleep with mother, mother well
Knows the charm for every spell.
Thou shalt be a hero as
Our good lord, great Stephen, was,
Brave in war, and strong in hand,
To protect thy fatherland.

Sleep, my baby, in thy bed ;
God upon thee blessings shed.
Be thou dark, and be thine eyes
Bright as stars that gem the skies.
Maidens' love be thine, and sweet
Blossoms spring beneath thy feet.

The last lines might be taken for a paraphrase
of—

.   .   .   . puellae
Hunc rapiant : quicquid calcaverit hic, rosa fiat

The Three Fates have still their cult at Athens.
When a child is three days old, the mother places by
its cot a little table spread with a clean linen cloth,
upon which she sets a pot of honey, sundry cakes and·
fruits, her wedding ring, and a few pieces of money
belonging to her husband. In the honey are stuck
three almonds. These are the preparations for the
visit of the Μοῖραι. In some places the Norns or
Parcæ have got transformed into the three Maries ;
in others they closely retain their original character.
A perfect sample of the mixing up of pagan and
Christian lore is to be found in a Bulgarian legend,
which shows the three Fates weaving the destiny of
the infant Saviour during a momentary absence of
the Virgin—the whole scene occurring in the middle
of a Balkan wood. In Sicily exists a belief in certain
strange ladies ("donni-di-fora"), who take charge of

the new-born babe, with or without permission. The Palermitan mother says aloud, when she lifts her child out of the cradle, " 'Nnome di Dio ! " (" In God's name ! ")—but she quickly adds *sotto voce :* " Cu licenzi, signuri miu ! " (" By your leave, ladies ").

At Noto, *Ronni-di-casa*, or house-women, take the place of the *Donni-di-fora*. They inhabit every house in which a fire burns. If offended by their host, they revenge themselves on the children : the mother finds the infant whom she left asleep and tucked into the cradle, rolling on the floor or screaming with sudden fright. When, however, the *Ronni-di-casa* are amiably disposed, they make the sleeping child smile, after the fashion of angels in other parts of the world. Should they wish to leave an unmistakable mark of their good will, they twist a lock of the baby's hair into an inextricable tress. In England, elves were supposed to tangle the hair during sleep (*vide King Lear :* " Elf all my hair in knots ; " and Mercutio's Mab speech). The favour of the Sicilian house-women is not without its drawbacks, for if by any mischance the knotted lock be cut off, they will probably twist the child's spine out of spite. " 'Ccussi lu lassurii li Ronni-di-casa," says an inhabitant of Noto when he points out to you a child suffering from spinal curvature. The voice is lowered in mentioning these questionable guests, and there are Noticiani who will use any amount of circumlocution to avoid actually naming them. The are often called "certi signuri," as in this characteristic lullaby :

> My love, I wish thee well ; so lullaby !
> Thy little eyes are like the cloudless sky,
> My little lovely girl, my pretty one,
> Mother will make of thee a little nun :

A sister of the Saviour's Priory
Where noble dames and ladies great there be.
Sleep, moon-faced treasure, sleep, the while I sing :
Thou hadst thy cradle from the Spanish king.
When thou hast slept, I'll love thee better still.
(Sleep to my daughter comes and goes at will
And in her slumber she is made to smile
By certain ladies whom I dare not style.)
Breath of my body, thou, my love, my care,
Thou art without a flaw, so wondrous fair.
Sleep then, thy mother's breath, sleep, sleep, and rest,
For thee my very soul forsakes my breast.
My very soul goes forth, and sore my heart :
Thou criest ; words of comfort I impart.
Daughter, my flame, lie still and take repose,
Thou art a nosegay culled from off the rose.

At Palermo, mothers dazzled their little girls with the prospect of entering the convent of Santa Zita or Santa Chiara. In announcing the birth of his child, a Sicilian peasant commonly says, " My wife has a daughter-abbess." "What! has your wife a daughter old enough to be an abbess?" has sometimes been the innocent rejoinder of a traveller from the mainland. The Convent of the Saviour, which is the destination of the paragon of beauty described in the above lullaby, was one of the wealthiest, and what is still more to the point, one of the most aristocratic religious houses in the island. To have a relation among its members was a distinction ardently coveted by the citizens of Noto ; a town which once rejoiced in thirty-three noble families, one loftier than the other. The number is now cut down, but according to Signor Avolio such as remain are regarded with undiminished reverence. There are households in which the whole conversation runs on the *Barone* and *Baronessa*, when

not absorbed by the *Baronello* and the *Baronessella.*
It is just possible that the same phenomenon might
be observed without going to Noto. *Tutto il mondo
è paese :* a proverb which would serve as an excellent
motto for the Folk-lore Society.

Outside Sicily the cradle-singer's ideal of felicity is
rather matrimonial than monastic. The Venetian is
convinced that who never loved before must succumb
to her daughter's incomparable charms. It seems, .
by-the-by, that the "fatal gift" can be praised without fear or scruple in modern Italy ; the visitors of a
new-born babe ejaculate in a chorus, "Quant' è
bellino ! O bimbo ! Bimbino !" and Italian lullabies,
far more than any others, are one long catalogue of
perfections, one drawn-out reiteration of the boast of
a Greek mother of Terra d'Otranto : "There are
children in the street, but like my boy there is not
one ; there are children before the house, but like my
child there are none at all." The Sardinian who
wishes to say something civil of a baby will not do
less than predict that "his fame will go round the
world." The cradle-singer of the Basilicata desires
for her nursling that he may outstrip the sun and
moon in their race. It has been seen that the Roumanian mother would have her son emulate the famous
hero of Moldavia ; for her daughter she cherishes a
gentler ambition :

> Sleep, my daughter, sleep an hour ; '
> Mother's darling gilliflower.
> Mother rocks thee, standing near,
> She will wash thee in the clear
> Waters that from fountains run,
> To protect thee from the sun.

2 B

Sleep, my darling, sleep an hour,
Grow thou as the gilliflower.
As a tear-drop be thou white,
As a willow, tall and slight ;
Gentle as the ring-doves are, .
And be lovely as a star !

This *nani-nani* calls to mind some words in a letter
of Sydney Dobell's : " A little girl-child ! The very
idea is the most exquisite of poems ! a child-daughter
—wherein it seems to me that the spirit of all dews
and flowers and springs and tender, sweet wonders
'strikes its being into bounds.'" "Tear drop"
(*lacrimiòra*) is the poetic Roumanian name for the
lily of the valley. It may be needful to add that
gilliflower is the English name for the clove-pink;
at least an explanatory foot-note is now attached to
the word in new editions of the old poets. Exiled
from the polite society of "bedding plants"—all
heads and no bodies—the "matted and clove gilli-
flowers" which Bacon wished to have in his garden,
must be sought for by the door of the cottager who
speaks of them fondly yet apologetically, as "old-
fashioned things." To the folk-singers of the small
Italy on the Danube and the great Italy on the Arno
they are still the type of the choicest excellence, of the
most healthful grace. Even the long stalk, which has
been the flower's undoing, from a worldly point of
view, gets praised by the unsophisticated Tuscan.
"See," he says, "with how lordly an air it holds itself
in the hand!" ("Guarda con quanta signoria si
tiene in mano!")

The anguish of the Hindu dying childless has its
root deeper down in the human heart than the reason

he gives for it, the foolish fear lest his funeral rites be not properly performed. No man quite knows what it is to die who leaves a child in the world; children are more than a link with the future—they *are* the future: the portion of ourselves that belongs not to this day but to to-morrow. To them may be transferred all the hopes sadly laid by, in our own case, as illusions; the "to be" of their young lives can be turned into a beautiful "arrangement in pink," even though experience has taught us that the common lot of humanity is "an Imbroglio in Whity-brown." Most parents do all this and much more; as lullabies would show were there any need for the showing of it. One cradle-song, however, faces the truth that of all sure things the surest is that sorrow and disappointment will fall upon the children as it has fallen upon the fathers. The song comes from Germany; the English version is by Mr C. G. Leland:

Sleep, little darling, an angel art thou!
Sleep, while I'm brushing the flies from your brow.
All is as silent as silent can be;
Close your blue eyes from the daylight and me.

This is the time, love, to sleep and to play;
Later, oh later, is not like to-day,
When care and trouble and sorrow come sore
You never will sleep, love, as sound as before.

Angels from heaven as lovely as thou
Sweep round thy bed, love, and smile on thee now;
Later, oh later, they'll come as to-day,
But only to wipe all the tear-drops away.

Sleep, little darling, while night's coming round,
Mother will still by her baby be found;
If it be early, or if it be late,
Still by her baby she'll watch and she'll wait.

The sad truth is there, but with what tenderness is it not hedged about! These Teutonic angels are worth more than the too sensitive little angels of Spain who fly away at the sight of tears. And the last verse conveys a second truth, as consoling as the first is sad; pass what must, change what may, the mother's love will not change or pass; its healing presence will remain till death; who knows? perhaps after. Signor Salomone-Marino records the cry of one, who out of the depths blesses the haven of maternal love:

> Mamma, Mammuzza mia, vu' siti l'arma,
> Lu mè rifugiu nni la sorti orrenna,
> Vui siti la culonna e la giurlanna,
> Lu celu chi vi guardi e vi mantegna!

The soul that directs and inspires, the refuge that shelters, the column that supports, the garland that crowns—such language would not be natural in the mouth of an English labourer. An Englishman who feels deeply is almost bound to hold his tongue; but the poor Sicilian can so express himself in perfect naturalness and simplicity.

There is a kind of sleep-song that has only the form in common with the rose-coloured fiction that makes the bulk of cradle literature. It is the song of the mother who lulls her child with the overflow of her own troubled heart. The child may be the very cause of her sorest perplexity: yet from it alone she gains the courage to live, from it alone she learns a lesson of duty:

> "The babe I carry on my arm,
> He saves for me my precious soul."

A Corsican mother says to the infant at her breast,
"Thou art my guardian angel!"—which is the same
thought spoken in another way.

The most lovely of all sad lullabies is that written
much more than two thousand years ago by Simonides of Ceos. Acrisius, king of Argos, was informed
by an oracle that he would be killed by the son of his
daughter Danaë, who was therefore shut up in a tower,
where Zeus visited her in the form of a shower of
gold. Afterwards, when she gave birth to Perseus,
Acrisius ordered mother and child to be exposed in a
wicker chest or coffin on the open sea. This is the
story which Simonides took as the subject of his
poem:

Whilst the wind blew and rattled on the decorated ark, and
the troubled deep tossed as though in terror—her own fair
cheek also not unwet—around Perseus Danaë threw her arms,
and cried: "O how grievous, my child, is my trouble; yet thou
sleepest, and with tranquil heart slumberest within this joyless
house, beneath the brazen-barred, black-gleaming, musky
heavens. Ah! little reckest thou, beloved object, of the howling of the tempest, nor of the brine wetting thy delicate hair, as
there thou liest, clad in thy little crimson mantle! But even
were this dire pass dreadful also to thee, yet lend thy soft ear to
my words: Sleep on, my babe, I say; sleep on, I charge thee;
nay, let the wild waters sleep, and sleep the immeasurable woe.
Let me, too, see some change of will on thy part, Zeus, father!
or if the speech be deemed too venturous, then, for thy child's
sake, I pray thee pardon."

This is not a folk-song, but it has a prescriptive
right to a place among lullabies.

Passing over the beautiful Widow's Song, quoted in
a former essay, we come to some Basque lines, which
bring before us the blank and vulgar ugliness of

modern misery with a realism that would please
M. Zola:

> Hush, poor child, hush thee to sleep :
> (See him lying in slumber deep !)
> Thou first, then following I,
> We will hush and hushaby.
>
> Thy bad father is at the inn ;
> Oh ! the shame of it, and the sin !
> Home at midnight he will fare,
> Drunk with strong wine of Navarre.

After each verse the singer repeats again and again :
Lo lo, lo lo, on three lingering notes that have the
plaintive monotony of the chiming of bells where
there are but three in the belfry.

Almost as dismal as the Basque ditty is the English
nursery rhyme :

> Bye, O my baby !
> When I was a lady
> O then my poor baby didn't cry ;
> But my baby is weeping
> For want of good keeping ;
> Oh ! I fear my poor baby will die !

—which may have been composed to fit in with some
particular story, as was the tearful little song occurring in the ballad of Childe Waters :

> She said : Lullabye, mine own dear child,
> Lullabye, my child so dear ;
> I would thy father were a king,
> Thy mother laid on a bier.

One feels glad that that story ends happily in a
"churching and bridal" that take place upon the
same day.

I have the copy of a lullaby for a sick child, written down from memory by Signor Lerda, of Turin, who reports it to be popular in Tuscany:

Sleep, dear child, as mother bids :
  If thou sleep thou shalt not die !
  Sleep, and death shall pass thee by.
Close worn eyes and aching lids,
  Yield to soft forgetfulness ;
  Let sweet sleep thy senses press :
Child, on whom my love doth dwell,
Sleep, sleep, and thou shalt be well.

See, I strew thee, soft and light,
  Bed of down that cannot pain ;
  Linen sheets have o'er it lain
More than snow new-fallen white.
  Perfume sweet, health-giving scent,
  The meadows' pride, is o'er it sprent :
Sleep, dear son, a little spell,
Sleep, sleep, and thou shalt be well.

Change thy side and rest thee there,
  Beauty I love ! turn on thy side,
  O my son, thou dost not bide
As of yore, so fresh and fair.
  Sickness mars thee with its spite,
  Cruel sickness changes quite ;
How, alas ! its traces tell !
Yet sleep, and thou shalt be well.

Sleep, thy mother's kisses poured
  On her darling son. Repose ;
  God give end to all our woes.
Sleep, and wake by sleep restored,
  Pangs that make thee faint shall fly !
  Sleep, my child, and lullaby !
Sleep, and fears of death dispel ;
Sleep, sleep, and thou shalt be well.

"Se tu dormi, non morrai!" In how many tongues are not these words spoken every day by trembling lips, whilst the heart seems to stand still, whilst the eyes dare not weep, for tears would mean the victory of hope or fear; whilst the watcher leans expectant over the beloved little wasted form, conscious that all that can be done has been done, that all that care or skill can try has been tried, that there are no other remedies to fall back upon, that there is no more strength left for battle, and that now, even in this very hour, sleep or his brother death will decide the issue.

When a Sicilian hears that a child is dead, he exclaims, "Glory and Paradise!" The phrase is jubilant almost to harshness; yet the underlying sentiment is not harsh. The thought of a dead child makes natural harmonies with thoughts of bright and shining things. A mother likes to dream of her lost babe as fair and spotless and little. If she is sad, with him it is surely well. He is gone to play with the Holy Boys. He has won the crown of innocence. There are folk-songs that reflect this radiancy with which love clothes dead children; songs for the last sleep full of all the confusion of fond epithets commonly addressed to living babies.

Only in one direction did my efforts to obtain lullabies prove fruitless. America has, it seems, no nursery rhymes but those which are still current in the Old World.[1] Mr Bret Harte told me: "Our

---

[1] This is confirmed by Mr W. Newell in his admirable book, "Games and Songs of American Children" (1885), which might be called with equal propriety, "Games and Songs of British Children." It is indeed the best collection of English nursery

lullabies are the same as in England, but there are also a few Dutch ones," and he went on to relate how, when he was at a small frontier town on the Rhine, he heard a woman singing a song to her child : it was the old story,—if the child would not sleep it would be punished, its shoes would be taken away ; if it would go to sleep at once, Santa Claus would bring it a beautiful gift. Words and air, said Mr Bret Harte, were strangely familiar to him ; then, after a moment's reflection, he remembered hearing this identical lullaby.sung amongst his own kindred in the Far West of America.

rhymes that exists. Thus America will have given the mother country the most satisfactory editions, both of her ballads (Prof. F. T. Child's splendid work, now in course of publication) and of her children's songs.

FOLK-DIRGES.

THERE are probably many persons who could repeat by heart the greater portion of the last scene in the last book of the *Iliad*, and who yet have never been struck by the fact, that not its least excellence consists in its setting before us a carefully accurate picture of a group of usages which for the antiquity of their origin, the wide area of their observance, and the tenacity with which they have been preserved, may be fairly said to occupy an unique position amongst popular customs and ceremonials. First, we are shown the citizens of Troy bearing their vanquished hero within the walls amidst vehement demonstrations of grief: the people cling to the chariot wheels, or prostrate themselves on the earth; the wife and the mother of the dead tear their hair and cast it to the winds. Then the body is laid on a bed of state, and the leaders of a choir of professional minstrels sing a dirge, which is at times interrupted by the wailing of the women. When this is done, Andromache, Hecuba, and Helen in turn give voice each one to the feelings awakened in her by their common loss; and afterwards—so soon as the proper interval has elapsed—the body is burnt, wine being poured over the embers of the pyre. Lastly, the ashes are consigned to the tomb, and the mourners sit down to a banquet. "Such honours paid they to the good knight Hector;" and such, in their main features, are the funeral rites which may be presumed to date back to a period not only anterior to the siege of Troy, granting for the moment that event to have veritably taken place, but also previous to the crystallisation of the Greek or any other of the Indo-European nationalities which flowed westward from the uplands of the Hindu Kush. The custom of hymning the dead, which is just now what more particularly concerns us, once prevailed over most if not all parts of Europe; and the firmness of its hold upon the affections of the people may be inferred from the persistency with which they adhered to it, even when it was opposed not only by the working of the gradual, though fatal, law of decay to which all old usages must in the end submit, but also by the active interposition of persons in authority. Charlemagne, for instance, tried to put it down in Provence —desiring that all those attending funerals, who did not know by rote any of the appropriate psalms, should recite aloud the *Kyrie eleison* instead of singing "profane songs" made to suit the occasion. But the edict seems to have met with a signal want of success ; for some five hundred years after it was issued, the Provençals still hired Præficæ, and still introduced within the very precincts of their churches, whole choirs of lay dirge-singers, frequently composed of young girls who were stationed in two companies, that chanted songs alternately to the accompaniment of instrumental music ; and this notwithstanding that the clergy of Provence showed the strongest objection to the performance of observances at funerals, other than such as were approved by ecclesiastical sanction.

The custom in question bears an obvious affinity to Highland coronachs and Irish keens, and here in England there is reason to believe it to have survived as late as the seventeenth century. That Shakespeare was well acquainted with it is amply testified by the fourth act of *Cymbeline;* for it is plain that the song pronounced by Guiderius and Arviragus over the supposed corpse of Imogene was no mere poetic outburst of regret, but a real and legitimate dirge, the singing or saying of which was held to constitute Fidele's obsequies. In the Cotton Library there is a MS., having reference to a Yorkshire village in the reign of Elizabeth, which relates: "When any dieth, certaine women sing a song to the dead bodie recyting the jorney that the partye deceased must goe." Unhappily the English Neniæ are nearly all lost and forgotten; I know of no genuine specimen extant, except the famous Lyke Wake (*i.e.*, Death Watch) dirge beginning :

> This ae nighte, this ae nighte,
> *Everie nighte and alle,*
> Fire and sleete and candle lighte,
> *And Christe receive thy saule,* &c.

To the present day we find practices closely analogous with those recounted in the *Iliad* scattered here and there from the shores of the Mediterranean to the banks of Lake Onega; and the Trojan threnody is even now reproduced in Ireland, in Corsica, Sardinia, and Roumania, in Russia, in Greece, and South Italy. Students who may be tempted to make observations on this strange survival of the old world, will do well, however, to set about it at once, in parts which are either already invaded or else threatened with an imminent invasion of railways, for the screech of the engine sounds the very death-knell of ancient customs. Thus the Irish practice of keening is becoming less and less general. On recently making inquiries of a gentleman residing in Leinster, I learnt that it had gone quite out in that province; he added that he had once seen keeners at a funeral at Clonmacnoise (King's County), but was told they came from the Connaught side of the Shannon. The keens must not be confused with the peculiar wail or death-cry known as the Ullagone; they are articulate utterances, in a strongly marked rhythm, extolling the merits of the dead, and reproaching him for leaving his family, with much more in the same strain. The keeners may or may not be professional, and the keens are more often of a traditional than of an improvised description. One or two specimens in Gaelic have appeared in the *Journal of the Irish Archæological Association,* but on the whole the subject is far from having received the attention it deserves. The Irish keeners are invariably women, as also are all the continental dirge-singers of modern times. Whether by reason of the somewhat new-fashioned sentiment which forbids a man to exhibit his feelings in public, or from other motives not unconnected with selfishness, the onus of discharging the more active and laborious obligations prescribed in popular funeral rites has bit by bit been altogether shifted upon the shoulders of the weaker sex; *e.g.,* in places where scratching and tearing of the face forms part of the traditional ritual, the women are expected to continue the performance of this unpleasant ceremony

which the men have long since abandoned. Together
with the dirge, a more or less serious measure of self-
disfigurement has come down from an early date. An
Etruscan funeral urn, discovered at Clusi, shows an
exact picture of the hired mourners who tear their hair
and rend their garments, whilst one stands apart, in a
prophetic attitude, and declaims to the accompaniment
of a flute. Of the precise origin of the employment of
Public Wailers, or Præficæ, not much has been ascertained. One distinguished writer on folk-lore suggests that it had its rise not in any lack of consideration for the dead, but in the apprehension lest the
repose of their ghosts should be disturbed by a display of grief on the part of those who had been
nearest and dearest to them in life; and his theory
gains support in the abundant evidence forthcoming
to attest the existence of a widely-spread notion that
the dead are pained, and even annoyed and exasper-
ated, by the tears of their kindred. Traces of this
belief are discoverable in Zend and Hindu writings;
also amongst the Sclavs, Germans, and Scandinavians
—and, to look nearer home, in Ireland and Scotland.
On the other hand, it is possible that the business of
singing before the dead sprang from the root of well-
nigh every trade—that its duties were at first exclusively performed by private persons, and their passing
into public hands resulted simply from people finding
out that they were executed with less trouble and
more efficiency by a professional functionary; a common-place view of the matter which is somewhat
borne out by the circumstance, that whenever a member of the family is qualified and disposed to under-
take the dirge-singing, there seems to be no prejudice

against her doing so. It is often far from easy to
determine whether such or such a death-song was
composed by a hired præfica who for the time being
assumed the character of one of the dead man's
relatives, or by the latter speaking in her own person.

In Corsica, the wailing and chanting are kept up, off
and on, from the hour of death to the hour of burial.
The news that the head of a family has expired is
quickly communicated to his relations and friends in
the surrounding hamlets, who hasten to form themselves into a troop or band locally called the Scirrata,
and thus advance in procession towards the house of
mourning. If the death was caused by violence, the
scirrata makes a halt when it arrives in sight of the
village; and then it is that the Corsican women tear
their hair and scratch their faces till the blood flows—
just as do their sisters in Dalmatia and Montenegro.
Shortly after this, the scirrata is met by the deceased's
fellow-villagers, accompanied by all his near relatives
with the exception of the widow, to whose abode the
whole party now proceeds with loud cries and lamentations. The widow awaits the scirrata by the door
of her house, and, as it draws near, the leader steps
forward and throws a black veil over her head to
symbolise her widowhood; the term of which must
offer a dreary prospect to a woman who has the misfortune to lose her husband while she is still in the
prime of life, for public opinion insists that she remain
for years in almost total seclusion. The mourners
and as many as can enter the room assemble round
the body, which lies stretched on a table or plank
supported by benches; it is draped in a long mantle,
or it is clothed in the dead man's best suit. Now

begins the dirge, or Vocero. Two persons will perhaps start off singing together, and in that case the words cannot be distinguished ; but more often only one gets up at a time. She will open her song with a quietly-delivered eulogy of the virtues of the dead, and a few pointed allusions to the most important events of his life ; but before long she warms to her work, and pours forth volleys of rhythmic lamentation with a fire and animation that stir up the women present into a frenzied delirium of grief, in which, as the præfica pauses to take breath, they howl, dig their nails into their flesh, throw themselves on the ground, and sometimes cover their heads with ashes. When the dirge is ended they join hands and dance frantically round the plank on which the body lies. More singing takes place on the way to the church, and thence to the graveyard. After the funeral the men do not shave for weeks, and the women let their hair go loose and occasionally cut it off at the grave—cutting off the hair being, by the way, a universal sign of female mourning ; it was done by the women of ancient Greece, and it is done by the women of India. A good deal of eating and drinking brings the ceremonials to a close. If the bill of fare comes short of that recorded of the funeral feast of Sir John Paston, of Barton, when 1300 eggs, 41 pigs, 40 calves, and 10 nete were but a few of the items—nevertheless the Corsican baked meats fall very heavily upon the pockets of such families as deem themselves compelled to "keep up a position." Sixty persons is not an extraordinary number to be entertained at the banquet, and there is, over and above, a general distribution of bread and meat to poorer neighbours.

Mutton in summer, and pork in winter, are esteemed the viands proper to the occasion. In happy contrast to all this lugubrious feasting is the simple cup of milk drunk by each kinsman of the shepherd who dies in the mountains; in which case his body is laid out, like Robin Hood's, in the open air, a green sod under his head, his loins begirt with the pistol belt, his gun at his side, his dog at his feet. Curious are the superstitions of the Corsican shepherds touching death. The dead, they say, call the living in the night time, and he who answers will soon follow them; they believe, too, that, if you listen attentively after dark, you may hear at times the low beating of a drum, which announces that a soul has passed.

A notable section of the voceri treats of that insatiable thirst after vengeance which formerly provided as fruitful a theme to French romancers as it presented a perplexing problem to French legislators. In these dirges we see the vendetta in its true character, as the outgrowth and relic of times when people were, in self-defence, almost coerced into lawlessness through the perpetual miscarriage of constituted justice, and they enable us to better understand the process by which what was at the outset something of the nature of a social necessity, developed into the ruling passion of the race, and led to the frightful abuses that are associated with its name. All that he held sacred in heaven or on earth became bound up in the Corsican's mind with the obligation to avenge the blood of his kindred. Thus he made Hate his deity, and the old inexorable spirit of the Greek *Oresteia* lived and breathed in him anew, the Furies themselves finding no bad counterpart in the frenzied women who officiated at his funeral rites. As is well known, when no man was to be found to do the deed a woman would often come forward in his stead, and this not only among the lower orders, but in the highest ranks of society. A lady of the noble house of Pozzo di Borgo once donned male attire, and in velvet-tasselled cap, red doublet, high sheepskin boots, with pistol, gun, and dagger for her weapons, started off in search of an assassin at the head of a band of partisans. When he was caught, however, after the guns had been two or three times levelled at his breast, she decided to give him his life. Another fair avenger whose name has come down to us was Maria Felice di Calacuccia, of Niolo. Her vocero may be cited here as affording a good idea of the tone and spirit of the vendetta dirges in general.

"I was spinning at my distaff when I heard a loud noise ; it was a gun-shot, it re-echoed in my heart. It seemed to say to me : 'Fly! thy brother dies.' I ran into the upper chamber. As I unlatched the door, 'I am struck to the heart,' he said ; and I fell senseless to the ground. If I too died not, it was that one thought sustained me. Whom wouldst thou have to avenge thee ? Our mother, nigh to death, or thy sister Maria ? If Lario was not dead surely all this would not end without bloodshed. But of so great a race, thou dost only leave thy sister: she has no cousins, she is poor, an orphan, young. Still be at rest—to avenge thee, she suffices ! "

A dramatic vocero, dealing with the same subject, is that of the sister of Canino, a renowned brigand, who fell at Nazza in an encounter with the military. She begins by regretting that she has not a voice of

thunder wherewith to rehearse his prowess. Alas!
one early morning the soldiers ("barbarous set of
bandits that they are!") sallied forth on his pursuit,
and pounced upon him like wolves upon a lamb.
When she heard the bustle of folks going to and fro
in the street, she put her head out of window and
asked what it was all about. "Thy brother has been
slaughtered in the mountains," they reply. Even so
it was; his arquebuse was of no use to him; no, nor
his dagger, nor his pistol, nor yet his amulet. When
they brought him in, and she beheld his wounds, the
bitterness of her grief redoubled. Why did he not
answer her—did he lack heart to do so? "Canino,
heart of thy sister," she cries, "how thou art grown
pale! Thou that wert so stalwart and so full of grace,
thou who didst appear like unto a nosegay of flowers.
Canino, heart of thy sister, they have taken thy life.
I will plant a blackthorn in the land of Nazza, that
none of our house may henceforth pass that way—for
there were not three or four, but seven men against
one. Would I could make my bed at the foot of the
chestnut tree beneath whose shade they fired upon
thy breast. I desire to cast aside these women's
skirts, to arm me with poniard, and pistol, and gun,
to gird me with the belt and pouch; Canino, heart
of thy sister, I desire to avenge thy death." In the
lamentations over one Matteo, a doctor who was
murdered in 1745, we have an example of the songs
improvised along the road to the grave. This time
there are plenty of male relatives—brothers, brothers-
in-law, and cousins — to accomplish the vendetta.
The funeral procession passes through the village
where the crime was committed, and one of the

inhabitants, perhaps as a peace-offering, invites the whole party to come in and refresh themselves. To this a young girl replies : "We want none of your bread and wine ; what we do want is your blood." She invokes a thunderbolt to exterminate every soul in the blood-guilty place. But an aged dame interposes, for a wonder, with milder counsels ; she bids her savage sisters calm their wrath : "Is not Matteo in heaven with the Lord ?   Look at his winding sheet," says she, "and learn from it that Christ dwells above, who teaches forgiveness. The waters are troubled enough already without your goading on your men to violence." It is not unlikely that the Corsicans may have been in the habit, like the Irish, of intentionally parading the coffin of a murdered man past the door of the suspected murderer, in order that they might have a public opportunity of branding the latter with infamy.

Having glanced at these hymns of the avenger, we will turn to the laments expressive of grief unmixed with threats or anger. In these, also, Corsica is very rich. Sometimes it is a wife who deplores her husband struck down by no human hand, but by fever or accident. In one such vocero the widow pathetically crowds epithet on epithet, in the attempt to give words to her affection and her sorrow. "You were my flower, my thornless rose, my stalwart one, my column, my brother, my hope, my prop, my eastern gem, my most beautiful treasure," she says to her lost "Petru Francescu !" She curses fate which in a brief moment has deprived her of her paladin—she prayed so hard that he might be spared, but it was all in vain. He was laid low, the greatly courageous

one, who seemed so strong! Is it indeed true, that
he, the clever-headed, the handy-handed, will leave
his Nunziola all alone? Then she bids Mari, her
little daughter, come hither to where papa lies, and
beg him to pray God in paradise that she may have
a better lot than her little mother. She wishes her
eyes may change into two fountains ere she forgets
his name; for ever would she call him her Petru
Francescu. But most of all she wishes that her heart
might break so that her poor little soul could go with
his, and quit this treacherous world where is no more
joy. The typical keen given in Carleton's *Traits and
Stories of the Irish Peasantry* is so like Nunziola's
vocero, that in parts it might be taken for a translation of it. Sometimes it is a plaint of a mother whose
child has met the fate of those "whom the gods love."
That saying about the gods has its equivalent in the
Corsican lines:

> Chi nasci pe u paradisu
> A stu mondu un po' imbecchia,

which occur in the lament of La Dariola Danesi, of
Zuani, who mourns her sixteen-year-old daughter
Romana. Decked in feast-day raiment the damsel
sleeps in the rest of death, after all her sufferings.
Her sweet face has lost its hues of red and white; it
is like a gone-out sun. Romana was the fairest of
all the young girls, a rose among flowers; the youths
of the country round were consumed by love of her,
but in her presence they were filled with decorous
respect. She was courteous to all, familiar with none;
in church everybody gazed at her, but she looked at
no one; and the minute mass was over she would

say: "Mamma, let us go." Never can the mother
be consoled, albeit she knows her darling fares well
up there in heaven where all things smile and are
glad. Of a surety this earth was not worthy to contain so fair a face. "Ah! how much more beautiful
Paradise will be now she is in it!" cries the voceratrice, with the sublime audacity of maternal love. In
another dirge we have pictured a troop of girls coming
early to the house of Maria, their young companion,
to escort her to the Church of St Elia: for this morning the father of her betrothed has settled the marriage portion, and it is seemly that she should hear
mass, and make an offering of wax tapers. But the
maiden's mother comes forth to tell the gladsome
band that to-day's offering to St Elia is not of waxen
tapers; it is a peerless flower, a bouquet adorned
with ribands—surely the saint will be well pleased
with such a fine gift! For the bride elect lies dead;
who will now profit by her possessions—the twelve
mattresses, the twenty-four lambs? "I will pray the
Virgin," says the mother, "I will pray my God that
I may go hence this morning, pressing my flower to
my heart." The playfellows bathe Maria's face with
tears: sees she not those who loved her? Will she
leave them in their sadness? One runs to pluck
flowers, a second to gather roses; they twine her a
garland, a bridal crown—will she depart all the same,
lying upon her bier? But, after all, why should there
be all this grief? "To-day little Maria becomes the
spouse of the Lord; with what honour will she not
be greeted in paradise!" Alas for broken hearts!
they were never yet healed by that line of argument.
Up the street steals the chilling sound of the funeral

chant, *Ora pro eâ.* They are come to bear the maiden
to St Elia's Church; the mother sinks to the ground;
.fain would she follow the body to the grave, but she
faints with sorrow; only her streaming tears can pay
the tribute of her love.

It will be observed that it is usual for the survivors
to be held up as objects of pity rather than the dead,
who are generally regarded as well off; but now and
then we come across less optimist presages of the
future life. A woman named Maddelè complains
that they have taken her blonde daughter, her snow-
white dove, her "Chili, cara di Mamma," to the worst
possible of places, where no sun penetrates, and no
fire is lit.

Sometimes to a young girl is assigned the task of
bewailing her playmate. "This morning my companion is all adorned," begins a maiden dirge-singer;
"one would think she was going to be married." But
the ceremony about to take place differs sadly from
that other. The bell tolls slowly, the cross and
banner arrive at the door; the dead companion is
setting out on a long journey, she is going to find
their ancestors—the voceratrice's father, and her uncle
the curé—in the land whither each one must go in
his turn and remain for ever. Since she has made
up her mind thus to change country and climate
(though it be all too soon, for she has not yet done
growing), will she at any rate listen for an instant to
her friend of other days? She wishes to give her a
little letter to carry to her father; and, besides the
letter, she would like her to take him a message, and
give him news of the family he left so young, all
weeping round his hearth. She is to tell him that all

goes well; that his eldest daughter is married and has a boy, a flowering lily, who already knows his father, and points at him with his finger. The boy is called after the grandpapa, and old friends declare him to be his very image. To the curé she is to say that his flock flourish and do not forget him. Now the priest enters, bringing the holy water; everyone lifts his hat; they bear the body away: "Go to heaven, dear; the Lord awaits you."

It is hardly necessary to add that the voceri of Corsica are without exception composed in the native speech of the country, which the accomplished scholar, lexicographer, and poet, Niccolò Tommaseo, spoke of with perfect truth as one of "the most Italian of the dialects of Italy." The time may come when the people will renounce their own language in favour of the idiom of their rulers, but it has not come yet; nor do they show much disposition to abandon their old usages, as may be guessed from the fact that even in their Gallicanised capital the dead are considered slighted if the due amount of wailing is left undone.

The Sardinian Attitido—a word which has been thought to have some connection with the Greek ororoi, and the Latin *atat*—is made on exactly the same pattern as the Corsican vocero. I have been told on trustworthy authority that in some districts in the island the keening over a married man is performed not by a dirge-singer but by his own children, who chant a string of homely sentences, such as: "Why art thou dead, papa? Thou didst not want for bread or wine!" A practice may here be mentioned which recalls the milk and honey and nuts of the Roman Inferiæ, and which, so far as I am aware, lingers on nowhere excepting Sardinia; the attidora whilst she sings, scatters on the bier handfuls of almonds or—if the family is well-to-do—of sweet-meats, to be subsequently buried with the body.

Very few specimens of the attitido have found their way into print; but amongst these few, in Canon Spano's *Canti popolari Tempiesi*, there is one that is highly interesting. Doubts have been raised as to whether the bulk of the songs in Canon Spano's collection are of purely illiterate origin; but even if the author of the dirge to which I allude was guilty of that heinous offence in the eyes of the strict·folk-lore gleaner—the knowledge of the alphabet—it must still be judged a remarkable production. The attidora laments the death of a much-beloved bishop :—

" It was the pleasure of this good father, this gentle pastor," she says, " at all hours to nourish his flock ; to the bread of the soul he joined the bread of the body. Was the wife naked, her sons starving and destitute? He laboured unceasingly to console them all. The one he clothed, the others he fed. None can tell the number of the poor whom he succoured. The naked came to him that they might be clothed, the hungry came to him that they might be fed, and all went their way comforted. How many had suffered hunger in the winter's cold, had not his tender heart proffered them help! It was a grand sight to behold so many poor gathered together in his house —above, below, they were so numerous there was no room to pass. And these were the comers of every day. I do not count those to whom once a month he supplied the needful food, nor yet those other poor to whose necessities he ministered in secret. By the needy rogue he let himself be deceived with shut eyes : he recognised the fraud, but he esteemed it gain so to lose. Ah, dear father, father to us all, I ought not to weep for thee! I mourn our common bereavement, for thy death this day has been a blow to all of us, even to the strongest men."

It would be hard to conceive a more lovely portrait of the Christian priest ; it is scarcely surpassed by that of Monseigneur Bienvenu in *Les Misérables*, of whose conduct in the matter of the silver candlesticks we are not a little reminded by the good Sardinian bishop's compassion for the needy rogue. Neither the one nor the other realises an ideal which would win the unconditional approval of the Charity Organisation Society, and we must perhaps admit that humane proclivities which indirectly encourage swindling are more a mischief than an advantage to the State. Yet who can be insensible to the beauty of this unconquerable pity for the evil-doer, this charity that believeth all things, hopeth all things, endureth all things? Who can say how much it has done to make society possible, to keep the world on its wheels? It is the bond that binds together all religions. Six thousand years ago the ancient Egyptian dirge-singers chanted before their dead : "There is no fault in him. No answer riseth up against him. In the truth he liveth, with the truth he nourisheth himself. The gods are satisfied with all he hath done. . . . He succoured the afflicted, he gave bread to the hungry, drink to the thirsty, clothes to the naked, he sheltered the outcast, his doors were open to the stranger, he was a father to the fatherless."

The part of France where dirge-singing stayed the

longest seems to have been the south-west. The old
women of Gascony still preserve the memory of a
good many songs, some of which have been fortunately placed on record by M. Bladé in his collec
tion of Gascon folk-lore. The Gascon dirge is a kin l
of prose recitative made up of distinct exclamatioor
that fall into irregular strophes. Each has a burden
of this description :

Ah !

Ah ! Ah ! Ah !

Ah ! Praube !

Ah ! Praube !

Moun Diu !

Moun Diu ! Moun Diu !

The wife mourns for the loss of " Praube Jan ; "
when she was a young girl she loved only him.   " No,
no ! I will not have it ! I will not have them take thee
to the graveyard !"   " What will become of us ? "
asks the daughter ; " my poor mother is infirm, my
brothers and sisters are too small ; there is only me
to rule the house."   The mother bewails her boy :
" Poor little one ! I loved thee so much, thou wert so
pretty, thou wert so good.   Thou didst work so well ;
all I bid thee do, thou didst ; all I told thee, didst
thou believe ; thou wert very young, yet already didst
thou earn thy bread.   Poor little one, thou art dead ;
they carry thee to the grave, with the cross going
before.   They put thee into the earth. . . . Poor
little one, I shall see thee no more ; never ! never !
never !   Thou goest and I stay.   My God ! thou wilt
be very lonely in the graveyard this night ; and I, I
shall weep at home."

If we transport ourselves to the government of Olonetz, we discover the first cousin of the Corsican voceratrice in the Russian Voplénitsa ("the sobbing one"). But the jurisdiction of this functionary is of wider extent; she is mistress of the ceremonies at marriages as well as at funerals, and in both cases either improvises new songs or adapts old ones. Mr Ralston has familiarised English readers with some excellent samples of the Russian neniæ in his work on the *Songs of the Russian People.* In Montenegro dirge-singing survives in its most primitive form. During the war of 1877 there were frequent opportunities of observing it. One such occurred at Ostrog. A wounded man arrived at that place, which was made a sort of hospital station, with his father and mother, his sisters and a brother. Another brother and a cousin had fallen by his side in the last fight— the Montenegrins have always gone into battle in families—and the women had their faces covered with scratches, self-inflicted in their mourning for these kindred. The man was young, lively, and courageous; he might have got well but there were no surgical instruments to extract the ball in his back, and so in a day or two he was dead. At three in the morning the women began shrieking in spite of the orders given by the doctors in the interest of the other wounded ; the noise was horrible, and no sooner were they driven away than they came back and renewed it. The Prince, who has tried to put down the custom as barbarous, was quartered at Ostrog, and he suc- ceeded in having the wailers quieted for a moment, but when the body was borne to the cemetery the uproar began again. The women beat their breasts, scratched their faces, and screamed at a pitch that could be heard a mile off. It is usual to return to the house where the person died—they made their way therefore back into the hospital (the Prince being absent), and it was only after immense efforts on the part of the sisters of charity and those who were in authority that they were expelled. Then they seated themselves in the courtyard, and continued beating their breasts and reciting their death-song. An eye-witness of the scene described the dirge as a monotonous chant. One of the dead man's sisters had worked herself up into a state of hysterical frenzy, in which she seemed to have lost all control over her words and actions; she led the dirge, and her rhythmic ejaculations flowed forth as if she had no power to contain them. The father and brother went to salute the Prince the day after the funeral; the old man appeared to be extremely cheerful, but was doggedly inattentive to the advice to go home and fight no more, as his family had suffered enough losses. He had a son of ten, he said, who could accompany him now as there was a gun to spare, which before had not been the case. He wished he had ten sons to bring them all to fight the Turks.

The Sclavs are everywhere very strict in all that regards the cult of the dead, and the observances which have to be gone through by Russians who have lost friends or relations are by no means confined to the date of death and burial. Even when they have experienced no personal loss, they are still thought called upon to visit the cemeteries on the second Tuesday after Easter, and howl lustily over the tombs of their ancestors. Nor would it be held sufficient to strew flowers upon the graves, as is done on the Catholic All Souls' day; the most orthodox ghosts want something more substantial, and libations of beer and spirits are poured over their resting-places. Furthermore, disagreeable consequences have been said to result upon an omission of like marks of respect due to "the rude forefathers of the hamlet;" there is no making sure that a highly estimable individual will not, when thus incensed, re-enter an appearance on life's stage in the shape of a vampire. A small volume might be written on the preventive measures adopted to procure immunity from such-like visitations. The people of Havelland and Altmark put a small coin into the mouths of the dead in the hope that, so appeased, they will not assume vampire form; but this time the superstition, like a vast number of others, is clearly a later invention to explain a custom, the original significance of which is forgotten. The peasants of Roumelia also place pieces of money in the coffins, not as an insurance against vampires —who they think may be best avoided by burning instead of burying the mortal remains of any person they credit with the prospect of becoming one—but to pay the entrance fee into Paradise; a more authentic version of the old fable. The setting apart of a day, fixed by the Church or varying according to private anniversaries, for the special commemoration of the dead, is a world-wide custom.

If, as Mr Herbert Spencer thinks, the rudimentary form of all religion is the propitiation of dead ancestors who are supposed still to exist, some kind of *fête des morts* was probably the oldest of religious feasts. A theory has been started, to the effect that

the time of its appointment has been widely influenced
by the rising of the Pleiades, in support of which is
cited the curious fact that the Australians and Society
Islanders keep the celebration in November, though
with them November is a spring month. But this
may be no more than a coincidence. In ancient
Rome, in Russia, in China, the tendency has been to
commemorate the dead in the season of resurrection.

The Letts and Esthonians observe the Feast of
Souls, by spreading a banquet of which they suppose
their spirit relatives to partake ; they put torches on
the graves to light the ghosts to the repast, and they
imagine every sound they hear through the day to be
caused by the movements of the invisible guests.
Both these people celebrate death-watches with much
singing and drinking, the Esthonians addressing long
speeches to the dead, and asking him why he did not
stay longer, if his puddro (gruel) was not to his taste,
&c., precisely after the style of the keeners of less
remote parts. In some countries the entire system of
life would seem to be planned and organised mainly
with a view to honouring the dead. In Albania, for
example, one of the foremost objects pursued by the
peasantry is that of marrying their daughters near
home ; not so much from any affectionate unwilling-
ness to part with them, as in order to secure their
attendance at the *vaï* or lamentations which take
place on the death of a member of the family ; and
so rigorous are the mourning regulations, that even
married women who have lost their fathers remain
year after year shut up in houses deprived of light
and draped in black—they may not even go out to
church. The Albanian keens are not always versi-

fied; they sometimes consist simply in the endless reiteration of a single phrase. M. Auguste Dozon reports that he was at one time constantly hearing "les hurlements" of a poor Mussulman widow who bewailed two sons; on certain anniversaries she took their clothes out of a chest, and, placing them before her, she repeated, without intermission, χαλασια μου. The Greeks have the somewhat analogous practice, on the recurrence of the death-days of their dear ones, of putting their lips close to the graves and whispering to their silent tenants that they still love them.

The near relations in Greece leave their dwelling, as soon as they have closed the eyes of the dead, to take refuge in the house of a friend, with whom they sojourn till the more distant connections have had time to arrive, and the body is dressed in holiday gear. Then they return, clothe themselves in white dresses, and take up their position beside the bier. After some inarticulate wailing, which is strenuously echoed back by the neighbours, the dirge is sung, the chief female mourner usually leading off, and whosoever feels disposed following wake. When the body is lowered into the earth, the best-beloved of the dead—his mother or perhaps his betrothed—stoops down to the ground and imploringly utters his name, together with the word "Come!" On his making no reply, he is declared to be indeed dead, and the grave is closed.[1] The usage points to a

---

[1] "Calling the dead" was without doubt once general amongst all classes—which may be true of all the customs that we are now inclined to associate with only the very poor. In the striking mediæval ceremonial performed at the entombment of King Alfonso in the vault at the Escurial, the final act was that

probability that all the exhortations to awaken and to return with which the dirges of every nation are interlarded are remnants of ancient makeshifts for a medical certificate of death; and we may fancy with what breathless excitement these apostrophes were spoken in former days when they were accompanied by an actual, if faint, expectation that they would be heard and answered. It is conceivable that the complete system of making as much noise as possible at funerals may be derived from some sort of notion that the uproar would wake the dead if he were not dead at all, but sleeping. As elsewhere, so in Greece, the men take no part in the proceedings beyond bidding one last farewell just before they retire from the scene. Præficæ are still employed now and then; but the art of improvisation seems to be the natural birthright of Greek peasant women, nor do they require the inspiration of strong grief to call their poetic gifts into operation; it is stated to be no unusual thing to hear a girl stringing elegies over some lamb, or bird, or flower, which may have died, while she works in the fields. The Greeks send communications and even flowers by the dead to the dead : "·Now is the time," the folk-poet makes one say whose body is about to be buried, "for you to give me any messages or commissions ; and if your grief is too poignant for utterance, write it down on paper and bring me the letter." The Greek neniæ are marked by great vigour and variety of imagery

of the Lord Chamberlain, who unlocked the coffin, and in the midst of profound silence shouted into the king's ear, "Señor, Señor, Señor." After which he rose, saying, "His majesty does not answer. Then it is true the king is dead."

as is apparent in the subjoined extract from the dirge
of a poor young country-woman who was left a widow
with two children :—

"The other day I beheld at our threshold a youth
of lofty stature and threatening mien ; he had out-
stretched wings of gleaming white, and in his hand
was a sword. 'Woman, is thy husband in the house?'
'Yes ; he combs our Nicos' hair, and caresses him so
he may not cry. Go not in, terrible youth ; do not
frighten our babe.' The white-winged would not
listen ; I tried to drive him back, but I could not ; he
darted past me, and ran to thy side, O my beloved.
Hapless one, he smote thee ; and here is thy little
son, thy tiny Nicos, whom likewise he was fain to
strike." . . .

So vivid was the impression created by the woman's
fantasy that some of the spectators looked towards
the door, half expecting the white-winged visitant to
advance in their midst ; others turned to the child,
huddled by his mother's knees. She, coming down
from flights of imagination to the bitter realities of
her condition, exclaimed, as she flung herself sobbing
upon the bier : "How can I maintain the children?
How will they be able to live ? What will they not
suffer in the contrast between the rough lot in store
for them and the tender care which guarded them in
the happy days when their father lived ? " At last,
worn out by the force of her emotions, she sank senseless to the floor. The laments of widows, which are
very rare in some localities, are often to be met with
in Greece. In one of them we come upon an original
idea respecting the requirements of spirits : the singer
prays that her tears may swell into a lake or a sea, so

they may trickle through the earth to the nether
regions, to moisten those who get no rain, to be drink
to those who thirst, and—to fill up the dry inkstands
of the writers! "Then will they be able to chronicle
the chagrins of the loved ones who cross the river,
taste its wave, and forget their homes and their poor
orphans." Every species of Grecian peasant-song
abounds in classical reminiscences, which are easy to
identify, although they betray some mental confusion
of the attributes and functions belonging to the personages of antiquity. Of all the early myths, that of
the Stygian ferryman is the one which has shown
greatest longevity. Far from falling into oblivion,
the son of Erebus has gone on diligently accumulat-
ing honours till he has managed to get the arbitra-
ment of life and death into his power, and to enlist
the birds of the air as a staff of spies, to give him
prompt information should any unlucky individual
refer to him in a tone of mockery or defiance. Perhaps this is not development but reversion. Charon
may have been a great Infernal deity before he was a
boatman. The Charun of the Etruscans could destroy
life and torment the guilty—the office of conducting
shades to the other world forming only one part of
his duties.

The opinion of Achilles, that it was better to be a
slave amongst men than a king over ghosts, is very
much that which prevails in the Greece of to-day.
Visions of a Christian paradise above the skies have
much less hold on the popular mind than dread of a
pagan Tartarus under the earth; and that full conviction that after all it was a very bad thing to die,
that tendency to attach a paramount value to life,

per se, and *quand même*, which constituted so significant a feature of the old Greeks, is equally characteristic of their modern representatives. The next
world of the Romaic songs is far from being a place
" where all smiles and is glad ;" the forebodings of
the Corsican's Chilina's mother are common enough
here in Greece. " Rejoice in the present world, rejoice in the passing day," runs a μυρολόγιον, quoted
by Fauriel ; "to-morrow you will be under the sod,
and will behold the day no more." Down in Tartarus youths and maidens spend their time dismally
in asking if there be yet an earth and a sky up above.
Are there still churches and golden icons ? Do people
continue to work at their several trades ? " Blessed
are the mountains and the pastures," it is said, " where
we meet not Charon." The parents of a dying girl
ask of her why she is resolved to hasten into the
other world where the cock crows not, and the hen
clucks not ; where there is no water and no grass,
and where the hungry find it impossible to eat, and
the tired are incapable of sleep. Why is she not
content to abide at home ? The girl replies she
cannot, for yesterday, in the late evening, she was
married, and her consort is the tomb. That is the
peasant elegist's way of speaking of a sudden death,
caused very likely by the chill of nightfall. Of
another damsel, who succumbed to a long illness,
" who had suffered as none before suffered under
the sun," he narrates how she pressed her father's
hand to her heart, saying : " Alas ! my father, I am
about to die." She clasped her mother's hand to her
breast, saying : " Alas ! my mother, I am about to
die." Then she sent for her betrothed, and she bent

over him and kissed him, and whispered softly into
his ear: "Oh, my friend, when I am dead deck my
grave as you would have decked my nuptial bed."
We find in Greek poesy the universal legend of the
lover who kills himself on hearing of the death of his
mistress; but, as a rule, the regret of survivors is
depicted as neither desperate nor durable. Long ago,
three gallant youths plotted together to contrive an
escape from Hades, and a fair-haired maiden prayed
that they would take her with them; she did so wish
to see her mother mourning her loss, her brothers weeping because she is no more. They answered: "As
to thy brothers, poor girl, they are dancing, and thy
mother diverts herself with gossiping in the street."
The mournfully beautiful music that Schubert wedded
to Claudius's little poem *Der Tod und das Mädchen*
might serve as melodious expression to many a one
of these Grecian lays of dead damsels. Death will
not halt because he hears a voice crying: "Tarry, I
am still so young!" The future is as irrevocably
fixed as the past; and if fate deals hardly by mortals,
there is nothing to fall back upon but the sorry
resignation of despair; such is the sombre folk philo-
sophy of the land of eternal summer. Perhaps it is
the very brightness of the sky and air that makes the
quitting of this mortal coil so unspeakably grievous.
The most horribly painful idea associated with death
in the mind of the modern as of the ancient Greek is
the idea of darkness, of separation from what Dante,
yet more Greek than Italian in his passionate sun-
worship, describes in a line which seems somehow to
hold incarnate the thing it tells of—

. . . l'aer dolce che dal sol s'allegra.

It is worth noting that, whether the view entertained of immortality be cheerful or the reverse, in the songs of Western nations the disembodied soul is universally taken to be the exact duplicate of the creature of flesh and blood, in wants, tastes, and semblance. The European folk-singer could no more grasp a metaphysical conception of the eternity of spirit, such as that implied in the grand Indian dirge which craves everlasting good for the " unborn part " in man, than he would know what to make of the scientific theory of the indestructibility of matter shadowed forth in the ordinary Sanskrit periphrases for death, signifying " the resolution of the body into its five elementary constituents."

Among the Greek-speaking inhabitants of Southern Italy a peculiar metre is set apart to the composition of the neniæ, and the office of public wailer is transmitted from mother to daughter ; so that the living præficæ are the lineal descendants of the præficæ who lived of old in the Grecian Motherland. Unrivalled in the matter of her improvisations as in the manner of their delivery, the hereditary dirge-singer no doubt, like a good actress, keenly realises at the moment the sorrow not her own, of which she undertakes the interpretation in return for a trifling gratuity, and to her hearers she appears as the genius or high priestess of woe : she excites them into a whirlwind of ecstatic paroxysms not greatly differing from kindred phenomena vouched for by the historians of religious mysticism. There are, however, one or two of the Græco-Italic death-songs which bear too clear and touching a stamp of sincerity for us to attribute them even to the most skilled of hired " sobbing ones." There is

no savour of vicarious mourning in the plaint of the
desolate girl, who says to her dead mother that she
will wait for her, so that she may tell her how she has
passed the day: at eight she will await her, and if she
does not come she will begin to weep; at nine she
will await her, and if she comes not she will grow
black as soot; at ten she will await her, and if she
does not come at ten she will turn to earth, to earth
that may be sown in. And it is difficult to believe
that aught save the anguish of a mother's broken
heart could have quickened the senses of an ignorant
peasant to the tragic intensity of the following
lament:

> Now they have buried thee, my little one,
>> Who will make thy little bed?
>> Black Death will make it for me
>> For a very long night.
> Who will arrange thy pillows,
>> So thou mayst sleep softly?
>> Black Death will arrange them for me
>> With hard stones.
> Who will awake thee, my daughter,
>> When day is up?
>> Down here it is always sleep,
>> Always dark night.
> This my daughter was fair.
> When I went (with her) to high mass,
> The columns shone,
> The way grew bright.

The neniæ of Terra d'Otranto and of Calabria are
not uncommonly composed in a semi-dramatic form.
Professor Comparetti cites one, in which the friend
of a dead girl is represented as going to pay her a
visit, in ignorance of the misfortune that has happened.

She sees a crowd at the door, and she exclaims :
" How many folks are in thy house I they come from
all the neighbourhood ; they are bidden by thy mother,
who shows thee the bridal array I " But on crossing
the threshold she finds that the shutters are closed :
" Alas I " she cries, " I deceive myself—I enter into
darkness." Again she repeats : " How many folks
are in thy house! All Corigliano is there." The
mother says : " My daughter has bidden them by the
tolling of the bell." Then the daughter is made to
ask : " What ails thee, what ails thee, my mother?
wherefore dost thou rend thy hair ? " The mother
rejoins : " I think of thee, my daughter, of how thou
liest down in darkness." " What ails thee, what ails
thee, my mother, that all around one can hear thee
wailing ? " " I think of thee, my daughter, of how
thou art turned black as soot." A sort of chorus
is appended : " All, all the mothers weep and rend
their hair : let them weep, the poor mothers who lose
their children." Here are the last four lines as they
were originally set on paper :

> Ole sole i mane i cluene
> Isirnune anapota ta maddia,
> Afi nà clapsune tio mane misere
> Pu ichannune ta pedia !

Professor Comparetti has shaped them into looking
more like Greek :

> Ολαις, ὅλαις ἡ μάναι ἠκλαίουνε
> Ἡσύρνουνε ἀνάποδα τὰ μαλλίd
> Ἀφησε νὰ κλάψουνε ταῖς μάναις misere
> Ἡοῦ ἠχδνουνε τὰ παιδίd !

In his "Tour through the Southern Provinces of

the Kingdom of Naples," the Hon. R. Keppel Craven gave an account of a funeral at Corigliano. The deceased, a stout, swarthy man of about fifty, had been fond of field sports; he was, therefore, laid on his open bier in the dress of a hunter. When the procession passed the house of a friend of the dead man, it halted as a mark of respect, and the friend got up from his dinner and looked out for a few minutes, afterwards philosophically returning to the interrupted meal. The busy people in the street, carpenters, blacksmiths, cobblers, and fruitsellers, paused from their several occupations—all carried on, as usual, in the open air, when the dismal chant of the priests announced the approach of the funeral, resuming them with redoubled energy as soon as it had moved on. A group of weeping women led the widow, whose face was pale and motionless as a statue; her black tresses descended to her knees, and at regular intervals she pulled out two or three hairs—the women instantly taking hold of her hands and replacing them by her side, where they hung till the operation was next repeated.

The practice of plucking out the hair was so general in the last century that even at Naples the old women had hardly a hair left from out-living many relations. It was proper also to observe the day of burial as a fast day. Two unlucky women near Salerno lost their characters for ever because the dog of a visitor who had come to condole, sniffed out a dish of tripe which had been hastily thrust into a corner.

The Italian, or rather Calabrese-speaking population of Calabria, call their preficæ—where they still have any—*Reputatrici.* Some remarkable songs have been collected in the commune of Pizzo, the place of dubious fame by whose peasants Murat was caught and betrayed. There is something Dantesque in the image of Death as *'nu gran levreri* crouching in a mountain defile:

Joy, I saw death ; Joy, I saw her yesterday ; I beheld her in a narrow way, like unto a great greyhound, and I was very curious. " Death, whence comest thou ? " " I am come from Germany, going thence to Count Roger. I have killed princes, counts, and cavaliers ; and now I am come for a young maiden so that with me she may go.

Weep, mamma, weep for me, weep and never rest ; weep for me Sunday, Easter, and Christmas Day ; for no more wilt thou see thy daughter sit down at thy board to eat, and no more shalt thou await me.

One conclusion forced upon us incidentally by folk-dirges must seem strange when we remember how few are the cultured poetesses who have attained eminence—to wit, that with the unlettered multitude the poetic faculty is equally the property of women as of men.

In various parts of Italy the funerals of the poor are conducted exclusively by those of like sex with the dead—a custom of which I first took note at Varese in the year 1879. The funeral procession came up slowly by the shady paths near the lake ; long before it appeared one could hear the sound of shrill voices chanting a litany. When it got near to the little church of S. Vittore, it was seen that only women followed the bier, which was carried by women. "Una povera donna morta in parto," said a peasant standing by, as she pointed to the coffin with a gesture of sympathy. The mourners had black shawls thrown over their heads and bore tapers. A sight yet stranger to unaccustomed eyes is the funeral of a child at Spezia. A number of little girls, none older than eleven or twelve, some as young as five, carry the small coffin to the cemetery. Some of the children hold candles; they are nicely dressed in their best frocks; the sun plays on their bare black or golden curls. They have the little serious look of children engaged in some business of work or play, but no look of gloom or sadness. The coffin is covered with a white pall on which lies a large nosegay. No priests or elder persons are there except one man, walking apart, who has to see that the children go the right way. About twenty children is the average number, but there may be sometimes a hundred. When they return, running across the grass between the road and the sea-wall, they tumble over one another in the scramble to snatch daisies from the ground.

It is still common in Lombardy to ring the bells *d'allegrezza* on the death of an infant, "because its soul goes straight to Paradise." This way of ringing, or, rather, chiming, consists in striking the bell with a clapper held in the hand, when a light, dancing sound is produced, something like that of hand-bells. On a high *festa* all the bells are used; for dead babies, only two. I have often heard the sad message sounding gaily from the belfry at Salò.

Were I sure that all these songs of the Last Parting would have for others the same interest that they have had for me, I should be tempted to add a study dedicated solely to the dirges of savage nations and of those nations whose civilization has not followed the same course as ours. I must, at all events, indicate the wonderfully strange and wild Polynesian "Death-talks" and "Evas" (dirges proper) collected by the Rev. W. W. Gill. The South Pacific Islanders say of the dying, "he is passing over the sea." Their dead set out in a canoe on a long and perilous voyage to the regions of the sun-setting. When they get there, alas!— when they reach the mysterious spirit-land, a horrid doom awaits them: children and old men and women —all, in short, who have not died in battle, are devoured by a dreadful deity, and perish for ever. But this fate does not overtake them immediately; for a time they remain in a shadowy intermediate state till their turn comes. The spirit-journey is described in a dirge for two little children, composed by their father about the year 1796:

"Thy god,[1] pet-child, is a bad one;
  For thy body is attenuated;
  This wasting sickness must end thy days.
  Thy form, once so plump, now how changed!
  Ah! that god, that bad god!
  Inexpressibly bad, my child!

  Thou hast entered the expanse;
  And wilt visit 'the land of red parrot feathers,'
  Where Oārangi was once a guest.
  Thou feedest now on ocean spray,
  And sippest fresh water out of the rocks,
  Travelling over rugged cliffs,
  To the music of murmuring billows.
  Thy exile spirit is overtaken
  By darkness at the ocean's edge.
  Fourapapa[2] there sleeps. All three[3]
  Stood awhile to gaze wistfully
  At the glories of the setting sun."

[1] The child's "personal fate."   [2] The brother.
        [3] A little sister had died before.

There is much more, but this is perhaps sufficient to show the particular note struck.

I will give, in its entirety, one more dirge—the death-chant of the tribe of Badagas, in the Neilgherry Hills—because it is unique, so far as I know, in reversing the rule *de mortius*, and in charging, instead, the dead man with every sin, to make sure that none are omitted of which he is actually guilty. It is accompanied by a singular ceremony. An unblemished buffalo-calf is led into the midst of the mourners, and as after each verse they catch up and repeat the refrain, " It is a sin! " the performer of the dirge lays his hand upon the calf, to which the guilt is transferred. At the end the calf is let loose; like the Jewish scape-goat, it must be used for no secular work; it bears the sins of a human being, and is sacred till death. The English version is by Mr C. E. Gover, who has done so much for the preservation of South-Indian folk-songs.

INVOCATION.

In the presence of the great Bassava,
Who sprang from Banigé the holy cow.

The dead has sinned a thousand times.
E'en all the thirteen hundred sins
That can be done by mortal men
May stain the soul that fled to-day.
Stay not their flight to God's pure feet.
　　　　　Chorus—Stay not their flight.

He killed the crawling snake
　　　　　　Chorus—It is a sin.
The creeping lizard slew.
　　　　　　It is a sin.

Also the harmless frog.

It is a sin.

Of brothers he told tales.

It is a sin.

The landmark stone he moved.

It is a sin.

Called in the Sircar's aid.[1]

It is a sin.

Put poison in the milk.

It is a sin.

To strangers straying on the hills,
He offered aid but guided wrong.

It is a sin.

His sister's tender love he spurned
And showed his teeth to her in rage.

It is a sin.

He dared to drain the pendent teats
Of holy cow in sacred fold.

It is a sin.

The glorious sun shone warm and bright
He turned its back towards its beams.[2]

It is a sin.

Ere drinking from the babbling brook,
He made no bow of gratitude.

It is a sin.

His envy rose against the man
Who owned a fruitful buffalo.

It is a sin.

He bound with cords and made to plough
The budding ox too young to work.

It is a sin.

While yet his wife dwelt in his house
He lusted for a younger bride.

It is a sin.

---

[1] He had recourse to the Rajahs, whose courts under the old régime, had become a byeword for oppression and corruption.

[2] Compare *Inferno*, Canto vii.

The hungry begged—he gave no meat,
The cold asked warmth—he lent no fire.
               It is a sin.
He turned relations from his door,
Yet asked unworthy strangers home.
               It is a sin.
The weak and poor called for his aid,
He gave no alms, denied their woe.
               It is a sin.
When caught by thorns, in useless rage
He tore his cloth from side to side.
               It is a sin.
The father of his wife sat on the floor
Yet he reclined on bench or couch.
               It is a sin.
He cut the bund around a tank,
Set free the living water's store.
               It is a sin.

What though he sinned so much,
Or that his parents sinned?
What though the sins' long score
Was thirteen hundred crimes?
O let them every one,
Fly swift to Bas'va's feet.
             Chorus—Fly swift.

The chamber dark of death
Shall open to his soul.
The sea shall rise in waves ;
Surround on every side,
But yet that awful bridge
No thicker than a thread,
Shall stand both firm and strong.
The dragon's yawning mouth
Is shut—it brings no fear.
The palaces of heaven
Throw open wide their doors.
             Chorus—Open wide their doors.

> The thorny path is steep,
> Yet shall his soul go safe.
> The silver pillar stands
> So near—he touches it.
> He may approach the wall
> The golden wall of heaven.
> The burning pillar's flame
> Shall have no heat for him.
> > Chorus—Shall have no heat.
>
> Oh let us never doubt
> That all his sins are gone,
> That Bassava forgives.
> May it be well with him!
> > Chorus—May it be well!
> Let all be well with him!
> > Chorus—Let all be well.

Surely an impressive burial service to have been found in use amongst a poor little obscure tribe of Indian mountaineers!

It cannot be said that this moral attitude is often reached. Research into funeral rites, of whatever nature, confronts us with much that would be ludicrous were it not so very pitiful, for humanity has displayed a fatal tendency to rush into the committal of ghastly absurdities by way of showing the most sacred kind of grief. Yet, take them all in all, the death laments of the people form a striking and beautiful manifestation of such homage as " Life may give for love to death."

BOOKS OF REFERENCE.

Alecsandri, Vasile. Poesii Populare ale Romanilor. 1867.
—— Les Doïnas. Poésies Moldaves. 1855.
Alexander, Francesca. Roadside Songs of Tuscany (in ten parts, edited by John Ruskin, LL.D.). 1885.
Arbaud, Damase. Chants Populaires de la Provence. 2 vols 1864.
Armana Provençau. 1870.
Avolio, Corrado. Canti Popolari di Noto. 1875.

Bernoni, Dom. Giuseppe. Canti Populari Veneziani. 1873.
—— Preghiere Populari Veneziane. 1873.
—— Leggende Fantastiche Populari Veneziane. 1873.
Bladé, J. Poésies Populaires de la Gascogne. 3 vols.
Boullier, Auguste. Le Dialecte et les Chants Populaires de la Sardaigne. 1864.
Burton, Richard. Wit and Wisdom from West Arica. 1865.
Cardona, Enrico. Dell' Antica Letteratura Catalana. 1878.
Champfleury. Chansons Populaires des Provinces de France. 1860.
Comparetti, Prof. D. Saggi de' Dialetti Greci dell' Italia Meridionale. 1866.
Constantinescu, Dr B. Probe de Limba si Literatura Tiganilor din Romania. 1878.
Dalmedico, A. Canti del Popolo di Chioggia. 1872.
—— Ninne-Nanne e Giuochi Infantile Veneziani. 1871.
Davies, William. The Pilgrimage of the Tiber. 1874. (Popular Songs of the Tiberine District.)
D'Ancona, Prof. A. Origini del Teatro in Italia. 2 vols. 1877.
—— La Poesia Popolare Italiana. 1878.
Day, Rev. Lal Behari. Folk-Tales of Bengal. 1883.

Dorsa, Prof. V. La Tradizione Greco-Latina negli usi e nelle Credenze Popolari della Calabria Citeriore. 2d Ed. 1884.

Dozon, Auguste. Poésies Populaires Serbes. 1859.

—— Chansons Populaires Bulgares Inédites. 1875.

Dumersan et Colet. Chants et Chansons Populaires de la France.

Fauriel, C. Chansons Populaires de la Grèce. 2 vols. 1824.

Ferraro, Dr G. Canti Popolari Monferrini. 1870.

Fissore, G. Canti Popolari dell' Allemagna. 1857.

Flugi, Alfons von. Die Volkslieder des Engadin. 1873.

Gill, Rev. W. W. Myths and Songs from the South Pacific. 1876.

Gonzenbach, Laura. Sicilianische Märchen. 1870.

Gover, Charles E. The Folk-Songs of Southern India. 1872.

Grimm, Jacob. Deutsche Mythologie. Vierte Ausgabe Besorgt von Elard Hugo Meyer. 3 vols. 1875-7-8.

Gubernatis, Conte A. de. Storia Comparata degli usi Natalizi in Italia e presso gli altri Popoli Indo-Europei. 1878.

Imbriani, V., and Casetti, A. Canti Popolari delle Provincie Meridionali. 2 vols. 1871.

Issaverdenz, Dr G. Armenian Popular Songs. 1867.

Ive, Antonio. Canti Popolari Istriani. 1877.

Kolberg, Oskar. Piésni Luder Polskiego. 1857.

Kuhff, Prof. P. Les Enfantines du "Bon Pays de France." 1878.

Latham, R. G. The Nationalities of Europe (Estonian Poetry). 1863.

Leger, Louis. Chants Héroïques et Chansons Populaires des Slaves de Bohême. 1866.

Lizio-Bruno, Prof. Canti Popolari delle Isole Eolie. 1871.

Mandalari, Mario. Canti del Popolo Reggino. 1881.

Marcellus, Cte de. Chants Populaires de la Grèce Moderne. 1860.

Marcoaldi, Oreste. Canti Popolari inediti. 1855.

Marmier, X. Chants Populaires du Nord. 1842.

Moncaut, Cénac. Littérature Populaire de la Gascogne. 1868.

Morosi, Dr Giuseppe. Studi sui Dialetti Greci della Terra d'Otranto. 187c.

—— I Dialetti Romaici del Dialetto di Bova in Calabria. 1874.

Nerucci, G. Sessanta Novelle Popolari Montalesi. 1880.

Nigra, Conte Constantino. Canzone Popolari del Piemonte. Rivista Contemporanea : fascicoli lxxiv. and lxxxvi. 1860-1.

Nino, A. de. Usi Abruzzesi. 3 vols. 1879, 1881-3.

Ortoli, Frédéric. Les Contes Populaires de l'île de Corse. 1883.

Pellegrini, Prof. Astorre. Il Dialetto Greco-Calabro di Bova. 1880.

—— La Poesia di Bova. 1881.

Pitrè, Cav. Dr Giuseppe. Studi di Poesia Popolare. 1872.

—— Biblioteca delle Tradizioni Popolari Siciliane. 13 vols.

Ralston, W. R. S. The Songs of the Russian People. 1872.

Righi, Ettore-Scipione. Canti Popolari Veronesi. 1863.

Rink, Dr R. Tales and Traditions of the Eskimo. 1875.

Rosa, Gabriele. Dialetti, Costumi e Tradizioni nelle Provincie di Bergamo e di Brescia. Jerza edizione. 1870.

Salomone-Marino, S. Canti Popolari Siciliani. 1867.

Stokes, Maive. Indian Fairy Tales. 1880.

Symonds, T. Addington. Sketches in Italy and Greece. (Popular Songs of Tuscany.) 1874.

Thorpe, B. Northern Mythology. 1851.

Tigri, G. Canti Popolari Toscani. Terza ediz. 1869.

Tommaseo, N. Canti Popolari Toscani, Corsi, Illirici, Greci. 1841.

TURNBULL AND SPEARS, PRINTERS, EDINBURGH.